"Ted tells me I'm prissy an[...] should get over the incide[nt...] and our daughter. He actually said he's nuts about Francine because, even though my IQ is higher, she's fun to be with, she has big boobs and a nice butt and—get this—when they have sex, he feels he's died and gone to heaven." She threw up her hands, then dropped them to her sides in bafflement. "All vestiges of sanity have disappeared from my life."

"C'mere." Before she realized his intent, Cam had his arms around her, enveloping her in sympathy and warm masculine strength. Instinct made her resist…but only for a heartbeat. She was still all worked up over the sheer unfairness of life at the moment, and the appeal of a friendly hug was simply too much to resist. Tears started in her eyes and she blinked furiously to hold them back. She sniffed.

"Without a doubt you have the higher IQ," he told her softly.

She heard the smile in his voice and, turning her nose into his nice clean shirt, gave a shaky chuckle. "Ted said that, I didn't."

"Because you would never boast about your IQ."

"No, never." Then, in a bewildered voice, she added, "But what good does having a high IQ do if you can't keep a husband?"

"You would keep a decent one without even trying."

KAREN YOUNG
IN CONFIDENCE

MIRA®

ISBN 0-7783-2024-3

IN CONFIDENCE

Visit us at www.mirabooks.com

Printed in U.S.A.

Dear Reader,

If you have read any of my previous books, you'll know that I invariably come up with stories of women just like you and me, women who are dealing with the problems of contemporary life.

My heroines face the ups and downs of courtship or marriage, the stresses of parenting and family crises, divorce...and just about anything else you can think of. And all the while, of course, they're usually pursuing a career with its thorny challenges.

I almost always throw in something more to complicate my heroine's already complicated life. Rachel Forrester, the woman I write about in *In Confidence,* is certainly besieged by a host of unexpected—and painful—changes in her life. Her marriage of seventeen years ends when she discovers her husband's infidelity. As a high school guidance counselor, she isn't supposed to fail at this most basic relationship, so it is a struggle to handle such a deep personal betrayal and at the same time maintain a loving and secure environment for her children.

She is also conflicted by her attraction to a true-crime writer who lives next door, but he blames her for failing to anticipate his teenage son's suicide five years earlier. But much worse is her growing suspicion that something evil exists in her world, something that threatens the very fabric of her life, something that has already taken one young victim.

So settle back and prepare yourself for a story I've written about a shocking secret in a small Texas town...but it could happen anywhere.

Karen Young

I love to hear from readers. Please write me at P. O. Box 450947, Houston, Texas 77245. Or visit my Web site at authorkarenyoung.com.

Prologue

Rose Hill, Texas
April 1998

Right on time, the door opened and the interview Rachel Forrester had dreaded all morning was at hand. She often faced trying situations, but this was surely the worst in her experience.

"Mr. Ford?" Rachel Forrester stood behind her desk, extending her hand in formal greeting to the father of the boy. "I'm terribly sorry for your loss. I liked Jack so much, everyone who knew him did. He was a fine boy and a gifted athlete. He will be sorely missed here at Rose Hill High."

Cameron Ford grunted a reply and barely touched her palm before saying abruptly, "I have a few questions."

"Won't you please have a seat?" She gestured to the chair in front of her desk.

"I'll stand."

She nodded, bracing for a difficult interview. As she eased down on her chair, he swiped a hand over a face ravaged with grief, fatigue and sleep deprivation. He was a tall man of rangy build with dark brown hair and gray eyes hooded at the moment. He seemed to vibrate with energy, which probably explained how he carried not a spare ounce of flesh on him. His clothes were rumpled, as if he'd thrown them on without giving much thought to the way he'd look, or to any first impression he made. He wouldn't have recalled seeing her at Jack's funeral. In his shoes, she certainly wouldn't, she thought.

"I'll be glad to answer your questions as best I can," she told him.

He looked directly at her then from eyes that burned with accusation. "Why didn't you do your job with Jack?"

"I beg your pardon?"

"I'm telling you right up front that I think you dropped the ball with Jack. You're a shrink, right? I was told by Preston Ramsey that, as his guidance counselor, you saw my son no less than six times this semester. What's your job if it's not to spot troubled kids and step in before they wind up—" He turned away and paced to the window, keeping his back to her. "I want to know what went on in those six sessions that you didn't guess he was suicidal."

"Mr. Ford, won't you please take a seat so we can talk calmly."

He turned and took a step toward her desk. "I am calm. But I'm mad as hell and I intend to get answers, if not from you, then I'll go beyond you and Ramsey. You were privy to his confidences and Ramsey was his principal. Are you honestly telling me you didn't have a clue—either one of you—that Jack was contemplating suicide?"

Wary of his rage, Rachel felt her heartbeat up a bit, but she kept her tone even. "Yes, I'm telling you exactly that," she said, folding her hands in front of her. "I didn't think—"

"Yeah, what the hell *were* you thinking!" The sound of his hand slapped on her desktop was like a shot in the small office. "Do you people only notice when a kid winds up dead?"

"Please, Mr. Ford." Rachel rose from her chair on shaky legs. "If you want to talk about this, I'm more than willing, but it's not helpful to scream at me."

"It seems to me the time for talking is about a week late," he told her in a grim tone. "You had plenty of opportunities to get a fix on Jack in six sessions. Weren't you listening?

Isn't that what shrinks do? Or did you hear what he said and just ignored it?''

"Nobody ignored Jack, Mr. Ford," she said patiently, watching him pace. "His grades were slipping. I noticed he was withdrawing from his peers. He was skipping classes. His teachers were concerned. I was concerned. And I saw him for those sessions only because I dragged him in in an attempt to reach him. It wasn't his choice.''

He stopped momentarily. "So what did the two of you talk about, the weather?" he asked sarcastically.

He was hurting, she knew that. Rightfully. He was entitled. He needed someone, something on which to focus his rage and pain. In that, he was no different from the other parents she saw who were bewildered and frustrated over their kids' behavior. How much worse must it be to suffer the ultimate loss as Cameron Ford had? She drew a deep breath. "Something was going on, but he wasn't willing to share it. At least, not with me.''

His eyes were icy with disdain. "And didn't that tell you something?''

"What should it have told me, Mr. Ford?''

"Maybe you're in the wrong business. Maybe these kids need someone who's more skillful in connecting with them.''

She answered him coolly. "I can't force a teenage boy to share his deepest thoughts.'' Even knowing he needed to lash out, there was a limit to what she'd tolerate. "We can only do our best," she said.

"Yeah, well, your best wasn't enough to keep my son alive, was it?''

Out of compassion and professional restraint, Rachel bit back a sharp response. As the boy's guidance counselor, she knew she'd done her best. She could have asked if Ford had done his best as a father. Where was he in Jack's time of need? "I don't think there's anything to be gained by continuing our discussion just now, Mr. Ford," she said quietly. "Maybe you need to give yourself some time to adjust to your loss, and then, if you'd like to talk, you know where to reach me.'' Even before she'd finished, he was stalking to the door. ''Just call the school to make an appointment.''

''Don't hold your breath,'' he said. Then, with his hand on the catch, he suddenly turned back. ''Instead of answers all I got from you today was a lot of evasion and bullshit. If this session is an example of your expertise, I think I understand why, when Jack was in trouble, you failed him. God help other kids in your care.''

One

Rose Hill, Texas
Five years later

Nothing about the start of the day hinted at the way it would end. Rachel Forrester's routine didn't vary from the moment she got out of bed at six in the morning. She showered first, as always, then she headed downstairs to get the coffee started and fix breakfast for the kids. When that was done, she took two steaming mugs back to the bedroom, timing it just as Ted was toweling off. Her husband was slow to get going unless he had an early surgery scheduled. Neither made much conversation. Ted didn't like early-morning chatter.

"Is my black suit—the Armani—back from the cleaners?" he asked from the depths of the walk-in closet.

Rachel pulled the suit from half a dozen plastic-shrouded items hanging on her side of the closet. "It's here with all this stuff that was delivered yesterday. I haven't had a chance to separate it."

Ted took it after she stripped away the plastic, then chose two dress shirts from the twenty-or-so hanging in his closet and walked to the large sliding glass doors where the light was better. "What looks best?" he asked, critically studying the effects of both shirts with the Armani jacket.

"Depends on the tie."

He held up a smart black-and-gray tie. "This one."

"Okay, the white French cuffs." She paused in the act of buttoning her denim skirt and watched him put the shirt on. "Something special going on today?"

"I'll be in Dallas. Walter finally convinced me that we should interview that internist out of Baylor. Fat chance persuading him to leave Houston to come to a town the size of Rose Hill."

Rachel smiled. "Well, you'll make a terrific impression." Ted was an attractive man, still trim at forty-two, with just enough silver at the temples in his dark hair to add a distinguished touch. She walked over and took the cuff link he was fumbling with in his left hand and deftly fastened it.

"Thanks," he said, then picked up his jacket.

"Will you be back in time to have dinner with us?"

He seldom did lately and she wasn't surprised when he said he wouldn't. After he left, forgetting the goodbye kiss she no longer expected, she stood looking at nothing in particular for a moment. She'd been thinking for a while that she needed to impress upon Ted the fact that he needed to make a little more time for his family. He was very busy, all physicians were nowadays, what with the strictures of HMOs and PPOs cutting into the profits and time off that doctors used to enjoy. It meant taking on more patients, and more patients meant more time at the practice and at the hospital. Still, Nick and Kendall needed their father. At fifteen, Nick, particularly, would benefit from seeing more of his dad. Maybe Kendall wasn't quite so needy, but a nine-year-old girl deserved more from her daddy than she was getting.

With a sigh, she pulled a cotton-knit sweater over the denim skirt and added a leather belt anchored at her tummy. She quickly brushed her short, dark hair into its casual style, added a bit of blush on her cheeks and some soft plum lip gloss and—her one vanity—sprayed a bit of perfume near her throat. All done, she stood back and surveyed herself. No designer look to her, alas, more like a librarian. Still, if Ted had aged well, she hadn't done too badly herself, she thought, even if she had to cover her best feature—unique amber-colored eyes—with reading glasses. At Rose Hill High School, her students were more comfortable sitting down with a guidance counselor in denim and a casual sweater than the latest designer fashions.

"Mom, where's my CD player?" Nick appeared at the door of her bedroom. Tall and lanky, black-haired, with strong male features, her son was on the brink of manhood. She still couldn't get used to her firstborn being six inches taller than she was!

"The last time I saw it was in the sunroom."

"I had it after that."

"Sorry, son. You know you're supposed to be—"

"Responsible for my own stuff. I know, Mom." He stood with his face wrinkled in thought. "I gotta find it. We're—"

"It's in the game room on the pool table," Kendall called out from her room down the hall.

"Right!" Nick snapped his fingers. "Thanks, brat."

Rachel made an exasperated sound. "Don't call her—"

"Brat. I know. It slipped out." Nick turned, headed down the hall. As he passed his sister's room, he gave her door a friendly thump. "Thanks, sissy."

"Ni-i-ick!" Kendall appeared, frowning ferociously, small fists propped on her hips.

"Oops." He grinned and gave her ponytail a yank. "Thank you, Kendall Kate Forrester."

"To the car in five minutes," Rachel said, shoving her feet into a pair of Birkenstocks. Moving to the sitting area of her bedroom, she gathered up the dozen or so folders she'd worked on last evening. Each was labeled with a student's name on a bright blue sticker. She often worked at night, as trying to concentrate in her busy office was often impossible. She paused a moment, taking in the chintz-covered love seat, the coffee table she'd restored herself, the pretty view of her backyard from the window beyond. She loved her bedroom. The design was hers alone. When she and Ted had built the house five years before, she'd planned for the master bedroom to be a retreat for both of them. Unfortunately, he spent only the time it took to shower, shave and get dressed there. Or to sleep.

Downstairs, Kendall was pouring kitty pebbles into the cat's dish while a yellow-striped tomcat purred and circled in and out of her ankles. "Graham, be patient!" she scolded. "You're gonna make me have an accident." She set the bowl on the floor and stroked the cat a few times before standing up. She had chosen his name when they'd adopted him from the Humane Society, explaining that he was exactly the color of graham crackers. Rachel, feeling the push of the clock, found her purse and settled the strap on her shoulder.

"All set?" she asked Kendall. "Got your lunch money? Homework?" In her backpack and little denim jumper paired with a pink shirt, and sneakers that looked out of proportion, her baby appeared ready to go.

"Can I take my camera, Mommy?" She held up the inexpensive digital model she'd begged for on her birthday.

"You know you can't, honey."

"Puleeze, Mommy…"

"Do you want your teacher to confiscate it?" Rachel grabbed her coffee in a travel cup and opened the door.

"What's *conferskate* mean?"

"Take it away from you."

Mouth in a dejected droop, Kendall reluctantly placed the camera on the counter. She had probably gone through a dozen throwaway cameras before getting the digital for her birthday, and she treasured it above anything she possessed. At first, Rachel had been amused at a nine-year-old's interest in snapping photos right and left, thinking the novelty of it all would soon fade. Then she'd realized Kendall's interest went beyond a child's obsession with a new toy. The pictures were sometimes quite good. To the little girl, photography was no longer a novelty, but a passion. Still, taking her camera to school was out.

Rachel shooed her through the kitchen and out the door that led to the garage, where Nick sat behind the wheel of the BMW, waiting for them with the motor running. Rachel hadn't driven to school a single day since he'd gotten his student permit three months ago. She wasn't sure how much longer he'd be satisfied to ride with her and Kendall, but a car of his own was not in his immediate future, no matter how intensely he lobbied for it. A camera for Kendall was one thing. A car for Nick was another entirely.

"Is Daddy gonna come home tonight and eat with us?" Kendall asked, studying the empty space in the garage where Ted's Lexus belonged.

"I don't think so, sweetie," Rachel told her.

"So, what's new?" Nick muttered as he backed out of the garage.

Finding no reply to her children that wouldn't sound lame, Rachel turned her gaze to the spacious, upscale homes lining their street and said nothing.

Thirty minutes later, she was at her desk gazing into the pale face of a teenage girl. Ashley had been observed vomiting in the shrubs along the north side of the school before the morning bell. Had the observer been anyone but another teacher, Rachel probably wouldn't have had this chance to talk to the girl. Fortunately, it had been a teacher.

"How are you feeling now, Ashley?"

A glance down at knotted fingers in her lap. "I'm okay."

"Do you think you've picked up a stomach virus?"

"Probably." Gaze still fixed on her hands.

"Then we should call your mom to pick you up. These things are contagious, you know. They spread like wildfire among the other students."

"No!" Ashley's head jerked up. "I mean…ah, it's okay. I don't think I have a virus. I'm feeling better now."

"Did you have any breakfast this morning, Ashley?" Rachel opened a drawer in her desk and offered a blueberry muffin she'd picked up in the cafeteria.

The girl's face went from pearl white to pea green. She put both hands to her mouth and closed her eyes, breathing deep. Rachel stood up and quickly brought her waste can within reach just in time to catch another spate of vomiting. However, this time, there was little left in her stomach for the girl to throw up. Rachel waited with a handful of tissues until the retching stopped, then poured a small amount of ice water from a Thermos carafe on her desk and urged her to take it. "Don't drink much, honey. Just a taste."

"Thank you," Ashley whispered, then after using the tissues, she took a tiny sip or two, grimacing.

"Here, I think you'll feel better lying down." Rachel helped her to her feet, then led her over to an oversize sofa—one she'd purchased herself—and gently urged her down on the big cushions. She took an afghan and spread it over the girl, then watched her dab at tears, now trickling from the corners of her eyes. She looked absolutely miserable.

Rachel spoke with quiet understanding. "Are you pregnant, Ashley?"

The girl didn't respond for a moment or two, then closing her eyes, she nodded.

"Have you told anyone?"

One bleak negative move of her head.

"Do you have any idea how far along you are?"

"Four months, I think."

Rachel winced at the reply. Ashley wore an oversize sweater and jeans that she was probably having difficulty zipping all the way, but only a practiced eye would spot the signs. She was a bit overweight to begin with and apparently concealing her condition had not presented a problem. Unfortunately, she wasn't able to conceal the bouts of nausea that sometimes accompanied pregnancy.

"Have you been to a clinic, seen a doctor?"

"No."

"Have you told your boyfriend?" Ashley and Mike Reynolds, a star football jock, had been dating steadily since they were in eighth grade. Things, apparently, had progressed naturally when two healthy, sexually active kids had been unable to resist going all the way. Without protection.

"Mike knows." Her face was turned away now. "He said I should get an abortion."

"And you disagree?"

"I don't know."

"And since you haven't told your parents, I'm assuming you don't need to hear what they might think about such a decision."

"They'll hate me."

Rachel sighed, pulled the chair over that Ashley had just vacated, sat down and took the girl's hand. "They won't hate you, Ashley. Just because you've made a mistake in judgment doesn't mean your parents are going to stop loving you. And you need them now. You shouldn't have to handle such a momentous decision on your own."

"I know all that, Ms. Forrester," she said, beginning to cry again. "But they're gonna be so disappointed in me. I—I was supposed to g-go to college and now I've ruined everything. Besides, I think I've waited almost too late, as it is. Last night—" she gulped, wiping hard at her eyes with the tissue "—last night, I felt the baby move."

"Then the sooner you talk with your parents, the better." Rachel reached over and, with a gentle touch, brought the girl's chin around to look into her eyes. "I will be happy to call your mother or both your parents—whatever makes you more comfortable—and help you tell them. Would you want to do that?"

"I guess so."

"Is your mother at home today?"

"No, she's in Dallas shopping with my aunt. But maybe she could come in Monday."

Rachel stood up. "Tell you what. I'll phone her now and leave a message. Then, when she calls, we'll arrange to meet at a time we both agree on, okay? I'll let her know that it's urgent."

"Okay." Ashley was sitting up now. Her color was better. She brushed her mane of straight blond hair away from her face with both hands. Her blue eyes were red and slightly puffed, but she got to her feet easily, then stood with both hands cradling her tummy. Cautiously, she took a step toward the door.

"You're welcome to stay and rest awhile until you feel able to take on the day," Rachel said.

Now at the door, Ashley turned back. "No, that's the funny thing. When this happens—the nausea, I mean—I just feel horrible, like I want to die. But then when it's over, it's completely over and I feel just fine."

Rachel smiled, knowing the feeling after giving birth twice herself. "Pregnancy's like that, Ashley."

"I hate it."

"Which is all the more reason to have this discussion with your parents and try to work something out."

She nodded. "Thanks, Ms. Forrester."

"You're welcome, Ashley."

After the door closed, Rachel sank back in her chair with a sigh and put her head in her hands. Sixteen years old and four months pregnant. She'd put a positive spin on it for Ashley's sake, but the teenager's life was drastically changed, no matter what her decision about the abortion might be. The only bright spot was that she'd been able to talk the girl into confiding in her parents.

A quick knock at her door brought her head up.

"Got a minute, Rachel?" Preston Ramsey, the school principal, pushed the door open and waited for her to wave him inside. She did, pointing to a chair, which he refused. "No time to sit. I've got a killer schedule today and that's why I'm here. Is there anything of vital importance on yours? I need someone to go to Dallas."

Rose Hill was located southeast of Dallas, about an hour-and-a-half drive. Rachel enjoyed an occasional trip into the city. She glanced at her watch. "If I stay in my office, something will come up, as you know. If you want me to go, I should leave before that happens. What's the problem?"

"One of Coach Monk's kids was picked up in Dallas last night on a DUI. It's Jason Pate. Parents are divorced, lives with his mom, who's single with three more kids, all younger than Jason. Anyway, Monk made some calls and arranged for Jason's release if a representative of the school will vouch for him. Monk's got a conflict today, a conference call with a college that wants to sign Pete Freidman.''

"The quarterback who performed so well this season," Rachel murmured. "Monk's doing the deal today?"

"Apparently."

"And his record for signing his athletes to major universities is impressive."

"He takes a personal interest in these kids, Rachel." He was instantly on the defensive. It was well known to Preston that Rachel and Monk Tyson had had fierce disagreements several times over his blind ambition. To Tyson, performance at sports—whether football, basketball, baseball or track—took precedence over his athletes' academic performance. Preston had had to step in more than once to mediate when neither Rachel nor Tyson would give an inch.

"Anyway," he said now, "if you could go to juvenile detention—I've got the address here—and pick up Jason, it would help us out of a jam."

"Not a problem," Rachel said, getting to her feet. "When are they willing to release him?"

Preston glanced at the note in his hand. "The paperwork will take a while to process, but according to Coach Monk, he'll be ready to leave around ten."

"Then I'd better get going," Rachel said, taking her purse out of her desk drawer. "I wish they'd release him later as Ted's in Dallas today, and if I could find him, I'd let him buy my lunch."

"Oh, too bad."

"It's okay. It's a long shot, anyway."

"I owe you one for this, Rachel," her boss said, handing over the note with the address.

"No, Monk owes me." She snapped off the light in her office and smiled at him. "File that for the next time we lock horns and you're dragged into the fray."

* * *

When dealing with bureaucrats, Rachel thought as she turned into the parking lot of a trendy restaurant in Dallas's Turtle Creek area, nothing goes according to plan. She'd negotiated the city's freeway, then fought a tangle of traffic to get to a maze of municipal buildings, finally found a place to park, only to be told that there was a glitch in the get-along with Jason's paperwork, but they'd have it worked out by 2:00 p.m. She'd wished for a later departure time, so the glitch wasn't a total lost cause. She called the practice, found out where Ted had reservations for lunch and decided to take a chance that she'd be able to join him and the interviewee they were considering. Rachel didn't feel she'd be intruding. She'd been Ted's office manager when the practice was just getting started and had left after several years in the practice only when her responsibilities there began to encroach on her responsibilities at home. She'd replaced herself with a hotshot MBA type and then looked around for another venue for her skills and found it as the guidance counselor at Rose Hill High. There she had the same hours and holidays as her children. That had been eight years ago, and she truly enjoyed her job now. In spite of the fact that her "clients" were teenagers and their hormones were raging, she loved the challenge. Sadly, as happened with Ashley today, too many of the kids she saw were dealing with stress beyond their ability or experience to cope.

Ted, she was told by the receptionist at the practice, was having lunch at the Mansion in Turtle Creek. She was familiar with the area and easily found the restaurant. As she got out of the car, she glanced down at her denim skirt and Birkenstocks and thought, belatedly, that she was a bit too casually dressed for such a posh place, but a chance to have lunch with Ted was too rare to pass up.

"Do you have a reservation?" asked the elegantly clad hostess, a stunning blonde with flawless skin.

"No, but my husband is here somewhere," Rachel said,

looking beyond the woman to the crowded dining area. "I thought I'd surprise him."

"Of course," the hostess murmured. Leaving Rachel to do just that, she turned her attention to the party of four waiting to be seated.

Rachel moved just inside the dining room, scanned the crowd and was on the verge of leaving, thinking Ted must have changed his plans, when she spotted him at a table in the rear of the restaurant. His back was to the door, which explained why she'd almost missed him. Moving forward with a smile, she was almost upon him when she realized his lunch partner wasn't the prospective internist for the practice, but a woman, one whom she recognized instantly. It was Francine, wife of Ted's partner in the practice, Walter Dalton. What on earth...

Neither had yet seen Rachel and her pace slowed, almost to a full stop. In a heartbeat, her pleasure in surprising Ted vanished. She watched in disbelief as he reached for Francine's hand, closing his fingers around hers in a way that could only be described as intimate. Ted had not touched her that way for a long time. She saw Francine's face go soft and flush with arousal when Ted brought her hand up for what Rachel could tell was a slow, sensual kiss on her palm.

Rachel had stopped now, rooted in place with sheer surprise. She put her hand to her chest, felt her heart beating so hard that her head was filled with it, her ears rang with it. She could not see her husband's face, but the look on Francine's was unmistakable. Still, Rachel resisted what she was seeing. It could not be what it appeared.

"Excuse me, ma'am." A waiter burdened with a large tray paused, needing to thread the narrow space between the tables. With a murmured sound, Rachel shifted and let him pass. Then, drawing a deep, painful breath, she moved directly to Ted's table and stopped. It was a beat or two before he became aware of her. His eyes went wide with shock and he flushed a ruddy crimson.

"Surprise," she said, and gripped the back of one of the unoccupied chairs before her knees gave way.

"Rachel—" Dropping Francine's hand, he made to rise clumsily, then had to grab at his wineglass to keep it from tipping over.

"Is this a private party, or is there room for one more?" she said in a voice that wobbled a little.

"It isn't what you think," Ted said.

"Really." She glanced from him to Francine and back again. "Then what is it, Ted?"

Francine stood up, laid her napkin on the table and groped for a small Chanel handbag on the seat of the chair. "I'll wait for you outside," she said to Ted, and walked away without once looking at Rachel.

"This is not the time or place, Rachel," Ted said, with a warning look toward the other diners. A few nearby had picked up on the unfolding drama and were openly curious. Some watched with amusement, enjoying the show.

"What is it if it isn't what I think?" Rachel demanded in a low but fierce tone.

Ted had his wallet in his hands now, pulling out cash. He dropped a number of twenties on the table and reached for her arm, intending to guide her out of the restaurant. "Rachel—"

Rachel jerked away. "Don't...touch me." Lifting her chin, she turned on her heel and strode through the tables, mortified beyond anything that strangers had witnessed her humiliation. Her color high, she looked neither right nor left until she cleared the room. Now at the entrance, she pushed blindly at the double doors before Ted could assist her, desperate to breathe fresh air. She was aware that he said something to her before addressing the attendant who'd valet-parked his car, but she was intent only on escape. Almost running now, she sought the refuge of her car and dashed across the circular drive into the parking area. In her shocked state, however, she forgot where she had parked.

She reversed direction suddenly and almost ran into Ted,

who'd caught up with her. "What are you doing here?" he asked tersely.

"Looking for my car." Rooting through her handbag, she found her car keys and, in a panic, pushed the remote. Somewhere to her left, she heard the chirp of her vehicle.

"I mean, what are you doing at this restaurant? How did you—"

"Find you?" Heading for her car, she simply shook her head. "What does it matter, Ted?"

"Were you following me?"

She stopped then and looked at him. "I didn't think until ten minutes ago that I had any reason to follow you, Ted."

He gave a sigh and, bending his head, began to rub a place between his eyes. Ted was prone to migraines and she suspected he'd be in real pain by nightfall. Come to think of it, his migraines had come more frequently in the past few months. She thought back rapidly—six months? Longer? "How long have you been seeing her?"

"This is not the time, Rachel."

"How…long?" she repeated deliberately.

"Awhile."

She felt a pain in her chest that was as sharp as if he'd actually struck her. He wasn't denying it. Had she been thinking there was any other explanation for finding him in so compromising a situation?

"We were planning to tell you soon," he said, not meeting her eyes.

"Tell me what? That you're having an affair with the wife of your partner and friend in your practice? That you've decided to ignore the fact that you're a married man? Were you going to tell me that you've broken the vows you took to be faithful?"

It was midday and sunny. Overhead, the vast Texas sky was a surreal blue with stunning formations of soft white clouds. Ted's brown eyes crinkled at the corners as he squinted upward. "I know it looks bad," he said. "Francine and I—well, we didn't plan for this to happen. We tried to fight it. We—''

"You tried to fight it." She gave him a look of disgust. "I didn't see any sign of struggle when you swiped her palm with your tongue a few minutes ago. I haven't noticed any battles with your conscience when you've made excuses to miss Nick's ball games or Kendall's recitals. And I'll bet you haven't fought the urge to hop into bed with her, either, right? So just what do you mean, you've tried to fight it, Ted?''

"Would you keep your voice down, for God's sake? We're in a parking lot, Rachel. I know we're going to have to talk about this, but not here, okay?'' He drove his fingers through his expensively styled hair. She suddenly recalled finding the two-hundred-dollar charge on their American Express card at one of Dallas's premier hair stylists. She'd teased him about it, as his hair was obviously thinning and she'd assumed it was simply male ego. Well, it was ego and a lot more, she knew now.

She felt tears well up and she looked away quickly, not giving him the satisfaction of knowing how much it hurt. Through a haze, she saw Francine standing beneath the canopy at the entrance of the restaurant. She noted the trim black suit, the sleek, long legs made even more stunning by shoes with three-inch heels that had cost at least two hundred dollars. Rachel could afford to pay hundreds of dollars for a pair of shoes, too, but she felt there was something intrinsically...vulgar in such self-indulgence. Obviously, Francine felt no such reluctance.

"Is there an internist from Baylor interested in joining the practice,'' she asked quietly, "or was that a lie, too?''

"He was interviewed last night.''

She nodded, her gaze still fixed on Francine now being helped into Ted's car by a valet. They were so comfortable in their illicit affair that they didn't even bother coming in separate vehicles. Where did they meet in Rose Hill? she wondered. Had Ted found time when she was at school to screw Francine in their bed at home?

She turned back and looked her husband in the eye. "Why, Ted?"

"He's qualified. He's young. He'll build up a nice patient base in no time flat."

"I'm not talking about the internist. I'm talking about us. Why? How did this happen?"

Now his gaze found Francine, who watched him from the passenger seat of his Lexus. It was a long moment before he shrugged and said, with his eyes still on his lover, "I couldn't help myself."

Rachel drove back to Rose Hill with a silent and sullen Jason Pate. He sat slumped in the seat beside her, the headset of his CD player vibrating at a decibel level that was certain to damage his eardrums. Accepting the silence as a missed opportunity on her part to try to do some good with the boy, Rachel's own emotions were also in turmoil, and it was all she could do to hold herself together.

Actually, she felt numb. But she knew, as a professional, that when something shocking or hurtful or grievous strikes an individual, going numb is a temporary coping mechanism sometimes necessary for survival. She needed time to decide how best to deal with this. A part of her was still clinging to shocked disbelief. To denial. Ted couldn't possibly be serious. This was a crazy, midlife crisis thing and he would get over it. Then, maybe the horror of telling Nick and Kendall, destroying their illusions about their father, would not be necessary.

On the other hand, if he was determined to carry on the affair, what then? She hadn't asked him if he was planning on getting a divorce. In the first shock of discovering Ted's infidelity, she didn't think she was ready to consider ending her marriage.

Definitely denial.

Considering she'd left Dallas later than planned, she didn't arrive in Rose Hill until after school was over for the day. She'd reached Nick on his cell phone after arranging with her friend, Marta Ruiz, a teacher at Rose Hill High, to pick up the kids and see that they were settled at home until she got back, leaving Nick in charge. Marta had been happy to oblige. Widowed after a brief marriage and childless, Marta had been Rachel's friend since her first day on the job at Rose Hill High. At thirty-three, Marta was an award-winning honors English teacher and a great favorite with the kids, even while forcing them to read Thomas Mann and Shakespeare.

"Is everything okay?" she'd wanted to know. "You sound funny, Ray."

"Everything's fine," Rachel had lied. "It's been a hassle fighting bureaucrats in the Texas legal system."

"We're bureaucrats, too," Marta pointed out dryly. "I'd think you'd have a leg up, being entrenched yourself."

"Yes, but we don't have to deal with lawyers," Rachel said. "Anyway, I've got Jason now, and after I drop him off at school where Coach Monk awaits, I'll go straight home. Are you sure it's not an inconvenience to pick up the kids and drop them at my house?"

"Don't be ridiculous. I'll even stay awhile and watch Kendall if Nick wants to hang out with his buddies." She paused. "I guess Ted couldn't get away."

It wasn't exactly a question. "No, he's tied up...into the evening."

"Hmm."

Marta never bothered to hide her disapproval of Ted. She considered him neglectful as a father and selfish as a husband. "It's a doctor-thing," she was fond of saying. "They've got too much ego and you're so attuned to everybody else's needs that you never stop to consider your own."

"I don't have any needs that go unfulfilled," she'd disputed on the day of that conversation, "or at least none that cause me much heartburn."

Now, recalling her words, she felt like a complete idiot. Of course she had needs, and now that she'd been slapped in the face with her husband's infidelity, she admitted to sensing something wrong in her marriage for quite a while. Was this the prelude to divorce? Were she and Ted destined to go their separate ways? Would Nick and Kendall wind up as part of two "blended" families one day?

At a traffic light, she fought off a wave of despair. One thing she had decided during her soul-search on the way home—she wasn't going to mention anything to the kids just yet. Before tearing their lives apart, she and Ted would have to talk, but it would not be tonight. She was too filled with conflicting emotions to face it tonight.

Her cell phone rang as the light turned green. She reached for it, glancing at the number without recognition. "Hello?"

"Is this Rachel Forrester?"

It was a man's voice. She frowned, trying to place it. "Yes, who is this?"

"It's Cameron Ford. Dinah gave me your number," he said.

Cameron Ford. She was momentarily speechless. Why would he be calling her? They hadn't spoken since that distressing confrontation in her office five years ago.

"I'm at the hospital," he said.

"Yes?" She waited, still in the dark.

"It's your mother."

"My mother?" Her heart stopped. "Oh, Lord. What is it? What's wrong?"

"She's in the emergency room. She wanted me to let you know."

Two

Cameron Ford ended the call to Rachel Forrester and stood, grim-faced, in the waiting room of the ER to wait for her. It had been a helluva shock to look out his kitchen window and see his elderly neighbor lying unconscious in her azaleas. It had been another shock—and this one almost as unpleasant— to learn that she was Rachel Forrester's mother. Dinah Hunt had moved next door a couple of months before, but he had not made any of the usual hospitable gestures that he might have done to welcome her. He was pretty much a solitary type to begin with, plus he'd been on deadline with his book and, as always, nothing and no one got much more than momentary interest until he was done. He'd noticed the woman and felt relieved that she lived alone and would probably be a quiet, unobtrusive neighbor.

Which was his excuse for not being more attentive. But what, he wondered, was Rachel's excuse? He did not recall seeing her over there in the weeks since Dinah moved in. You'd think her daughter would have put in an appearance or two. Too busy sticking her nose into other people's lives to put in time with her aging mother, he thought. But he'd heard real panic in her voice when he'd called just now. He'd been unable to give her any information since he hadn't been told anything himself when he'd arrived at the hospital with Dinah, incoherent and pale as the white gardenias she prized. But at least she'd been conscious, sort of. When he'd reached her after spotting her lying at the edge of the flower beds separating their two houses, he had been pretty close to panic himself.

"Sir? Excuse me, sir."

He turned to find a woman beckoning to him from a cubicle behind a sliding glass partition. With a last look outside, he went to her. "What's the problem?"

"We need some insurance information on Mrs. Hunt."

"I'm sorry, I can't help you. She's my next-door neighbor, not a relative. I happened to see her when she fainted out in the yard."

The clerk frowned. "I need to know how to bill this, sir."

"If you'll wait a few minutes, you can probably get everything you need from her daughter, who should be here any minute. Dinah told me flat-out that she wasn't staying. I had a heck of a time just getting her here."

The clerk sniffed and shuffled forms. "You should have called 911. EMTs are trained to deal with the elderly."

"I'll remember that next time," he said dryly. He glanced again at the entrance just as Rachel rushed inside looking flustered and anxious. "Here's her daughter now." Cameron lifted his hand, catching her eye, and she hurried over.

"Where is she? What's wrong? Is it a heart attack?"

"They haven't given me any information, but maybe the clerk here can tell you something. For what it's worth, your mother regained consciousness in the car and did her best to talk me out of bringing her here. She claimed she wasn't having chest pains, so I don't think it's a heart attack."

Rachel turned quickly to the woman. "Is that right? Is she okay? Can I see her?"

"Someone will be out soon to answer your questions," the clerk said. "Meanwhile, I need—"

"What happened?" Rachel asked Cameron. "What do you mean, she was conscious and talking? When was she unconscious?"

"When she was flat on her back in her azaleas," he said, making no effort to be gentle. "Once I got her up and on her feet, she was dizzy and disoriented, but after a few minutes, she seemed to rally.''

Rachel was still confused. ''I don't understand. How did you... I mean, are you saying you were at her house?''

''I was on my porch. I looked over and saw her.''

''Your porch. You looked over and saw her.'' Rachel put a hand to her forehead before looking at him and asking incredulously, ''You...live nearby?''

''I live in the house next door.'' She didn't look any happier hearing that than he did knowing it.

''How could that be?'' She was asking herself, not him. ''How did I not know that?''

''Because you don't show much interest in your mother's affairs?'' It was a cheap shot, but Rachel Forrester had that effect on him. He had nothing against her mother, but he didn't owe Rachel anything. Just the opposite, in fact. His feelings for her hadn't changed since that day they had talked in her office after Jack's funeral, five years ago. Seeing her now was like taking the lid off a pot that still simmered with bitterness.

''Did you call the EMTs?'' she asked, ignoring his remark.

''I drove her. She wouldn't let me call the EMTs.''

''I—thank you.'' Rachel pressed the fingers of both hands hard against her lips. ''Maybe it's a stroke,'' she whispered. ''But the last time I was over there—''

''Yeah, when was that, Rachel?'' he asked, fixing her with a hard look. ''I see the neighbors dropping by, I see the postman chatting her up, I see the guy delivering her prescriptions from the pharmacy, but I don't see much of you.''

He could see he had her attention now. She stared at him. ''I do not neglect my mother,'' she said stiffly.

''Yeah, well, you could have fooled me.''

''Dinah Hunt. Someone for Dinah Hunt?'' Both turned as a young resident appeared and stood looking over the occupants in the waiting room.

''Here,'' Rachel said, moving toward him. ''I'm Rachel Forrester. Dinah Hunt is my mother. How is she?''

"I'm Dr. Carruthers." He smiled at both Rachel and Cameron, who'd followed her. "Your mom's just fine. In fact, she'll probably be out here demanding to be taken home before I finish talking. She told me in no uncertain terms that she wasn't about to spend a night in a hospital bed."

"What on earth happened?" Rachel asked anxiously. "Mr. Ford said he found her unconscious outside where she was working in her garden."

Carruthers nodded. "That's her story, too. And it's not uncommon in patients with hypoglycemia."

"Hypoglycemia?" Rachel repeated blankly.

"We don't have the results of her blood work yet, but she tells me she's been diagnosed as borderline hypoglycemic and she confessed to spending most of the day doing yard work without stopping for lunch or even taking a break." He paused. "How old is your mother?"

"Sixty-two."

"Amazing. Couple that with her medical condition and the fact that she worked in full sun without a hat and you have a recipe for a blackout."

"Hypoglycemia means low blood sugar, doesn't it?" Rachel asked.

"Yes. You knew, of course?"

She was shaking her head. "No. No, I didn't."

"Well, now that you do, try to persuade her to make a few concessions to her body's need for frequent, small meals, preferably high in protein." He smiled again. "And perhaps pacing herself a bit when she plans to do yard work."

"Is this a serious illness?"

"Not particularly, so long as a few common-sense precautions are observed." He included both Rachel and Cameron in his next words. "If she seems reluctant to discuss it with you, just stop by my office and pick up a pamphlet. You need to be aware so that you can help her adjust. The pamphlet lists some suggestions that help prevent sudden drops in blood sugar, which is what caused her to faint. Again, I don't have the results of her blood work and I might be jumping the gun here, but chances are we're on the right track.''

Just then, Dinah emerged from a treatment cubicle and, spotting Rachel, headed directly over. She was dressed for gardening in a pair of loose-fitting denim overalls over a faded tie-dyed T-shirt and muddy, once-white sneakers. A neat size eight, she ordinarily looked ten years younger than her age, but her collapse had taken a toll. There was a liberal sprinkling of gray in her hair, which had probably once been the same rich, near-black shade as Rachel's, Cameron noticed now. But whereas Rachel's cut was short, sleek and smooth, Dinah's style was wildly curly and much longer. She'd probably started the day with it confined at her nape in a leather thong, circa the sixties, but much of it had long since worked itself loose and the overall effect was one of a slightly aging flower child.

''As I mentioned,'' Dr. Carruthers said with a chuckle, ''I guessed she'd be out here before I was done.''

''Thank you, Doctor,'' Rachel murmured, turning back to Carruthers and extending her hand.

''My pleasure,'' he said, shaking it. He looked then at Cameron. ''You did the right thing insisting on having her checked out, Mr. Forrester.''

''Ford, not Forrester,'' Cameron said, shaking the doctor's hand. ''And I'm just a neighbor.''

''Oh.'' Carruthers paused for an awkward beat or two, then turned again to Rachel. ''The results of the blood work should be available sometime tomorrow, Ms. Forrester. If there's anything unusual, I'll call you. Otherwise, the results will be mailed.''

''Call me, Dr. Carruthers,'' Dinah instructed firmly, ''not Rachel. I'm not too fragile to hear bad news, at least not yet.''

''I don't anticipate giving you bad news, Mrs. Hunt,'' he said, with a grin. ''And remember, no working in the sun without a hat and no skipping meals.''

Dinah gave him a droll look. ''I'll try to remember that,

as I sure don't want to wake up looking at the underside of azalea leaves again.''

Still chuckling, he left them to enter another cubicle a few steps down the hall.

"Let's go, Mom," Rachel said, taking Dinah's arm. "The insurance—"

"In a minute." Dinah resisted being hustled away. "First, I need to thank Cameron."

"You don't owe me any thanks," he said. Now that he knew the older woman wasn't suffering a stroke or worse, he itched to get back to his work. He was only half done with the proposal for his next book.

"Well, of course I do. And I meant what I said in the car, Cameron. Anytime you feel like having a break, come over for coffee or some iced tea. I like to bake and usually have a little something on hand—cake or cookies. Nick and Kendall can vouch for that.''

"Nick and Kendall?"

"My grandchildren, Rachel's babies." Dinah moved over toward the area where the insurance clerk waited and presented the appropriate cards before looking back at him. "And thanks again for giving me a ride to the hospital, although I still say it was not necessary. I knew what was wrong the minute I began to feel dizzy. But by then, it was too late and I just keeled over. Plain bad judgment on my part," she said, taking the clipboard that was passed through the partition by the clerk.

"You should have waited until the weekend, Mom," Rachel scolded. "That's the kind of work Nick can do for you. And this just proves what I was telling you about moving out of your apartment. The upkeep on a house and yard is arduous. You should have gotten a condominium."

"Do I advise you where to live, Rachel?"

"No, of course not, but—"

"Then when I become senile, you can start advising me. Until then, I make my own decisions. Now," she said briskly, "as I said, I exercised bad judgment today, but the day dawned so sunny and clear and the ground was nice and soft from that shower Wednesday. I knew I wouldn't have a better chance to get those shrubs relocated and to tackle the weeds in that bed where the daylilies are planted.'' She studied the form to be completed on the clipboard for a moment. ''My word, I'm going to have to sit down to fill this thing out. Must be fifty questions on it.''

''Let me do that for you, Mom.'' Rachel reached for the clipboard.

''I'm still capable of filling out my own medical history, Rachel.'' She moved to a line of chairs against the wall, sat down and began writing.

Rachel drew a frustrated breath, then looked gamely into Cameron's eyes. When she spoke, it was in a tone that Dinah couldn't hear. ''It's frustrating trying to keep my mother from taking on more than she can handle, and since you believe that I neglect her, I'll say nothing more about that. Nevertheless, I appreciate what you did this afternoon. Thank you.''

''No thanks necessary,'' he told her, just as he'd told her mother. ''I did what any decent neighbor would do.'' She simply looked at him and something in her expression prodded the devil inside him. ''Your mother's not getting any younger. She bought the house she wanted and you should be gracious enough to help her enjoy it. An occasional visit would be nice.''

She flushed as his barb found its mark but, as good as her word, she didn't offer any defense. Something flashed in her eyes and he caught it just before it was veiled by her lashes—very long lashes, he noted. Then whatever he'd glimpsed was gone. Still stonily silent, she gave him a curt nod—just a quick dip of her head—before turning on her heel and striding to a chair on the far side of her mother and taking a seat. She didn't look at him again.

''Mom, won't you please reconsider and come home with me tonight?'' Frustrated, Rachel watched Dinah strip the leather thong from her hair and run her hands through the unruly curls. A couple of dried leaves and a broken twig landed on the bedroom carpet.

"For the tenth time, Rachel, I'm perfectly fine." Sitting on the side of her bed, Dinah pulled off her dirty sneakers and handed them to Rachel. "Will you drop these in my washing machine on your way out, please? Don't turn it on. I'll need to throw in the overalls when I'm done with my shower."

"You won't forget to eat before going to bed then, will you?"

"How could I? I'm as hungry as a bear."

Rachel went to the door. "I'll make you something while you shower. How about an omelette?"

"Not necessary, Rachel. And instead of feeding me, shouldn't you be worrying about Nick and Kendall?" Their eyes met in the mirror. "It's dinnertime and I'll bet Ted isn't home yet, is he?"

"No, he's...he has a meeting. He'll be late. And I've called Marta. She'll look out for the kids until I get home."

Dinah held her gaze for a moment, then with a skeptical sound, began to work at the snaps on her overalls. "That man has so many night meetings, you'd think he was a politician instead of a doctor. If he doesn't watch out, the kids are going to grow up not knowing him any better than they know the town's mayor!"

"I can't disagree with you on that, Mom."

Holding the overalls against her, Dinah studied Rachel's face. "Have you two talked about this? How long is he going to neglect his responsibilities? Have you discussed the importance of Nick and Kendall having both a mother and a father?"

"I wouldn't define our encounters as discussions," Rachel said frankly. "They usually wind up with me nagging and Ted clamming up."

Dinah sank with a sigh onto the side of the bed. "I guess

it's not helpful to hear me harping on it, either, is it? I'm sorry, Rachel, but you'd think—''

"Speaking of the kids, I'd better be going." Rachel stood in the shadows of the hall where her mother couldn't see how her words had stung, especially tonight. "You're sure you won't reconsider and come with me?"

Dinah didn't reply for a moment, but Rachel knew she wasn't finished. "I'm sure." She cocked her head, studying her intently. "How was your day? Those kids giving you more than the usual grief lately?"

"No more than usual. I counseled a pregnant sixteen-year-old this morning and then I drove to Dallas and picked up Jason Pate, Coach Monk's star quarterback. He was being held by the Juvenile authorities on a DUI charge."

"Oops."

"Uh-huh. Jason is the heart and soul of the Mustangs. Hence, Coach Monk's concern. Or rather the play-offs, which are in full swing, are his main concern and Jason is key to that."

"And then you came home to find your ditzy mom had landed herself in the ER," Dinah said with a grimace.

Rachel rubbed her temple with two fingers and managed a weak smile. "I suppose it has been one of those days."

"And that's all?" Dinah said, still trying to define something more she had sensed in Rachel's mood.

"Unless you want to count the lecture I got from Cameron Ford." She was still stinging from his unflattering assessment of her as a daughter. Five years ago, he'd been brutally judgmental about her ability as a counselor, now it appeared she hadn't risen a jot in his estimation. Bad counselor then, bad daughter now. It made no sense for her to care what he thought. She must be particularly vulnerable and he'd hit a nerve.

"I guess I'm shocked to learn you've moved next door to a man who hates me," she told her mother with a weak laugh. "If I'd known he was going to be your neighbor, I would have argued even more fiercely against you buying a house instead of a condo.''

She knew the man's reputation as a gifted author and she bought all his books—on the sly, of course, as it seemed inappropriate somehow, considering how brutal and accusatory he'd been about her job. It would be awkward having him right next door every time she visited her mother, although she supposed he wasn't any different from other Rose Hill residents who'd sampled life elsewhere before coming back home to live.

They'd both attended Rose Hill High, but Cameron had been four years older than Rachel, which made him as remote from her world as seniors are from lowly freshman girls. Even then, he'd been a brooding, nonconformist sort and she thought he wasn't much changed today. It was silly to be bothered that he had a low opinion of her. She knew him to be a decent person, if somewhat aloof—if his press was accurate—which should be all she needed to know since he was going to be her mother's neighbor. It wasn't as if he'd be *her* neighbor. Thank God.

Dinah was frowning. ''A lecture from Cameron? About what?''

''He thinks I neglect you. He told me I should find more time to visit. He thinks you get more attention from the postman and your neighbors than you get from me.''

''Ridiculous,'' Dinah said with a dismissive click of her tongue. ''Ignore him. Besides, we both know where his hostility is coming from.''

''His son,'' Rachel said, giving a sigh. ''He must still believe that I should have picked up on Jack's depression and done something before it was too late.'' She paused a long moment. ''Maybe I should have, Mom. I've relived those last few weeks of Jack's life many times. Maybe Cameron's right.''

Dinah made an impatient sound. ''If you could read the mind of every kid in an emotional tailspin at Rose Hill High, you'd wind up in one yourself. You do a good job with those children, Rachel. God knows, Jack's suicide was a tragedy, and what makes it even more tragic for you is that you were in the process of working with the boy, but sometimes there's just no foreseeing these things. Cam's reaction today was simply that he wasn't prepared to see you and it reminded him of what he'd like to forget.''

"Cam?'' she questioned dryly.

"He told me to call him Cam,'' Dinah said, rubbing at a smudge on her elbow. "Try not to dwell on what you may or may not have done. I, for one, know you always do your best.''

Rachel stared at the muddy sneakers in her hand, thinking back to that time. "Jack just didn't strike me as suicidal, Mom. I must have spent a hundred hours going over those last few weeks of his life. There was something troubling him, I knew that. His grades were slipping and he seemed distracted. His teachers had noticed a change in him. Of course, he was adjusting to a new school in a new state. Big difference between New York and Texas. And his parents were recently divorced, so he had a lot to contend with. It made sense that he was unhappy. Almost any teenager would be. I had a talk with him the day before he…before it happened. Why didn't I see it coming? If I could have just—''

"Could just what, Rachel? Live that day over? Be all things to all kids?'' Dinah removed her socks. "This wasn't the first tragedy that will happen on your watch, hon. And it won't be the last. Cam is unable to let it go and maybe that's understandable, but you're in a different place. You must let it go.''

Rachel drew in a deep breath and managed a fleeting smile. "I know.'' She scooped up the overalls that Dinah had tossed on the bed. "I'll put these in the washing machine for you and then I'm going to make you an omelette before I leave. And don't bother arguing, Mom.''

"If you must.'' Dinah rolled her eyes and pulled her T-shirt over her head. "May as well throw this in with everything else.'' Then, as if still trying to put her finger on something else in Rachel's mood, she added, "Is everything okay with you and Ted?"

Rachel stopped with the washables bundled in her arms and smiled brightly. "Define 'everything.'"

Dinah frowned in the act of donning a robe and looked hard at her. "You tell me, Rachel."

"Maybe, as you say, Mom, I am feeling a little neglected."

"Well, it's about time," Dinah said flatly. "You've been willing to put your own needs aside to accommodate Ted almost from the moment the two of you met. I'll always resent that you dropped your own plans for medical school to help him get his M.D. and a specialty. And now, after all you've done—" Dinah was pacing, her hands waving and slashing with heartfelt emotion. It was no secret that she'd long believed Rachel's sacrifice of her original plan for a career in medicine was a big mistake. She stopped suddenly. "You know what the problem is, Rachel? You've spoiled Ted rotten. You haven't demanded enough from him. I'm happy to hear you finally say you're feeling neglected. All you have to do now is tell him that."

Rachel made a short, futile attempt to laugh. "Yeah, that's all I have to do."

Dinah gave her a hug. "Go home, hon. Forget my laundry and the omelette. Tend to your babies and then take a long, hot soak in the tub and practice how best to let him have it. I promise you won't have another call to the ER about me."

"You should have told me about the onset of hypoglycemia, Mother," Rachel said with a chiding look.

"I know, but that would be just one more thing on your worry list."

"You're my mother. I'm supposed to worry about you."

"Not if I can help it." She gave Rachel a gentle shove toward the stairs. "Kiss the kids for me and tell that spoiled rotten husband of yours when he finally gets home that there're going to be some changes made."

* * *

Rachel wasn't the only one thinking of changes. Ted stood at the glass doors in the master bedroom of the lake cabin in deep thought. Moonlight dancing on the surface of the lake hinted at the chill of the night, but inside it was cozy. He'd built a fire in the fireplace and had knocked back a couple of stiff drinks. It had helped erase the bad taste he had in his mouth over the scene with Rachel at the restaurant, but he had a headache now, not the beginning of a migraine, which struck him sometimes in the throes of stress or crisis, but a nagging, unpleasant nuisance of a headache. And the euphoria he usually felt when he was with Francine hadn't quite anesthetized it.

He should be feeling good, he thought. The moment he'd dreaded for months had come and gone. Rachel knew about the affair now. She'd been shocked, as expected, and mad as hell, as she'd had a right. But all in all, it hadn't been as difficult as it could have been. For a moment, in the parking lot, he'd thought she might turn really mean, but it hadn't happened. There had been a horrific incident a couple of years ago in Houston when a woman caught her husband with another woman and after an argument in the parking lot of a swank restaurant, she'd climbed in her car and run him over. Not satisfied that she'd hurt him enough, she'd backed up and rolled over him again, killing him. No chance of that with Rachel. She was too practical to do something that would jeopardize the kids and their future. Or herself, for that matter.

Rubbing a hand over his face, he turned away from the view. The site for the cabin had been carefully chosen by Rachel when they'd decided to invest in real estate on the lake. She'd researched every lot available, looking for just the right one, and she'd hit a home run, as usual. She was good at that sort of thing. She managed time and her responsibilities so well that he often thought she could run the Pentagon if she wanted. The trouble was that she wasn't what he wanted anymore. The type of person she'd been when he was in med school and then setting up the practice was okay, but now he wanted—needed—a woman who was more feminine, more hip, sexier. A woman who needed him and made him feel as if he was special. Sometimes he thought Rachel went for weeks without really looking at him. But when Francine gazed up at him, impressed by his opinions, interested in his experiences, and so damn responsive as a lover, God, he felt incredible.

She stood smiling at him now, shedding the black suit one piece at a time, moving slowly, her body language sensual and provocative. Apparently, she wasn't feeling the same conflicting emotions as he about having their affair out in the open, but then they hadn't faced the major hurdle of telling Walter yet. When she wriggled out of her skirt, all she had left were thigh-high stockings—black—a wisp of a bra and thong panties. When he looked at her delectable little ass in that thong, it never failed that his dick went hard and his mouth went dry.

Like a cat, Francine put a knee on the bed and with a playful growl began a provocative crawl over the mattress toward him. "You're looking too serious, sugar," she murmured, puckering her lips at him in a wind-kiss. "Get naked and let me make you smile."

His brain went numb and his erection throbbed at the look of her stalking him across the bed, her sweet butt in the air and the heavy globes of her breasts threatening to burst out of that excuse for a bra. He knew she'd had breast enhancement, but it only made her more voluptuous, sexier. She was a wet dream come to life and she was his.

He pressed a palm against his erection and pushed thoughts of Rachel and Walter from his mind. Francine was across the bed now and her hands were at work unfastening his belt. Next, she'd have him freed of his pants, and with her already in position, one touch from her pink tongue would send him over the edge. He wondered if she gave Walter…

"Wait, Franny," he told her as she reached for the zipper

on his pants. "Hold on, baby." He caught her hands and squeezed them, stopping her.

She looked up at him, moist lips parted. Seeing his expression, she sighed with resignation and rested her forehead against his abdomen. "What?" There was impatience in her voice. She didn't like being interrupted.

"We need to talk about it, Franny."

She moved away, drew her knees up and wrapped her arms around them. Her sexy mouth was now in a pout. "What's to discuss, Teddy? She saw us, she knows now. There's no turning back. It'll make everything easier."

"How do you figure that?" he asked. "Walter will find out, my kids will soon know. Everyone in the practice will be buzzing with it. Hell, within twenty-four hours, all of Rose Hill will be buzzing with it, trust me."

"They'll get over it, Teddy," she said, speaking as if he was slightly dim. Her way of focusing solely on herself made him uncomfortable sometimes.

"It was easier before when nobody knew but us, Francine. Complications will begin to multiply, big time. We need to be prepared."

"For what?"

She couldn't be as unconcerned by the consequences as she seemed, he thought. He drew a breath and spoke patiently. "What I'm trying to say is that both of us need to be on the same page, especially with Walter. He'll have questions. We need to settle between us what we're going to answer."

"Forget Walter. I'll think of something. Whatever he says, I'll handle it."

"He's not going to accept you sleeping with me, Franny. You need to make him understand this isn't just some meaningless affair that'll play itself out if he's patient. You need to tell him it's serious between us." Ted rubbed at a temple, now throbbing. Maybe it was the onset of a migraine. He wished for a couple of Darvon tablets, but he'd taken the last of them just a couple of days ago. "Has it occurred to you that Rachel may be talking to him right now?"

"Rachel wouldn't do that," Francine said. She lifted one long leg and began removing the black stockings. It was an invitation, but he still wanted to try to settle this. She dropped the nylons delicately onto the floor. "She's too..."

"Too decent?"

"Yeah, decent. Too nice for the real world. People like Rachel will always get the short end of the stick."

Ted felt a prickle of unease at her attitude. She was a maddening, irresistible mix of female charm, sexy allure and street smarts. And the package was captivating. It made him uncomfortable to admit it, but he felt almost enslaved. He couldn't get enough of her.

Sensing she'd crossed a line, Francine reached out and, with a wicked little smile, ran a finger down the opening of his fly. "C'mon, you worry too much."

He removed her hand and sat down beside her. "You don't worry enough. We've got to talk about Walter. When he finds out, he's going to be one pissed-off son of a bitch. I'm not sure he'll be able to control himself. He's crazy where you're concerned." As crazy as Ted himself was, which was another fact that worried him.

She unhooked her bra and tossed it on the floor. "Like I said, let me worry about controlling Walter, sugar." Up on her knees now, she slipped her arms around him from behind and began unbuttoning his shirt. She got it off him and pressed her naked breasts against his back as her hands moved all over the front of him. "Hmm, I love doing this," she crooned, sifting through the hair on his chest. "Walter's got a gut and he's about fifty pounds overweight," she complained, tweaking his nipples with her fingers. "Show me a man with muscles and a flat belly and I get really hot, sugar." She was nibbling on his ear now and he felt himself weakening.

His lust for Francine had been a keen motivating factor in the exercise program Ted had undertaken a year ago. As a result of hours in the gym, his abdomen was as flat as that of a man fifteen years younger, and his reward was the uninhibited enjoyment Francine took in letting him know it. God, it was a turn-on knowing he excited a woman like this.

One of her hands wandered lower now, slipped beneath the waistband of his briefs. He groaned as her fingers curled around him, and he gave up trying to have a practical discussion. Later, he promised himself as he fell back on the bed and let her strip off his pants and briefs. They could work on the practicalities of continuing their relationship later. Rachel might prove difficult once she'd had some time to come to terms with the fact that he was in love with Francine. And Walter was definitely a wild card. He was one possessive bastard where Francine was concerned and Ted could identify with that. But he'd go to hell and back before giving her up.

She had climbed on top now, smiling and tempting him with her lush, heavy breasts cupped in both hands. She still wore the thong and she moved like a belly dancer on top of him, bewitching and utterly sexual, an enticing siren of a woman. Francine called to something deep within him that he'd never known was there and that no other woman had ever tapped. With a groan, he fumbled at the thong, tore it off her and violently buried himself to the hilt. She might deny they were in for trouble, but Ted knew stormy times were ahead. But that thought was lost as he gave himself up to the lust of the moment.

Three

Rachel never had a chance to lay down the law to Ted that night, even if the opportunity had presented itself. Which it didn't. Marta had fixed dinner for Nick and Kendall, but her loyalty as a friend did not extend to doing the dishes, and without Rachel's supervision, neither had the kids. So, by the time Rachel had tidied up, supervised homework, monitored television time and urged the kids upstairs to shower and get into bed, it was late. Taking a minute for herself—finally—she had barely begun filling the tub for a long soak and some deep thinking about her marriage and Ted's infidelity when the phone rang. It was Monk Tyson. She was in no fit shape to discuss Jason Pate's problems, which she assumed was the reason for his call. She was swamped by her own problems. But Monk was insistent. Consequently, she was tied up for another half hour sharing the details of the boy's arrest and release from Juvenile in Dallas. It was almost eleven when the call finally ended. And still no word from Ted.

She showered—forgoing the long soak—and turned the covers back on her bed. Waiting up for Ted was something she usually did, or rather, she'd been in the habit of doing so until his hours became so erratic. Now that she knew about the affair, that intimate little ritual of marriage was ended. She felt a pang, knowing Ted probably hadn't valued that effort on her part for the past year, anyway, considering his infatuation with another woman. He'd be sleeping in the guest room now and was probably relieved to do it. She lay flat on her back, dry-eyed, her gaze fixed on the ceiling. She vowed he wouldn't see her desolation or find her red-eyed and weepy when he finally showed up. But hours later as the clock struck two and then three, she realized he wasn't coming home at all.

The numbness that had gripped her until then suddenly disappeared. Since the moment Ted had admitted the affair, her stomach had been in a knot, but she'd crammed so many other things into her day that her personal problems had been crowded out. How could he be in love with someone else, and Francine Dalton, of all people? Francine and Walter were their friends. Walter, older and more settled in Rose Hill, had partnered up with Ted when they'd first started the practice. A few years later, he'd married Francine, who'd been twenty years younger than Walter. Francine, Rachel thought now, was twelve years younger than Ted. It was ludicrous.

It was crushing. A sob caught in her throat. Just last month, she and Ted had celebrated their eighteenth anniversary at a restaurant with Walter and Francine. Had there been signs of Ted's infidelity then? She thought of the new suits he'd suddenly decided he needed, the silk boxer shorts he'd begun wearing, the diet he'd undertaken to lose weight, the ambitious exercise program he'd been fixated on at the gym. Moments of sexual intimacy between them had become increasingly rare. She remembered the ongoing search for an additional partner in the practice that required trips to Dallas or Houston or Los Angeles, Boston, New York. Always excluding her. How had she been so blind? Didn't a wife sense these things? Didn't she somehow know deep down in her heart that her husband had fallen out of love with her? Is that what had happened? Had Ted fallen out of love with her and she hadn't noticed? But how could that be? She was a psychologist. She was supposed to be able to read people, to see beyond the obvious. Was she a failure there, as Cameron Ford seemed to think, as well as in her role as Ted's wife?

And now, what next?

There was no school the next day, Saturday, and fortunately Nick and Kendall were still sleeping when Ted finally came home. Standing on the sunporch drinking a cup of black coffee, Rachel waited while he went into the kitchen, poured himself some coffee and then went looking for her. At least, she assumed he was looking for her. She said nothing, unwilling to call out to him as she once would have done to let him know she was in the sunroom. After a few minutes, he found her.

For a moment, as he stood in the door, they simply looked at each other. He still wore the Armani suit from yesterday, she noticed, although it was somewhat wilted and he'd removed his tie. The ends of it dangled from his jacket pocket. His shirt was open at the throat and she saw a faint mark near the collar. Francine's lipstick, she guessed, and felt a surge of raw rage. She took some satisfaction that he looked tired and his eyes were red-rimmed as if he'd had little sleep. She could guess the reason now.

"Where were you last night, Ted?"

"I stayed in the cabin at the lake."

"And you didn't think to call and let us—the kids and me—know that?"

He didn't answer, but shrugged out of the jacket and tossed it onto a rattan chair. "We need to talk, Rachel."

"Was Francine with you at the cabin?"

"For a while. Then I took her home." He shrugged, rubbing the back of his neck. "I apologize for not calling. I should have. I thought it was for the best last night...now that you know, I mean. I figured you'd need some time to come to terms with—"

"With the fact that my husband is a liar and a cheat?" She set her coffee down before he could see her unsteady hands. "After eighteen years, it takes more than a few hours to come to terms with something like that, Ted," she said bitterly.

"I didn't plan this, Rachel, I swear to God." He eased himself down onto the chair. "And neither did Francine. I can't explain it, how one day we were just friends, and then…the next thing we knew, it was something else. It just…happened. She and I—''

"It just happened that both of you ignored sacred vows? It just happened that you schemed and planned ways to sneak around? It just happened that you forgot what was at stake for you, the father of two children?''

"I know it sounds bad.'' With his gaze fixed on his coffee mug, he shook his head. "I don't expect you to understand, but what we need to do now is figure out how best to handle it.''

Rachel sat gingerly on the edge of the rattan settee. She was thinking back to the countless times they'd been together with the Daltons, two couples, compatible, friends as well as business associates. "How long has this been going on? How long have the two of you been sleeping together?''

Ted turned his face away, flushing with discomfort. "I don't see any point in going down that road, Rachel.''

She gave him an incredulous look. "You don't see the point? You tell me you're in love with another woman and you can't help yourself, but I'm not supposed to ask whether or not you were having sex with her at the same time you've been having sex with me? Then let me put it this way, Ted. Either you answer that question or this conversation is over and any hope you had that we can—'' she used her fingers as quote marks "'figure out how best to handle it' is zero. So I ask again, how long have you been sleeping with her?''

"A year,'' he replied tightly.

A year. Shocked, she stood up quickly and moved across the room. She and Ted hadn't made love often lately, but they had certainly not given up sex altogether. Now she wondered how she could have been unaware that his heart wasn't in it. Had he been imagining Francine as his partner? She was sickened at the thought.

"You say you spent the night at our lake house thinking,'' she said, her tone quiet and just a bit unsteady. "You said we needed to discuss how to handle…it. I need to know what we're to handle, the aftermath of your affair or a divorce?''

"It's not that simple, Rachel."

"Why not? The way I see it, there are only two options. You end the affair and we'll see if it's possible to save our marriage. Or, you continue the affair and I file for a divorce." Her heart was pounding. Was this the end? Could he really be serious?

"I don't want to give her up, Rachel. I can't give her up."

She stared at him. So his desire for Francine was that overwhelming. "Then you want a divorce." White-hot pain settled in her chest. Rachel tried to imagine being so enthralled by passion that Nick and Kendall didn't matter. Or being able to ignore her marriage vows when it was convenient. But she simply couldn't.

"I thought we'd try a separation." He rose and went to stand at the glass wall looking out. "Like I said, it's not as simple considering the circumstances. There's the practice. And Walter…Walter doesn't know yet."

"Yet?"

"Francine plans to tell him."

"When?"

"When the time is right."

Rachel laughed bitterly. "Would the time have been right for you if I hadn't surprised you at lunch yesterday?"

"We knew we were on borrowed time," Ted said, turning back. "What I'm asking for now is just that…some time. Let me try to figure out the best way to handle this. Hell, Rachel, I spent the whole night worrying about what to tell you, what—"

"After having sex with Francine, I assume."

"—what to say to the kids," he plowed on doggedly, "whether to move out, wondering what Walter will do when he's told. It's going to be a big mess. I don't have to tell you that."

"No, you don't have to tell me that," she repeated. "And as for Walter, I can guess what his reaction will be. He's twenty years older than Francine and tends to be possessive. If you recall, she was married when they met. She got a divorce to marry Walter. He's crazy about her. He's an old fashioned guy. He likes the idea that she belongs to him. He's not going to take this lying down.''

Ted shrugged. ''What can he do? She doesn't love him anymore.''

''Oh, she loves you now?''

He looked her in the eye. ''Is that so hard to believe?''

Was it? Was he saying he felt unloved by Rachel? Had they drifted into the familiar rut of married couples who took each other for granted? Did she no longer see Ted as sexy and desirable? Was it her fault that he'd looked for someone who did see him that way? But…Francine?

''How long will it be,'' she asked him, ''once the two of you finally get together, that she gets bored with you as she apparently has with Walter and begins looking for someone new?''

''That won't happen.''

''Really.''

''Really.'' After a moment, he sighed. ''I don't expect you to understand.''

Their gazes held, Ted's defensive and stubborn, Rachel's filled with disbelief and disgust. Then the moment was broken by the sound of the doorbell. But before either could react, it rang again. And then again.

Ted swore, glancing at his watch as Rachel hurried away to answer. ''Who the hell can that be so early?''

Before she reached the foyer, the sound of the chimes gave way to the crash of a fist pounding on the door. At the peephole now, Rachel peered out, her eyes going wide with dismay. Walter Dalton. Quickly, she turned the deadbolt and before opening the door, said to Ted, who'd followed on her heels, ''It's Walter, and if I were you, I'd get ready for a very dicey encounter.''

To Rachel, Walter Dalton had always looked more like a boxer than a physician. He was fifty-two years old and no more than five eight or nine in his stocking feet, with heavy shoulders and a neck thick from his years as an athlete in high school. But his short, iron-gray haircut and pugnacious features belied a gentle manner that sick children seemed to sense instinctively. There was nothing gentle about his demeanor now. Just the opposite.

He looked beyond Rachel to Ted. "What the hell's going on with you and my wife, Ted?" he growled.

Rachel glanced quickly to check that no neighbors were out, then reached for Walter's arm and pulled him over the threshold. "Come in, Walter," she said, trying for a calm tone. "I've got fresh coffee in the kitchen. The kids are still asleep."

"I don't want any goddamned coffee. I want some answers." He lowered his head on his neck and looked narrow-eyed at Ted. "When I got home last night, my wife met me at the door with some kind of crazy talk about you and her. I better hear you say it's a lie or I swear to God, Ted, I'm gonna kick your ass from here to Dallas after I've sliced your dick off."

"Calm down, for God's sake, Walter," Ted said, glancing toward the stairs. He reached for his partner's arm, but Walter shook him off. "We can talk in the sunroom."

"You're not denying it?" he bellowed.

Rachel put her finger to her lips. "Please, Walter. The kids. I don't want—"

Still breathing fire, he gave Ted a ferocious glare before muttering a gruff apology to Rachel and sending a quick glance to the stairs, still mercifully sans the children. Lowering his tone somewhat, he said to her, "Do you know what this son of a bitch has been doing with Francine behind our backs?"

She sighed, urging him along toward the sunroom. "I do."

He frowned darkly. "You know they've been screwing around and you didn't say anything?"

"I only found out yesterday, Walter." They entered the sunroom, she still keeping a cautionary hand on Walter's arm, Ted following warily. "Let me get you a cup of coffee and we'll try to straighten all this out."

"I don't want any coffee. Make it bourbon instead."

"I'll get it," Ted said, moving hastily to the small portable bar they kept stocked in the sunroom. He found the bottle of Jack Daniel's and took a glass from a hanging rack, then tipped to pour it with a shaky hand. Warning him with a look, Rachel took the drink from Ted and handed it to Walter, who knocked almost all of it back in a single swallow. His eyes locked with Ted's as he wiped his mouth with the back of his hand. "You better have a good story, *partner*. Otherwise, life as you once knew it is over."

"Let's all sit down," Rachel said, telling Ted with a look to find a seat across the room. Then, patting the place beside her on the settee, she managed a smile at Walter. "This is going to be difficult for all of us. And I think you're right, Walter. Our lives are changed."

Walter ignored the invitation to sit and instead looked hard at Ted. "It's true, then? You've been screwing my wife?"

"We didn't plan it, Walt," Ted said. Sweat now glistened on his forehead and his face was pale. "Sometimes these things just happen."

"Tell me, Ted, just how long have you been screwing her?" Walter's tone was soft with menace.

Ted stood up. "I think you should discuss those details with Francine. She—"

Walter slammed his glass on the bar, took three steps across the room and grabbed the front of Ted's shirt. "If I ask you for details, you bastard, then you be man enough to answer," he said between clenched teeth. Although he was three inches shorter than Ted, he outweighed him by a good forty pounds. Tightening his grip, he gave a twist to the shirt and Ted suddenly couldn't breathe. Feet scrabbling, he made a strangled sound, trying to keep his balance and loosen Walter's hold at the same time.

"Walter!" Rachel pulled frantically at his elbow, but it was like trying to move a stone statue. "Please, Walter, stop! Don't, please, don't!" But Walter was past hearing…or caring. He drew his fist back and let fly a hard right at Ted's face.

"Oh, my God!" Rachel watched helplessly as the two men crashed over the coffee table. The glass top shattered. Books, photos, a potted orchid and mementos went flying. Blood spurted from Ted's nose. Both men rolled about, grunting and gouging and kicking, each trying to find an opening to strike a blow.

"Dad! Mom! Jeez, what's going on?"

Rachel turned to find Nick in the doorway, staring in amazement. "Nick, oh, thank God, help me stop them!"

The boy hesitated only a second before dashing into action. "You take Dad and I'll take Dr. Walt." Wading into the fray, he got a good grip on the back of Walt's collar and pulled tight, momentarily choking off the older man's breath. Rachel didn't need to do more than grab at Ted's arm. Once he had a chance, he scrambled out of Walter's reach and got hastily to his feet, swiping at his bloody nose with the sleeve of his expensive shirt. He stood heaving and trying to catch his breath, watching warily as Nick kept a firm hold on Walter.

"I'm okay," Walter said to Nick, shaking free of the boy's grip. "Sorry about that, Rachel. Nick." Then he turned back to Ted. "No apology to you, you prick. And don't think I'm done with you yet. Francine may be determined to leave me, but it'll be a cold day in hell before she ever belongs to you." Giving his shoulders a quick hunch, he straightened the collar of his golf shirt and began tucking in the tails. That done, he looked briefly at Rachel and Nick, standing stunned and silent before turning back to Ted. "What the hell's the matter with you, you dickhead? You've got everything a man could want right here in Rachel and your kids and still you go poaching my territory. What, you think the grass is greener on the other side? *My* side," he emphasized, jabbing his thumb toward his chest. Then, shaking his head, he crossed the room to leave, but at the door, he turned back for one final shot. "You're a goddamn fool, Ted."

Four

"Dad, Mom, what was that all about?" Nick demanded in bewilderment. "I heard the commotion and when I get downstairs I find my dad and his partner at fist city! Jeez."

"It's nothing," Ted said curtly, tearing a paper towel from a roll behind the bar. "Go on back upstairs."

He dampened the towel and pressed it to his nose, unaware of a cut near his eye, which Rachel could see beginning to swell. Walter's first blow got him square on his nose, but he must have landed a blow that glanced high off the cheekbone. He'd have a shiner soon that wouldn't fade before Monday, when he'd have to show his face at the practice. She wondered how he'd explain it to the staff.

"Go upstairs?" Hands propped on his hips, Nick stared at his father. "You're kidding, right? You were in a fight, Dad. A real knock-down, drag-out with Dr. Walt. Jeez, he's supposed to be your best friend."

"Nick—" Rachel began, but he wasn't finished.

"The coffee table is smashed," the boy said, waving an arm at the desecration in the room, "you've got a busted nose and a shiner, and you say it's nothing? I don't think so."

"It's personal," Ted said, talking through the towel. "I'll explain later."

Nick made a disgusted sound and turned to his mother. "What did Dr. Walt mean, that Francine would never belong to Dad?"

"Nick—" She put out a hand and felt something twist

near her heart. "I'm sorry you had to see this. I don't think—"

"Is Dad having an affair with Francine?" Nick's face was pale, but his eyes burned.

Rachel looked at Ted. "Now is not the time for this discussion," Ted said, grimacing at the bloodstains on the towel. "I can't believe this! I've probably got a broken nose."

"That's it, isn't it, Mom?" Nick persisted. "He's screwing Francine."

"Nick, please…" Rachel caught his hand and tried to guide him over to the settee. "You know we don't allow that language. Sit down and I'll try to explain." But Nick stayed stiffly on his feet, glaring at his father. No one noticed Kendall standing in the doorway until she spoke.

"I want to hear, too."

All eyes went to the little girl looking sweetly innocent in a nightie sprinkled with a pattern of tiny red hearts. Bunny faces on her bedroom slippers peeked from beneath the ruffle at the bottom and her camera hung by a cord around her neck. Gingerly avoiding the glass on the floor, she went to her mother. "I heard someone banging on the door and I wanted my camera, but it took a minute to find it. Then Dr. Walt started yelling, all mad and everything. I almost didn't remember to take pictures when him and Daddy started to fight, but then I did. Why were they fighting?"

"You took pictures?" Rachel said faintly.

Kendall nodded, then looked at her dad. "So why were you and Dr. Walt mad at each other, Daddy?"

Rachel slipped an arm around the little girl's waist and gave Ted another compelling look.

"I'm going to have to take care of this bleeding," he mumbled. Face down, he ducked past his family. "Sorry."

"I'm right, huh, Mom?" Nick persisted as Ted escaped. "He's fooling around with Francine."

Rachel took one of each of her children's hands and paused for a moment, praying that she'd be able to tell them what was necessary in a way that would do them the least harm. "Sometimes," she began, "people who are married to each other discover that even though they have many good things together, such as wonderful children and a lovely house and good jobs, that somehow they need something different. A change, maybe. Your…your dad—" she cleared her throat as it threatened to close "—your dad is experiencing something like that."

"So the something different Dad needed," Nick said, cutting to the chase as always, "was an affair with his best friend's wife? Have I got it right?"

Rachel closed her eyes in momentary pain. "It…it appears that…he and Francine are involved, yes. At the moment."

"What a dumb shit!" Nick stood up abruptly. He hadn't put on a shirt before heading downstairs, so he wore only the bottoms of his Joe Boxer shorts. His sleek young torso heaved with emotion. Arms stiff at his sides, he clenched both hands into fists, working them open and closed. "Dr. Walt should have done more than coldcock him one. What he should have done—"

"Nick." Rachel held up her hand. "It might feel good to rant and rave at your dad for the moment, but he is, and always will be, your father."

"He's sure acting like a piss-poor one, then," the boy said bitterly.

"I don't understand," Kendall said, her small brow wrinkled in confusion. "What's Daddy doing that's wrong?"

"He's fooling around with Dr. Walt's wife, brat. That's a big no-no."

"It's not okay for Daddy to be friends with Ms. Francine?" Kendall looked in bewilderment first at Rachel, then at Nick.

"They're more than friends, Kendy," Nick said, softening his tone.

"Dad and Ms. Francine have special feelings for each other," Rachel explained. "They want to be together…like Nick says…as more than friends."

"But what about you if they want to be together like that?" Kendall asked, her frown returning.

"Dad has decided that he wants some time to live apart from me right now, Kendall. He'll probably move to our cabin on the lake, so he won't be here with us like he has been."

Kendall's eyes widened. "He's going to sleep there and eat and...and everything?"

"For the time being, yes," Rachel said, nodding. "But he'll be close by when you want to see him. The cabin is only an hour from Rose Hill. It's just that he won't be living in this house."

Kendall studied her mother's face for a long moment. "Are we getting a divorce?"

Rachel brought the little girl's hand up to her cheek. "Who said anything about a divorce, sweetheart?"

Kendy looked worried. "But you won't, will you, Mom? I have friends who're divorced and it's not good."

How Rachel wished she could make that promise. "I don't think your dad is going to move to Dallas or any place other than Rose Hill, Kendy," she said, trying to sound reassuring. "His practice is here and he won't be leaving that. So even though he's living at the lake, he's still here for you when you need him."

"Yeah," Nick muttered, glancing at the door where Ted had escaped. Then he added in a tone not overheard by his little sister, "Just don't count on him when the going gets tough."

"Francine? He's having an affair with the wife of his partner?" Marta stood up and began pacing the length of the sunroom. "Has he lost his freakin' mind? Walter Dalton will kill him!"

"He came close to it this morning," Rachel muttered dryly.

Marta stopped. "What? Walter knows?"

Rachel sat with her arms wrapped around her knees. "He

appeared before seven today, not ten minutes after Ted, who'd spent the night at the lake cabin. And you're right. He was so furious when Ted didn't deny the affair that he lost it, Marta. One minute he was hurling threats and insults and the next, he was at Ted's throat, literally. If Nick hadn't appeared just then and helped break them up, I don't know how the fracas would have ended.''

Marta motioned toward the coffee table. ''Is that why you have a coffee table with no top?''

''Glass went everywhere. They were like two schoolboys, Marta. It was dreadful. And to have Nick and Kendall see it all made it ten times worse.''

''They fought in front of the kids?''

Rachel sighed. ''Kendall took pictures. You know she carries that camera everywhere she goes.''

''Oh, boy.''

Rachel rested her cheek on her knees, looking beyond Marta to her beautifully landscaped yard. ''I had no choice but to tell them, Marta. Or, at least, I had to try to give them some kind of explanation once they saw what happened between Ted and Walt, plus they heard what Walt said. I'm not sure they're convinced things are as dire as they really are, but personally, I believe Ted's serious.''

''Classic male midlife crisis,'' Marta muttered with disgust. ''Or just your basic male propensity to cheat.'' Marta, who had been engaged several years ago to a cop, had walked into his apartment unexpectedly one day and found him with his partner, a pretty brunette rookie fresh out of the police academy. She'd immediately broken the engagement and in less than six months had married Jorge Ruiz, a quiet, mild-mannered music teacher at RHH, who'd died of Hodgkin's disease eighteen months later.

''Whatever you call it,'' Rachel said, ''he's definitely infatuated with Francine right now, so much so that he seems blind to what it ultimately means to his children.''

''Or to you.''

''That, too.''

"What are you going to do?"

She shrugged. "What can I do? I think I owe it to the kids not to do anything rash just yet."

"You mean in case he changes his mind and decides to let you forgive him and y'all just pick up where you left off?"

"I guess I'd be a dope to do that. You certainly didn't give Pete a second chance."

"Ted's the dope, not you," Marta said. "And Pete didn't ask for a second chance, not that I would have considered it for one minute." She reached over and patted Rachel's knee. "I know you're hurt and in a state of shock right now, Ray, but for too many years Ted's been a selfish, narcissistic bastard—pardon me, but it's true. You've spoiled him rotten."

"Now you sound like my mother."

"An astute woman. At least she's never looked at Ted through rose-colored glasses."

"The feeling was mutual," Rachel said, thinking of the tension that had existed between the two for years. It had been difficult, as she'd felt pulled in opposite directions. "Mom and Ted are almost always disagreeing over something."

"The miracle is that Ted's found someone else willing to put up with his ego. I give it six months, max." Marta straddled a chair and folded her arms on the back. "Can we assume this is the first time he's cheated?"

That thought had been on Rachel's mind ever since the scene in the Dallas restaurant. "I'm not sure," she murmured, recalling the sexy, young workout coach Ted had been very friendly with at their club a few years ago. Rachel, whose weight had crept up a bit, had talked Ted into enrolling as they both needed more exercise. Kendall had been entering preschool and Rachel had been run ragged trying to juggle her responsibilities managing Ted and Walt's practice and caring for the kids. Ted had admired cute little Wendy from the start, and although Rachel did whittle down to a size eight, Ted had thrown himself into the fitness program a hundred and ten percent. After six months, he was as buff as a college boy. Without admitting to herself that he showed more interest in Wendy than was appropriate, Rachel had concentrated on giving him extra attention. She'd planned special outings, a five-day cruise, a surprise birthday party for him, an intimate candlelight dinner on their anniversary.

Then Wendy had moved to Denver.

But what if Wendy hadn't moved? she wondered now. Had she failed to heed signs that he didn't hold his vows to be as sacred as she did? Had she closed her eyes to Ted's true character then? Had circumstances alone saved the day when Wendy left town?

Marta took a sip of cola. "If the kids know, there's no way you can keep this from your mom," she said, adding dryly, "I'd love to hear her take on the situation. Dinah's gonna want to hang him by his cheatin' balls."

"I know." Rachel sighed and glanced at her watch. "Kendall has a soccer game at two, then the whole team's going somewhere for Amy Milton's birthday. As soon as the game's over, I'll stop by and tell her. I need to check on her, anyway, but I'll have to do it after Kendall's game. No chance of Ted showing up for that. As for telling Mom, best just to get it over with. I can imagine her reaction and it won't be pretty." Lifting her hand, she studied the wedding ring on her finger somberly. "I wish there was some way to avoid having the world know what's happened, Marta. It's painful and humiliating for me, but it's going to be worse for Nick and Kendall. I see kids at school coping with the breakup of their parents' marriage. The reaction of their peers is not always sympathetic. I hate subjecting Nick and Kendall to that."

"It'll be rocky at first, sure. But they're tough, Rachel, and your relationship with them is great. Plus, you're strong, and you'll need that strength now. You'll come through this well, whether your marriage survives or not. As for the kids, there'll be as much moral support from their friends as otherwise. Even more. For the others—" she finished her drink and stood up "—when shitty people speak, just consider the source. The worst thing is, it's all Ted's doing and he'll be distanced from a lot of the fallout living at the lake, the rat. Not fair, but that's the way real life works." She grabbed her keys, leaned over and gave Rachel a kiss on the cheek. "Call me if you need me."

Cam seldom took a break for lunch as it tended to break his concentration, but he'd been interrupted this morning by a call from his agent, Ben Eckstein, who was hot to start negotiations for a new contract. Nothing distracted Cam like contract negotiations. So, after firmly quelling Ben's enthusiasm—and failing to pick up after Ben had interrupted—he remembered he hadn't eaten the night before, so he wandered into the kitchen and made himself a sandwich. He was standing on his back porch eating it when he saw the kid leave Dinah Hunt's patio and start across the lawn.

The boy was lean and lanky, in his mid-teens, Cam guessed, feeling a catch in his chest. Looked athletic, too, moving with an easy gait in spite of the fact that he hadn't yet grown into those long limbs and big hands and feet. A lot like Jack. And just about Jack's age when—

Dark memories instantly killed his appetite and he tossed the sandwich, food for the squirrels. Standing motionless, he watched the kid step around Dinah's newly planted herb garden, then move through the thick growth of azaleas that separated the boundaries of her property and his own. Her grandson, Rachel's boy? No sign of a car in the driveway, so apparently it took more for Rachel to find a moment for visiting her mother than a brief collapse in the garden.

As the kid drew closer, he tried to come up with a name. Dinah had mentioned it. Nick. Yeah, Nick. And no mistake about it, he thought with a scowl, the kid was heading straight for his porch.

"'Scuse me, sir." He stood looking at Cam, hesitant and polite. But determined.

Shit. It was too late to turn on his heel and go inside. "Nick, right?"

"Yes, sir." The boy ventured closer, stopped at the bottom step. Dark hair like his mother's and those same odd gold eyes, Cam noted. "Dinah Hunt is my grandmother."

"Yeah, I know."

Nick glanced down at his feet, as if to gather his thoughts. Or courage. Then he looked back up at Cam. "My mom told me how you happened to see Gran when she fainted yesterday and that you took her to the hospital. I just wanted to come over and thank you for doing that."

"No need." Cam took a couple of steps down to bring himself more in line with the boy. While inside, the memory of Jack was as heavy as lead, only a robot would be unmoved by the appeal in the boy's face. "It was sheer luck that I happened to be out when it happened. You would have done the same. Anyone would."

"Maybe. But I just wanted to, you know, say thanks. I mean, I know my mom was grateful. And Gran, too, of course." Fiddling with a smooth stone he'd picked up, he gazed at his grandmother's house a moment before turning back to Cam. "And I need to ask you a favor."

Ah, Jesus, what now? Warily, Cam braced himself. He was promising nothing. "A favor?"

"Yes, sir." Nick tossed the stone. "My mom…she's got a lot of things on her mind lately. She's a guidance counselor at RHHS. I don't know if you knew that, but—"

"I knew."

"Well, a lot of kids sort of rely on her when they get in trouble or have personal problems and stuff." He shrugged. "Not that she complains. She says it comes with the territory, but it can get so that she doesn't have a lot of time left over for—"

"For her mother?"

He gave Cam a startled look. "No, sir. Well, not exactly. Gran's pretty independent about that. Doesn't want any advice most of the time." He hesitated, then went on. "What

I mean about my mom is she doesn't have much time left over for anyone, not even herself. And if she did, she wouldn't do much for herself, anyway. She'd be thinking of Kendy or me or...or Dad. Gran, too.'' He paused, watching a squirrel eyeing the tossed sandwich. ''And my dad, he's...ah, kind of...I guess you could say...preoccupied right now.''

''Preoccupied.''

''It's a long story.'' Nick shifted so that he faced Cam squarely. ''Anyway, Mom's going to be really maxed out for some time because of this, uh, personal stuff that's come up.'' He paused and then went on in a rush, ''And so the favor I had in mind was this. If you could just sort of keep an eye on Gran when Mom isn't around—or me—it would mean a lot.''

''Does your Gran know about this?''

''You mean that I'm asking you to keep an eye on her? Jeez, no! She'd kill me. She'd come after me with my own bat. Mom, too. Anyway, Gran doesn't think she needs any help, but where would she have been yesterday if you hadn't just lucked out and happened to see her faint?''

She would have come around in a few minutes and fixed herself something to eat, Cam thought. And it would have taught her a lesson. But then again, if it had been the heart attack he'd feared at the time, then this boy's concern was well placed. ''It isn't necessary to ask me to keep an eye on your grandmother, Nick,'' he said. ''After what happened, I was planning on it. Within reason. But just so you'll know, I'm a writer and I often get caught up in what I'm doing and lose track of time. You can't depend on me exclusively.''

''Yes, sir, I understand that. I'll be checking on her myself. A lot.''

They both watched the squirrel scamper across the ground and up into a tree, carrying a piece of Cam's sandwich. ''Speaking of bats,'' Cam said, ''do you play sports?''

''Yes, sir, baseball.'' He propped a foot on the bottom

step. "I started with T-ball when I was six and I've been playing ever since."

"What's your position?"

"First base. For the B team, right now. I mean, I'm in the ninth grade and I won't have a shot at varsity till next year. Maybe not even then, but by eleventh I should be in." At ease now, Nick slid his hands into his hip pockets, comfortable talking about a subject he knew well. "Now, my buddy, Ward—Ward Rivers—he's real good. He's a pitcher. He might even get a shot at varsity this year, he's so good. His brother Jimbo's five years older and he got a scholarship to play for UT."

He knew him. Jimbo Rivers had been a pallbearer at Jack's funeral. "I've heard of him," Cam said.

"Well, Coach told us he'll probably be tapped by one of the majors at the end of this season. Is that cool or what?"

Yeah, cool. Cam clenched his jaw hard. His chest actually hurt, deep down where he kept a lock on everything that made him think of Jack. "The coach would be Monk Tyson," he said.

"Yes, sir. You know him?"

"We've met."

Nick nodded. "He's put a lot of athletes into the majors. I mean, they play college sports and then move right on up to the big leagues."

"Remarkable for a small town like Rose Hill," Cam said.

"That's what everybody says. Well…I need to get back. I didn't tell Gran where I was headed and she'll be breakin' out the blueberry muffins any minute now." He flashed a quick grin. "She likes to push food at me when I come and I'm sure not complaining. You should try her pecan pie. Man, it's to die for!" He hesitated, then stepped forward and stuck out his hand. "Thanks, Mr. Ford."

Drawing a deep breath, Cam took the boy's hand. Bony, young, strong. Like Jack's. "Cam, not Mr. Ford. And, like I said, don't rely on me exclusively regarding your gran."

"Yes, sir. I mean, no, sir, I won't." He started off, but then stopped and looked back. "If you notice anything that me or Mom should know about, will you let us know?"

"Yeah, I'll do that."

Five

Rachel had an eye out for Nick at Kendall's soccer game, but he didn't show, which was unusual. Since the beginning of the season, he'd made it a point to go to nearly every game because somehow Ted never could. Kendall always beamed after spotting Nick in the bleachers, and her teammates almost swooned with delight over her big brother. But today there was no sign of Nick.

The team won, anyway, and Rachel saw Kendall off in an SUV with Amy Milton's mom driving, then headed over to see Dinah. As she got out of her car in her mother's driveway, she glanced with new interest at the house next door, now that she knew it belonged to Cameron Ford. A rambling forties-style cottage, it was a soft shade of buttery yellow with elaborate gingerbread trim painted white. Clearly, it had been added on to more than once over the years and the result was charming, she had to admit. In the front yard, a huge oak with wide-spread limbs furnished deep shade and beauty that no amount of professional landscaping could match. Underneath the ancient tree was a white wrought-iron lawn set, a table and four chairs that would be the perfect place to enjoy morning coffee while reading the paper or to laze away a summer afternoon with a book and a glass of ice-cold lemonade.

She'd noticed the house a couple of years ago when she'd called on a student's parents who lived nearby, never dreaming her mother would one day decide to move to the neighborhood. At the time, she seemed to recall this particular house showing dire signs of neglect. Cameron must have decided to restore it.

She saw movement of the lace curtain at the upstairs window and wondered if he was watching her now, probably thinking her visit to her mother was in response to his lecture about neglecting Dinah. Turning away, she hurried up the flagstone walk to her mother's front door.

As soon as she got inside, Dinah called out from somewhere in the rear of the house. ''I'm back here! Pour yourself some wine, Rachel. It's six o'clock somewhere.''

Not a bad idea, Rachel thought. An opened bottle of a good cabernet sat breathing on the kitchen counter with one of Dinah's unique wineglasses ready and waiting. She poured the wine and went in search of her mother.

''Hi,'' she said, upon finding Dinah curled up on a chaise on her patio. Afternoon sun had taken the chill off the day, not unusual in this part of Texas in February. Rachel held up the wine. ''Were you expecting someone?''

''You,'' Dinah said. ''Nick dropped by earlier.''

''Oh.''

''He's mad as hell at Ted.''

''Well, that makes five of us, I guess.''

''Who's the fifth?'' Dinah ticked off on her fingers, ''Me, Nick, Kendy, you and—''

''Marta.'' Rachel sat down on the porch swing. ''I should have guessed Nick would come straight to you. I hoped I would get over here before you heard it from one of the kids. And you're right, he was very angry. It may be a long time before Ted can mend what was destroyed this morning. If ever.''

''Hmm.'' Dinah took a sip of wine. ''The only thing that surprised me was the fight with Walter. It's hard to imagine Ted actually getting into a physical confrontation with anyone. Over anything. I wish I'd been there.''

''It wasn't Ted's doing, believe me.'' Rachel rubbed her left temple and added in an unsteady voice, ''And, trust me, Mom, you wouldn't want to see it. I was already dreading having to tell the kids their father is having an affair and wants to move out, but to have them learn it that way made it even more traumatic. The whole thing still seems so unbelievable.'' Tears started in her eyes and she abruptly leaned over and set her glass on a small wrought-iron table. ''Ted with another woman,'' she murmured, pressing her fingers to her lips. ''I'm still in a state of shock.''

''Excuse me, ladies.''

Rachel looked around, startled to find Cameron Ford at the edge of the patio. She turned away, quickly swiping at both eyes as Dinah greeted him. How long had he been there, she wondered frantically. How much had he heard?

''Are you knocking off early today, Cam?'' Dinah asked.

After a keen look at Rachel's face, he replied to Dinah. ''Just taking a break. I realized when I got home from the hospital that I had some personal items of yours. When they removed your watch and earrings, they gave them to me for safekeeping.'' He handed her a small plastic bag.

''Thank you,'' Dinah said, peeking into the bag. ''I realized this morning that I'd left them at the hospital, so I would have wasted a trip going back for them.''

''I spotted you sitting out here from my kitchen window and didn't realize that you weren't alone. I can see my timing's off.''

''Not at all,'' Dinah spoke, stopping him as he turned to go. ''There's more wine. Rachel, go inside and pour a glass for Cam. Or there's beer, if you'd prefer that.''

He looked directly at Rachel then. ''No, thanks.'' He seemed to hesitate, then he blew out a breath and squared his shoulders. ''I suppose now's as good a time as any to apologize.''

''Apologize?'' Rachel knew traces of tears were still in her eyes and wished she had a tissue. Almost as the thought was born, he produced a neatly folded handkerchief.

''Here, looks like you've had some bad news.''

She hesitated briefly, then took the handkerchief, murmuring thanks before pressing it to her eyes. There was no hiding the fact that she'd been crying. "What are you apologizing for?"

"For being out of line at the hospital yesterday. It was the wrong time to jump you about something that's none of my business."

Dinah chuckled. "But you'll reserve the right to jump her at another time, huh?"

A smile threatened before he bent down to pick up a leafy twig that had blown onto the flagstone surface. "Maybe if I count to ten, it'll save me from sticking my foot in my mouth again," he replied, settling his gaze again on Rachel.

"Just so you'll know, Cam, Rachel makes more time for me than I deserve." Dinah disregarded a murmured denial from Rachel. "And if I felt neglected, she knows I wouldn't be shy about saying so."

"Like I said, I was over the line."

"Forget it," Rachel said, wishing he'd go.

"One more thing," Cam said, studying the twig in his hands before looking up into her eyes. "I've spit out the apology, so I might as well be in for a penny as in for a pound. I couldn't help overhearing the reason you're upset. For what it's worth, if Ted has screwed around and messed up your life and his kids', too, then he's a bigger fool than I figured."

Rachel stared, unsure how to respond to such a straight-on insult to Ted, even if she'd been in a mood to defend him. A more tactful person would have ignored what was clearly a personal conversation, wouldn't he? While she was trying to think of a reply, he straightened, adding as he was half-turned to leave again, "Did it really come as a shock to you?"

"Yes. Of course." And was instantly shocked that she'd answered. The subject was devastatingly personal and he was, after all, a virtual stranger. Frowning, she gave a confused shake of her head. "Do you know Ted? Have the two of you met?"

"It's a small town. I've seen him on the golf course

and…around here and there. He's a jerk. Beats me what you saw in him to begin with, but with two kids and a pretty solid history together, he's the loser in this, not you.''

''Why don't you tell us what you really think?'' Dinah put in dryly.

Rachel hardly noticed, she was so riveted by what he was telling her. Later, she'd probably figure out that he still felt so hostile toward her that it had been easy to speak with brutal honesty. Which gave her more information than she'd get from her friends, even if they'd known about Ted. ''Since you're into plain speaking about my husband,'' she said stiffly, ''I'd like to know if you were aware of other times when he…he…''

''Cheated?'' Cam broke the twig in half and tossed it in the grass. ''If I did, I wouldn't tell you. What good would it do? You'd only feel worse than you do already.''

''My sentiments exactly,'' Dinah said.

Again ignoring her mother, Rachel rose slowly from the swing. ''Then you do know something?''

''What you need to do now,'' he said, ignoring her question, ''is to beat him to the punch in case my reading of his character holds. Go to the bank and make sure he doesn't clean out your accounts, which would leave you in a financial bind just when you don't need that kind of grief. And since he's caused the upheaval in your life, you and your kids shouldn't be forced to alter your lifestyle. Do you have a lawyer?''

''A lawyer?''

''Yeah, trust me. You need a lawyer.''

Her expression turned frosty. ''I don't see what concern—''

''It's not my concern. I'm just telling you that your first step should be to call a lawyer. And not someone used to handling both your business affairs. Get someone new, and while you're at it, get someone who's good.''

''You should call Stephanie Roscoe, Rachel,'' Dinah suggested.

"Wait—" Rachel pressed her fingers against both temples. "Enough, please. This is crazy. We—I—don't know if any of this is necessary. Ted's probably going through a midlife crisis. That's usually a temporary thing. It's common for men of his age." She glanced at them and got only bland stares in return. "And even so, I don't think Ted would take advantage that way. He—"

She was interrupted by her mother's snort of disgust. "You just found out he's been cheating on you for a year, honey. And until you saw it with your own eyes, you probably didn't think he'd do something like that, did you?"

Rachel sat back down again. "This is insane," she murmured.

Cam propped a foot on the edge of the patio. "It happens all the time."

She looked up at that, hearing more than a trite cliché in his tone. "It happened to you?" It was a personal question, but he'd opened the door himself.

"Call it the voice of experience." He shrugged, stepping back to leave. "And if I had it to do over again, I'd react differently. I wouldn't waste time in denial. You sound as if you're ready to defend Ted, but he's not showing the same sensitivity to you or your kids, so forget him and think about the kids and…just in case…take some common-sense precautions, that's all I'm saying."

He brushed grit from his hands. "And since I'm so full of advice today, I'll just make this one other suggestion. Don't waste time wondering what you did or didn't do that made him cheat. That's mostly a road to nowhere when you need to be concentrating on what you and the kids'll do with the rest of your life." He then stepped off the patio and walked away as abruptly as he'd appeared.

"Whoa," Dinah said softly as soon as he was out of earshot. "And here we thought he was surly and insensitive and had a deep-seated grudge against you."

"I still think that," Rachel said, watching him make his way across the lawn, setting a fast clip to cover the distance between her mother's property and his. "Yesterday, he could barely be civil to me and today he's doling out advice, but not in a very loving way. He's probably getting some kind of sick satisfaction knowing my life is falling apart." She gave a push on the swing with one foot and settled back while it swayed gently. "Whatever his motives, I don't need his advice."

"I wouldn't dismiss it so lightly, hon. To hear him tell it, he's been there, done that. Besides, it can't hurt to call Stephanie and simply run the situation by her, just to hear what she might suggest."

Rachel looked at her mother. "Mom, for Ted to do what Cameron said would be a betrayal as bad as his cheating in the first place. Do you really think he would be so…so lowdown?"

"I'm hardly unbiased, but I've seen some pretty sneaky things done when couples begin talking divorce. You—"

"We haven't decided to divorce! Ted's moving to the lake cabin, but it's more like a separation. He'll come to his senses, I'm sure of it. The consequences of an affair with Francine are just too dire. For one thing—if we're talking assets—Ted's whole financial life is tied up in the practice and the affair jeopardizes his position there. He had a taste of Walter's reaction this morning, for heaven's sake. He can't think Walter will simply stand aside while Ted steals his wife and yet expects to continue to work alongside him every day, can he?"

"Betcha a dollar to doughnuts that he's telling himself he'll figure a way to get around that sticky issue."

"I grant you his behavior is pretty disgusting," Rachel said as she bent forward and picked up her wineglass, "but he won't just dismiss eighteen years of marriage and our two children like one of his used suits. You'll see."

"Just promise me you'll call Stephanie."

That lowlife, Cam thought as he made his way back across the lawn. And stupid to boot, screwing around with his partner's wife. Although he didn't know Ted Forrester beyond a few casual encounters at the golf course, he'd seen him a couple of months ago at a restaurant in Dallas with a woman and it wasn't Rachel. With no connection to Rachel other than the few minutes he'd spent in her office five years before, he'd thought nothing of it. But now...somehow after overhearing her talking to her mother and knowing the boy's concern, he couldn't quite manage the detachment it took to stay clear of sticky situations.

Back inside his house now, he went to the fridge for a beer. Unscrewing the cap, he headed back onto the porch and stood squinting through the afternoon sun at Dinah's patio where both women still sat talking. Ever since Nick's surprise visit this morning, he'd been trying to figure what in hell was behind the boy's request. Well, now he knew. With his father shirking his responsibilities as keeper of the Forrester cave, the son felt obliged to assume the man-of-the-house role. Apparently that included helping his mom manage things on the home front and seeing to the welfare of his little sister and his grandmother...even if it meant forgoing his pride and seeking help from someone who was a virtual stranger. A daunting task for a fifteen-year-old.

His beer forgotten, he stared at the two women as thoughts of Jack and his own desolated family rushed back. He'd spent five years wishing he could turn back the clock, wishing especially that he wasn't haunted by that last telephone call from Jack.

It had been late at night and he'd been in the throes of his usual deadline angst, trying to work through a book that was giving him problems. He'd rewritten the dialogue of the killer at least four times, trying to get it right. It was a crucial scene, one that would shed a glimmer of understanding about a man who had murdered half a dozen teenagers in the local lover's lane of a small town in California. The crime had actually happened, and only God—or the devil—knew for certain what the killer said or thought as he prepared his young victims for sexual torture and death. Cam's extensive research

into the case had provided a lot of facts, but little psycho
logical insight. If he'd pulled the story out of his imagination
he could invent whatever drove a monster to kill. But h
genre was true crime, and his evaluation of the killer's psych
had to be solid. After three bestsellers, nothing less for h
next book would satisfy his fans or Cam himself.

In the back of his mind, he'd heard his phone ringing bu
ignored it. Everyone knew to leave him alone when he wa
working to a deadline. The book had to be on his editor
desk in two weeks, and even working fourteen-hour day
he'd have to push to get it done. It was on the fifth ring tha
the answering machine picked up.

"Hi, Dad. It's me."

Jack. Cam dropped his head and groaned. It was the thir
time this week that his son had called, and Cam was sti
clueless over the reason for the calls. Lately when Jac
phoned, he seemed to have something on his mind beside
playing ball and the latest movie or rock group. When Cam
tried probing deeper, all he got was evasion or Jack sudden
had to hang up.

Now Cam turned to look at the answering machine, silen
except for Jack's breathing. It could simply be that Jac
wanted to see Cam, whether in a visit to New York or i
Texas, where he lived with his mother. He hadn't come ou
and said so, but that had to be it. He knew it was not possibl
It was the middle of the school year. Besides, he knew Cam
was on deadline. Jack understood these things. Or he used t
understand these things.

"Dad, will you pick up?" There was urgency in his ton
now. "I need to talk to you."

Maybe it was Cara. Now that Jack was in the full throe
of adolescence, maybe they were at odds over some thing
Girls. Sex. Algebra. But, hell, it would kill Cara if Jack ac
tually pushed to come and live with Cam in New York an
leave her.

"I know you're on deadline, Dad, but—" Jack's voic
caught on something that sounded like a sob.

Cam picked up. "Hey, Jack. What's up, son?"

"Not too much." Cam heard a sniff, then in a muffled tone, Jack said, "I guess you're working, huh?"

Cam looked at the blinking cursor on his monitor. "I'm trying to wrap this one up, yeah, but maybe taking a break's a good thing. How's it going with you, son?"

"We had a game tonight. I scored eighteen points."

"Well, hey! Next year, you'll make the varsity team in a cakewalk."

"If I don't break a leg or something."

Cam smiled. "It's hard to break a leg that's only fifteen years old. Now, you take my legs—"

"Nah, Dad, thanks. You can keep both of 'em." Jack laughed, but to Cam's ears, it seemed shaky, not quite right.

"Is something wrong, Jack? Everything okay with your mom?"

"Mom's okay. I think she's serious about this guy Anthony."

"You like him?"

"He's cool, I guess."

"How about school? Those grades went a little south last term. Are you having a problem?"

"It was my own fault, Dad. I just…f—ah, messed up and it got away from me. I'll bring 'em around next term, okay?"

"I know you can do it, son." Cam rubbed a hand over his face, knowing he should be the one helping Jack, but how the hell could he when they were separated by the breadth of the whole country? It had been a stupid idea for Cara to move back to Texas after the divorce. What the hell had she been thinking? Why had he let her do it?

"Dad…"

"Yeah?"

"I—ah, I mean, I wish we could—" Jack made a strangled sound. "When do you think you'll finish your book?"

"Couple of weeks, Jack. I've run into some problems with this one, but I'll work them out eventually. Soon as it's done, I'm outta here and coming to see you." Using the mouse,

Cam idly scrolled back to the chapter he'd written the da
before and scanned the text. After a second or two, inspira
tion struck. Suddenly he knew how to write the scene he'
been wrestling with.

"...some trouble with the guys on the team," Jack wa
saying. "I was thinking maybe you could come dow
and—"

"Hold a second, Jack." Cam clicked the mouse and wrot
a couple of phrases before losing his thought. "Now, what'
that you were saying?"

"It's—oh, nothing, Dad," he replied in a deflated tone. "
guess you need to get back to work."

"I can tell there's something on your mind, son. The min
ute this book's done, I'll get on a plane and be there. W
can talk it over."

"You really think it won't be too long, Dad?"

"Two weeks, maximum, Jack. I promise."

"Well—"

"I'll get this thing in the mail and we'll spend some rea
time together. You know your grandparents' house is empt
now they're gone, so I don't see why I can't arrange to sta
for the summer. No reason why I have to be here in Nev
York. How 'bout that?"

"It's great, Dad." Jack spoke quietly and Cam thought h
heard a break in the boy's voice again, but the line went dea
before he had a chance to reply. And he was soon lost in th
scene that had been giving him trouble.

It was three o'clock in the morning when his phone ran
again. Groggy from a sixteen-hour marathon at his compute
and disoriented, he didn't pick up until it finally penetrate
who was speaking on the answering machine.

"Cara, what in hell—"

His ex-wife's reply was muffled with sobs. Cam sat u
then and said in a voice sharp with alarm, "What's wrong
Cara?"

"It's—it's Jack, Cam. Oh, my God, it's Jack." She mad

a small, despairing sound. "He's gone. Oh God, oh God, oh God, I can't bear it."

"What do you mean, he's gone? He's run away?"

"C-Cam..."

"Come on, Cara. What about Jack?"

Her voice steadied slightly as she managed to pull herself together. She breathed in and said dully, "Jack is dead, Cam. He's committed suicide."

He realized he was still standing on the porch, still focused on the two women with the pain of losing Jack a deep, black hole inside him. His life had been forever changed with that phone call. And what he wouldn't give to have what Forrester was idiotically jeopardizing. Still, it was none of his business and he'd already broken one of his hard-and-fast rules by even acknowledging Rachel's situation. He hadn't expected to find her sitting with her mother when he dropped off Dinah's jewelry, otherwise he'd have put off returning it. Then he'd compounded his mistake by apologizing. But he'd been out of line attacking her at the ER and he'd been out of line offering advice. Another stupid error. He'd made every mistake in the book handling his divorce and its consequences, so what could he offer that her vast circle of friends and family couldn't?

He raised the bottle to take another drink and looked thoughtfully across the lawn. He'd honor his promise to the kid to keep an eye on Dinah, he decided as he turned to go back inside, but that was as far as he would go.

When Rachel got home later that day, she found that Ted had moved out. In their bedroom, she stared in shocked disbelief at the empty racks in their closet. By seizing a moment when no one else was in the house, he'd avoided what was sure to be a difficult scene. And he'd left her with the task of dealing with Nick and Kendall when they came home and found their father had cleared out.

She stood with a torrent of emotion roiling in her chest. It was one thing for Ted to tire of her as a wife and to want to

avoid all the sticky stuff that women dished out to cheating
husbands, but it was sneaky and cowardly to walk out on
Nick and Kendall without at least taking a moment to sit
down and reassure them that they'd still have a father even
though he was no longer in the house with them. By leaving
this way, it looked like he was abandoning them along with
their mother. That was sure to be the way the kids would
feel.

Fury, like nothing she'd ever felt, rose in her. How *dare*
he! Since Friday, when she'd caught him red-handed, she'd
managed to keep her emotions under control. Except for a
few bewildered tears and some agonizing self-examination,
she'd tried to handle his infidelity without unraveling emotionally. She'd told herself that for the sake of the kids she
couldn't afford to fall apart.

But the kids weren't here right now, she thought, stalking
across the room. And she was tired of behaving like the only
grown-up in this farce. Stopping at Ted's armoire, she jerked
the doors open. Empty. In the bathroom, she discovered he'd
even cleaned out all his toiletries. Moving like a woman possessed, she dashed down the stairs, swept up her purse and
car keys and stormed out to her car. It was an hour's drive
to the lake cabin. Chest heaving with rage, she backed out
and, with a squeal of tires, drove off to confront him.

Forty minutes later, she was still fuming as she pulled up
in front of the cabin. Parking behind the small Porsche she
recognized as Francine's, she got out of her car, deliberately
blocking the Porsche. Unlike the scene at the restaurant, this
time, if Francine wanted to escape an uncomfortable confrontation, she was out of luck. She couldn't move her car
until Rachel was finished. And if the door was locked, Rachel
planned to use her keys and walk right in. She didn't give a
damn if she found them naked and having sex. In fact, she
wished exactly that would happen. Catching them in an embarrassing situation would give her unholy satisfaction.

She took the four porch steps in two quick strides and

without knocking, tried the unlocked door and went inside. There was an immediate let-down when she didn't see them right away in the great room, all of which was visible from the front door. The thought of barging into the bedroom where they might actually be having sex was suddenly too disgusting. But as she stood with some of her anger fading, she heard their voices. They were in the hot tub.

She was flooded with a fresh wave of fury. Ted hated the hot tub. It had been *her* idea to install it when they'd re-modeled the cabin. Ted hadn't wanted it, had argued against it. The lake was great for fishing and boating, and a swimming pool was impractical in the wooded location, but she'd finally persuaded him that a hot tub was relaxing, even therapeutic after the hours both spent in stressful occupations. It could also be romantic, she'd suggested. That had been around the time she'd sensed Ted's interest in Wendy at the health club. The hot tub had been one of the little gambits she'd dreamed up to add some spice to their love life. It hadn't worked for them, she thought, now moving through the cabin to the deck, but apparently it had worked for Ted and Francine.

They actually were naked.

Spotting Rachel, Francine shrieked. Ted turned. His jaw dropped, but surprise quickly changed to irritation. He stood up, scowling, and grabbed two robes lying within reach. Moving in front of Francine, he managed to shield her as she scrambled into it, giving Rachel only a glimpse of her in the buff. Then he climbed out without any obvious haste. Rachel avoided more than a glimpse of his shriveled penis by looking beyond him while he donned a robe. Francine hovered warily just behind him, looking as if she thought Rachel might be armed.

Later, in telling Marta about it, Rachel had found some humor in the situation, but she felt no inclination to laugh now. She knew suddenly with a sick, sad resignation that her marriage was truly over. It would not be possible to get beyond actually seeing Ted with Francine this way.

"What do you mean by barging in here like this, Rachel?" Thanks to Walter, his left eye was puffy and half closed, making his outrage seem almost comical. She could not tell if his nose was broken, but she could always hope.

"Isn't it obvious, Ted? I'm mad as hell and you're going to hear about it whether you like it or not."

"For God's sake!" he said in disgust. "What does it take to convince you? Didn't you hear anything I said this morning? I'm in love with Francine. She loves me and we want to be together. We're going to be together whether you like it or not. Go home and get a life."

Rachel mastered an urge to leap over the hot tub and scratch his other eye out. "I'm not here because I want anything from you, you thoughtless *bastard!* I'm here because of the sneaky way you packed up and left. Why didn't you wait until Nick and Kendall came home so you could at least try to reassure them? Don't you give a damn about your kids anymore? Is…is *this*—" she threw her arm out to include the house, the deck, the hot tub, Francine "—all you care about now?"

He looked irritated and anything but repentant. "I was planning on calling them later tonight."

Fresh from a romp in the hot tub, he was still too dazzled to feel any guilt, Rachel thought. "Are you sure you can spare the time?" she asked sarcastically.

"Give it a rest, Rachel." He stuck his feet into rubber slides and reached for his Rolex. "I still love my kids and I'll explain how this happened."

"How exactly will you explain it, Ted?" she asked, seeing that she wasn't getting through to him. "Like you explained it to me? One day you and Francine were friends and the next you were having sex together? I think they've got that part already, thanks to the scene in our home this morning. And Nick, for one, is mad as hell over it. Kendall is simply bewildered."

"It'll take some getting used to, but they'll be okay with it," he said, dismissing almost casually something that was going to turn his children's lives upside down. "That is, unless you go behind my back and paint me as evil incarnate."

"You know better than that, Ted."

His face was tight, his eyes hard. "These things happen a lot, Rachel. Probably half Nick and Kendy's friends are part of blended families."

"Blended families," she repeated. "That has such a benign sound, doesn't it? But I know from dealing with those kids every day that there's pain and depression and jealousy jockeying for position in 'blended families.'" She used her fingers to make quotation marks. "And you don't have a clue, Ted. So, don't try to spin the effect of what you're doing to me. It's going to be devastating for Nick and Kendy. Even the most amicable divorces do terrible damage to the children involved."

Ted let out an exasperated breath. "You sound like you're reading some kind of research paper, Rachel. You're exaggerating, as usual. You see only the screwed-up kids in your job. Nick and Kendy will be fine."

Was he really so obtuse? She stared at him, her husband of eighteen years. He seemed totally unaffected by her attempt to bring him to his senses. When had it happened that this man whom she'd known more intimately than any other had become a stranger? "And what if they aren't, Ted?"

"Ted..." Francine finally spoke, touching his arm. "Any discussion about your kids is between you and Rachel. It doesn't concern me. Why don't I—"

"Excuse me?" Rachel gave her an incredulous look. "You claim to be in love with Ted and the two of you want to be together, but you have no concern about the future of his children?"

"I don't know anything about kids," Francine said, looking uncomfortable. "Walter and I chose not to have any."

"Do you even like kids, Francine?"

She shrugged, said nothing.

"What about that, Ted?" Rachel asked.

"What about it?" he repeated with some resentment.

"Francine and I haven't decided on our own future yet, so all this talk about kids is premature."

"Is it premature to ask you to find an hour away from your love nest to talk to Nick and Kendall?"

"I told you I'm planning on it."

"Not on the phone. In person. It's the least you can do."

"All right, all right." He reached for Francine and slipped his arm around her waist. "But the next time you get a wild idea to come charging out here, have the decency to knock first."

Rachel was still furious as she drove away from the cabin. As much as she hated to admit it, Cameron Ford had been right. She needed a lawyer. Worse yet, she must have sounded like a naive twit defending Ted. Well, so be it. Since it was now obvious that she couldn't protect them from Ted's callousness, she could at least try to protect the lifestyle they were accustomed to. Knowing time was now of the essence, she picked up her cell phone, punched the information number and asked for a listing for Stephanie Roscoe.

Six

By the middle of the week, the news was all over town that Ted Forrester was having an affair and had left Rachel and the kids. It was impossible for word of the scandal not to reach into every nook and cranny of Rose Hill. Everywhere she went—from church to the grocery store, from the shopping mall to staff meetings at school—Rachel felt herself the object of pitying looks and worse, the morbid curiosity people had about infidelity when it struck someone they knew.

"I feel like an all-too-familiar cliché," she told Marta in the break room on Wednesday. "I'm the nearly forty, boring wife who's been dumped for the more exciting, sexy younger woman." She stirred powdered cream into her coffee. "And you know what, Marta? It happens so often that it doesn't even shock people anymore. I'm the only one who's shocked. What they say is true. The wife's the last to know. What galls me the most is that I should have seen it coming."

"How could you when you just don't think that way? And you aren't boring." Marta worked at the tab on a can of soda. "Besides, you'd never cheat even if you were bored to death and sexually frustrated to boot. You'd look for solutions." She stopped with the can at her mouth. "I guess you're thinking of suggesting counseling to him…or something like that, huh?"

Rachel leaned against the counter holding her coffee. "It takes two, Marta. And Ted's not interested in trying to save our marriage. He just wants to get on with the transition from husband and father to unfettered bachelor, ASAP."

"What a guy."

Rachel stood in silence for a few moments. "I've retained a lawyer."

Eyes wide, Marta set her can down hard. "Now you've surprised me. This is good. This is smart. What did he say?"

"She. It's Stephanie Roscoe. She urged me to be at the bank when it opened Monday morning. I thought Ted probably wouldn't be devious enough to fool around with our finances without consulting me, but after that scene at the lake, I wasn't willing to risk taking the chance. Besides, I'd only learned about the affair on Friday and I assumed he wouldn't have had time to do anything."

"I think I hear a 'but' coming."

Rachel still felt stunned. "But apparently, right after the scene with Walter, he went to a branch of our bank that's open on Saturday and drew out almost all our ready cash, then he fixed it so that nearly everything else is blocked. So until we work out some agreement for the division of our joint assets, I'm pretty much dependent on what he sees fit to dole out. It's humiliating to be the object of everyone's pity now that his affair is public, but this makes it even worse. On top of being infuriated, I'm frustrated as hell, Marta."

"What happened to 'I only want a separation,'" Marta asked, looking openly disgusted.

Rachel's effort to laugh fell short. "After I ripped into him at the cabin, I think he's probably rushing to have divorce papers drawn up. Which is fine with me." She was still furious over the sneaky way he'd moved out, but her tirade had prodded him into facing the kids. He had shown up soon after they came home that day and made a lame attempt to explain why he was leaving. Nick was stoic, for the most part. And Kendall was a little weepy, bless her heart. Rachel had remained silent, and after Ted left, she'd had a hard time keeping her own resentment from showing when they'd plied her with tons of questions.

"What does Stephanie say?"

"That I'm certainly not to sit still and let him take advantage of me. She and I worked out some terms of the separation on Sunday and he was served with the papers Monday morning at the practice." Making a face, she set her coffee aside. "I've tried to reach him ever since, but he's obviously avoiding me. I just hope there aren't any other stunning surprises in store."

Both looked up as the door to the break room opened and Monk Tyson entered.

"Hey, Rachel. Marta. How's it goin', gals?" Lifting the coffeepot, he poured himself a cup and turned, propping one hip against the small table, his feet crossed at the ankles.

"Just peachy," Marta said. "And you?"

"Same here. Couldn't be better." Rose Hill's coach and athletic director looked exactly what he was—an athlete just past his prime. His broad shoulders were a little too thick and he wasn't as buff as he'd once been. But he was a good-looking man with strong features, very light blue eyes and a full head of sandy-blond hair.

"Morning, Monk." Rachel was not in the mood for Monk's chitchat. Just the opposite. He'd ignored the last note she sent him about Ferdy Jordan, one of his athletes who was one point away from academic probation. As a coach, he needed to take a stronger hand in encouraging his athletes academically instead of helping them get around the standards established by the school. It was an ongoing battle between them that she was determined to win for the sake of the athletes.

He leaned against the counter with his coffee and spoke to Rachel. "Hey, I heard about Ted and it stinks to high heaven. What's wrong with that guy? He's got steak at home and he wants hamburger instead?" He shook his head. "I hope you don't let it get you down."

"I think I'll survive," she said coldly. Inside, she cringed with humiliation. She'd had no doubt that all of Rose Hill was buzzing with the scandal, but having Monk chatting about it so casually was particularly embarrassing.

"Hard to figure what comes over guys when they get to that stage," he said.

"What stage is that, Monk?" Marta asked in an even tone.

"Well, you know." He turned back to get a paper napkin. "They're forty-something, they get an itch, they spot a sweet thing and, wham, they lose their minds."

With both hands around her can of soda, Marta looked at him. "Hmm, that is deep."

Unfazed, he looked at Rachel. "I'm glad I ran into you, Rachel. I'd planned to drop by later today."

"You got my note about Ferdy?"

"Yeah, but he'll be okay. I'll jack him up and he'll get it together. It's Nick I wanted to talk about."

"Nick?" She paused, her cup in midair.

Using the napkin, he wiped at a few drops of coffee on his shirt. "He's been looking real good in practice lately, so much so, that I'm thinking he'll work into first-base position next year. It would hurt if he was to let this get next to him, trip him up enough to take the edge off his performance."

"Let what get next to him, Monk?" she asked carefully.

"The divorce. It sometimes takes the juice out of a kid. Trust me, I see it all the time."

Beyond winning ball games, Monk ranked low on a list of people she trusted to be sensitive to a boy in emotional turmoil. If Nick was too demoralized over Ted's abandonment to play baseball, then she didn't give a damn what Monk thought about it. She knew his priority was the athletic program. All that mattered now was Nick's survival.

"As for my alleged divorce, I don't know where you heard that, Monk, and I certainly don't intend to discuss my private life here," Rachel said. And with Monk, never, she wanted to say, but didn't. It was a struggle to keep her voice steady. "Ted and I are having some difficulties. It would be ludicrous to deny that, under the circumstances, but divorce…no." At least, not yet.

"Well, sure," Monk said easily. "But I just thought I'd mention it, in case it comes to that. Kids overreact to this stuff. And the hurt can extend to every little corner of a kid's life."

"You mean, as in his position on the team?" Rachel guessed. "I'm touched by the depth of your concern."

"Well, hell, Rachel, you know what I mean," he said, undeterred by her sarcasm. "It would hurt us all, Nick as well as the guys on the team. You know our stats are high so far this season and the Mustangs are gonna make the play-offs if all goes well and the creek don't rise. We need everybody to stay focused. So, what I'm saying is I hope you'll be on the lookout for trouble or for signs that he's not handling this too good, divorce or not. A kid sees separation of his parents as traumatic as the real thing."

"As a guidance counselor, trust me, I'm aware of that," Rachel said, now openly sarcastic.

"You bet. So if that happens, you call me. I stand ready to listen if he wants to talk. Better than that, I'm willing to spend extra time with him. I just want you to know that."

"Thank you, Monk," she said. "I appreciate your concern."

"Hey, I'm glad to do it." Hearing no irony in her voice, he turned to go.

"Just a minute...before you go..." Rachel set her cup down and followed him to the door. Tyson's remarks about Nick were out of line, but she couldn't let her personal bias about the man keep her from tending to the needs of at-risk students. And one of his athletes was definitely at risk. "I'm trying to persuade Jason Pate to come in and talk to me," she told him. "I have a feeling he's troubled about something and his drinking is a way of coping. But so far he's resisting. It's alcohol now, but drugs will be the next crutch if something isn't done, and I don't think his parents are going to be much support right now. Maybe you could suggest that talking to me is a good thing. From the little I got from him on our way home from Dallas, your approval would do it."

"Aw, I just think he's one of those kids who like to binge.

I don't think he's headed for alcoholism or anything. If that's what you're worrying about, you can let it go. He's okay.''

"Bingeing is an early-warning sign, Monk," she said stiffly.

"Well, we'll see." He flashed her a smile. "I'll mention it. The kid's got a future in pro ball if he doesn't screw it up."

"I'd really like to talk to him." She was pushing, but it was necessary. She'd misread Jack Ford with tragic consequences and she was determined not to make the same mistake with another boy ever again.

"Hey, I'll try." He shifted to see around her and, spotting the trash, tossed his empty cup toward the can in a basketball-like free throw. It went in smartly. "Gotta go, gals." He left, grinning.

"I have never been able to figure that guy out," Marta said as she and Rachel watched him stride confidently down the hall. "Have you ever noticed when you see him interact with those young athletes? They're all around him, buzzing like little bees around the queen." She grimaced at her own metaphor. "Planets, I guess I should say. They're like little planets around the sun, Monk being the sun."

"Yes, I've noticed," Rachel said, picking up her coffee. "He definitely has a way where they're concerned. Charisma, I suppose."

"Or something," Marta said dryly. "To tell the truth, I never got it. Too pushy and jocklike for my taste. But, whatever he has going for him, we know it works. Like he said, they're headed for the play-offs and will probably finish first in the division again this year."

Rachel gathered up paperwork she'd meant to scan and fell into step with Marta. "We know he'll do anything for his precious sports program, but does he care at all about those boys' future beyond sports? I wonder sometimes. I've dealt with him for the past five years and I still don't know the answer to that." She made a mental note not to depend on Monk to persuade Jason. She'd do it herself, somehow.

But even as she dismissed Tyson's disinterest about Jason, his remarks about Nick made her uneasy. So far, Nick had not shared what he felt about Ted's leaving with her, but she knew there was a lot going on inside him. He was moody and uncommunicative and Rachel guessed he needed time to get his head around such a drastic change. Ted had been neglectful lately, but at least he'd been in the house. Not being a presence anymore, albeit a shadowy one, was the new reality for Kendall and Nick. Coach Monk's offer might be a welcome distraction, she thought, frowning with concern over Nick again. The man seemed to have the right touch when it came to his players. And at least he'd recognized the fact that Nick's life was turned upside down, which was more than she could say about Ted.

Nick walked into the locker room, stripping off his practice jersey as he went. He'd been off his game today and there was nothing he hated worse. "I really sucked out there today," he complained to Ward in disgust. "I should never have let that grounder get past me."

"It happens." Ward Rivers, who'd been in the same class as Nick since kindergarten, pulled his locker door open and tossed his cleats inside, then stripped off his jersey. "Coach didn't say anything, so don't sweat it."

Nick sat down on a bench to remove his cleats. Coach had a reputation for being a hard-ass, but so far Nick hadn't seen that side of him. He'd always been pretty nice. He rose to put the cleats into his locker as three athletes rounded the corner. Jason Pate, in the act of removing his jersey as he walked, hardly noticed him or anyone else. But Ferdy Jordan, second-string outfielder, stopped and so did his butt-ugly sidekick, B. J. Folsom, who was practically Ferdy's shadow. Everybody knew B.J. didn't take a dump unless Ferdy told him how.

Ferdy grinned slyly, while idly passing a baseball from one hand to the other. "Hey, Forrester! Heard about your old man."

B.J. snickered. "Whoa, way to go, Forrester. Gettin' it on with the partner's wife."

"Knock it off, you jerks," Ward said with disgust. He slammed the door of his locker shut. "I think I hear your mothers calling."

"Wait, wait," Ferdy said, pointing to Nick. "*His* mom's supposed to have all the answers, right? She tells everybody what to do and how to do it, and now we find out she don't know how to run her own life. So, Nicky, what's her take on old Teddy-boy screwin' around?"

Nick dropped the cleats and leaped over the bench, bent on ripping Ferdy's face off, but before Ward could step in, Jason Pate suddenly appeared from the next bank of lockers and quickly got a choke hold on Ferdy's neck. "Get a life, you dumb shit," he told Ferdy, then gave a nod to Ward to force Nick, still bristling, back over the bench. When he saw that Nick was restrained, he let Ferdy go. "What the hell you guys doing?" The question was meant for Ferdy and B.J.

Ferdy, not dumb enough to challenge somebody of Jason's stature, moved backward with his hands up, palms out. "Hey, man, we were just horsin' around."

"Yeah, right." Jason shoved Ferdy's ball glove back into his hands with a little more force than was necessary. "Then next time, horse around with somebody who appreciates redneck humor." And with a disgusted look, he swept up his jersey and headed on back to the senior lockers.

Ward still kept a restraining hand on Nick and watched as both Ferdy and B.J. couldn't leave fast enough. "You okay, Nick?"

Nick tossed his cleats into the metal locker and slammed the door. Then he stood a moment just looking at the puke-green surface. His heart was pounding and he felt a deep, red rage building inside. He wanted to take somebody's head off and Ferdy Jordan was his first choice. Ferdy had no class. He had no talent on the field. He had nothing but a smart-ass mouth and one day—

"Sometimes I think I hate him, Ward."

"Yeah, well, Ferdy's the kind of jerk you do hate, man. He's worthless. Forget him."

"Not Ferdy. I meant my dad."

"Oh, jeez, Nick."

Nick pulled a towel from around his neck and stuffed it into his gym bag. "How could he do this? What was so awful about us that he'd want to cut out? I know it's happened to other people and all, but you don't know how it feels until it happens to you."

"Yeah, it's the shits, man."

Nick just stood holding his bag for a moment. "And you're right. Ferdy's a jerk. I guess I lost it there for a minute."

"Hey, shit happens." Ward gave him a punch on his shoulder and Nick felt some of his rage ease. He might not be able to depend on his dad any longer, but Ward would never let him down.

They'd been playing baseball together from the time that his mom had signed him up for T-ball when he was six. Ward's folks had been right here with him, too. And from the beginning, both had felt real passion for the game and a strong desire to win. After a loss, both would agonize over what had gone wrong, where had they messed up, how they could avoid it next time, and what each needed to do to get just that tiny edge that made the difference between winning and losing.

And both had watched Ward's brother, Jimbo, do the ultimate—after getting a scholarship at UT, he'd snagged a contract with one of the majors.

With a sigh, Nick opened his locker again to get his shirt. He could have ended his own chances of playing for Coach Monk when he went for Ferdy that way. He owed Jason Pate and Ward for stepping in. Coach would have shit a brick if he'd seen it. But, damn it all, it was embarrassing for Jason to overhear what Ferdy said.

Nick shook out his T-shirt, getting ready to put it on, when Coach Monk appeared from the area of the senior lockers.

Nick and Ward were instantly at attention. "You were lookin' good out there this afternoon, Ward-boy," he said, clamping a large hand on the boy's bare shoulder. "You want to spend some quality time perfecting your curve ball, son. It's breakin' a little short."

"Yes, sir. I will."

"I've got some time tomorrow, so plan to stay late. With me spotting, we'll correct the problem."

Ward managed to contain his grin. "Yes, sir," he said, and quickly pulled his shirt over his head.

"So, Nick," Coach turned, folding his arms across his chest, "I like the way you've been shaping up at first lately. 'Course, you had an off day today, but it happens. Yesterday, two doubles in one inning. That's good—" he was nodding "—very good. Plan to come tomorrow with Ward and we'll work out a couple of plays. The two of you make a solid pair, Ward pitching and you at first."

"Thanks, Coach."

"Hang in there."

"I plan on that, sir."

Then, leaning against the closed lockers, the coach sobered. "I heard about your folks, Nick. Too bad about that. It's tough."

Extremely embarrassed, Nick looked at his feet. "Yes, sir," he mumbled.

Tyson pushed away from the lockers and reached out to grip Nick's shoulder in a gesture of gruff sympathy. "Hey, it's one of those things, son. You don't want to think you're one of a kind there, no way. You ask around, you'll find a quarter of the kids in the school been through the same thing."

"Yes, sir."

"Your mom and I spoke about it this morning," he said. Nick looked up, startled.

"Yeah. I promised her I'd find time to talk if you want."

"That's okay, Coach," Nick said, mortified. "I'm okay. Honest."

"Well…" Smiling, Tyson stepped back. "If you need a friend—besides Ward here," he laughed heartily, "you know all you have to do is knock on my door."

"Yes, sir."

"Now, you two finish dressing and get your butts outta here. Practice is over, it's chow time."

Both boys were motionless, watching the coach head out past the shelves of neatly-stacked sports equipment. Just then, Jason emerged from the lockers, and when Tyson spotted him, he motioned him over and slung his arm around the quarterback's shoulder. Coach had a way of bonding with his athletes that paid off big time for them. Sportswise, he'd put Rose Hill High and the Mustangs on the map in Texas, and that was saying something, considering the size of the town and the passion that infused high school sports in the state. In a moment, three more varsity players appeared and fell into step with Jason and the coach. Like Jimbo and others before them, the four made up the core elite of the Mustangs, and with the magic of Monk Tyson's coaching setting the stage—barring any accidents or injuries—all were destined for outstanding careers in sports. Just like Jimbo.

"Jeezum-pete," Ward breathed as the group moved along with the coach like a god in their midst. "What do you make of special attention from The Man himself?"

Grimly, Nick pulled his shirt over his head, then grabbed his glove and stuffed it inside his gym bag. "I don't know."

Hearing something in his voice, Ward turned. "What's wrong?"

"Can you believe my mom?" he asked, zipping the gym bag with a vengeance. "Coach'll think I'm some kind of chickenshit weakling, like I need somebody to hold my hand and tell me everything's gonna be all right now that my dad's walked out on us."

"Aw, I think you've got him wrong, Nick. He's just being, you know, nice. Like, some of the guys here are closer to Coach Monk than to their own dads…those guys he's talking to now, f'r instance. He was probably just paving the way if you should need, you know, help...or something.''

Nick straightened up and looked at him. "Do I look like I need help?"

Ward shrugged. "Maybe not that kind of help. But he's offering to coach us, like privately, so I don't know about you, man, but me—just name the time and place and I'm there."

Standing with his gym bag in his hand, Nick eyed Coach's chosen few with a mix of awe for their talent and envy for their good luck in being part of a tight circle. All were older than Nick and Ward—juniors and seniors mostly. It would be tough to penetrate that clique, Nick thought, but Ward was right. Coach had opened a door just now and he wasn't about to refuse. The trouble with his mom and dad made him feel pretty rotten, but he couldn't do anything about it. Grown-ups were going to do what they were going to do and what he thought didn't count. He didn't have control over anything in his life anymore except here at school. Making varsity next year—a year earlier than ninety-nine percent of high school athletes—was a hard goal, but with Coach Monk's help, he was going to bust his butt to do it.

Nick slung the gym bag onto his shoulder. "Let's go, Ward. You heard Coach. It's chow time and I'm hungry."

It would have been easy for Rachel to slack off at her job because of the meltdown in her personal life, but she'd learned a lesson when she'd failed to sense Jack Ford's despair and a young life had ended tragically. As much as she'd like to take a leave of absence and devote herself to the care and comfort of her own children as her family tried to adjust to the change in their lives, there were kids at Rose Hill High whose needs were just as urgent. Jason Pate, to name one.

Not that Jason wanted her help. He sat across from her now in her office, polite, respectful and so bent on stonewalling her that she was truly tempted to give up and just point him to the door and dismiss him from her mind. She couldn't recall ever having a more arduous time trying to coax dialogue from a student. But there was something wrong when an eighteen-year-old star athlete had begun bingeing on beer every weekend—even sometimes during the week. So, with Jack Ford always lurking in the back of her mind, her own personal reminder that a beautiful, talented athlete and gifted student could shock everybody and go off the deep end, she couldn't give up on Jason. It wouldn't happen to this boy, she vowed. Not if she could help it.

"I see you have a sister, Jason," she said, attempting to draw from him a clue to his home life.

"Yes, ma'am. Jennifer." One knee bounced restlessly. He seemed to realize it suddenly and shifted in the chair, then put his hands on his knees as if to keep himself under control.

"She's thirteen," Rachel said, looking at his file, then up into his eyes. She smiled. "Some say that's a difficult age for girls."

"She's okay."

Dead end there. Okay. Rachel knew the boy's mother was battling breast cancer. The whole family was probably in crisis over that, which sometimes left the kids feeling adrift, even abandoned. "Are you worried about your mother?" It was a direct question, but she was fresh out of ideas on how to approach him subtly.

"I guess. The doctor said she's done great with the chemo treatments. He says her tests show her cured."

"That's really wonderful news," Rachel said warmly. "I'm as happy to hear that as you and Jennifer must be."

"Yes, ma'am."

She cast in her mind for more small talk in the effort to get him to open up. "Is she going to be able to get out now and see you play?"

"She's not much of a sports fan. And my dad's been real busy looking after her, but that's okay. I understand."

Did he really? As a result of his mother's cancer, they'd missed most of his games this season, which had probably overshadowed everything else in the family, Jason's sports career included. Was he drowning his disappointment? Could it be that simple? "Coach Monk tells me you're one of his most promising athletes. There's bound to be a scholarship when you graduate. Possibly more than one."

"Yes, ma'am. So he says."

She paused, picking up a note of…what, irony? "You don't doubt what he says, do you?"

He gave a short laugh. "Nobody doubts what The Man says."

"Do you have a problem with Coach Monk?"

He stared at his hands. "If I did, I wouldn't be playing varsity quarterback."

Okay, maybe there was something going on, possibly having to do with politics on the team or maybe trouble trying to please Monk Tyson. Hopefully that wasn't it, as this boy didn't need any more stress than he was already dealing with, considering that until lately he'd probably believed he might lose his mother. Rachel didn't think there was much chance that Jason would confide anything negative that might get back to "The Man." She was surprised he'd even given a hint of intrigue in Tyson's little kingdom. But if Jason was drinking to avoid dealing with whatever it was troubling him, the effect was still dangerous and it still put his future in jeopardy. Maybe it was time to quit beating around the bush.

"Drinking the way you do could destroy your chances at a professional career in sports, Jason. You must know that."

"I guess." His knee was bouncing again and he looked tense. Rachel sensed he was on the verge of springing up out of the chair and leaving.

"Jason." She rose, moved around the desk and sat down in the chair beside him. "Why would you keep on doing something that is going to have such dire consequences? Have you thought about that?"

"Yes, ma'am."

She waited. He said nothing. "And—" she prompted.

He shrugged, remaining mute.

She sighed. "There is help out there, Jason. Have you considered that? There's AA, there's—"

"I don't need any of that!" he said, finally showing real emotion. His face was suddenly flushed and he was breathing hard. Both hands were clenched into fists. "I don't need it because I know what—"

Rachel waited, holding her breath. He turned from her, but not before she'd caught a glimpse of tears in his eyes. "You know...what, Jason?" she urged softly.

He met her eyes then and her heart swelled with sympathy. There was anguish there, and such pain that she wanted to lean forward, put her arms around him, as she would if he were her own and tell him everything would be all right.

"How do you know if you're gay, Ms. Forrester?"

Seven

Just when Rachel was thinking Ted had apparently dropped off the face of the earth, she found him waiting for her when she got home that evening. The session with Jason had taken a lot out of her, and she really didn't feel up to a sparring match with Ted. But she'd driven out to the lake several times since discovering what he'd done with their finances with no luck, so if she wanted a conversation with him, it was probably going to be at his convenience, not hers. Apparently, he and Francine were taking no chances on being subjected to another of Rachel's temper tantrums and were making themselves scarce. There'd been no answer when she tried his cell phone, either. Frustrated, she'd left numerous voice mail messages asking him to name a time when they could talk. Now, four days later, it seemed he'd finally decided to come out of seclusion.

"Where have you been, Ted? I've been trying to reach you for days." What energy she had left might as well be used up front. She watched him pour himself a drink at the bar and down most of it in one swallow.

"I've been busy."

"I noticed that when I went to the bank and discovered you'd emptied our checking account and frozen most everything else. It's a despicable thing to do, letting me find out when my ATM card was rejected for insufficient funds. Why didn't you tell me when I saw you at the cabin? What's gotten into you, for heaven's sake! What do you expect the kids and me to live on?"

He removed his sunglasses and revealed a fading bruise around his eye. With a sigh, he massaged the bridge of his nose with thumb and forefinger. "I did it to avoid the possibility of us getting tangled in a financial squabble since I'd had a sample of the way you've decided to react about Francine and me."

"Oh, bullshit! You thought *I'd* rush to the bank and grab everything, so you acted to beat me to it."

"It's happened before when couples divorce."

She propped her hands on her hips. "So you've definitely decided. It's a divorce, not a trial separation?"

He sat down, dangling the half-empty drink between his knees. "I just know I want to be with Francine." Gone was the defiant lover he'd been at the cabin. Instead, he was now glum. He also looked as if a migraine was coming on. At one time, she would have been sympathetic. Now she felt no urge to find his pills or to say something soothing. Just the opposite.

"Listen to yourself, Ted! You sound like a teenage boy in the throes of a mad crush. Give me a break, please. I have to deal with adolescents every day at school. This is serious. This is the future of our children you're monkeying around with. Have you considered the consequences? Have you really thought through what you're doing?"

"I haven't been happy for a long time, Rachel."

She simply stared at him, wondering at his selfishness. "I think you've managed to convey that message now, Ted. But, just out of curiosity, if I hadn't seen you and Francine together, when were you going to tell me you were unhappy?"

"I knew you'd freak out. Or start a campaign designed to fix the problem." He took a drink. "Some things can't be fixed."

She gave a bitter laugh. "I don't know if my reaction over your infidelity was freaky or not, but I can tell you I certainly freaked out when you pulled the financial rug out from under me and your children. I'm not going to sit by while you grab everything we've worked for in eighteen years. I'm fighting you on this, Ted.''

"It's a moot point, anyway, now," he said, running a palm over his two-hundred-dollar haircut. "I'm the one who's had the financial rug pulled out from under me."

She frowned. "What are you talking about?"

"Walter. He talked the other doctors into voting me out of the practice. When I got there Monday morning, they'd already met over the weekend and had a document drafted with the buy-out terms. It's totally unacceptable. It'll be a cold day in hell before I let him grab my practice. I've spent twelve years building up that practice. Who the hell does he think he is?"

"I think that's pretty obvious. He's your partner and you stole his wife. It's a betrayal of the most hurtful kind."

"That wouldn't have happened if Francine had been getting what she needed from him," he said, staring into his drink.

Rachel sank back against the chair's cushions. "Then I can assume the same thing? You weren't getting what you needed from me and you could get it from Francine?"

"I told you, it just happened. We didn't plan it."

"Uh-huh. And I heard you the first time." She stood up. "As for the manner of Walter's revenge, you must have had a clue when he stormed over Saturday morning with blood in his eye. You can't steal a man's wife and expect him to have no hard feelings. And you can't expect the other doctors in the practice to turn a blind eye either. Everything that's happened is so predictable, Ted. How did you not assume there would be some negative fallout? Walter simply chose the most effective way to retaliate."

"I'm not taking this lying down. I'm fighting them in court." Setting his drink aside, he reached for an envelope in his jacket. "You've got a stake in this, too. Think about it. If their offer stands, it will affect you and the kids, too. If Walter screws me in this deal, our joint net worth is cut in half. No way is he getting away with this." He gave her the envelope. "Here, my lawyer drew this up."

She took it, frowning. "What is it?"

"It started out to be the terms of a tentative separation settlement, but it had to be revised after I arrived at the practice Monday morning. Everything's changed." He glanced toward the stairs. "Are the kids here?"

"No, Nick's still at baseball practice and it's Kendall's day for gymnastics." She glanced at her watch as she pulled the folded document from the envelope. "I have to pick her up at six-fifteen," she said, scanning the first page. She frowned, struggling through the usual legalese until she finally reached the meat of it. Then her eyes widened in disbelief. She looked up at Ted. "You can't be serious!"

"When have you ever known me to joke about money?"

She held the blue-bound papers as if they were poisonous. "You're seriously suggesting we sell the house? This house? What makes you think I'd even consider such a crazy thing? This is Nick and Kendall's home, Ted. It's not yours to use to get your tail out of a crack."

"If you can come up with a better idea, I'm open to suggestions."

As he rose from the chair to freshen his drink, the front door crashed open and Nick burst into the room. "Mom, I gotta talk to you!" He broke stride only momentarily when he spotted his dad, then ignored him to light into his mother. "You have really messed up."

She gave him a stern look. "Can't you see your dad and I are having a discussion now, Nick? We'll be done in—"

"Why did you tell Coach about Dad walking out on us?"

She gave him a startled look. "What are you talking about?"

"Coach saw me after practice and offered a shoulder to cry on, Mom. It was—" Tossing his jacket on a chair, he shook his head as words failed him. "Jeez, Mom. Ward heard it and I don't know who else. I can see it now, I'll be trying to live this down for the rest of my life. I don't believe you did something so bogus!''

"I did not tell Monk Tyson your father walked out."

"Then how'd he know it?" Nick demanded, his face filled with outrage.

"This is a small town. Word gets around, Nick." Rachel drew a deep breath, knowing this was not the last time she would have to try to ease the fallout from Ted's desertion. "Monk mentioned it in the break room this morning," she explained. "He expressed concern, nothing else."

"And you let him think I'm such a baby that I might not be able to handle what's happened?"

Ted finally spoke up. "Nobody thinks that, Nick. And of course you can handle it. If you ask me, it's a good coach who's aware of more than just a kid's stats on the ball team."

Nick turned on Ted furiously. "What the hell would you know about stats, Dad? You haven't made one of my ball games this season."

"Don't talk to me like that, boy," Ted ordered. "You know the rules around here about profanity."

"Yeah, and I guess you're going to leave it to Mom to enforce the rules as usual, right?"

"Please..." Rachel lifted a hand to stop them. "Let's all calm down. Nick, my conversation with Monk was not personal, so you have no need to feel embarrassed. He offered to help if you seemed to need it, that's all. There's nothing for you to be upset about."

"Except the whole team is thinking what a trip this is," Nick said bitterly. "You should have heard Ferdy, then you'd understand. You're a guidance counselor, Mom. This isn't supposed to happen to you. Everybody thinks you're supposed to fix things."

"Oh, for Christ's sake," Ted said. "You're looking at real trouble if you start listening to what everybody says."

"I'm sorry, Nick," Rachel said quietly, ignoring Ted. "I didn't see this coming and I can't fix it. But we'll get through it. Now, why don't you go to the kitchen and get yourself something to eat. I picked up a pizza on my way home. We'll talk later.''

Nick turned on his heel. "I'm not hungry." He snagged his jacket from the back of the chair and stalked out.

When he was gone, Rachel gave Ted a meaningful look. "What was that you were saying about the kids being fine with this?"

"They will. It'll take some getting used to, but Nick's tough. He'll adjust."

She looked briefly at the ceiling, praying for patience. "Okay, Ted. Whatever you say." She realized she still held the legal papers in her hand. "Was there anything else you wanted to tell me about this? Like Nick, is there anything more I need to adjust to besides the fact that you want to sell the house out from under us?"

"As I said, I've talked to my lawyer. According to the terms of the original agreement when the practice was established, if Walt and the others are unanimous in any decision—and that includes demanding the ouster of any partner—they can do it. The only negotiable is how much they'll agree the departing member is worth. And that's where it all gets sticky. If I don't accept what they offer—and I'm not about to—then I have to take them to court. Who knows how long that'll take. Could be months. A year. I'll need the money—" He paused, then started again. "We'll both need income while this is ongoing. Your salary at school won't cut it. The money's there…once we sell the house."

"What does Francine have to say about all this?"

"She's shocked, naturally. She says Walter's just doing it to hurt her."

"He's probably feeling pretty hurt himself, seeing his wife has been sleeping with a man he thought was his friend." She waved him quiet when he started to argue and said wearily, "Never mind trying to spin what you and Francine have done as anything except the trashy thing it is, Ted. What you and I have to do now is figure out what to do to survive this disaster and to help our children." She gestured with the

papers. "First of all, I hope there's some place in the fine
print here that establishes a regular income to the kids and
me while you pursue this lawsuit."

"There is, but it's not enough to maintain this house and
all the other perks of our current lifestyle."

"You're planning to stay in the cabin at the lake, I as
sume."

He nodded. "For the time being."

"We could sell that, I suppose," she said, looking beyond
him at nothing in particular as she considered various pos
sibilities.

"There's one obvious solution that will take care of ev
erything," Ted said. Something in his tone caught her atten
tion, but he turned away and, with his back to her, tossed off
the rest of his drink.

"And what would that be?" she asked.

"You and the kids could move in with Dinah."

"Excuse me?"

"It's the logical thing to do, Rachel." He tipped the bottle
and poured himself a fresh drink. "Now that Dinah's out of
her apartment and settled into her new house, I bet she'll be
happy to have you and the kids for a visit."

"A visit."

Hearing her lack of enthusiasm, he made an impatient
sound. "It won't be forever, goddamn it! Just phone her and
see what she says before you blow off the idea. That's all
I'm saying."

"It's an imposition, Ted. Think about it. She's a widow
in her sixties. She isn't used to young children. It's too much
to ask."

"Explain the problem. She'll understand."

She stood looking at him, wondering at his audacity.
"You're really serious about this," she remarked.

"Yeah."

"And is it really only a separation, Ted? Or have you
decided you want a divorce?"

"The only thing I've decided is that I want to be with

Francine right now. I don't know where that'll go." He brought the drink up, then set it down again. "It's Walter who's caused all this trouble, Rachel. He's being a first-class son of a bitch."

She stared. "Walter."

"I just told you what he's doing."

"Ted. Wake up and smell the coffee. Walter isn't the cause of your trouble. I can't believe you! The trouble is your own selfish insistence on having an affair and damning the consequences."

"Let's not get started on that again, Rachel. Just tell me you'll mention to Dinah the possibility of moving in with her temporarily. She's crazy about the kids. It'll be okay, you'll see. And by the way, I've talked to a real estate agent. We can make a ton of money on this house."

"You talked to an agent before even mentioning it to me?"

"I just asked," he said, shrugging. "I figured you'd be happy to hear what a good investment we're sitting on."

Rachel simply gazed at him in silence for a long moment. "If you thought I was freaked out over your shoddy affair, Ted," she said in a dangerously soft tone, "then you will really be shocked if you hang around another minute."

"Oh, for crying out loud, Rachel."

She pointed to the door. "Out, Ted. Now."

Muttering an obscenity, he slammed his drink on the bar in disgust and left.

Eight

Three months later

Cam's first job on his to-do list after finishing his book was to repaint the trim on his porch. Trying to keep the old place in good repair was a never-ending challenge, but he'd found that he liked tinkering around the house where he'd been raised. It was surprisingly satisfying. Not only was the house shaping up, but while doing the work, he found that with his hands occupied, his mind was free to flesh out the proposal for a new book. It was nearing midday now and he was almost finished repainting the trim when he heard the roaring sound of a huge moving van gearing down, then braking to make the turn at the corner of the street. New neighbors…and close by, he thought, since Morningside was a short street. He stopped what he was doing, balanced the paint brush on top of the can and reached for a rag soaked in turpentine to clean his hands.

The van appeared to be slowing to a stop. With a frown, he saw the driver peering at the number on his own house and then his neighbor's, Dinah Hunt. Cam watched, assuming the driver had stopped to get his bearings, but then a car turned the corner, pulled in front of the moving van and stopped at curbside. Out of it came Rachel Forrester, her son, Nick, another teenage boy in a baseball cap and a little girl. This couldn't be what it appeared, he thought, even as he watched Rachel approach the van driver.

With a sense of impending doom, he saw the driver's helper get out and head toward the back of the van. Once the doors were opened, he adjusted the load ramp and disappeared inside. The little girl raced up Dinah's sidewalk yelling, "We're here, Gran! We're all ready to move in!"

It couldn't be, but it was. Tossing his paint rag aside, Cam slapped the lid on the can and gave it a smart thump with a hammer, heedless of the color splattering his shoes. Scowling, he snatched up the newspaper he'd used to protect the porch floor and stuffed it into a plastic trash bag while out of the corner of his eye he saw the boy, Nick, break away from his buddy and head his way. Just what he needed right next door, Rachel Forrester and her son, highly visible and constant reminders of Jack and how he'd died.

"Hi, Mr. Ford."

He straightened slowly, scooping up the smelly rag. "Cam," he reminded the boy. "How's it goin', Nick?"

"I guess you can tell we're moving in with Gran today."

Looking up from scrubbing paint off his shoe, Cam saw the first load—three large boxes—was now being wheeled down the ramp on a dolly. "I figured that out."

Nick's gaze drifted back to the van where the helper was carefully handing a cat carrier over to the driver. Inside, a big yellow tom meowed in protest. "It's sort of a family emergency. Nobody's happy about it except Gran and Kendy."

"Kendy. That would be your little sister."

"Yes, sir. Kendall. She seems to think it's some kind of vacation, us going to live with Gran. The truth is, my mom and dad are getting a divorce."

And Rachel was screwed out of the house? Had she let him con her into using the same lawyer, playing on her denial that he wouldn't take advantage of her? His infidelity alone should have given her grounds to take him to the cleaners. Instead, here were Rachel and the kids being displaced, not Ted. Cam swiped one last time at his Nikes and tried to keep what he thought off his face. He found it gave him no satisfaction that he'd been right about Forrester. Straightening, he said, "I'm sorry about that."

Nick shrugged with a kid's fatalistic acceptance of having no power over grown-ups and their decisions. "Mom says the move's only temporary," he said, watching Kendall coax the scared cat out of the carrier. "We'll have to wait for the details of the divorce to be worked out before finding another house, but it'll be in Rose Hill." This he said with certainty, but a scowl darkened his face. "No way we'll move somewhere else."

"Then it's fortunate your Gran lives right here and that Rose Hill is a small town," Cam said, seeking to help put a positive spin on a sorry situation. "You and your sister won't have to change schools." At least these kids would stay on familiar turf with friends to help ease the pain of their parents' split. The stress of divorce plus the move from New York to Texas had apparently been more than Jack could handle.

"That's what my mom said when she told us that we had to sell the house." He was turned, watching the movers. "Because of the lawsuit."

Well, at least Rachel was suing his ass. Which would mean their assets were in limbo while she negotiated with Ted. Moving in with Dinah might have been a necessity, which meant she could hold out as long as it took. "Your mom is staying on at Rose Hill High, I assume."

"I guess."

"And your dad?" Cam didn't know why the hell he was asking. It definitely was nothing to him where Forrester went.

Nick's gaze swung about. "My dad won't be able to stay at his practice...with the lawsuit and all. He says he's gonna have to scope out another location."

Ted was setting up a new practice? Maybe it wasn't Rachel suing him, but Walter Dalton. Was he being kicked out of the practice? If so, Rachel and the family unit weren't the only casualties of his infidelity. Was he leaving town? Cam could tell him about the problems for his kids that would add to the situation. Presuming, of course, that Forrester had any concern about the welfare of his kids. So far, he hadn't shown much of anything except a juvenile infatuation for someone else's wife.

"Dad says his new practice will be here in Rose Hill," Nick added, but when Cam glanced over at the boy, he was chewing the inside of his lip. Worried, but trying to keep up a brave front, Cam thought. He wondered if Ted had anticipated quite so much fallout from his affair. And what did it mean for Rachel and her kids if the practice was kaput? Then he caught himself. No sense speculating about a situation that didn't concern him.

"How's the ball team doing this season?" he asked, moving to a safe subject.

"Okay, I guess. Varsity will probably make the play-offs if we keep on like we're going, so far. Coach says I could be at first base next year." Nick slipped his hands into his back pockets, looking as if he had a secret. His demeanor went from dark to light in a few seconds. "He's been great. He's been giving Ward and me extra coaching." Turning to look for his friend, he put two fingers to his lips and gave a shrill whistle, motioning the boy over. "Ward's over today helping me and my mom with the move."

Ward appeared, winded a little from the run. "Hi, Mr. Ford." Then, before Nick could introduce him, he added, "How ya doin'?"

"I'm good, Ward. And it's Cam. How's your dad?"

"Same as ever." Ward grinned. "Big as life and twice as tough."

"Wait, wait," Nick broke in, waving a hand. "You guys know each other?"

Ward's easy smile faltered. "Sort of," he said, with a hesitant look at Cam.

Cam flashed back to Jack's funeral, the day he'd met the boy, and found he could reply and sound almost normal. "My son and Jimbo were friends," he explained to Nick.

Forcing memory aside, he said to Ward, "I hear Jimbo's shaping up to go pro."

"You're not gonna believe it," Ward said with pride. "He's had a couple of interviews with scouts already, but Dad's trying to persuade him to stay at UT until he graduates. Problem is, he's got a whole year to go."

"A whole year," Cam said, knowing it sounded like a lifetime to Ward.

"Yeah, and what if he gets injured or something." Ward saw visions of big money floating out the window. "It's tough to turn your back on that."

"Yeah, injury is always a possibility."

"I didn't know you had a son," Nick said, looking interested. "Is he, like, living with his mom, or something?"

"Cool it, Nick," Ward said, jabbing him in the ribs with his elbow.

"Ow!" Nick looked at Ward. "What? What!"

"My son passed away five years ago," Cam said.

"Oh, jeez, I'm sorry," Nick said with a stricken look. "Ward never said—"

"I didn't know Mr. Ford was living here. You never mentioned knowing him," Ward explained, then looked at Cam. "Everyone thought you'd stay in New York, Mr....uh, Cam. You know, because of your work. Being a writer and all. And with Jack—" He broke off, cleared his throat, realizing he'd veered into deep water. "I mean, what's Rose Hill compared to New York City?"

"It's home," Cam said. "And to tell the truth, writers can pretty much write anywhere...as long as it doesn't get too noisy." He could tell them that memories haunted a man anywhere, anyplace. And maybe he'd wanted to be close to Jack.

"You won't even know we're here," Nick promised hastily.

Not a chance. Cam wished it was true. He looked at Ward. "So, which scouts are courting Jimbo?"

"St. Louis and Chicago." Ward beamed with brotherly

pride. "Hot and heavy, too. Me and Nick have a bet going whether he'll drop out of UT and sign with one of them or pass for right now. I mean, jeez, the offer will probably be six figures. Nick says he'll stay. I say he'll take the money."

"Tough decision," Cam agreed. "But keeping in mind that injury can happen whether Jimbo's playing at UT or in the pros, it makes sense to have that degree to fall back on. And whether an athlete is injured or not, he can't play ball after passing his prime, anyway."

"What about Nolan Ryan?" Ward argued, naming one of baseball's greats and Texas's favorite sons. "He was way into his forties when he retired."

"Nolan Ryan is a rare exception," Cam said. Then, after a pause, "So, how's it going with Coach Monk and the special attention?"

"I told Cam about Coach Monk giving both of us some pointers," Nick explained to Ward, making a mock overhand pitch to an imaginary target near the van. "My stats have improved big time. I couldn't believe it at first, him singling us out for special coaching, but he's been really great, huh, Ward?"

Ward didn't look quite as enthusiastic, but he gave a nod. "Yeah, he's great." He shifted from one foot to the other, gave a swipe to his nose and squinted off in the distance. "We're lucky, I guess. When I told Jimbo about it, he said that kind of help from Coach can be a real advantage, but to look out for some bad action from the other guys." He brought his gaze back to Nick. "You gotta admit, Nick, Ferdy and B.J. are acting really pissed off."

"Yeah, I guess," Nick said, shrugging, "but I'm blowin' 'em off. They're jerks." He turned back to Cam. "Ward's the one who's really lucked out with Coach. I mean, he's giving me some pointers, but he's spending a lot more time with Ward. Coach thinks Ward will be even better than Jimbo."

"Aw, c'mon, Nick. Can it." Ward's fair skin was flushed with embarrassment.

"He's shy," Nick said, grinning at Cam.

To Cam, it seemed there was more than shyness in Ward's demeanor. "You having any difficulty with...who is it? Ferdy and B.J., Ward?"

"Nothing I can't handle," Ward said.

"They're just jealous," Nick said. "I keep telling him that."

"Jealousy can show itself in pretty mean ways sometimes," Cam said, still studying Ward's face.

"It's okay. I'm cool." The look he gave Nick promised a reckoning later. Cam decided to let it go. If Ward and Nick were being singled out for preferential treatment from Monk Tyson, then they'd have to learn to handle the fallout.

"Uh-oh," Nick said, turning at the sound of his name. "Kendy-the-tiger's headed this way. Break time's over, guys."

Looking beyond them, Cam saw Kendall marching across the lawn, her gaze fixed on her brother. Dark hair, curly and wild like her grandmother's, he thought as she drew closer. Snub nose, big brown eyes, which came from Forrester, he decided, although her expression as she zeroed in on her brother put him in mind of Rachel in one of her no-nonsense moods. Looking closer, he saw that she had a camera hanging around her neck on a bright red strap.

"Nick, Mom says you've gotta come and help, right now." She had one small fist propped on her hip, the other hand held on to her camera.

Sure enough, Rachel was crossing the lawn. "We gotta go," Nick said to Ward. "We don't want to tick Mom off, otherwise, she'll nix the pizza she promised and we'll be eating pb and j instead." Flashing a grin and a friendly wave at Cam, he and Ward jogged off in Rachel's direction.

Cam watched them go, young, strong and healthy, their whole lives in front of them. He was forced to take a steadying breath and hold it until the pain was shoved back inside and a tight lid slapped on.

"'Scuse me, Mr. Ford."

Coming from a dark place, he looked down to find the little girl looking up at him from the bottom of the porch steps. The yellow tom wound in and out at her feet and the sound of his purring was so loud that Cam could hear it. "Hey, Kendall."

"You know my name?" She smiled widely.

"Nick mentioned it."

"Oh. Okay." Not waiting for an invitation, she climbed the porch steps. The cat followed. "This is my camera," she told him. "It's digital."

"It's cool," he said. Her face was heart-shaped, what he could see of it through her curly mop. Big eyes fixed on him. "Are you a photographer?"

"Yes. And I'd like to take a picture of your house, please. If you don't mind."

"My house?"

She glanced around the porch, taking in the leaded glass front door, the fanlights above the tall windows, the gingerbread trim glistening with fresh paint. "It's a special house. I've been noticing it for a long time...whenever I visit Gran. I like the way it looks, like it probably has secrets from way back."

"I don't know about secrets, but I've been told there's a ghost." What was he doing? he asked himself. First the boy, now the little girl. Open a door to kids and they were like puppy dogs, swarming all over.

"A ghost?" Her eyes went wide. "Really?"

Cam reached down and picked up the paint can. His grandfather had convinced him by the time he was six years old that the ghost of a renegade ancestor roamed the attic of the old house. "My great-great-great uncle was a gambler who was falsely accused of cheating while playing poker."

"It's his ghost?"

"Uh-huh, so they say. And he can't rest until his name is cleared."

"But how can he ever prove that he didn't do it?" Kendall

asked, frowning over practicalities. Another of her mother's traits.

Cam shrugged. "I don't know. Maybe that's why he hasn't gone on to that big gambling casino in the sky. He's holding out for justice."

"Maybe he expects you to prove him innocent," she said, her head cocked, considering. "That's what you do, isn't it? Write about crimes and try to figure out who did it if it isn't already solved?"

"I guess so, more or less."

She studied his face, long and hard. "I still want to take a picture of your house."

Now was the time to establish boundaries, but he made the mistake of looking into her big eyes. "Okay, go for it." But he told himself he didn't have to hang around and watch. He was reaching for the door to escape when she stopped him.

"No, wait. You have to be in it." Kendall ran back down the porch steps and stood looking critically at the front of the house through the digital lens of her camera, then back up at Cam. "You need to sit in that wicker chair. Actually," she added, "you look sort of like someone back in olden times. You know those pictures taken when cameras were first invented? They never smiled. Like you. You may be your great-great-great uncle come back to clear his name."

"You believe in reincarnation?"

"What's that mean?" she asked, momentarily distracted.

"Just what you said. Someone who died in the past comes back in the body of a present-day person."

"Hmm," she said, puckering up her face to think it over. "I'm not sure that could happen." She paused and he could almost see the wheels turning. He was thinking that Ted Forrester must be crazy as well as heartless for turning his back on these two kids. Nick seemed a nice boy and this little girl could steal a robot's heart. "I think I see your mom coming, so you'd better hurry with that photo," he said, spotting

Rachel making her way over with a decidedly stern look about her.

Kendall immediately focused the camera again, paying meticulous attention to the composition of the picture.

"Kendy—"

"Mom, Mr. Ford is letting me take a picture of his house. And him, too. There's a ghost, but unless I'm lucky, he probably won't show up in the picture."

Rachel looked once into Cam's gray eyes, then away. "Kendall, Mr. Ford is busy. And you need to go inside and unpack your things. The movers have taken in all the boxes marked with your name."

"This will only take a minute," Kendall said, refusing to be rushed. With the photo now set up, she turned her attention back to Cam. "Put that paint can down, Mr. Ford," she ordered. "Hide it behind that big pot plant."

"Yes, ma'am." Cam did as told and sat down in the wicker chair.

"Kendall—"

"I'm almost done, Mom." With all her attention focused on getting the perfect shot, Kendall carefully snapped several pictures. "Okay, that's perfect. Thanks, Mr. Ford." She flashed him a bright smile and dashed off with the cat at her heels.

"That cat must think he's a dog," Cam said, watching them.

"Graham," Rachel said. "And sometimes I think the same thing." She took a deep breath. "I apologize for both Nick and Kendall. I don't know why they headed over here, but—" She brought herself up short. "Don't worry, I'll establish ground rules right away. I'm aware of your occupation and your need for absolute privacy. It won't happen again."

"Nick tells me Ted's setting up a new practice," he said, ignoring her tense little speech. "Don't tell me, let me guess. When Walter got the news, he retaliated in the way it would hurt Ted the most."

Her color heightened, but her gaze held. "Do you always say exactly what you think, Mr. Ford, no matter how intrusive or insensitive? Or is there something about me and my situation that brings out the worst in you? I think it's obvious that my…our circumstances are changed," she said stiffly. "I'll leave it to the gossip mill in Rose Hill to fill you in on the details." She turned to go.

"Did you get legal representation?"

She stopped, turned back. "Why, do you expect me to thank you for suggesting it? Yes, of course, I engaged a lawyer. I'm not an idiot. You can't get a divorce without one."

"Not a separation after all, huh? What happened to your belief that Ted was simply having a midlife crisis?"

"I still suspect it, but I'm not waiting around for him to get over it."

He nodded slowly. "Ah, I think I hear a bit of good old-fashioned rage in your voice at last. Justifiable and about time, if you ask me."

"That's just it, Mr. Ford," she said, her tone rich with disgust. "Nobody asked you." Turning on her heel, she stalked off.

Cam watched her leave, as disgusted with himself as she was, even though he had every reason, because of Jack, to feel hostile toward her. But hell, there were a lot of people he should feel hostile to because of Jack, and he didn't lose his cool when they crossed paths. Cara, for one. And he damn sure hadn't forgiven his ex-wife for being more interested in her new lover than their son's problems, but reminding her was like kicking a puppy. Her anguish over Jack was, like his, a permanent burden, while Rachel Forrester had simply put the death of a kid in her care in a closed file and got on with her life.

He looked over where she, her kids, Ward, her mother and the cat mingled amid the contents of the moving van. He didn't want her living right next door, a bitter reminder of what he'd tried for five years to forget. He'd been in a dark, tormented place when he returned to Rose Hill, but with his work and the restoration of the old house, he'd managed to find a measure of peace. It was a matter of emotional survival to reject anything—or anybody—that screwed that up.

"Whoa, man, tell me about Jack. Was he in a car accident or something?" Accompanied by Eminem's rap on the CD player, Nick was in the process of stowing gear in a chest of drawers. Now he straightened and met Ward's eyes in the mirror above the chest. "And how come you knew about it and I didn't?"

"Jack and Jimbo were real tight." Ward shoved an empty suitcase under the bed and straightened up, dusting his hands. "So Jimbo was a pallbearer at the funeral. It was real sad, man."

"Jeez…"

"Yeah, but you don't know the worst part yet. It was no car accident. Jack committed suicide."

Nick's eyes went round with surprise. "So that was…what, a few years ago? How long?"

Ward shrugged. "I don't know. Seems like I was in the fourth or fifth grade."

Which meant Nick had been about ten or eleven years old. "I think I remember it," he said, frowning. "My mom was real upset that this student had died. I recall it, because we were here at Gran's house and Mom was crying. She never did that, so it kinda made an impression, you know?" He went quiet, thinking what a shock it would be if something like that happened to one of his friends and how much worse it would be if it were a close friend, someone like Ward, for instance. "So Jimbo took it real hard, huh?"

"Yeah. Even though Jack hadn't been at Rose Hill very long, him and Jimbo were, like, best friends." Ward frowned, thinking back. "I think Jack and his mom moved here because his folks got a divorce. Transferred from New York and Mr. Ford—Cam—stayed there. Jimbo said Jack was pretty messed up at first, but he seemed to settle in after a while, especially when he started playing ball." Ward watched Nick move to the CD player and pop out Eminem. "Probably helped a lot that he was so good he started out the next year playing varsity ball. Coach Monk really liked him. He would have snagged a scholarship like Jimbo, without a doubt. But…well…" Ward shrugged. "He ended it with a rope."

Nick winced, the CD in his hand forgotten. "Oh, man, you mean he hung himself?"

"Yeah. It was in a hotel when the team was playing-off somewhere. Anyway, he was supposed to share a room with Jimbo, but he never showed up that night. They found him in a room that was unoccupied, like he wanted to do it but didn't want Jimbo to find him. Weird, you know? Jimbo was all broken up. Lucky for him that my folks were there for the game, because it was my dad who told him about Jack. He hadn't cried since he broke his collarbone in seventh grade playing soccer, but he sure cried when he heard about Jack." Ward sat on the bed, elbows resting on his knees, and stared at his feet. "I'll never forget it."

There was silence in the room as both boys struggled with the unthinkable. Suicide happened, but never to someone you *knew*. It was, like, old people who did that. Or druggies. Or folks who were mental. Nick finally pegged something about Cameron Ford that he'd sensed. He hadn't actually put it into words, but he'd felt from their first meeting that there was something kind of dark about him. Something buried deep, and it made him sort of…unreachable. Dropping his gaze to the CD in his hand, he studied the label without really seeing it. No wonder. You would feel pretty dark and deep, Nick decided, if your kid killed himself.

Rachel waited until nightfall to call the family conference. They'd unloaded and placed their stuff where it belonged in her mother's house, although it would be several days—if not weeks—before everything was neat enough to ease her concern over invading Dinah's privacy.

"How many times do I have to tell you, Rachel? I'm more

than happy to have you and the kids staying here.'' Dinah opened the pizza box and set it in the middle of the table. ''We both know it's temporary. Stop beating up on yourself. You didn't choose this situation, but it's happened. Luckily, I'm in a position to help. Try thinking of it as being a bit easier on Nick and Kendy rather than you renting an apartment where people don't bother to say hi even if they live in the adjoining unit.''

''You're not telling me your neighbor is a warm-and-fuzzy, friendly type, are you?''

''Who, Cameron? Underneath that gruff exterior, he's a pussycat.''

Rachel, in the act of filling glasses with lemonade, made a sputtering sound. ''I've already had a run-in with him, Mom. He was insufferably rude.''

''Rude or blunt?''

''What's the difference?''

''Quite a bit.''

''Whatever, I'm going to have the kids steer clear of him.''

''Which is definitely overreacting.'' Dinah took a stack of paper plates from the cupboard. ''We know why he's testy around you, Rachel, but he's hardly going to take it out on your children.''

''Right, because I'm not giving him a chance. I'm establishing ground rules as of tonight. I don't want them bothering him.'' She walked to the doorway leading to the bedrooms and called out, ''Nick, Kendall, take a break! Pizza's here.''

Kendall responded promptly. She inspected the contents of the box on the table and wrinkled her nose. ''I wanted a Happy Meal,'' she said, poking out her bottom lip.

Rachel took a look at her grimy hands. ''Go wash up,'' she said as she mixed the ingredients for a salad. ''And tell your brother he's keeping others from eating dinner by holing up in his room. Tell Ward he's welcome to stay and eat with us, too.''

''He's gone. His mom called,'' Kendall said. ''And I don't

want to talk to Nick. He hollered at me when I just asked if he knew where my Dixie Chicks CD was. He's in a bad mood.''

"Aren't we all?" Rachel muttered, once her daughter was out of earshot.

"It's a difficult time," Dinah said sympathetically. "I'll go get him."

Rachel nodded mutely and felt a rush of gratitude mixed with bone-deep fatigue. Her mother had been an angel, going far beyond generosity in opening her house to her family. Before they arrived—and without consulting Rachel—Dinah had cleared the three bedrooms they would occupy, leaving nothing but the essentials, bed, dresser, chest, which left room for the kids' personal belongings. She'd insisted that Nick and Kendall would feel less uprooted if they were surrounded by their own things. Most of the furniture from the other house had, of necessity, gone into storage.

"Here we are," Dinah said, urging a surly-faced Nick into the kitchen. "I don't know about anybody else, but I'm famished."

"I need to get my stuff unpacked," Nick said, dropping into a chair only when Dinah put a hand on his shoulder. "I can always eat later."

And avoid his family, Rachel thought with a pang. The effect of his life being in upheaval was telling on Nick. He'd been acting out lately, staying in his room, missing meals, ignoring his curfew. She knew where his rebelliousness came from, but that didn't make it any easier to deal with.

"You can eat later if you want, Nick," she said, taking a seat at the head of the table. "But there are some ground rules to be established, now that we're going to be living here with Gran."

"Gimme a break, Mom. Save the lecture about keeping my room clean and picking up after myself. You gave it already.''

"I want to hear you say you'll do it, Nick."

"What do you think I am, a total jerk? I'm gonna do it."
He flicked at a crumb on the table. "Jeez..."

"I'm also counting on your basic good manners, so watch
your mouth. The least we can do in appreciation of Gran's
hospitality is to behave with common courtesy."

"So, what's the deal with the family conference?" he
asked. "That is, what's left of our family."

Rachel counted to ten. "This is about Gran's next-door
neighbor."

"Who, Cam?"

"Mr. Ford?" Kendall echoed, slipping into her chair.

"Yes, Mr. Ford." Rachel rested her folded hands on the
table. "Do not go over there without an invitation. Do not
trespass on his property for any reason. Kendy, keep Graham
away from there. He's probably the type to complain about
cats pooping in his flower beds. I don't want any complaints
from him that my children are a nuisance."

Nick eyed her with instant suspicion. "Did he tell you we
were bugging him?"

"No, but I don't want to give him a chance to make a
formal complaint."

Nick, slouched low in his chair, made a disgusted sound.
"He's an okay guy, Mom."

"He's an extremely private individual," she argued. "His
work requires absolute solitude. I don't want to warn either
of you again to keep your distance."

"Is the lecture finished?" Nick's fingers drummed on the
table while he gazed with boredom at nothing in particular.
"Can I go now?"

She looked at him in silence, then waved a hand in dis-
missal. "Go," she said wearily.

Nine

By the end of the month, they were settled in at Dinah's house, more or less. Kendall seemed to take to their new digs with little fuss, but Nick was increasingly surly and withdrawn. In spite of Dinah's attempts to reassure her, Rachel felt obliged to say often and apologetically that their stay was strictly temporary, and that as soon as she could manage it, she'd get a place of her own. Both knew that before Rachel could do anything, Ted and his ex-partners first had to settle the division of assets in the practice, and that would come only after a lengthy legal battle. Still, she worried over her mother's loss of privacy.

That would not be a problem for the next two days, Rachel thought one Saturday morning as she poured orange juice and went in search of Dinah. Nick and Kendall had been picked up last night by Ted to spend the entire weekend with him at the lake house. Their plan, as she understood it, was to head out early today for the rodeo in Fort Worth. Ted's change of heart surprised her, but it was more than welcome. Forever, it seemed, he'd been deaf to Rachel's pleas that he needed to pay more attention to Nick and Kendy. Since their separation, he hadn't spent more than a couple of hours at one time with his children, never for an overnight visit. Mostly, he picked them up for a quick fast-food meal on a school night, which meant he was forced to drop them off at an early hour, thus freeing him for weekends with Francine.

Guessing that Dinah was outside, Rachel headed for the backyard and found her in the greenhouse repotting African violets. She stood for a minute watching as Dinah snipped and pinched at the delicate tropicals, readying them for transplanting. Her hands were grubby with soil, as she never wore gloves. She said she preferred to feel plants as she handled them. Her frizzy hair was parted in the middle and haphazardly confined in scrunches that Rachel recognized as belonging to Kendall. The old flannel shirt worn over ragtag jeans she also recognized as belonging to her father. As Dinah worked, a stray curl fell into her line of vision and she gave it an impatient swipe, leaving a smudge on her cheek. Her mother might look disreputable, but there was nothing careless in the way she worked. Her face was intent as she set the African violets into soil she'd specifically formulated herself.

Rachel stepped into the close, humid confines of the greenhouse. She didn't share her mother's passion for gardening, but there was something soothing about Dinah's lively green world, carefully tended and heavy with fragrance. "I thought I'd find you here," Rachel said, looking around for a place reasonably free of grit and grime to set the orange juice. "Did you take time for breakfast?"

"No, but I'll break soon and have something, so don't nag."

"No nagging, but only if you drink this," Rachel said, offering the juice. She could see Dinah was tempted to refuse. "Don't even think it, Mom. You promised not to skip breakfast. That is why your blood sugar is—"

"Just fine, otherwise I'd be dizzy. And you are nagging." But Dinah took the glass after rubbing some of the grime from her hands on her shirttails and gulped it down as if it were medicine. Finished, she gave another futile swipe at her unruly hair and suddenly noticed Rachel's outfit. "Hmm, that's something new, isn't it? And you look terrific in that color."

"Thanks." Rachel glanced down at the turquoise pants matched with a tunic-length sweater of the same color. "I bought it on sale yesterday. I can't really afford to do any shopping, but—''

"But you finally noticed there's room for you and someone else in most of your clothes lately." Dinah hitched up her sagging jeans while giving Rachel a keen look. "How much weight have you lost?"

"Not too much, so get that look off your face. I needed to lose a few pounds."

"You didn't, but I don't suppose you'll believe me." She handed the empty juice glass back to Rachel and, turning, lifted a flat with four newly planted pots and led the way toward the door of the greenhouse. "C'mon, let's go to the patio and find a sunny place for these herbs. I don't think we'll have another frost, do you?"

Rachel hastily set the glasses down. "Here, let me carry that, Mom."

"No, no, you bring the glasses. I can manage this. You might get something on that nice outfit." Hanging on to the flat, Dinah left the greenhouse and headed up the winding path toward the house, giving Rachel no choice but to follow. The yard was alive with color and displays of Dinah's green thumb. In this climate zone, it was possible to have blooming plants almost all year round except in the coldest winter months, and she took full advantage of it. Hot-pink azaleas and bright white bridal wreath at the fence line formed the backdrop for a riot of colorful annuals, as well as pink snapdragons, purple and yellow pansies and bright red petunias. Her handiwork was truly a feast for the eyes.

At the patio, she set the herbs on a plant stand partially protected from unexpected chill and stood back, dusting soil from her hands. "I don't know about you, but I'm really missing those kids," she said.

"That's hard to believe." Rachel sat on the porch swing, using one foot to push herself gently. "Kendy's okay, but Nick has been so difficult lately that you must have been glad to see him go, Mom. I just wish that—"

"If wishes were gold, we'd all be rich." Dinah blew at a

stray curl dangling over one eye. "Nick is simply reacting to Ted's neglect. How could it be anything but hurtful and bewildering to see his dad lavishing most of his time and attention on a woman?"

"They do miss him," Rachel said, "even though he was never particularly attentive. That's why it's such an unexpected treat to have him to themselves for a whole weekend. Hopefully it'll work a miracle on Nick, so that by the time he gets home, his attitude will have improved."

"What time did he get in the other night?"

"It was late."

Dinah gave a sigh. And because Rachel didn't want her mother worrying, she didn't tell her that it had been past 1:00 a.m. when Nick finally came home. Rachel had been on the point of going out to search for him, but where? One look and she knew he'd been drinking, but he'd refused to tell her anything except that he'd been with his friends and they'd just been "hanging out." Not with Ward. She'd called the Rivers', pulling Dan, Ward's dad, out of a dead sleep. But Nick hadn't been drunk, which she supposed was a good thing. Still, the fact that he was even experimenting with alcohol was unacceptable. She planned to have a talk with Ted about it, but had decided it could wait until they returned from what she hoped would be a fun weekend.

"Maybe some time with his dad will improve his attitude," Rachel said dryly. "I know some time without him will certainly improve mine."

"Shame on you," her mother said, but she was smiling. "And speaking of free weekends, you should grab the opportunity to go somewhere special, indulge yourself while you have a chance."

"I'm way ahead of you." Rachel brushed a ladybug off her knee. "There's an art exhibit in the Galleria. Marta and I have already made plans to go. Is there anything you need in Dallas? I could pick it up. Just tell me what and where."

"No, forget about me. Forget everything. Have fun. I don't think you've had a single moment since Ted went crazy when you could just take off and do what you wanted." Dinah plucked a few spent blooms from a potted azalea. "Which reminds me. I've been meaning to ask where Francine is spending the weekend. Considering Ted's infatuation, I'm surprised he's able to tear himself away for a night, let alone two."

"He isn't. Francine is part of the plan."

Dinah straightened and studied her face for several seconds. "They're not going to be sleeping together with Nick and Kendy right there, are they?"

"Actually, that was the plan originally," Rachel said. "Silly me, I assumed Francine was busy elsewhere since I couldn't see her choosing to spend two days with the kids. But, just to be sure, I called Ted before he picked them up yesterday and was told that she would be with them. When I asked about sleeping arrangements, he seemed surprised. He expected me to be pleased that Francine was willing to spend time with Nick and Kendy, which included staying with them at the lake house. Of course, they'd be sleeping together. Why would I think otherwise?"

She nodded when Dinah rolled her eyes. "Can you believe how dense he can be? He saw nothing wrong with that. If it made his children uncomfortable, they'd soon get over it, he said."

Dinah stood with her hands on her hips. "Are you saying you approved his plans? He and Francine are shacking up in front of Nick and Kendy?"

"No, of course not. Francine's still going, but she'll be staying at her apartment overnight." Rachel had to smile, recalling the small victory. "The prospect of sleeping alone made Ted very grumpy."

"I'll bet." Dinah turned her attention to an asparagus fern. "How did you change his mind? I can't see him giving in just on general principles. We know he hasn't got any."

"He's behind in child support payments and I threatened to drag him into court."

"Ah." Dinah nodded.

Rachel grinned. "He's strapped for cash right now, thanks to Walter pushing the lawsuit, so he was forced to deal. But mainly, he wouldn't want the publicity. I heard from a source in the practice that he's been shopping his résumé around looking for an attractive situation in Dallas."

"Big-city practice, big-city income," Dinah said, unsurprised. "Francine's pushing for that, I bet."

"Without a doubt. But it wouldn't be Ted's first choice. If he joins a large practice, he'll be forced to spend several years before making partner status," Rachel said. "Francine may favor a move to the city, but I know he's still hoping to set up his own practice. Any hint of dishonorable personal behavior would be a serious impediment."

"Meanwhile, he still owes you money. So you're damned if you do and damned if you don't." Dinah scowled while snipping away on the fern.

"True, but at least the kids won't be exposed to the sexual aspect of his affair with Francine." She watched her mother move the large pot to a different spot. "It amazes me that Ted doesn't seem to see how his behavior sends the wrong message to a boy of Nick's age. And Kendy. My gosh, she's still a complete innocent. What was he *thinking?*"

"Who knows?" Dinah stood back to judge the effect of her tinkering. "But it's clear what he's thinking with."

"Which is why I'm glad he's devoting a weekend to the kids." Rachel's gaze wandered from the swing to the neighboring house across the way. "If he keeps this up, Nick and Kendy may look elsewhere for a replacement."

"Cam," Dinah guessed, following her gaze.

"Go figure." In spite of Rachel doing her best to keep Nick and Kendy away from their prickly neighbor, both kids seemed as drawn to him as if he was the embodiment of Santa Claus and the Easter Bunny combined. "I swear Kendy has a crush on him, Mother. No matter what I do, she finds opportunities to chat with him. She acts as if he's a favorite uncle and she's known him forever. When I try laying down the law, she gives me that big-eyed, bewildered look and says

Cam's her friend, and then she tells me I'd like him, too, if I'd just try. 'Buy one of his books,' she told me a couple of days ago. 'He'll autograph it and then you can have coffee and stuff.''' Rachel rolled her eyes.

"You want to have coffee and stuff with him?"

Rachel put her hand on her chest and patted it dramatically. "I'm just panting for the opportunity. Not."

Chuckling, Dinah moved a low stool to a corner of the patio. "Nick's pretty taken with him, too, I think."

"Even more so. But it takes two, Mother. If Cam would discourage them, neither Nick nor Kendy would be over there. But if he's outside puttering around in his garage or doing repairs to his house, it's like an open invitation and they're over like a shot."

"I can't see any harm in this, Rachel. As you say, if he doesn't like it, all he has to do is send them home." Dinah gazed thoughtfully at the yellow house. "Authors can be reclusive. It's not uncommon in his profession, and by holing up inside it would be easy to avoid people. In fact, that's mostly how it used to be before you moved in."

"You were here only a couple of months before we moved in, Mother," Rachel pointed out.

"Long enough for me to see that Cam was a man closed off from the world," Dinah said. "There are people who can lose themselves in their work and it strikes me that in his particular profession, that might easily happen. And who knows, with the loss of his son and a failed marriage, he had a lot on his plate. But, lately, he's been more accessible. So if the kids are drawn to him and he's receptive, everyone benefits. At least, that's the way I see it."

Rachel was still looking at Cam's house. "Speaking of his puttering in the garage, what's up with that, do you know? He's in and out of it a lot lately. I hear him sawing and then he's painting. Next, he's hammering away. Is he building something?"

"Could be he's making a project of restoring that old

house," Dinah said, studying her daughter's face. "If you're so interested, why don't you ask him?"

Hearing something in her mother's tone, Rachel quickly brought her gaze back to the patio. "I'm not that interested. Besides, can you imagine anyone having the nerve to question him about anything?"

"Actually, I can." She moved about, collecting bits and pieces she'd pruned and putting them in a plastic bag. "We've just discussed how approachable he is to Nick and Kendy. And I've found him to be quite neighborly."

"Even an un-neighborly neighbor would have come to your aid when you fainted in your flowers, Mother," Rachel said.

"He was a good neighbor even before I fainted in my flowers." Dinah closed the bag with a twist.

"Meaning he nodded coolly if the two of you happened to pass near the petunias," Rachel said. "Next you'll be telling me I broke up a beautiful friendship." Looking peevish, she increased the pace of the swing.

Holding the bag, Dinah looked at her daughter and chuckled. "Is that a complaint? If so, maybe you should take a leaf out of Nick and Kendy's book."

"What?"

"Maybe Nick and Kendy aren't the only ones drawn to Cam."

Rachel stopped the swing abruptly. "That is absurd!"

"Why is it absurd to be attracted to a man like Cam? He's successful, he's unattached, he's sexy." She dropped the tone of her voice and waggled her eyebrows suggestively. "And he has a past. What's not to like?"

"I'm in the midst of a divorce, if you haven't noticed. I'm up to my ears adjusting to that and to the fact that Ted has had a mistress for a year. Plus, my financial situation is so dismal that my kids and I are homeless. I know, I know—" she waved off Dinah's instant objection "—you don't have to say it. *Mi casa, es su casa.* I appreciate it, more than I can ever say. But you must admit, I have a lot on my mind."

"All the more reason to have a little fun."

"What, like an affair with Cam Ford?"

Dinah's expression was devilish. "Sounds good to me."

Rachel gave herself another push and started the swing again. "You're the flower child, not me." Dinah's college years during the sixties had given her a loosey-goosey outlook that Rachel had simply never had any desire to emulate. "I've just had a big row with Ted over the example he's setting by living in sin with Francine. Are you now suggesting that I do the same thing?"

Dinah laughed and picked up the two glasses to take inside. "I wasn't suggesting anything of the sort and you know it. But I do think—" She broke off at the sound of a commotion. Somewhere in the front of the house, a door slammed and loud voices could be heard all the way out to the porch. Rachel sprang up from the swing in alarm.

"That's Nick," Rachel said, rushing to the door. "And Ted. Oh, my God, something's happened." She hurried inside just as Nick burst into the kitchen. He was flushed, his face set and angry. Kendall, who was with him, looked pale and scared. Catching sight of Rachel, she burst into tears and rushed into her mother's arms. There was no sign of Ted.

With Kendall's face pressed to her breast, Rachel looked at Nick. "What's wrong? What happened, Nick?"

"We're not going back with him, Mom. I don't care what he says!" His eyes flashed with defiance, but the hand he used to rake his hair away from his eyes was shaky. "This whole thing was a stupid idea to start with. Look at Kendy. She's really freaked and I don't blame her."

Rachel tried pulling back to get a look at Kendall's face, but the little girl's arms were tight around her waist and she was sobbing wildly. "Is she hurt?" she asked Nick. "Was there an accident?"

"It was no accident," Nick said bitterly. He slapped a hand flat on the countertop, rattling dishes and cutlery. "I don't understand why Dad is so, like, ga-ga over her, but he is. Anybody can see she sucks!"

"Nick. Watch your language," Rachel ordered. "Now, calm down and tell me what happened. And where is Ted? Did he just drop you at the door and leave?"

Nick's mouth twisted with disgust. "No, but I bet that's what Francine wants. What gets me is why Dad planned a whole weekend with me and Kendy if she was gonna be there. Francine was miserable from the minute he picked us up yesterday." He kicked at the leg of a chair. "She's a real bitch, Mom."

"That's enough, Nick." Ted stood in the door, scowling at his son. "I know you don't like Francine, but you will show some respect."

"She doesn't deserve respect!" Nick shot back angrily. "She hurt Kendy."

Rachel's eyes widened. "Hurt her? How?" Prying Kendall loose, she examined the little girl's face. "Are you hurt, Kendy?"

"It's nothing, barely a scratch," Ted said in a dismissive tone. "It was all a misunderstanding. Francine…" He took a deep breath to calm himself, then spoke stiffly, "Francine may have been a bit harsh. She sends her apologies, Kendall. She says to tell you she's sorry."

"Oh, yeah, now she's sorry," Nick said with heavy sarcasm.

"I hate her!" Kendall said hotly.

"Oh, for pity's sake!" Ted said, throwing up his hands. "She lost her temper. It happens."

"What happened?" Rachel cried. "Will somebody please tell me."

"We were having breakfast at a restaurant," Nick said, shooting a glare at his father. "Nobody wanted to go there, but his precious Francine insisted. It was a stupid place not meant for kids, but whatever Francine wants, Francine gets." More heavy sarcasm. "And then Kendy accidentally spills her orange juice, which goes into Francine's lap and ruins her dress, she says. Beats me why she even wore something like that to go to a rodeo. She looked more like she was going to a party or something instead of the rodeo, but Dad seems blind to anything except her boobs and her butt!''

"Nicholas!" Ted roared. "I told you to watch your mouth and I won't tell you again."

"Nick," Rachel chided in a lesser tone, "you know better. Just tell me how she hurt Kendall."

"She jerked her by the arm and dragged her off to the rest room, and Dad just let her!" Nick cried, giving his father an accusing look.

"I certainly couldn't take her into the men's room," Ted said.

"And then the minute they got out of sight," Nick said, ignoring him, "she pinched the hell out of her!"

"I didn't want to go with her!" Kendall looked tearfully at Rachel. "But she made me, Mom. I started to cry because she doesn't like me. She didn't want me to take my camera, that's why I know she doesn't like me. And she told me to shut up and don't embarrass her and that's when she pinched me with her long fingernails just the minute we got inside the rest room. See?" She stuck out an arm, shoved the sleeve of her shirt back and displayed an angry bruise just above the elbow. "It really, really hurt, Mom."

Rachel looked at the purple mark and turned instantly to Ted. "Is this true, Ted?" she asked evenly.

He gave an impatient sigh. "They've made it sound worse than it was."

"In what way? Kendall has an ugly bruise. The skin is broken. Was Francine's version of the way it happened different from what Nick and Kendy say?"

"That's it, more or less," he admitted reluctantly. "Francine's not used to kids. And it was embarrassing to have juice dumped in her lap."

"I'll tell you what's embarrassing," Nick said, looking angrily at Ted. "It's watching my old man make a big fool of himself over some stupid woman whom he's almost old enough to be her father and then when she does something that's mean and cruel to his kid, he pretends it's okay because he doesn't want to piss her off.'' It wasn't simply disgust on Nick's face. It was utter contempt. "What's the matter, Dad? Are you afraid she won't be ready to screw tonight if you stand up for Kendy?''

With a muttered oath, Ted came at Nick with his hand raised, but Rachel moved faster. She stepped in front of him and warned, "Don't even think it, Ted." Then, still holding Ted's gaze, she said to Nick, "Go somewhere and cool off, Nick. Your father and I need to talk privately.''

Nick hesitated, both hands fisted at his sides. Chest heaving, his eyes teemed with the hot accusations he longed to throw at his father. But after a moment, he muttered something under his breath, turned abruptly and stalked out of the kitchen.

Dinah, who'd been watching in silence, moved quickly to Kendall. She slipped an arm around the little girl's shoulders and urged her toward the door. "C'mon, Kendy, let's go to the greenhouse and check on those zinnia seeds we planted. I've got a first aid kit in there, too. I bet there's something in it that'll take the sting out of that bruise.''

With everyone else gone, Rachel struggled to control her outrage. She wasn't sure what made her more angry—that Francine had dared to hurt Kendall or that Ted had allowed it. She took a deep breath. "I'll make this short, Ted, as we know Francine's patience is wearing thin today. I assume she's waiting for you outside.''

"She left in my car. I told her I'd call her on my cell phone after I dropped the kids off. I knew you'd overreact, just like they did." He leaned against the counter, crossing his arms. "Say it so we can discuss it and I can get the hell out of here.''

"At least you admit we need to discuss it.''

"You don't discuss anything, Rachel," he told her. "You lecture. So, let's have the sermon where you tell me what a pig I am when, in fact, this whole thing was a simple accident. And don't bother to say you don't accept that Francine was upset and reacted as she did because she's not used to kids. You've already expressed your opinion on that. We both know what you think."

Rachel didn't allow herself to be distracted by his attack on her. "Being unused to kids doesn't excuse hurting Kendy, Ted. Surely you see that. Most people who aren't used to children don't resort to violence, especially in response to a minor accident." Rachel raised her hand to stop his reply. "No. Don't make it worse by trying to defend what she did, or I'll have to agree with Nick that you are so besotted that you've forgotten your first duty is to your children. What possessed you to include Francine in a trip to the rodeo, anyway? It strikes me as the last place she'd choose."

"It seemed a fun way to introduce her to Nick and Kendy." He moved, turning away with his shoulders hunched against her disapproval.

"They've been introduced, you know that. We've had Francine and Walter in our home on several occasions while the kids were around. This past Christmas, to name the most recent." She was shaking her head. "But that's beside the point. You realize, don't you, that after what's happened it will probably be a long time before Kendy is willing to go anywhere with you if Francine's included? That would be a very normal reaction for a nine-year-old."

"She'll soon forget it if you don't poison her mind first."

She gave him an exasperated look. "You've accused me of that before and it's just as ridiculous now as then, and I'm beginning to think it's a smoke screen, Ted, something you use to obscure your role in this mess. Our children's home has been destroyed and their security threatened. The last thing I want is to add to their distress, and being nasty about you and Francine behind your back would do just that. The divorce has been horrible for them, but you're still their father and they love you. They need you. It's confusing and scary to them when you seem to forget that."

"I have not forgotten that! Why do you think I planned this freaking weekend?" he demanded, angry now at being put on the defensive.

"Ted. You failed to come to Kendy's rescue today when Francine hurt her," Rachel said, stating the obvious. "That made a powerful impression and neither of them will get over it anytime soon."

"And you certainly won't do anything to help, will you?" His mouth was set in a grim line.

"If you mean I won't allow Francine to get near Kendall again, then you're right. Because if you can't be trusted to look out for her, then both of us are negligent."

"So now I'm negligent!"

She threw up her hands. "Francine bruised Kendall's arm and you did nothing. Nothing, Ted. I call that negligence, and I'm not going to put my little girl in a situation where it could happen again."

"Things got out of hand, I'm telling you," he snapped. "It was a first-rate restaurant and people were staring when she spilled her juice. It was a mess. Francine was upset and embarrassed. She just wanted to escape to the bathroom and Kendall had to go with her. As I said, I could hardly take her to the men's room, could I? But with Kendall crying and carrying on, Francine was rattled. She overreacted. She admits it. She's apologized. Like I said, it won't happen again."

"She was embarrassed and she was rattled, so she's excused? She hurt Kendy. She pinched her hard enough to break the skin and leave a bruise, Ted. That was just plain mean of her."

"She apologized," he repeated through his teeth. "What more do you expect?"

"What more? Well, first of all, once Kendy came out of that rest room in tears bearing the marks of Francine's temper, it was your place to comfort your daughter, not to make excuses for Francine! You should have let her know you won't tolerate it. And just because she apologized doesn't mean she won't fly off the handle and hurt Kendy again. Kids have accidents. They're messy. Noisy. Demanding. Are you telling me Francine's not going to overreact again?"

He simply stared at her in silence for a moment. "What

does it take to please you, Rachel? You've done nothing but nag me constantly about spending time with the kids, and at the first sign that things didn't go exactly like a Disney movie, you decide I've screwed up and therefore no more visits.'' He paced a few steps away and then turned back, pointing a finger at her. ''I know what this is all about and it isn't that Kendall took a little pinch from Francine. Uh-uh, it's about the divorce. It's about Francine and me and the fact that we want to be together. You see a chance to stick it to me and you've grabbed it.''

Rachel stared at him with her mouth open. ''This has nothing to do with the divorce, Ted! It's about Kendall being abused by Francine. She's nine years old. I won't put her in a position to be hurt again. Period. If you choose to think that's some kind of petty payback on my part, so be it. You're free to think whatever. But the bottom line is this. Francine isn't going to get another chance to abuse Kendall.''

''Well, I can see we're going nowhere with this,'' Ted said, stalking out of the kitchen and heading angrily for the front door. He jerked it open and crossed the threshold, then suddenly he stopped and turned back to glare at Rachel. ''I should have known not to expect any understanding from you, Rachel. With you, things are black or white. Always were. No room for a little human misstep here or a screw-up there. Well, Francine's just the opposite and it's refreshing. She's not perfect, she drinks a little too much and she can't quite quit smoking. She doesn't have your IQ and she's damn sure not as organized. So, according to your standards, I guess that makes me shallow and shameless for loving her. But you know what? Nick's right. I'm turned on by her boobs and her ass, and when we have sex, she makes me feel like I've died and gone to heaven. And before you start another lecture, think about this. I bet there's not another man on the planet who wouldn't trade places with me!''

Speechless, Rachel watched him descend the steps, reaching for his cell phone as he walked. He glanced at it, hit a single digit—Francine's number programmed, she guessed—

and was talking before he reached the end of the sidewalk.
Before her eyes, the grim look on his face instantly morphed
into something different, gentler. As he spoke, even the pace
of his stride slowed. And by the time he reached the street,
he was actually smiling. Rachel stepped back and quietly
closed the door.

While his parents were arguing, Nick was prowling Dinah's backyard, fantasizing the many ways he'd like to see
Francine wiped off the face of the earth. Or fried in oil. Or
run over by a truck. No matter how hard he tried, he couldn't
understand why his dad had deserted everybody to be with
a ditz like Francine. She was hot, yeah, he could see that,
but how much time could a man spend screwing around?
Sooner or later, there had to be something else to pass the
time, was the way he saw it. Francine talked mostly about
what was hip in fashion and the latest movies and where the
best restaurants were in Dallas. Jeez, to hear her tell it, she
knew the best restaurants in the whole state of Texas and
what to order when you got there. But so what? Nick could
tell she was bored when Kendy wanted to tell her about her
digital and the photos she liked to take. And as for sports,
man, she was, like, a total zero.

His dad had walked away from his mom for that? No way
Nick could ever understand it. No way he could get used to
the changes that had happened because his dad split, either.
He bent and picked up a penny that lay on the ground. If
you found a penny, it meant good luck, he thought. He could
sure use some good luck. Lately his life just plain sucked.

Hearing the sound of a car, he turned to see Cam pull into
his driveway and begin unloading groceries from his SUV.
He straightened and looked at Nick over the top of his vehicle, but didn't make much of a sign of welcome. Nick
wondered, now that he knew about Cam losing his son, Jack,
whether he'd been cheerier before that happened. The taste
of the fiasco with his dad and Francine had just about ruined
his day, and in spite of his mom frowning on him talking to

Cam, he felt in the right mood for Cam's kind of dark personality. So he headed over there.

"Hey," he said, approaching the SUV.

"Nick." Busy with the groceries, Cam barely glanced up.

"Can I give you a hand?"

Cam hesitated. "Yeah, sure." He had one bag beneath his arm already and a couple more in each hand. "You can bring in the twelve-pack and that bag with the fragile stuff in it. Careful with the chips. Nothing worse than crushed nachos."

"Tell me." With the twelve-pack wedged between his knee and the bumper of the SUV and the sack in his other hand, Nick pulled the hatch down.

"Weren't you supposed to be at the rodeo today?" Cam asked when they were inside.

"Yeah, I didn't know if you remembered." That's what he liked about Cam. You told him stuff and he actually heard it. You could talk to him.

"Back early, aren't you?"

"We never made it." Nick didn't wait for permission but began removing cans of chili, tuna, chicken and dumplings and spaghetti sauce from a sack. Cam's diet came mostly from a can. "This stuff go in the pantry over there?"

"Except for the spaghetti sauce. That's tonight's dinner." Cam took two cans of soda from the twelve-pack, tossed one to Nick and popped the second open for himself. "You can have chips with that drink if you want."

"Thanks." Nick tore the bag open and helped himself. "Francine screwed up the trip."

"Huh." With his back to Nick, Cam placed stuff on the pantry shelves.

"Yeah, she made us stop at this snooty restaurant for brunch." He made a face just saying the word. "Then Kendy dumped her OJ into the queen's lap. Big row over that, so she took Kendy inside the bathroom where she pinched the hell out of her and made a nasty bruise, which sort of took the shine off the trip, so Dad got pissed and drove us all back here and dumped us. Goodbye, rodeo."

Cam frowned. "She actually bruised Kendy?"

"Uh-huh. How's that for being plumb mean? Which she is."

"You said Kendy dumped her OJ. Was it an accident?"

"Yeah, sure. You know, it happens. Kendy was, like, bummed over doing it. But you don't get the bejesus pinched out of you for an accident, right?"

Cam took a dairy carton out of a bag and held it up. "I've got dip. You want some?"

"Nah, I'm good with just the chips." He ate a few, then popped the top off the can of Coke. "You want to know what really ruined the trip?"

"Hmm."

"That Dad didn't take up for Kendy." Nick worked the bottom of the can on the tabletop, making concentric circles. "He was more worried about the queen and how upset she was than his own kid. And Kendy's only nine. She was real upset, crying and all."

"Was your mother around when Ted brought you back?"

"Yeah. I think she had plans to go somewhere with Marta, but she hadn't left yet. Good thing, too. I guess I said a few things when we first went inside 'cause I was really ticked off. I mean, wouldn't you be? And then Mom banished me while Gran took Kendy, so she and Dad could talk privately." He crunched into a chip. "I bet she lit into him, big time."

"Hmm."

Nick shifted in the chair and, with one leg stretched out, gazed thoughtfully at the window above Cam's kitchen sink. "I used to wish my mom and dad would patch things up and get back together," he said, still twirling the can. "But now I wonder if it's even possible. May not be the best thing, considering."

Cam, fitting a roll of paper towels on a spindle, turned to look at him. "Considering what?"

"My dad has never been much of a family man, to tell the truth." He hesitated and, as if wanting to be fair, added,

"Well, he's a doctor and they perform a noble service to mankind, I guess, or at least that's the line Mom's fed us all these years when he never found time to be with us. Always claims he's got a bunch of other stuff going. Like, he travels a lot and he plays golf and tennis, and there's always the professional garbage. Plus, doctors keep pretty long hours. Like I said, with all that stuff going, there's not much left over for hanging out with us."

"Uh-huh."

"I mean, when you stop and think about it, it's surprising that my mom wasn't the one to have an affair first."

"I don't see your mother doing anything like that."

"I know, but I'm just saying, she had more reason to do it than my dad."

Cam turned from his task and, leaning against the counter, said, "I wouldn't be so quick to judge, Nick. Every marriage is unique. It's like finding yourself in a game where you don't know the rules. There are two players, both with different backgrounds and personalities. You go at it the best you can, making mistakes along the way. And there aren't any guarantees that you'll win. You just—"

"Pay your money and take your chances?"

Cam straightened and reached for the empty grocery bags. "Something like that. And remember, I'm hardly one to be advising anybody about marriage. Mine ended in divorce, too."

Nick studied the logo on the can. "I guess I'm a little bitter about the weekend turning out to be a bust because I had a couple things I wanted to mention to Dad. I mean, we haven't spent much time together lately because of the divorce, and like I said, his schedule makes it tough for him to go to my games as much as some of the guys' dads on the team, but—" Nick lifted his shoulders in a wry shrug. "Anyway, maybe you could…you know, sort of give me your take on something." He shot a quick, questioning look at Cam.

Cam hesitated only briefly. "Sure," he said. "Shoot."

"It's about me and Ward and the situation with Coach giving us special help."

"There's a problem?"

Nick rose and went to the window above the sink. With his back to Cam, he said, "You said once that we might get some static from other guys and it could become a problem."

"And has it?"

"Well, it's nothing that's out in the open, at least not yet, but I can sort of feel it, you know?" He turned but stayed put at the sink. "There's nothing outright, no crap on the field during practice or messages left where you can't miss them, but there's this…stuff kinda hanging in the air, if you know what I mean. It's got me wondering whether getting special attention from Coach Monk is the way to go. I mean, Ward's getting the same thing and I guess he's okay with it. But I'm thinking I'd just as soon be like most of the other guys on the team. I make it on my own, or I don't. That way, nobody can ever say I had special treatment."

"Monk Tyson's good at spotting talent. He's not just killing time coaching you, and the boost you get from his training might mean the difference between a fantastic scholarship and none at all. I guess you've thought of that."

"Yeah, sure, but how many athletes make it into pro sports, anyway? One half of one percent, even if you're really good." Back in his chair, Nick hunched forward, both arms on the tabletop. "There's something else that I guess is kinda making me rethink whether I want the special coaching. I know it might sound, like, weird or something, but when I'm with Coach Monk and we're all alone, you know, just the two of us, I'm not, like, really easy."

"Not easy," Cam repeated. "How…exactly?"

Nick shrugged. "It's nothing I can explain. I just get this…feeling. And to tell the truth, it's kinda…creepy, I guess. I mean, I know he's doing me a real favor, but the truth is, I wish I could think of a way to tell him I appreciate it, but—"

"But no thank you?"

"Yeah." Nick frowned at his hands a long minute, then looked up at Cam again. "And hey, I do something like that and the fallout's gonna be big. I mean, telling Monk Tyson no means he might just possibly decide to bench me, like, forever."

"And you're prepared to accept that?"

"Well, shoot! What do you think? Heck, no." He worked up a smile, sort of. "That's why I'm in the market for advice from a grown-up."

"Your mom's a grown-up, Nick. Have you considered talking to her about this?"

"Nah, she's got a lot of things on her mind right now. And, let's face it, she'd have a female point of view on the sports aspect of my problem, right? I mean, she'd immediately say there are other fabulous career possibilities for me—medicine, law, engineering, writing."

Cam's gaze sharpened. "You have some interest in writing?"

Nick grinned. "No way, I just threw that in to see if you were listening."

"I'm listening." Cam opened the dishwasher and began removing the items inside.

"So, what do you think?" Nick prodded.

"I am thinking," Cam said, placing a stack of plates in an overhead cabinet.

Nick watched him sort the silverware and drop it into a drawer to the left of the sink. This was a chore his mom assigned to Kendy, but if you were a guy living alone, he guessed, you'd have to do the kitchen chores, including cooking, by yourself.

"Okay, how about this?" Cam faced him, resting against the cabinet with his arms crossed. "You've just mentioned how your mom's got a lot on her plate. Maybe you could use that as your excuse to pull away from Tyson. Tell him that with the move to your grandmother's house, plus adjusting to the divorce, and having the full brunt of household responsibilities on your mother's shoulders now, you need to take up some of the slack. Tell him playing ball is still a high priority and you'll do your dead-level best to stay competitive on the team, but putting in extra hours is adding a hardship to your mom. Blame it on the divorce and your changed circumstances, Nick. I don't think he can dish you for taking the high road.''

"Man, that's great!'' Nick looked at him with real admiration before adding wryly, "He might even buy it.''

Cam nodded, understanding as Nick did, that there was an even chance Tyson would see right through the bullshit and Nick would be benched out of sheer spite. In his gut, Cam thought Tyson was probably capable of that sort of mean-spirited retaliation to an athlete who somehow displeased him. From his window, he watched Nick's easy lope across the lawn, heading home. The thought of Nick being singled out didn't set well, he realized. But after a few minutes, he put the boy and his problems out of his mind by focusing on his book, a tactic guaranteed to distract him.

The tactic worked for the hours that Cam spent writing that day, but later, as he threw together a few ingredients to improve the canned red sauce, he found himself again thinking of his conversation with Nick. He didn't like the idea of Nick going up against a man with Tyson's power without parental support. Which wasn't his job, he reminded himself as he chopped an onion. Here was a kid needing his dad and Ted was too busy chasing a woman to notice. And the kid was just plain heroic for not wanting to add to his mother's burdens by telling her. Nick was grappling with a decision that might well affect his entire future and both his parents were blissfully unaware.

As unaware as Cam had been when Jack was in trouble.

The knife went still in Cam's hand. He stood looking at nothing in particular, but thinking of the irony that he should be the one Nick confided in. It was not his problem, he told himself again. And unlike Jack, Nick wasn't suicidal, just conflicted. He laid the knife aside and tossed the onions in a skillet. What was more of a puzzle was whether Nick had been totally candid about what had driven him to consider rejecting an opportunity that most athletes would kill for. Cam sensed there was more, and if so, what was it? He adjusted the heat under the skillet and went to the fridge to get the meat. The person who should know the answer to that was the kid's mother. In spite of Nick wanting to spare her, Cam thought, maybe he ought to give her a heads-up, let her do some nosing around in Monk Tyson's little kingdom.

Cam had just slapped a lid on the skillet where his red sauce bubbled and spat when Rachel knocked on his back door. First Nick, now his mom. His plan to distance himself from his neighbors, these neighbors in particular, was going to require something with more teeth in it. But hell, he needed to talk to her about the kid, anyway.

On his way to let her in, he grabbed at a wet sponge and dabbed at several tomatoey splotches on his shirt, but succeeded only in doing more damage. Tossing the sponge in the sink, he motioned her to come in as he pulled the shirt off over his head.

"Is this a bad time?" she asked after a startled glance at his naked torso.

"No, I was just painting myself with red sauce," he said, heading for the laundry area just off the kitchen where his once-a-week cleaning lady folded clean clothes. Pointing to the breakfast nook, he said, "Have a seat while I try to find a shirt. It'll only take me a second."

"Thanks, but I'm not staying. I just wanted—"

"How about some wine? I'm having spaghetti, so it's Chianti." His head emerged from the neck of the pullover on his way back to the kitchen. "It's pretty good."

"The spaghetti?"

"No, the wine." He took two glasses from a hanging rack. "I bought a couple bottles on the recommendation of the guy at the liquor store, thinking he ought to know, and he did."

She was still standing. "No, really, I just came over to—"

"Here, try it." He set her wineglass on the table and touched her shoulder, urging her to sit. "I was just thinking of giving you a call,'' he told her. ''I wanted to talk to you about Nick.''

She sighed and seemed to wilt a little. ''I know. I'm sorry. That's why I came. I don't know why he seems so determined to pester you. As soon as I realized he'd been over here, I let him know—again—that he is not to drop in on you like that. But he—''

''He doesn't pester me. He talks. I listen. I'd send him home if it was a problem.'' Knocking him out of six or eight pages of his work in progress was a problem, but he found he didn't want to tell her that. For some reason.

She looked puzzled. ''Then what is it you wanted to say about him?''

He slid the wine closer to her hand and pulled out a chair for himself. ''Did you know that Monk Tyson is giving him special coaching?''

''Yes, of course. He's thrilled over it.''

''When is the last time the two of you talked about it?''

''Talked—'' She made a small, uncertain gesture. ''Not lately. I know he's just as wild about baseball as most of Monk's athletes. Why? What makes you ask?''

''Something he said today about feeling uneasy—his word, not mine—about the situation. He's aware of the advantages in accepting special treatment from Tyson, but now he's thinking of the drawbacks. He didn't tell me anything specific, but I'm guessing he's had a taste of sour grapes from some of his teammates. He's considering backing off and he's braced for Tyson being very unhappy about it.''

She rose. ''I appreciate you telling me. I'll have a talk with him.''

Without getting up, Cam caught her hand and gently urged her back into her chair. ''I wish you wouldn't do that. First, he'll think he can't trust me to keep what he tells me private. Second, he said his dad doesn't have time for him right now and he'd planned to get Ted's take on the situation sometime during the weekend outing. I guess, being male, I'm sort of a stand-in,'' Cam said, rubbing his neck and giving her a wry look. ''Do you really want to take that away?''

''No, of course not.'' With her fingers pressed against her brow, she sighed. ''Divorce. It's such a mess.''

''Yeah, he had high hopes for the weekend.''

Not looking at him, she fiddled with the stem of the wineglass. ''So he confided his problems with Tyson, trouble with his teammates, his unhappiness with Ted and…what else?''

''That almost covers it.''

She glanced up at him. ''No details of the breakfast from hell?''

He chuckled. ''He may have made a comment or two about Francine's shortcomings.''

Shaking her head, she simply sat for a moment. ''It has been one of those days.''

''Good reason to drink up.'' He lifted his glass toward her. ''Here's to a better tomorrow.''

''Well, it has to be.'' She took a tiny sip of Chianti. ''Hmm, you're right, this is good.''

''Uh-huh.'' He found himself relaxing back in his chair. ''Want to talk about it?''

''Then I'd be the one pestering you, not Nick.''

''No, actually you won't, since I owe you one.''

She frowned. ''What?''

''I was rude—'' He paused. ''Hell, I'm trying to make amends. Here it is. I admit I was more than rude when I barged into your office five years ago. As a psychologist, you must have guessed I was angry and grieving—''

''It happens.''

''And I took it out on you.''

She gave a forgiving shrug. ''It's okay. I've had worse.''

''Then you're a saint for not shooting somebody before now.'' His smile was slightly off center. ''So, go ahead, pester me.''

With a similar half smile, she ran a finger around the rim of the wineglass, but then her face sobered. ''I guess Nick told you the plans for the weekend with Ted didn't work out.

It's especially troubling that it ended the way it did, since, from what you tell me, he needed more from Ted than a couple of days of fun. I knew he was upset, but I needed to talk to Ted first, and when we were done, Nick had disappeared. Besides, I'm not sure he would have opened up to me as he did you. It's hard to get him to tell me anything lately.''

"His reaction was more about Kendall than himself. He's protective where his little sister is concerned, and the way Nick told it, Ted screwed up there royally.''

"He really did open up to you, didn't he?'' She rubbed a spot between her eyes. "He had good reason to be angry with his dad. Ted seemed more interested in defending Francine than in looking out for Kendy.''

Cam nodded. "So he came over here to vent a little. I've got no problem with that.'' If Jack had found someone to vent to, he might be here today.

She sighed again. "But frankly, he's doing more than his share of venting lately. Some of it's just the normal angst that comes with being fifteen years old, I suppose, but a lot of it is reaction to the divorce. I'm trying to be patient, but—''

"From what I see, he's a good kid,'' Cam said.

"He is.'' There was a small, soft smile on her face now. "In spite of mood swings and rebelliousness, which I understand, I'm basically crazy about him.'' She looked away, troubled. "That's why it's so hard to understand Ted's—'' She stopped herself, gave a brief shrug. "I'm sorry, you don't want to hear me vent, too. If you really are okay with Nick coming over to talk, it's a good thing. I'm glad he feels he has someone other than me. Being female, there's a gender gap, as you might imagine. Ted, of course, is preoccupied with the lawsuit,'' she added, "plus, he's trying to figure out what he's going to do about getting reestablished in another practice, so he has practically no time left over for Nick and Kendy.''

"His loss,'' Cam said.

Their eyes met and lingered and, for a few long moments, drifted into territory that had nothing to do with kids or Ted. Cam was making a prolonged study of her face, thinking her coloring—pale ivory skin and true black hair—made a striking combination that any model would envy. He'd never seen eyes quite like hers, either, so light a brown that they looked like amber. For a moment, he indulged himself by wondering what the rest of her looked like. Rachel, meanwhile, found herself thinking of her reaction when he'd answered the door half in, half out of his shirt. She'd only glimpsed his bare torso, but it had been enough to give her a jolt, a purely sexual response.

She stood up abruptly. "Well, I'll let you get back to your dinner."

He rose, but more slowly. "Don't worry about Nick. He has his head screwed on right."

"At least he used to," she said, heading toward the door. "I reminded myself of that last week when I learned he failed to turn in a biology assignment and made two D's on math quizzes." Mystified, she raised her shoulders in a shrug. "He used to love science and ace math."

"A lot going on in his head," Cam suggested.

"And a lot going right over Ted's head," she said, showing outrage for just a second. A beat later, her brows were knitted in a frown. "I know you won't believe this because Ted's being such a jerk lately, but he wasn't always such a...a—"

"Jerk? Just one more question," he added, not waiting for her reply. "Did Francine really pinch Kendall hard enough to make a bruise?"

"Yes!" The thought of it had Rachel's ire rising again. "And I was ready to show her how it feels, but Ted was sneaky enough to let her escape in his car after dropping him and the kids off."

He smiled, leaning against the doorjamb. "Somehow I can't see you in a catfight. It would be more like you to give her a piece of your mind, then suggest she have counseling to manage her anger.''

She hesitated, frowning at her hand on the doorknob before looking up at him. ''May I ask you something?''

''Sure.''

''By giving her a piece of my mind, I assume you mean lecturing her, which Ted has already accused me of doing. But suggesting counseling for anger management, is that a bad thing?''

''No.'' He studied her face, sensing he'd hit a nerve. ''What kind of question is that? Why would you think it's bad?''

''I don't think it's bad to try to avoid violence. I think it's, well, civilized, I guess. After all, I am a psychologist. Positive dialogue is what we're supposed to suggest to resolve conflict, isn't it?''

''When you can get the parties involved to talk, I suppose it is.''

''Well, there's the problem,'' she said with a note of irony. ''Lately, it seems to me that the people I'm dealing with prefer hitting first and talking later.''

''Who's hitting whom?'' he asked in a sharp tone.

She put a hand to her cheek. ''What am I doing? This is so inappropriate.'' What could she have been thinking, she asked herself. The man was Nick's confidant, not hers.

''Who is hitting whom, Rachel?''

''Families in crisis have episodes when people simply explode,'' she explained, ''and as much as it bothers me, mine is no different.'' She turned to go. ''I've said more than I should have. I need—''

Cam stopped her with a hand on her arm. ''Nick was on a tear today when we talked, but the only violence he mentioned was Francine pinching Kendall. Was there more?''

She'd gone this far, Rachel thought. She may as well finish it. ''Nick said some rude things to his dad. Ted came at him and I don't know what would have happened if they'd actually connected, but I stepped between them. I was sickened at the thought of them coming to blows. What was Ted thinking? Would he have used his fists to hit his son? Besides being taller than Nick and much heavier, how unthinkable is that?'' She plowed ahead, now on a roll. "This is not the first episode, either. The day that Walter found out about the affair, he came to our house and he and Ted actually did come to blows. They were like two animals, thrashing about in the sunroom, crashing into a glass table, breaking things. Ted got a black eye and Walter reminded me of a…a pro wrestler! It was terrible. Nick had to help me break it up. Kendall saw it all, too. She took pictures!''

"Cute," he muttered.

She barely heard him. "So, today I learn about Francine's cruelty to Kendall. Call me a bit biased, but I thought Ted should have been mad at his lover, not his little girl. So when I say that, Ted tells me I'm prissy and uptight, that it was an accident, to get over it. That he's nuts about Francine because, even though my IQ is higher, she's fun to be with, she has big boobs and a nice butt and—get this—when they have sex, he feels he's died and gone to heaven.'' She threw up her hands, then dropped them to her sides in bafflement. "All vestige of sanity has disappeared from my life.''

"C'mere." Before she realized his intent, Cam had his arms around her, enveloping her in sympathy and warm masculine strength. Instinct made her resist…but only for a heartbeat. Still all het up as she was over the sheer unfairness of life at the moment, the appeal of a friendly hug was simply too much to resist. Tears started in her eyes and she blinked furiously to hold them back. She sniffed.

"Without a doubt, you have the higher IQ," he told her softly.

She heard the smile in his voice and, turning her nose into his nice, clean shirt, gave a shaky chuckle. "Ted said that, I didn't.''

"Because you would never boast about your IQ.''

"No, never." Then, in a bewildered voice she asked, "But

what good does having a nice IQ do if you can't keep a husband?''

"You would keep a decent one without even trying.''

"Thank you.'' It struck her that Cam was a very unlikely champion, a man whose marriage had failed, whose son had committed suicide, and who'd lived almost as a recluse for the past five years. Yet in spite of all that, everyone closest to her, Nick, Kendall and even her mother, seemed drawn to him, while to her, he'd been prickly and standoffish from the start...until today. Now, standing in the circle of his arms, she was beginning to appreciate a few of his good points.

"And you know what?'' His chin rested on top of her head.

"What?''

"I'd bet my next advance that you are as terrific in the sack as Francine.''

Her smile was shaky, but real. She pulled away from him and walked back to the kitchen counter to get a paper towel. Not quite able to meet his eyes, she blotted her tears away, blew her nose and went back to the door. "I am really leaving now. My dignity is shattered and I've seriously undermined my vow to keep Kendy and Nick from pestering you.''

"Relax. They'll only pester me when I allow it.'' As he held the door for her, she brushed past him, head down, cheeks still a little pink. Then, when she was at the bottom of the steps, he spoke. "Just one more question...''

She looked up. "What?''

"Are you absolutely sure Ted's their father?''

She stared at him for a second, then saw he was joking and burst out laughing. "Thanks, I needed that.''

Ten

Before trying to get anything out of Nick himself, Rachel decided to see what Monk might have to say. On Monday, when he hadn't responded by noon to her voice mail message, she went in search of him. Leaving the main building right after lunch, she walked over to the gym. Tyson had an office a couple of doors from her own, but as he preferred being on his own territory, he was seldom there.

As most of their discussions—encounters would be more accurate, she thought—were held on her territory, it was the first time she'd seen his office at the gym. She was impressed. The leather couch and plush carpet were expensive. An upscale desk and good art on the wall made it seem more like the domain of an executive than the office of a small town coach. The walls, she noted, were studded with photos of Tyson with various VIPs, as well as numerous awards, some his own, others won by his athletes.

"Don't tell me, let me guess," he said after offering her a seat. "You bring bad news. Which one of my boys won't graduate?"

"Ferdy Jordan," she told him, having come armed with a plausible excuse for seeking him out, "unless he manages by some miracle to improve in both Algebra II and English."

He made a derisive sound. "It may be difficult to teach him to read at this late date."

She sighed. "Monk, I've been telling you for months now that he's in trouble. If he wants to play sports, he has to graduate. To graduate, he must pick up those grades."

"I'll get on his butt."

"You promised to do that at the beginning of the semester when he was in only a little trouble. It'll be a lot harder now."

"I'll line up a tutor. No way his folks would be any help there." His pencil was doing rat-a-tats on the desk. "Who else?"

"Jason Pate. As always."

He frowned. "I jacked him up over that DUI in Dallas. Damn it, what's he done now?"

"I'm not here to discuss his drinking problem. How would we know, anyway? He's been absent for three days. Haven't you noticed?"

"No problem here. He's been dressing out. If he was skipping practice, I'd bench his ass and he knows it."

"Then see if you can persuade him to attend class with the same commitment," she said tartly. "Otherwise, he's another one whose plans for college will be over." Regardless of what he said, she vowed to talk to Jason herself, even if she had to show up after baseball practice to do it. Which would certainly not win her any points with Nick, she thought ruefully.

"Anybody else? A couple more screwups and I'll be out of business."

"Nobody except—" She shifted a bit in the chair, crossed her legs and clasped both hands on one knee. "Since I'm here and we're talking, how about Nick? He's very flattered that you're spending extra time with him. How's he doing?"

Monk leaned back in his chair, more relaxed now. "He's doing great. And I'm glad to see you're interested."

"Of course I'm interested. He's my son."

"Yeah, but I mean interested in his sports career. He's got a real future in baseball, Rachel. I've got him at first, but he's versatile enough to play other positions." His gaze sharpened. "He's okay, isn't he? Not letting the split between you and his dad mess with his head, is he?"

"He's not as happy as he was before it happened, but

we're doing okay.'' She was here fishing for a reason to explain Nick's ''unease'' over accepting favors from Monk. She didn't consider it any of his business that he was having trouble doing his class work. Or breaking curfew. ''I wondered if you've noticed anything, any change in his playing, anything like that?''

''Nope. Nothing.''

''Good,'' she said after a moment, then got to her feet. ''I'm glad he's coming along if it makes him happy. Baseball has been Nick's passion since he first learned to throw a ball.''

''Yeah, a kid like Nick is a natural.''

His expression was bland and she read nothing in it. If there was anything going on, she wasn't going to learn about it from Monk. She glanced at her watch. ''I've got a one-thirty appointment, so I'd better be going.''

Monk stood up. ''Hey, if all my boys were as together as Nick, you'd be out of a job. Don't worry about him. He's got his head screwed on right.''

''That seems to be the general consensus,'' she said dryly, and headed for the door. ''Thanks, Monk.''

She almost bumped into Ward Rivers as she turned the corner leaving the gym. ''Ward, don't you have a class scheduled for this hour?''

''Yes, ma'am, social studies.'' His fair skin turned bright pink. ''Coach called and got me excused.''

''Why? It's too early for practice, isn't it?''

''I'm getting some special coaching,'' he said, not quite meeting her eyes. ''Me and Nick.''

She frowned. ''You're not supposed to be using class time to do it. Does this happen often?''

He looked at his feet, obviously uncomfortable with her questions. ''Coach has a pretty tight schedule.''

Something about his demeanor bothered her. Was Ward, as well as Nick, feeling—what was Cam's word—*uneasy* over these special sessions with Monk? But even so, Ward would probably go along with anything Tyson dictated, just as all his athletes would. She conjured up a smile for the boy. "Well, go ahead, Ward, but I wouldn't like for you to make a habit of this. I'll speak to Coach Tyson myself."

"Yes, ma'am."

She made a mental note to ask Nick whether or not any of the private coaching he got from Tyson had taken place during class time. Although, if he made good on his vow to quit, she supposed it didn't matter. But really, Monk was impossible, enticing these athletes to break rules, not to mention that they missed important class work. The man behaved as if he was running a little empire here. With a sigh of disgust, she left, glad to be off his territory.

The next couple of weeks passed without another incident. Ted skipped his usual midweek pizza treat for the kids twice in a row, but since neither Nick nor Kendall were quite ready to forgive him for the disastrous rodeo weekend, nobody cared. On Saturday, Rachel insisted that Nick go with her to Home Depot to help her choose ready-to-assemble shelving to install in Dinah's garage. Although they'd found room for a lot of their things, there was still sports gear and bikes, plus other odds and ends that rightfully belonged in a garage. Dinah simply wasn't equipped for a family with two kids.

"I'm told it doesn't require a skilled carpenter to install shelves," Rachel said to Nick upon entering the huge warehouse-like building, and hoped it was true. Ted had never been the handy type, and now with money being scarce, she tried to avoid paying someone for simple projects. Nick could do it, although he certainly hadn't been happy at the prospect. She hoped that by including him in shopping for the shelves, he'd be less negative about having to install them. Negative or not, he was going to do it.

"They're over there, Mom, aisle twelve," he told her, pointing in the opposite direction from where she headed. Like most males, he knew the layout of Home Depot almost as well as he knew the layout of his bedroom. Rachel had long ago decided it must be a gender thing. "We're gonna need a heavy-duty cart to carry the stuff,'' he informed her without making a move to go get one.

''I'll find the shelves while you get the cart,'' she said, ''but don't dawdle. There are several different kinds. We'll need to look them over to see what's available, and then decide.''

''Steel shelving's best,'' he told her, with his hands shoved deep in his pockets. ''But you'll probably want to go with the snap-together plastic stuff. It's lightweight and any female can do it.''

''We've discussed this, Nick. I won't have to do it, you will.''

Rolling his eyes, he turned and left.

''And let's hope you're better at it than you were when you were five years old and insisted on putting together your first bike,'' she muttered to his disappearing backside as she searched the overhead signs. Where *was* aisle twelve?

More and more, Nick's bad attitude troubled her. The rodeo debacle seemed to have crystallized the reality of divorce for both her kids, but neither of them were open to talking about it, at least not to her. In fact, neither had mentioned Ted or Francine since. Maybe Ted's defense of Francine had resigned them to his new priorities and they figured what's the use. But contrary to what Ted said, Rachel was open to trying to mend the rift between them, especially since he said he was going to marry Francine. It would take time and effort by all, scarce commodities for Ted at the moment. He was much too busy trying to save his career.

The odds against him were formidable. He needed to retain as many of his patients as possible, even as he pulled out of the practice he'd shared with Walter and their partners. Meanwhile, word was that Francine was still pushing him to take a position in an established practice in Dallas. How long he could stall her on that was anyone's guess. Hovering over all was the lawsuit. Yes, indeed, Ted had his problems, which meant he had little time to devote to Nick or Kendall.

After the last bitter words he'd flung at her, Rachel found

she had little sympathy for him. It had stung to hear him say that what she'd always considered her strengths were, in his mind, faults. And she'd naturally assumed that sex played a big part in his decision to leave her for another woman, but she hadn't realized how unsatisfactory in bed he thought she was. She found herself recalling how Cam had dismissed Ted's opinion and it eased her wounded pride.

Otherwise, she shied away from thinking too much about Cam.

Fortunately, as a divorced woman, there was plenty to occupy her mind in the mountain of things for which she now assumed full responsibility. At night, she shuffled through bills and legal papers defining the division of assets shared by her and Ted. She realized that she'd been assuming more and more of the details of their married life long before Ted decided to leave. Had he been unconsciously distancing himself or had his loss of interest in their personal affairs been planned, knowing he would soon want out? And when would she have finally noticed?

As she stood puzzling over that thought and the store layout, someone spoke close behind her. "Shelving is down four aisles, past the lawn equipment and turn left."

She knew that voice and hearing it made her heart do a little dip. Turning, she found herself looking into Cam's eyes. Today they were a cool, smoky hue, not the silvery shade of blue. "Um, hi. Was I looking lost?"

"Maybe just a little. And you would have been lost had you kept on in the direction you're headed."

"How did you know I was looking for shelving?"

"I passed Nick on his way to get a cart." He took her arm and gently turned her around. "Go thataway."

Her pulse hummed at his touch while something deeply feminine in her stirred as if emerging from a long, wintry chill. He wore a sweatshirt with a Houston *Texans* logo on it, jeans faded to a washed-out shade and running shoes that looked as if they had major mileage on them. She'd taken barely a split second look at him directly, so how, she wondered, had she taken it all in? She blinked, realizing that she was staring, and remarked inanely, "I'm not too familiar with the store."

He nodded, a hint of a smile teasing the corner of his mouth. "I guessed that. When you get to know it, you'll love it." He touched her waist to steer her in the right direction and, to her surprise, fell into step beside her.

He tended to look a little rumpled most of the time, she realized, noting from a sidelong glance that his near-black hair needed a trim. It was as if his physical appearance was of minimum concern to him. And why would it be otherwise, a voice in her head retorted, when a man looked that good no matter what he wore? Dodging a man wheeling a cart loaded with lumber, she said, "We need space in the garage to store overload. We seem to have brought more stuff than Mom has room for. I'm counting on Nick to install shelves." She sounded breathless and flustered. Actually, she felt breathless and flustered. *Good gracious!*

"He can," Cam said. "For that matter, you can, too. You don't have to be handy. You just have to be able to read instructions and fit part A into part B." They'd reached their destination now and he closed his fingers on her elbow, guiding her midway down the aisle. "But if you find you still need more room, I've got storage space to spare, both in the loft of my garage and in the basement in the house. It's unused. I don't have nearly enough stuff to fill up a house that size."

She gave him a startled glance but recovered enough to say, "Thanks, I appreciate it, but I'm hoping it won't be necessary." They'd reached the shelving section now and she saw immediately that there was, indeed, a lot to choose from.

"What're you planning to put on the shelves?" Cam asked, watching her face.

"Toys, Nick's sports stuff, some boxed china that I didn't feel comfortable storing in the commercial storage we rented." She shrugged. "Just the general junk people put in garages."

"Steel is best and permanent, but in your case, the heavy-duty plastic would work," he said, pointing it out. "It's strong and quick to install. Cheap, too, since it isn't your house you're equipping."

"Actually, plastic is what Nick expected me to choose. He—" She stopped, suddenly recognizing the man coming down the aisle toward them. "Pete! Pete Singletary," she said, her face lighting up. "What a nice surprise."

"Hi, Rachel. I was at the checkout and saw you heading this way." Tall, broad-shouldered and blond, Marta's former fiancé was dressed for work in jeans and a leather bomber jacket. It had been some time since she'd seen him, at least five years ago when Marta abruptly broke off their engagement. Living in Dallas and no longer engaged to Marta, he'd had little reason to be in Rose Hill.

"What are you doing here?" she asked. "Dallas must have half a dozen Home Depots."

"I'm living here now. I've bought a house in Olde Towne, but nothing's in it yet, just a few clothes, a bedroll and a TV set. The movers were scheduled to arrive Monday, but I've got a conflict and it'll have to be Tuesday."

Rachel's surprise showed on her face. "Have you given up police work?"

"I think he's the new police chief," Cam said, stepping forward and putting out his hand. "Cam Ford. Welcome to Rose Hill."

Rachel's jaw dropped as they shook hands. "Well, for heaven's sake, Pete. I had no idea." Pete had been on the police force in Dallas and very ambitious when he and Marta were engaged. The last she heard, he'd been on a fast track there careerwise. She couldn't imagine him leaving DPD for the slower pace of a town like Rose Hill. "When did this happen? How did it happen?"

"Two days ago and I lobbied like hell for the job," Pete admitted with a wry grin. Then he turned to Cam. "How did you know? I wasn't notified myself until the middle of the week and the official announcement isn't happening until Monday morning.''

"I've got some connections at city hall," Cam explained. "You've stirred some excitement there. I should warn you, they're expecting good things."

"I'll try not to disappoint them, then." Pete shifted the bag containing his purchases to the opposite hand and looked at Rachel. "How's Marta?"

Breaking the engagement had not been Pete's idea, but Marta had been unable to get beyond the fact of his betrayal and had cut him out of her life. She hadn't bought his argument that it was "just that one time and meant nothing."

"She's well, Pete. As sassy as ever. She's teaching honors English now."

"Good, good." He looked away. "She wanted that spot and worked hard for it. I'm glad the school board came around."

"Yes. They know she's a terrific teacher."

He shifted from one foot to the other, looking a little uncomfortable before adding, "I didn't hear about Jorge dying until months afterward. That must have been really tough, them being married only a year and a half."

"It was tough. And very sudden. Jorge got sick just a few months after they were married and he went steadily downhill in spite of very aggressive treatment. It happened so fast, they never really had a chance to experience much married life."

"Yeah. Well…" He cleared his throat, as if preparing to say something else, but whatever it was, it went unsaid as he shifted his purchases yet again. "I guess I'd better go get started. I'm installing a ceiling fan in the bedroom." He gave Rachel a smile and nodded to Cam, then paused. His expression changed and he snapped his fingers. "Cam Ford. Wait a minute, you're the guy who wrote the book about Ray David Jenkins, right?"

"Right."

"You did a great job on that. I once saw a tape of his interrogation when he began describing how he killed his victims. He was as casual as if he was talking about the weather. Gave me the creeps, just listening to him.''

''Gave me the creeps writing about him,'' Cam said, giving a grimace at the recollection. ''He was definitely thinking and playing outside the box.''

''But maybe not as prolific a killer as he pretended to be, huh? You built a good case for questioning many of his confessions,'' Pete said. ''A damn good case. Are you working on a book now?''

''In a sense. I'm doing some preliminary research.''

''Anybody I know?'' Pete asked, looking intrigued. ''I worked in Homicide in Dallas.''

Listening, Rachel recalled now that Pete had been slated for management at Homicide in Dallas, which made his appearance in Rose Hill even more puzzling. Why in the world had he walked away from that kind of career opportunity?

''You wouldn't remember this case,'' Cam said. ''The crime occurred in Texas, but it was over seventy-five years ago on a huge ranch near San Antonio. The owner of the ranch and his paramour, who'd once been a dance hall girl, were murdered and his wife was believed to have done it, although it was never proved.''

''A woman scorned,'' Rachel said.

''That was the conventional wisdom at the time,'' Cam said, giving her a wry smile.

Pete snapped his fingers. ''Diablo D Ranch. Way back in the thirties, right?''

''That's the one.'' Cam moved to allow a customer with a loaded cart to pass.

''As I recall, she was never convicted,'' Pete said.

''Never even arrested.'' Cam turned to Rachel. ''The wife had more motive than the fact that her husband was cheating on her. About that time, oil was discovered on the property. She stood to be one of the richest women in Texas…and that was saying something in those early days of the depression.''

''If you write the book,'' Rachel said, ''will you build a case that proves she did it?''

"I don't think she did it, just as I don't think Ray David Jenkins committed all the crimes the police claimed he did."

"Cops can be overzealous trying to close cases when they get a likely killer," Pete said, backing away. "I'll look forward to reading it, and if you need insight into the methods of a homicide cop, feel free to call me. Or better yet, drop by and I'll offer you a cup of what's bound to be the worst coffee you ever had."

"I'll do that," Cam said, putting out his hand for a shake. "Thanks. Nice to meet you."

"Same here." Turning to go, Pete waved to Rachel. "Good to see you, Rachel. My place is going to need a lot of fixing up, but I bought a barbecue grill yesterday. As soon as I get settled, I'll have you and Ted over. We'll cook some steaks."

She hesitated only a moment before telling the truth. "You'll have to settle for me by myself," she said. "Ted and I are getting a divorce."

He looked at her in astonishment. "Are you serious?" Then, shaking his head, "Dumb question, I guess. I'm sorry, Rachel. When—" He glanced at Cam helplessly, then back at Rachel. "Hell, I hate to hear that."

She shrugged. "It happens, Pete. Thanks." She summoned a smile. "But I just may take you up on that offer of a steak one day."

"Just name the day, lady." He studied her face for another moment, then lifted the bag with his purchases. "Ceiling fan. It's waiting."

"Bye," she said, and watched him leave, her smile lingering until she felt Cam's gaze on her face. "What?"

"Your first post-divorce date?"

"Excuse me?"

"I think he's interested."

She shook her head, rolling her eyes. "That's absurd." She gave an impatient look toward the opposite end of the aisle. "What is keeping Nick? He knows we can't load these shelves without that cart."

"Why is it ridiculous?"

She looked at him. "Because Pete's just a friend. And he used to be Marta's fiancé. And he still loves her."

"Oh? You know that?"

"I do."

"So, what happened?"

"It's ancient history, but if you're so interested, you can always ask him." She turned to go. "You two can have a chat over really bad coffee. And right now, if I'm going to get these shelves bought before nightfall, I guess I'll have to find that cart myself."

Nick was headed for the rear of the store in search of the heavy-duty carts when two people fell into step with him, one on each side.

"Hey, my man," Ferdy Jordan said, draping an arm around Nick's shoulder. "We saw you come in. You have a lot of fun shopping with your mommy?"

Nick shrugged free of Ferdy's arm. "Screw you, Ferdy."

"Ooh—ooh, did you hear that, B.J.? He's talkin' tough."

B.J. gave a snicker. "Yeah, real tough."

Ferdy jerked Nick's baseball cap from his head and danced backward, just out of Nick's reach as he grabbed for it. Then he tossed it to B.J., who leaped up, caught it and sailed it up into the air where it landed on top of a stack of fertilizer high in the nether regions of the store. Seeing the uselessness of making an issue of his cap, Nick turned abruptly, ignoring both, and headed for the carts parked nearby. It was plain bad luck running into them. They wouldn't miss giving him a taste of their idea of fun.

Ignoring them, he struggled to get the unwieldy cart turned around while Ferdy grabbed the handle of another one. "Hey," he exclaimed gleefully, "let's play bumper cars!" With a motion to B.J. to clear a path, he made a beeline for Nick. With both boys pushing, the heavy metal cart was traveling at breakneck speed. Nick barely managed to jump aside with a second to spare.

"Are you nuts!" he yelled, confronting them. "That thing weighs a ton. You can do some damage horsing around like that."

Ferdy feigned remorse. "Oh, gee. Did it almost get Mommy's boy?" His expression morphed into malicious spite. "Or is it Coach's boy now?" Ferdy looked at his sidekick. "Have you noticed Nicky and Ward getting real chummy with Coach lately, B.J.?"

"Yeah, I've noticed," B.J. said with a sly grin. "They're plumb tight."

"It's disgusting." Ferdy lifted a bag of pesticide and tossed it casually from hand to hand. "You know, B.J., the way Nicky and Ward are so tight sharing Coach's time and attention like that...well, it makes a person wonder what else they share. You ever think of that, B.J.?"

"Yeah, all the time."

Nick stood them down, legs in an aggressive stance, fists stiff at his sides. "Does your mind stay in the gutter twenty-four hours a day, Ferdy, or just when you're awake?"

Ferdy was still leering. "Did I get it right, Nicky?"

Bent on leaving, Nick reached for the handle of the cart in disgust. But Ferdy wasn't ready to quit. His grin faded and his eyes went cold. "I wouldn't count on moving into the first-base slot if I were you," he said in a tone that had now lost all trace of humor.

"Yeah, and when you get to be coach, your opinion will count," Nick said, refusing to be spooked. He shoved the second cart aside, clearing a path. "Until then, you know what you can do with it." Turning his back on them both, he started again up the aisle. But he'd taken no more than three steps when Ferdy drew back and hurled the bag of fertilizer. Nick was hit hard in the center of his back. Caught off guard, he went down in a sprawl of arms and a shower of Triple 13, yelping when his elbow glanced painfully off the concrete.

"Oops," Ferdy said, his voice soft and menacing, "Mommy's boy has hurt himself, B.J."

"Yeah, too bad," B.J. giggled, his color high with excitement. Dancing from one foot to the other, his eyes darted nervously to the far end of the aisle.

With B.J. on the lookout for witnesses, Ferdy moved unhurriedly to shove the cart aside with one foot. "Coach is not gonna be happy to find Nicky all banged up on Monday when it comes time for those special lessons." Shaking his head in mock sympathy, he reached down to give Nick a hand up.

"Go to hell." Nick knocked his hand aside. His ears were ringing, but he'd be damned if he'd let these two goons know it.

"Nick!"

Shit. It was his mother. In a flash, Ferdy and B.J. sprinted to the corner in the opposite direction and disappeared. Shit again! Cam Ford was with his mom and just in time to see him sprawled on his butt, covered in fertilizer. He must look like a dumb dork.

"What is going on, Nick?" His mother stood with her hands on her hips looking royally pissed. Then, as he raised his eyes to explain, her expression changed. With a shocked cry, she went down on one knee and reached out a hand to touch his face. "You're bleeding! What happened? Who were those kids we saw running away?"

"Two of the biggest jerks in the whole school," he muttered. And, pushing his mother's hand aside, he got to his feet, a little shaky and a lot embarrassed. "Hi, Cam."

Eyes narrowed, Cam's gaze was directed toward the aisle where Ferdy and B.J. had split. "You know those two?"

"Yeah." Nick was busy dusting pellets from his hands and off the seat of his jeans. "Like I said, they're stupid and they like to try acting tough."

"Why would they single you out, Nick?" Rachel asked with just enough motherly concern to make Nick squirm as she dug in her purse for a tissue.

"It's no big deal, Mom." He reached for the handle of the

cart. "C'mon, let's go load up those shelves and get this show on the road."

"Nick—" His mother was planted firmly in front of the cart. "I asked you a question."

"They were just looking for trouble and I was handy."

"I think that was obvious, but they must have a reason. Tell me their names," she ordered, coming at him with the tissue.

"Like I said, two jerks." He turned his face from her but took the tissue and gave a swipe at his forehead, then stuffed it into his pocket. "Leave it alone, Mom."

Cam touched Rachel's arm to hold her off, but his eyes were on Nick. It had been some time since he'd dealt with a teenage boy, but he remembered enough to know that Nick wouldn't appreciate any show of motherly concern in public. He was already embarrassed at Rachel stumbling upon the scuffle in the first place. "Looks like you're coming up against some of the meanness we mentioned a while back," he remarked.

"I can handle it," Nick muttered, and reached for the cart.

"We'll have to pay for the damaged bag," Rachel said, still eyeing Nick anxiously.

Cam bent to get the bag and toss it onto the cart, then he caught Rachel's arm and urged her forward. Even if he hadn't seen how distressed she was, he could feel the tension in her.

Rachel allowed Nick to pass and followed him up the aisle with a troubled look in her eye. Cam guessed Nick would have to answer a boatload of questions when they got back home. He had a few questions himself, but not for Nick. It looked like problems were brewing in Monk Tyson's sports program, and as they headed for the checkout, he decided to pay a visit to the coach and get a firsthand look at the situation.

Eleven

"What are you doing?" Marta asked. She stood in the doorway of Dinah's garage where Rachel sat on a stack of cardboard cartons studying what appeared to be an illustrated instruction sheet for something. A slew of nuts and bolts were strewn about on the floor amid steel shelving and the connecting apparatus that went with it.

"What does it look like?" Rachel muttered, tossing the instructions down in disgust. "I'm installing shelves in the garage…if I can ever manage to figure out how to begin." She stood up, looking at the scattered contents of the first carton as if studying the markings on a rattlesnake.

"Apparently you were correct in rejecting a career in engineering." Marta, hands propped on her hips, surveyed the chaos. "This looks like a job for Nick. Where is he?"

Rachel threw up her hands. "Ward called. Kristin Gates and about six other hotties—their description, not mine—are hanging out at the mall. Both boys were practically panting to get over there, so I caved. They would have been useless, anyway."

"True," Marta said dryly. She bent and retrieved the instructions, scanned the paper briefly and began organizing the articles strewn around the garage floor. "These things are designed so anybody can put them together. Between the two of us, we can do it."

Marta was known at school for being handy with a screwdriver. "Where were you going? I'd hate to ruin a fun afternoon," she lied.

"Just killing time at the mall, but not with the same glee that drives Nick and Ward." On her haunches now, Marta deftly sorted through the items once contained in a plastic bag. "According to the instructions, you should have forty-two bolts with nuts and washers. You'll need a wrench, too. I hope you have regular tools, not metric."

"Who knows?" Rachel muttered, and without a clue as to what kind of tools Dinah kept in the tall storage bin, began searching for something that wasn't designed for pruning live plants or digging in dirt. Before her divorce, she'd hired professionals to do most household repairs or installations, and today she longed to pick up the phone and call Buddy's Fix-It. Alas, such indulgences were no longer in the budget. "I should have taken Cam up on his offer to help," she grumbled, shoving aside gardening gloves, a small trowel and the remains of a dead chrysanthemum in a pot. "He certainly had an opinion while I was trying to decide which type to buy."

"Cam Ford, the brooding and brilliant novelist, went with you to Home Depot?" Now Marta was incredulous.

"No, of course not. Nick and I ran into him there."

"Well, why didn't you take him up if he offered, for Pete's sake?" Resting on her heels, Marta glanced across the way to where Cam was doing something to the windows on his front porch. "Look, he's on his porch right now. We can just give him a shout."

"He was just being polite, Marta."

"I don't see Cam as a man who offers to do something just to be polite. Most of the time he's anything but polite."

"He's not so bad…once you get to know him." Rachel threw up her hands in defeat. "I can't find anything that looks like real tools."

Marta took another moment to study Rachel's face, then turned to search for a small container to hold the nuts and bolts. "Dinah's bound to have the basic stuff somewhere. It's just a matter of looking hard enough."

"Yeah," Rachel said, and pulled at an innocent-looking

box, thinking she'd found the tools, but the bottom had rotted out of the box and loose potting soil cascaded out, landing on her feet. Wrinkling her nose, she stomped dirt off her sneakers. "This, I assume, is not it. Doggone it, where's Nick when I need him?"

"Like all men at that point, otherwise occupied," Marta said, and, with a wide smile, suddenly pulled a long brace punctuated with holes from the pile on the floor. "Hah!" she said, falling into a warrior position and brandishing the steel bar like a pirate with a cutlass. "Bring on those pesky shelves, woman. Who needs men when we have intelligence, strength of purpose and feminine ingenuity to get the job done?"

"Maybe we don't need them," Rachel said, "but they sure would come in handy."

"Not a problem," Marta said, returning to her task. "I tell you, we can do this."

Reading the printed instructions again, Marta picked up the first of the steel shelves, ready to begin assembling. "Where do you want them set up?" she asked.

"Anywhere but my bedroom," Rachel said, finally locating a small box that had to be Dinah's tools. She set it on the floor and popped it open. "Pray that what we need is in here."

"That flat plastic tray holds the wrenches," Marta said, appearing beside her. Rachel let her help herself, and to her intense relief, Marta unhesitatingly plucked the proper tool from the motley collection. "We're all set," she said. "How 'bout you start opening the other cartons, but don't scatter the hardware like you did from the first one."

"I didn't do that, Nick did!"

"Whatever. We don't have extra pieces. The Chinese expect Americans to be able to follow instructions, therefore, from their thrifty point of view, there is no need to supply more than forty-two nuts and bolts if that's what it takes to do the job."

"So that's why it looks like a Chinese puzzle," Rachel muttered.

Marta laughed. "C'mon, it'll be a piece of cake."

"No, the piece-of-cake-type shelves were plastic," Rachel grumbled. "I foolishly let myself be persuaded by three macho men to get the steel variety."

"Three?" Marta questioned. "Nick, Cam and who else?"

"Oh." She gave Marta a sly glance. "Didn't I mention I also ran into Pete?"

"Pete who?" Marta stood holding one of the shelves, ready to attach it to the brace.

"How many men do we know named Pete?" Rachel asked, leaning casually against the counter, her feet in dirty sneakers crossed at the ankles.

"Pete Singletary was at Home Depot in Rose Hill?" Marta asked, setting the shelf down slowly.

"Big as life and twice as sexy."

Marta made a contemptuous sound. "Isn't Rose Hill a bit out of his jurisdiction?"

"It's very much in his jurisdiction now," Rachel said, enjoying herself. She still believed that Marta had never truly gotten over Pete, in spite of her decision to break her engagement and her hasty marriage to Jorge Ruiz a few months later. Infidelity, she now knew, was a cruel betrayal, but Marta and Pete had been dealing with some sticky problems that might have been worked through. "Pete is our new police chief," she told Marta.

Marta's mouth dropped. "You're kidding."

Rachel put both hands on her chest. "Cross my heart."

Shelves forgotten, Marta sat down on top of a short stepladder. "What happened? He would never voluntarily leave DPD and especially not to relocate to sleepy little Rose Hill. He lived and breathed that job in Dallas. What's up with him leaving? Did you ask?"

"No, I didn't. But you'll get a chance to ask him yourself," Rachel said, looking beyond Marta's shoulder. "He's walking up the driveway as we speak."

Marta whipped around just as Pete Singletary stepped around Kendall's bike—left on the driveway as usual—and entered Dinah's garage. The afternoon sun was at his back, so it was impossible to read the expression on his face. But Rachel guessed he must have recognized Marta's car and stopped.

"Afternoon, ladies." He glanced at the litter on the garage floor. "Looks like the two of you have a major project going."

"Hi, Pete," Rachel said, and for the second time that day, flashed him a warm smile. "I guess you had less trouble installing your ceiling fan than I'm having with these shelves."

"I guess," he said, before turning to his ex-fiancée. "Marta. Good to see you."

"Hello, Pete." Marta's cheeks were flushed and she looked as if she'd like to escape, but Pete's six-foot-two-inch frame blocked the only way out.

He glanced at the wrench in her hand. "I see Rachel's got you working."

"Um, right." She gave a quick look around at the material strewn on the garage floor. "We were just about to get started."

A hint for him to clear out, Rachel guessed. But not if she could help it. "I was just telling Marta about seeing you at Home Depot today."

"Yeah," Marta said, with a tilt to her chin. "And she mentioned your new job. Are congratulations in order...or not?"

His smile was slightly off center. "I guess you might think that, considering. It took a while, but I've managed to overcome my obsession with DPD." He studied his feet a second or two, then met her eyes. "So yeah, congratulations are in order. I never wanted a job more than I wanted this one."

She studied him in silence. "In that case, congratulations."

He held her gaze, then said softly, "Thanks. So," he added, turning back to Rachel, "can I give you gals a hand here? I put these exact shelves up at my fishing camp a few weeks ago. They're a little tricky and I found it goes a lot faster if there's a helper.''

"And did you have one?" Marta asked in a tart tone.

"Nope, which is why I know I needed one."

"Luckily, there are two of us," Marta said. "We can manage."

Rachel handed him a screwdriver. "Don't listen to her. I don't even know if my mother's got the right tools to get the job done, but if you need anything that's not on hand, I'll be happy to jump in my car and make another run to Home Depot to get it. Heck, I'll run to Dallas to get it if you'll help."

"Then you don't need me," Marta said, ready to toss the wrench in her hand on the floor.

"I do," Rachel said, catching her by the arm. "You heard him. It takes two. If I have to go get something, he'll need you to stay and help."

"What's the problem, Marta?" Pete said in a tone that made even Rachel's heart quiver. "I promise not to bring up the past."

"Bring up anything you please," she said, snatching up the pot with nuts and bolts. "Nothing you say or do matters to me anymore."

"If that's true, you won't object if I lend a hand here," he said in a tone as bland as milk. He bent and lifted a single shelf. "We always worked well together, so I'll just put this piece in place and hold it steady while you fasten the first of the braces to it. Or would you rather be the helper and let me handle the tools?"

He was amused, although he wasn't about to let Marta see him smile. Rachel, however, could see it in his eyes, hear it in his voice. And so could Marta.

"I don't make a good second banana anymore," Marta snapped.

Rachel had to fight to keep her own smile from showing. It was such an intriguing turn of events, spiced with the real possibility that the tension between the two of them might suddenly erupt like spontaneous combustion. She hoped there wouldn't be bloodshed. "What can I do?" she asked in an innocent tone.

"How about you mind your own business," Marta muttered, but in a voice meant only for Rachel.

"Right. Okay." Rachel dusted her hands and gladly withdrew from the project. "I'll just go to fix us something to drink," she said brightly. "What'll it be, guys? Coffee? Iced tea? Beer?"

"Beer for me," Pete said without hesitation.

"Diet. Soda," Marta gritted. To Pete, she gave a lift of her chin, indicating the next piece she needed. Pete did as instructed, but took his own sweet time doing it, letting his gaze travel over Marta from the top of her head to her neat white sneakers before releasing the piece to her.

"Diet soda? What the hell are you drinking diet stuff for? You don't need to lose an ounce. You're a perfect size."

"I wouldn't be if I didn't." Color high, she slapped the brace in place with a clang of steel against steel. "Do you know how many grams of sugar are in a can of soda? And calories? Not to mention the caffeine."

"Whoa, you make it sound like poison," he said, openly teasing her now.

"It *is* poison. One of the things that bugs me most is that the kids at school—"

Rachel left them to it. Besides, she could have been one of the host of garden implements mounted on the wall for all the notice they took of her at the moment as Marta launched into her favorite pet peeve and Pete, apparently, was inclined to listen.

She'd wished for some way to bring Marta and Pete together for a long time now, believing Marta needed to deal with the issues that had torn her and Pete apart. In Rachel's opinion, she'd married Jorge too close on the heels of her broken engagement. But Marta had always denied Rachel's suggestion that she carried around a lot of unresolved pain from her breakup with Pete. It brought a smile to her lips that fate, and not Rachel, had intervened. However it happened, she thought, opening the refrigerator to get beer and the diet drink, it was about time.

Cam had been wrapping up a job recaulking windows and the door on his front porch when Pete Singletary pulled to the curb in front of Dinah's home. He'd watched the new police chief saunter up the driveway and enter the garage where Rachel and her friend were wrestling with the assembly of her new shelves. Irritation and a feeling he couldn't nail down caused him to turn away. Actually, he did know what he felt, but he wasn't sure what to do about it. He was attracted to Rachel and getting nowhere fast trying to tell himself he wasn't. And seeing some other dude sniffing around her made him testy. Rachel was way off in dismissing the notion that Singletary was interested in her, he thought, closing the lid of his toolbox with a hard snap. Why else would he show up now? As far as Singletary knew after running into her at Home Depot, the plan was for Nick to install the shelves.

Cam, of course, had seen Nick leave with his buddy and assumed Rachel would wait to put up the shelves until the boy got back, but that stubborn streak he was coming to know all too well had kicked in and she'd apparently decided to tackle the job on her own. He'd been on the verge of offering help himself, but then Marta had shown up and killed his excuse for going over. He'd gone back to caulking, but with less concentration than when he'd begun.

As he cleared away the caulking debris, he avoided looking over, but he couldn't avoid hearing the voices that drifted across the lawn. Rachel's comments, sounding husky and musical, were easily distinguished from Marta's more clipped words, but setting Cam's teeth on edge was Singletary, whose voice was as smooth as snake oil. The three of them might as well break out the beer and the barbecue grill, he decided grumpily. Make it a real party. Scowling, he gathered up the caulking gun and his toolbox. Hell, it should be nothing to him if Rachel wanted to enjoy the company of a man. She was as good as divorced from that cheating bastard of a husband and better off for it, even if she was a long way from seeing it yet.

With his jaw set, he left the porch carrying his equipment. To get to his own garage, he had to walk between his place and Dinah's, but halfway there, he heard another burst of laughter from Singletary and stopped midstride, set his equipment down, turned and started across the lawn.

Rachel spotted him before the other two, who were struggling with what looked like the top tier on one of the sets of shelves. "Hi, Cam. Come and join the fun, but don't volunteer to help. Marta just told me in no uncertain terms that they didn't need any."

"I didn't say nobody could help." Marta spoke around two screws clamped between her teeth. "Just that you couldn't. You've already mashed your finger and dropped a wrench on my toe."

Rachel grinned at him, looking as if she didn't much regret being banished from the workforce. "Would you like a beer?"

"Sounds good." Instead of waiting for her to bring it out, he followed her into the house. "Where's Dinah?"

"In Dallas, attending some kind of daylily show with one of her garden club friends. They took Kendall along. She'll be in heaven."

"She got her camera with her?"

"Is grass green? Is the sky blue? Of course, she has her camera." She opened the fridge and pulled out a long-neck beer. "Corona okay?"

"It's fine." He took it, uncapped it and, holding her gaze, savored the first cold bite at the back of his throat. Now that he was inside with her and Singletary was outside, he felt less...testy. He motioned toward the garage with his beer and said, "So, what's with those two? I thought you said they were busted up for good."

"No, I said they were busted up, but not necessarily for good. And didn't I say if you were interested in the reasons their engagement was broken off all those years ago, you should ask them, not me?" She leaned against the counter. "And why are you so hung up on Pete and Marta?"

"I'm not hung up on them, but it seems to me if Singletary's interested in rekindling a romance with Marta, why isn't he knocking on her door instead of yours?"

"You could ask him that, too," she said. Turning, she opened a cabinet, reached up and took out a bag of nachos and a large bottle of picante sauce. The bottom of her sweater hiked up, revealing a slim waist and the intriguing flare of her hips in low-slung jeans. She wasn't pencil thin, but he didn't particularly like his women skinny. Not that she was his woman, or likely to be, although he didn't have any difficulty recalling how neatly she'd fit when he hugged her last Saturday. But she had baggage in the form of kids, one of them rebellious, a contentious ex, an ailing mother and financial woes, plus a passel of problems stemming from all of the above.

He watched her remove something in two pieces from underneath the counter, one shaped like the state of Texas and the other a star for serving the chips and sauce. She handed him the jar of picante. "Here, open this for me, will you?"

"Are we having a party?"

"No, but the least I can do is provide snacks while Pete and Marta put up those shelves."

Setting his beer aside, he twisted the sealed cap from the picante sauce while she tore the bag of nachos open and dumped them into the Texas dish. Since he had the sauce in his hand, he emptied it into the star shape. She took the jar from him and tossed it into the trash. Then, instead of heading for the door with the goodies, she paused. "Before we go outside, there's something I'd like to ask you."

"Sure." But he was warned by the way she looked at him. He raised the long neck to his lips and took a slow swallow. "I think."

"It's personal." She reached for a chip in the bowl.

"How personal?"

"I need to know if you can recall when Jack was—"

He swung away at the mention of Jack's name and moved to the window above the sink. His first instinct was to get away, get out of her kitchen and stay the hell away from her. "No, the answer's no," he told her. "No questions about Jack."

"Not even if it might help another boy?"

Blind to the view from the window, he imagined another parent getting that fearsome phone call in the middle of the night. He thought of the impact on another parent of a message so grievous that life was changed forever. Real joy was never quite possible and the future was dark as far ahead as you looked. He set the long-neck bottle on the counter carefully and drew a deep breath. "What do you want to know?"

"I know it's hard," she said. "I wouldn't—"

He turned and looked at her. "The question, Rachel. What is it?"

She hesitated but only for a heartbeat. "I counseled a boy who was—is—one of Monk Tyson's star athletes. If he doesn't screw up he's sure to be offered a scholarship so fantastic that most high school football players can only dream of. But I'm worried he's going to do just that. I sense he's dealing with a personal crisis. His grades are slipping, he's skipping school, he's binge drinking. He's had one DUI already and I'm afraid it's just a matter of time before he has another." The chip in her hand snapped. "Or worse."

"You think he's contemplating escape the same way Jack did?"

"No, I don't think he's that desperate. Yet."

"Then what?"

"Do you…" She looked away, deeply thoughtful. "After talking to him, I just have this feeling…" The chip was now in pieces as she struggled to put her concern into words. Frowning now, she bit off a tiny piece of the nacho. "Something is tormenting this boy."

"I don't see how this relates to Jack."

"I'm wondering if playing sports is right for this student."

"The kid is unhappy over the prospect of a future of fame and fortune beyond his wildest dreams?"

"No." She licked a bit of salt from one finger, unconscious of the effect on Cam. "But something's...wrong. Monk Tyson is obsessed with those athletes, especially the gifted ones."

"Is that how this relates to Jack in your mind?"

She raised her eyes to his. "Did you ever get a feeling from Jack that he was being pressured? Or that there was anything...unusual...or—I don't know—anything at all that troubled him about Monk Tyson's sports program?"

"...some trouble with guys on the team. I was thinking maybe you could come down and—"

The words in Jack's last phone call were seared into Cam's mind. He'd been too distracted to listen then, but after it was too late, he'd been unable to turn them off. He'd replayed their conversations, studied every e-mail, relived their visits, all as he searched for a clue...anything that would have—should have—alerted him that his son was in crisis. He'd found nothing.

"Did Jack ever say that he suspected something more was happening in Monk's organization than simply playing ball?" Rachel asked.

"What are we talking about here, a weird club of some sort? Devil worship? Sex, drugs, porn? Stuff like that?"

Rachel spread her hands, mystified. "Again...I don't know. But I keep thinking about Nick telling you he was uneasy when he should be feeling just the opposite. I know how much baseball means to him. Do you think he's sensing something that's...I don't know, not right? Is that what he was hinting at that day when he was in your kitchen?"

"I don't know. Didn't you ask? You said you planned to talk to him."

She was shaking her head. "He was instantly defensive

when I brought it up, as he is when I try to talk to him now about anything. Even the most trivial stuff.''

"Tell you what," he said, knowing he was digging himself a hole that might swallow him up, "why don't I try to have a conversation with him? If he's comfortable talking to me, then it seems reasonable to take advantage of it.''

"Would you?" she said, looking relieved, then added, 'But only on the condition that you tell me exactly what he ays." She studied the bowl of chips, frowning. "I may be off in left field here, but I've felt some uneasiness for a while now, and after talking with this particular student, it's stronger than ever.''

"You had this uneasy feeling before Jack died?"

"No, not then, no. It was afterward." She turned and rinsed her hands, then ripped off a paper towel. "Or maybe after losing Jack, I was simply more alert.''

"Jack tested positive for drugs at the autopsy," Cam said. The words were as caustic as acid in his mouth. "You must know that.''

"Yes, but Jack was not a user, I *know* it. I never believed the answer to the mystery of…what he did was due to drugs. I don't know why he took whatever it was that night, but from what I knew of Jack, I really don't think he had a problem.''

"Thank you," he muttered. She looked as if she wanted to give him a hug and he knew it would feel good to get a hug from Rachel. He didn't have any trouble recalling how she'd felt snuggled against his chest in his kitchen last week, soft, womanly and, at that moment, a little fragile. He'd wanted to do a helluva lot more than hug her. Still did.

Unnerved at how far he'd let his libido take him since last week, Cam grabbed his beer. "I had a lot of trouble trying to fit in that part of the puzzle myself," he said. "I talked to several of the boys Jack had mentioned when we were together talking about school and ball, girls and dates. Nobody admitted ever seeing him take drugs. He had too much to lose, if you think about it. Monk Tyson runs a tight ship and nobody who wants his approval fools around with drugs. Or at least, that was the word I got.''

''Not even steroids?''

''Not even steroids.'' And no amount of digging had unearthed a clue that proved otherwise. Immediately after Jack's death, Cam had spoken to Tyson directly and had heard the same thing from ''The Man'' himself. Tyson had seemed genuinely baffled by the suicide of one of his most promising athletes. Same thing with Preston Ramsey. The principal had actually been shocked that Cam searched for anything behind Jack's suicide other than the usual, which was a troubled teenager unable to cope. Tragic, but not really uncommon. Clearly, he'd believed Cam to be in the throes of major denial. Cam, dissatisfied and sensing there was something if only he could isolate it or find a kid willing to talk, had then fallen back on what he, as a writer, did best: research. Still, his poking and prying had turned up nothing. Zip. Nada. He'd scrutinized everything about the school, its faculty, after-hours social events, clubs, incidences in the past, you name it. Finally, he'd been forced to admit he was at a dead end.

''Have you ever discussed this with Ramsey?'' he asked Rachel now.

She tossed the paper towel. ''What would I say? Preston would have dismissed a hunch as vague and unproductive. And if I were to stir up anything that reflected negatively on the school without being able to point clearly to facts as opposed to 'a feeling,' it would not bode well for the future of my job.''

''So you didn't make the effort.'' He didn't give her a chance to reply, but added, ''So, if there was, or is, something weird going on—your word, not mine—aren't you concerned that another boy might wind up like Jack?''

''That's the only reason I risked mentioning it, since I knew it would upset you.''

''Hmm.'' Cam, thoughtful and less defensive now, leaned

gainst the countertop, idly turning the long-neck bottle ound and round. "How much more digging did you do?"

"I spoke to Jack's mother." At his sharp look, she gave nother spread-hands-so-sue-me movement and barely aused. "I hoped to get some insight into Jack's state of nind at the time, but she was not helpful. She was too hocked and stunned by what happened and still deeply rieving. Understandably so. I waited a while—a month or o—then called her again, but she still couldn't come up with nything. I asked her to call me if she thought of anything, ut she never did."

"Cara was probably even less aware of Jack's state of nind at the time than me," Cam said, trying to keep the old itterness out of his voice. "She was all caught up in reeling n the new man in her life. Jack and his problems were a listant second."

"Sometimes it's hard to read teenagers, regardless of vhat's going on in your personal life," Rachel pointed out ,ently, then added, "even when the signs are right under our nose."

She was in her psychologist mode, Cam thought, probably eading in his face the fact that he still had not forgiven Cara or screwing around with Anthony Rosetti while Jack needed er. "For what it's worth, she later married the guy," he aid, making an effort to sound less unreasonable. "I guess hey're happy."

"If that's true, then I'm glad," Rachel said. "She surely eserves to be happy, considering her loss. For a mother to ose a child is—" She stopped, making a small, apologetic esture. "I'm sorry, that goes for fathers, too. I didn't mean o suggest—"

"It's okay. Cara seems to have adjusted. It's a good thing. Vlore power to her."

"Yes, a very good thing."

And why haven't you adjusted? Cam could see the thought n her face. And what he felt was probably hanging out there or her to make whatever psychologists made of these things.

He didn't like her reading his face…or his mind, but he'd brought it on himself by talking about Jack. Anytime he went there, a toddler could tell what he felt.

Rachel busied herself taking down a tray from an overhead cabinet and placing napkins on it. "I was wondering…considering that she seems to be getting on with her life, if she might have a clearer perspective now about what was going on before Jack died."

"Who, Cara?"

She smiled. "Weren't we talking about Cara?"

"Yeah, but you threw me a curve with that 'perspective' business."

"What I was getting at," she said with gentle patience, "is that Cara might be able to tell you something now that escaped her then. A person's reaction to grief and shock is never predictable. Some go into a self-preservation mode that excludes anything except the basics of life—eating, sleeping, working, simply getting through the day. Most eventually work through it and life goes on. Memory returns."

Definitely wearing her psychologist hat. "Okay, I'll accept that. What about it?"

"Assuming she might have remembered something, you won't know what it is if you don't ask."

He crossed his arms over his chest, not giving a damn what she read into his body language. "You're actually suggesting that I go over and ask Cara if she's willing to answer some questions about Jack, five years too late?"

"It's never too late and I think it makes sense, don't you?"

"That's assuming she'll let me inside the door," he said, openly sarcastic. "This is a woman who cheated on me, who neglected Jack while setting up the next sucker, who spends most of her time making her life as cushy as possible for herself, and you want me to pay a visit and make nice?"

"If she was that bad, I'm surprised you liked her well enough to marry her."

"I was an idiot."

She smiled. "Aren't we all?"

He shot her a narrow-eyed look. "At least Ted managed to behave most of the time you were married."

"I'm not so sure about that anymore."

Huh. He'd suspected that, but didn't know Rachel did. And dragging Ted's sleazy behavior into this to avoid her questions was hitting below the belt. Besides, she was just going to stand there and shoot back one-liners for every reason he gave to stay away from Cara. Rachel wouldn't see things the way he did, regardless of what Cara might say now. And for him, it wouldn't change anything. He was convinced that if Jack had been living with him and not Cara, he would still be alive today. Which was small comfort. No comfort.

"What could it hurt to try?" Rachel said, relentless now that she had him against the ropes.

Her eyes were soft and full of understanding, silently urging. It made him think of escape again, and though he didn't move, he wanted to. She had an uncanny way of reaching something inside him, which probably accounted for her success as a psychologist. No, damn it, she hadn't been insightful with Jack, he reminded himself. Just the opposite. She'd been as blind as Cara, when you got right down to it.

"And think of the payoff if she is able to shed some light," Rachel said, driving home one more point. "You've tortured yourself for years, being in the dark. You may learn something that—"

"For God's sake, Rachel!"

"I'm sorry," she said instantly. "I can see that it's still too difficult for you to—"

"No. No," he said, blowing out a defeated sigh. "It's logical. It makes perfect sense. It's just—" He stared at his shoes for a beat or two, then looked at her. "I'm the one who should apologize," he said. "I know you mean well. I'm sorry." Almost choking on the words. Unfamiliar words. He didn't remember the last time he'd said them. Living as he did, avoiding anything resembling intimacy, he didn't ever have to apologize. To anybody.

"Then just think about it, that's all I'm suggesting."

He gave a reluctant laugh, watching her load up the tray. "Why do I get the feeling that I won the argument but lost the battle?" he mused.

"This is not a battle, Cam," she said, adding the picante to the tray. "Aren't we both working toward the same goal? Don't we both want to prevent another tragedy at school?" Sensing the question was rhetorical, Cam was silent. "So, to get back to my original question," she said, "you picked up nothing from Jack to make you think something might have been going on in Monk's organization?"

"Actually, there was something and he wanted to talk about it. He phoned me the night he…died." He took the loaded tray from her and they walked to the door. "I don't know what was on his mind, except that he said it was something about the team and 'some trouble.' Those were his exact words. I went to see Monk Tyson after the funeral, but he claimed to be clueless. No trouble of any kind with his kids, he assured me."

"I would hardly expect him to admit to trouble," Rachel said dryly. "He's going to hang on to his little kingdom until he's offered something bigger and better."

"He appears very loyal to Rose Hill," Cam said. "I'm told he's been offered opportunities to go to bigger, more visible schools where the money is considerably more, but has turned them down."

Rachel frowned. "That really surprises me. It's odd, if true. A bigger school with higher visibility means more celebrity and Monk thrives on that. He's unmarried, so there's no wife and kids who might object to being uprooted. In fact, I hardly ever see him in a social setting unless it relates to something going on at school. On the other hand, I know nothing about his private life. Or if he even has a life separate from Rose Hill's sports program."

"Enough about Monk Tyson." Cam motioned her to open the door, eager to get with other people before she could zero in on him again. "Let's go check if your friends need help with those shelves."

Twelve

Nick hit the back door in a rush of male teenage energy, smelling like popcorn and a potpourri of expensive men's cologne. "Hey, didn't I tell you the shelves would be a piece of cake, Mom? Me and Ward couldn't do it any better."

"Then you can do it next time," Rachel said, giving him a whack on his arm. Then, making a big thing of the way he smelled, she backed up, waving a hand back and forth in front of her face. "Been at the cologne counter in Dillard's, right?"

"It was Kristin," Nick said, snagging a banana from a bowl of fruit on his way to the fridge. Noticing Cam propped on a bar stool, he grinned with real welcome. Then, something about the situation struck him. They both looked kinda…funny. Was Cam interested in his mom…that way? If so, he was wasting his time. Mom was totally deaf, dumb and blind to that stuff, in Nick's opinion. Clueless. Her every thought these days was about how to straighten out their lives since his dad had split.

"Nick. How's it hangin'?"

"Loose, very loose."

"Glad to hear it." Nick finished the banana, tossed the peel overhand into the trash and studied the contents of the fridge. Spotting leftover pizza, he grabbed the box. Nothing better than leftover pizza except a fresh, hot one. "Kristin loves this cologne by Ralph Lauren," he said, chomping into a cheesy wedge. "You can get it for girls or guys."

"So you tested that one and a few others," Rachel guessed.

"Yeah, but we learned in bio that the human nose can only distinguish between about four different smells at once, even though Kristin said no way, she didn't believe it. So then Ward volunteered to be her guinea pig, which surprised me. He's been kinda moody lately, but he let Kristin squirt him down pretty good, too. He's hot for Kristin, but he denies it." He finished a wedge of pizza and started in on another. "Anyway, between us, we musta tested about ten flavors." He pulled at his sweatshirt with two fingers, wrinkling his nose. "I guess I need a shower."

"I guess you do," Rachel said, stopping him midstride as he moved past her carrying the pizza box. "And don't take that to your room, buddy-boy. Finish it here in the kitchen or forget it."

"Aw, Mom, those are your rules, not Gran's. She knows I'm not gonna leave anything lying around for the roaches."

"That's true, because no food is leaving this kitchen, Nicholas."

Nick, with his eyebrows raised in mock alarm, looked at Cam. "Uh-oh, when Mom goes into three-syllable mode, look out."

Cam slipped off the stool. "What's the rule for eating in the garage?"

"There's not one, as far as I know." Nick chewed noisily on his way back to the fridge for a can of soda. "Yet."

"Close your mouth when you chew," his mother ordered.

"How 'bout we go out there and finish the job your mom's friends started," Cam suggested as Nick popped the top on a root beer. "They're assembled and standing, but they still need to be fastened to the wall. You don't want to take a chance they'll topple over once they're loaded."

"Nobody mentioned that possibility!" Rachel said. She tossed her dish towel down, ready to go out in the garage and, Nick assumed, use her body, if necessary, to hold the shelves in place. But Cam stopped her before she got to the door.

"Nick and I can take care of it, Rachel. You've been on the go most of the day. Why don't you pour yourself a glass of wine, crank up a good CD and relax for a few minutes?"

Nick recognized the look on his mother's face. It was her I-know-something's-up-but-not-exactly-what-but-just-give-me-a-minute expression. Not as simple as trying to read Cam, Nick thought, making a stab at it, anyway, with a sharp study of the man's face. For some reason, Cam wanted him outside, away from his mom. With a shrug, he snagged the last piece of pizza, stuffed the box in the trash and followed the man outside.

"Let's walk across to my place," Cam said. "I've got some brackets that'll work to secure the shelves to the wall, plus it'll go easier with my power drill."

"Okay," Nick said, unable to read anything in his profile. Cam was pretty good at keeping a poker face.

They trudged in silence across the space that separated the two properties. Nick had always liked Cam's house, even though it was old-fashioned. Something about it was really interesting. Like it had history. It suited Cam, like they both had a sort of dark streak, him and his house.

"I'm thinking of putting up a basketball hoop," Cam said, indicating a space in the center of the garage's pitched roof.

"Cool," Nick said. "We had one at our other house. I miss it."

"I bet. So once I get it up, feel free to use it. With your friends."

"Hey, that's—well, thanks."

Cam went into his garage and took a sturdy black case from a shelf. The power drill, Nick guessed. Next, he opened a drawer in a big wood cabinet, rummaged around until he found the brackets and handed them over to Nick. "Here, you carry these while I see if I can find screws the right size. They should be here somewhere." Another neat little cubbyhole thing mounted to the wall held about a dozen small drawers, each one labeled with screws, bolts, nails, washers. The guy was organized. Must come with his type of work. Nick didn't see how anybody could string together all the facts in a real murder case, taking about five hundred pages to do it and have it make any sense…unless you were real organized, like inside-your-head organized. He watched Cam sort through the screws he'd need for fixing the brackets in place.

"This is a really cool workshop," he said.

"When I lived in New York, I had so few tools that one metal box held everything I owned and still fit under the kitchen sink with room to spare." Cam closed the drawer and put the screws in the pocket of his jeans. "When I decided to move back here, the house needed a lot of repairs. I decided to do it myself. Turned out, I liked it so much that—although I didn't plan it—it turned into a restoration of the original house." He gave a chuckle. "It's been, as they say, a learning experience. For instance, to replace the stained glass and do it myself from scratch, I had to take a course."

Nick moved to a piece of machinery across the floor. "This is a lathe, isn't it?"

"Yeah. I'm working on replacement dowels for the banisters, which requires a lathe. That, I didn't have to take a class to do." He smiled. "I bought a how-to video."

Nick stroked a piece of wood sanded as smooth as satin. "This is really neat."

Cam smiled. "I think so now, but when I was your age, all I knew about carpentry I learned in a year of wood shop in high school." He stood looking around at the collection of machinery and projects in progress. "It's a challenge, restoring the house and making things look the way they did almost a century ago. Fortunately, I don't have to work to a schedule, just do what comes up when it comes up."

"It's a great old house," Nick said. "Maybe I could lend a hand sometimes, that is, if you need a helper. Pay you back for installing the shelves for my mom, me taking off like I did and going to the mall.''

''Actually, Marta and Pete installed the shelves.''

''Pete? Who's Pete?''

''According to your mom, he's Marta's ex-fiancé.''

Nick's jaw dropped. ''Whoa, *that* Pete. Man, as long as I can remember, I've heard Ms. Marta rant and rave about what a jerk he was! How'd it happen that he was here?''

''Your mother ran into him at Home Depot today while you were getting the cart.''

''And she invited him over?''

''I think he just showed up.''

''And Ms. Marta didn't shoot him?''

Smiling, Cam brushed a few wood shavings into the trash. ''No, but she didn't seem thrilled, either.'' And if Nick was reading him right, neither did Cam.

Man, you never could tell about grown-ups. Well, women. Nick studied the brackets in his hand, thinking it was pretty unlikely that Pete, the ex-fiancé, would have been invited to the house under any circumstances, considering Ms. Marta's bad attitude all these years. ''I guess this means I owe him, too.''

Cam went to an apartment-size fridge and took out two canned drinks. ''You don't owe either one of us, but I'll take you up on your offer to help and be glad of it. I'm going to lay some flooring in the attic soon and I could use help getting the sheets of plywood up those stairs. In fact, if you want to mention it to Ward, I could use both of you.'' He tossed a can to Nick and popped open his own. ''The pay's nothing to brag about, but it beats minimum wage.''

''Um, great. Wow. Just let us know what time.'' So the reason for wanting to get him out of range of his mom was to offer him a job? Uh-uh, the way Cam was studying the top of that can, he still had something on his mind.

''I'll call or tell your mom,'' he said, after tasting the soda. Definitely something else on his mind. ''Cool.''

Cam propped an elbow on the tool cabinet. "How're things going for you at school?"

"You mean, did I have that talk with Coach Monk?"

"Did you?"

"Yeah." He bent and picked up a small wood chip. "To tell the truth, I made up some excuses like I had to take a makeup test and my mom was overloaded with moving and the divorce, plus my dad needed me for something—which was a crock, as you know."

"How did he take it?"

"Coach? Well, he didn't throw me off the team, which he could have. He told me to give it a while and when things ease off with my situation at home and stuff, he'd still find time to help me work out some kinks."

"Huh." Cam was noncommittal. "So, otherwise, how are things?"

Nick shrugged. "Okay. Same old, same old."

"Did Ward quit, too?"

"Uh-uh. He had some stuff to say when I told him I was backing off from the coach. Thinks I'm nuts. Told me he wasn't gonna toss away a chance to get into the big leagues like his brother, Jimbo, and Coach Tyson is the way to get there."

"What did you mean when you said Ward was kind of moody lately?"

Nick leaned back against a nearby sawhorse, thinking. With his eyes on the can, he frowned. "I don't know exactly, just that he used to be a lot more fun, not so...*moody* is the best word. He used to, you know, blow off stuff. Now he's real touchy. His temper's right out there. One minute he's okay, the next he's like, um, somebody set a match to him."

"And this is out of character for Ward?"

"Well, sure. He never used to be so...up and down."

Cam crossed his arms, balancing the can of soda on one bicep. "You think it has something to do with Monk's demands on him?" When Nick's frown deepened, thinking it over, Cam added, "Just because his brother excelled under Monk's coaching doesn't mean that Ward has the same gift. Maybe he's feeling pressure. Maybe it's too much pressure."

"I don't know. Ward was really thrilled when Coach Monk first told us he'd give us some special help and, like I said, way more than I was. I mean, I realized the significance of being chosen by The Man, but to Ward, it meant the chance to shine like Jimbo."

"Shine like his brother," Cam said, "or outshine his brother?"

"You guessed it. Outshine him. Which would be a surefire way of making his dad sit up and take notice. Finally."

Cam smiled. "Ward 'doesn't get no respect,' is that it?"

"Yeah, that's it. Most of the time he feels he's, like, a runner-up. Always comes in second to Jimbo."

"So, could it be that Monk isn't particularly pleased with how Ward's shaping up, which means his dad won't be impressed, either, and he'll continue to walk in Jimbo's shadow? Could that be what's making him moody?"

"If Ward's thinking that, he's nuts," Nick said, dismissing the notion. "He's lookin' great out there on the field."

"But you aren't with him all the time he's getting coached by Monk, are you?"

"Well…no." Nick frowned, making a stab at analyzing Ward's situation for the first time. "But to tell the truth, I don't think it's that. If Coach Monk was disappointed in Ward and how he's shaping up, The Man would let it be known. It's like he uses people who screw up to push everyone else to their maximum best. Makes 'em an example of where not to go."

"Nobody likes to be labeled a loser," Cam murmured.

"You got it." Nick drank some soda, trying to get a fix on Cam's interest in what was happening in the sports program at Rose Hill. He sensed it was related in some way to Cam's son who'd committed suicide.

"How about yourself, Nick? Have you ever felt as if something wasn't quite right in Monk's sports program? I mean, the overall program. Have you ever suspected that some of the athletes were overly pressured?''

"They're pressured, sure. You hear people say winning's not everything, it's how you play the game, right?'' Nick gave a short laugh and rolled his eyes. "Bullshit. Winning is all it's about.''

"Well, have you ever sensed anything like…say, fear on the part of the athletes?''

This time, Nick's laugh was genuine. "Yeah. Coach will climb their rear ends if he doesn't get a hundred and ten percent.''

"Everything you've said applies to any athletic program and to most coaches,'' Cam said. He spotted a loose nail on the garage floor and bent to pick it up. "I'm not hearing anything unusual. Are you saying you backed away from Tyson's teaching because you don't want to look as if you're receiving special favors?''

"Yeah, mostly that.''

Cam gave him a quick look. "There's something else?''

"I sometimes do get a feeling that there's an air, you know, a kind of thing that's happening, but not out in the open—'' He broke off, shaking his head. "That sounds pretty goofy, like some of the stuff John Edward 'sees'—'' he used his fingers as quotes "—on his TV program, doesn't it?''

"Such as?''

"Well, Coach is running a really competitive sports program. That might explain it. I don't know whether or not there's more pressure than you'd expect, considering,'' he said, back to staring at his drink. "Maybe it's 'out of the ordinary,' like you say, maybe not. Maybe it's that they're taking steroids. Wouldn't be a big surprise, you gotta know that.'' He thought of Ferdy and B.J. He'd bet his new cleats that they'd been popping steroids like candy this season. "They say steroids make you act all kinds of weird ways,'' he told Cam. "Is that what you were getting at?''

"I don't know what I'm getting at, Nick. Yet.'' He raised

his drink and drained what was left in the can. "Tell me about Jimbo, Ward's brother."

"He's cool. Really cool. A great athlete. Smart, too. He's gonna be a lawyer after his baseball career is over."

"Does he ever reminisce about his days here at Rose Hill High?"

"Not when I've been around, but with Ward, maybe."

"Have you ever heard him mention my son, Jack?"

Jeez. Nick found it tough to hold the man's gaze. "No, sir. Never."

"Don't you think that's odd, seeing they were best friends?"

"Yeah, I even mentioned it to Ward once, but he brushed it off. Said with Jack…you know, gone now, Jimbo sort of closed down on that. He took it real hard when Jack…when he was told about Jack."

Cam nodded, just a quick dip of his head. Nick had a feeling that talking about Jack was something he didn't do often, but he was on some kind of mission that forced him to go there. As Cam shut down his shop and turned off lights, Nick pushed up from the sawhorse, tossed his drink can and headed with him out of the garage. Monday, at school, he was gonna see if he could pick up on anything…weird. With Cam's questions bouncing around in his head, his own suspicions didn't feel so off-the-wall. He'd had a funny feeling lately, but nothing definite enough to put a label on. So, except for backing off the special coaching, he'd ignored it. Now, after talking with Cam, he was thinking his instincts might not be so off-the-wall after all. Wouldn't hurt to keep his eyes and ears open. See what turned up. Whatever, he was positive that Cam, for one, did think something was going on.

What the heck could it be?

Rachel heard the whine of a power drill coming from the garage and guessed that Nick and Cam were back, doing whatever else was necessary to secure the shelves to the wall.

She thought about going out and pretending she could be of some help, but short of holding a screwdriver and passing it to whichever of them needed it—or fetching beer or soda— she would be useless. Instead, she took another sip of wine, settled back against the soft cushions and continued to indulge herself by surfing the TV channels. She almost never had an opportunity to watch what she preferred. Even on the rare times when she had a couple of hours to kill, she usually gave in to Kendy or Nick or her mother, all of whom seemed to care more than she did about what was on the tube. Now, stretched out on the sofa with her wineglass balanced on her tummy, she found the cooking channel and watched Emeril go about concocting a really incredible meat loaf, of all things.

Keeping the volume low, she could hear Nick and Cam in conversation. Nick had never been as big a chatterbox as Kendall, but in the company of Cam, he became almost gabby. And he laughed, for which she was profoundly thankful. He'd had little to laugh about since his father left. Cam's low chuckles were less frequent, but the two seemed to be enjoying each other. It should be Ted out there with Nick, she thought, but after the scene with Francine, she feared his spotty interest in Nick and Kendy might sputter out altogether.

Losing interest in Emeril's meat loaf, she muted the sound altogether and took a sip of wine. Even before Ted had chosen to abandon his family, he'd shown little interest in spending time with his children. She'd bought into his excuse that, as a physician, he had precious little free time, overlooking the fact that when he did manage time off, he usually spent it doing something apart from his family. But had she ever really taken Ted to task over it? It was troubling to look back and see that she'd been as passive about his neglect of Nick and Kendy as she'd been about his neglect of her. Seeing that now, it shouldn't be a surprise that he viewed her passivity as disinterest. As boredom. Taking it one step further, was it so surprising that he'd looked around for someone who *did* care? Had Francine's admiration felt as good to Ted as Cam's support felt to her?

"Emeril has finally stooped to making meat loaf?"

"Oh!" Startled, she made a grab for the wine before it tipped over. Cam stood in the doorway, palms tucked in the back pockets of his jeans. The sweatshirt wasn't as neat as it had been earlier today, so how was it that looking scruffy and rumpled only made him seem more appealing? Thinking it brought her up straight on the sofa. Thoughts like *that* could lead to more dangerous ones.

"Don't get up," he said, crossing the room. "I'm not staying. I just wanted to—"

"Would you like something? Beer? Some wine?" Flustered, she fumbled for the remote and turned the TV off.

"No, thanks."

"I didn't realize you and Nick were done out there." Dinah's den was not as roomy as the one in the house she'd shared with Ted, and Cam, well above six feet, broad-shouldered and so...male, seemed to fill it. Especially from her vantage point looking up at him from the sofa. And she'd slipped her shoes off, too, which made her feel even more rattled. Where the heck were they?

Cam scooped them out from beneath the ottoman. "It was just a matter of screwing a few brackets into the wall. It didn't take long."

"Well, thanks for doing it, just the same," she said, and bent over to slip her shoes on. Glancing beyond him to the kitchen, she saw no sign of her son. "What happened to Nick?"

He smiled. "I think he's taking a shower."

"And not before he needed it." Rachel reached for a cushion and curled herself into the corner of the sofa. "Well, don't keep me waiting. What did he tell you?"

"Not much other than a vague feeling that something's not right, almost the same thing you said yourself."

"That's all? Nothing he's seen, nothing he's been told?"

"He's reluctant to believe anything negative about the

sports program because it means so much to him. Same thing for the coach, I think.''

''He and Ward both have their hearts set on being part of Monk's core elite. I wish he had the same burning ambition to do well in class.''

''Dissecting frogs versus the challenge of playing ball? No contest, Mom.'' He rose from the ottoman and crossed the den, checking the kitchen to see that Nick hadn't returned, then came back. ''I know when you counsel those kids that you're bound by the rules of your profession to keep everything confidential and I respect that. So, I hope this doesn't violate your code of ethics, but I need to ask. Is Ward the boy you mentioned earlier today, the boy you're concerned about?''

She sat up, laying the cushion aside. ''No, he's not. Why do you ask?''

''Nick mentioned the way Ward has changed lately. Says he's moody, has a hair-trigger temper now and, according to Nick, that's out of character. Plus, I don't think Nick would have mentioned Ward in that context if the changes hadn't been pretty noticeable.''

''Funny you should mention Ward,'' Rachel said, frowning. She rose quickly from the sofa and set her wineglass on the coffee table. ''I saw him at the gym when I went to see Monk. He was red-faced and obviously uncomfortable that I caught him.''

''Why? What was going on?''

''He was supposed to be in class. Of course, it was Monk who'd pulled him out of class, which made it legitimate, if not wise. Ward said Monk was a very busy guy and it was plain that he'd convinced him—and maybe Nick as well— that their 'special coaching' took precedence over class work.''

''It's irrelevant as far as Nick is concerned. One thing I did learn. He found the courage to tell Tyson thanks, but no thanks. He won't be on the receiving end of special favors from the coach. It took a lot of guts, Rachel.''

"Yes, it did. And I'm not sure he would have been able to do it if you hadn't encouraged him. So, thanks."

He shrugged off her thanks. "I think I'll have a talk with Monk Tyson myself," he told her. "See if I pick up any of those vibes you and Nick seem to feel. If something is going on, I'm not going to sit on my hands and wait until we have another tragedy. And I promise to see you afterward and fill you in."

"I want to know everything, no matter how trivial it may seem," Rachel said. "Promise me."

"You have my word on it."

She pushed her hair back from her face, knowing he could see that she was upset. "This is very…troubling, isn't it, Cam?"

He skimmed her face with eyes that echoed her concern. "Yeah. But we may be seeing trouble where there is none." His gaze drifted to the window where dusk had now fallen. Outside, the sights and sounds of evening were coming alive. The neighborhood, almost picturesque in its simplicity and innocence, was settling in for the night. If there was evil, it was well hidden.

Cam glanced at her wineglass. "I think I will have some of that wine, if it's not too late."

"Not at all." She found herself smiling as she went to get it. She wasn't sure why she'd been so flustered when he'd first appeared, except that she'd been intensely aware of Cam ever since that impulsive hug in his kitchen. She told herself her reaction was perfectly understandable, considering she hadn't been in the arms of any man except Ted for eighteen years, but still—

Carrying both her wineglass, which she'd replenished, and his, she made her way back to the den and handed it over. But his smile, she noticed now, had faded away. "What's the matter?" she asked, handing him the wine.

"Nothing, just the opposite. I was thinking.…" Running a hand over the back of his neck, he looked down at his feet. She could see the tension in him and wondered if there was something more he'd learned from Nick and it was so awful he needed a drink to tell her. "You were right, what you said in the kitchen."

"The kitchen?" She looked at him blankly.

"Yeah, this afternoon. About Cara."

"Oh, that." She nodded, feeling relief and a little surprise. Talking about his ex-wife had been her idea, not Cam's, and he'd hated it. She couldn't imagine why he'd bring it up again.

"I've decided to try seeing her."

She smiled, thinking he looked as if he'd rather drink turpentine. "I think that's a great idea."

He hooked a thumb in the belt loop of his jeans and looked immeasurably more relaxed. "Yeah, it's possible that once she sees it's me, she'll refuse to tell me anything…if she'll even hear me out. Our divorce wasn't exactly amicable."

"Is there such a thing?"

"Probably not." He looked as if he'd figured that out long ago. "I reacted pretty viscerally when I found out she was having an affair. I was insulted, humiliated and mad as hell. I went through all the stages you psychologists talk about and then some. I didn't give a damn that she and that particular guy broke up even before our divorce was final and she probably would have agreed to try to fix whatever was wrong in our marriage. But no, I was too pissed off to feel anything except righteous rage. I just wanted her out of my life." He met her eyes as if he expected her to be shocked or disgusted. "I don't think anything she could have done at that point would have been enough to change my mind."

"Infidelity is a horrendous problem to overcome in a marriage."

He smiled then, somewhat. "Is that the psychologist talking or the voice of experience?"

She took a sip of wine. "Both. And I don't think anything Ted could do or say at this point would be enough to make me change my mind, either. I'm still just so damn mad at him for doing this."

"Just don't let your anger blind you to the needs of your kids, Rachel. That's where Cara and I screwed up."

She searched his face, sensing more than words of wisdom from someone who'd been there and done that. "Why? Did Nick tell you something else that I should know?"

"No, nothing. This isn't about Nick, it's about me and my awkward attempt to share what I did wrong." He glanced at the sofa. "Can we sit down?"

"Yes, of course." She went over and did exactly that, but he sat on the edge of the ottoman facing her, his wineglass dangling between his knees.

"I guess I'm just getting around to admitting that while I was nursing my pride, I lost sight of the fact that I wasn't the only one who was hurt."

"Jack," she guessed, pleased to see that he appeared to be working his way out of a long period of denial.

"Yeah." He studied the wine. "This business with Monk's athletes has me thinking a lot about my son." His mouth went soft with sadness. "Which is something I've avoided since he...since I lost him."

"I can only imagine how hard it would be for me, God forbid," she said gently.

"I don't know if Cara can tell me anything to shed any light on what might have been going on with Jack, but I'm going to give it a shot."

"Good for you."

"I was obsessed with getting answers when it first happened," he said, again with his gaze fixed on the wine in his hand. "But after a while and so many dead ends, my initial belief that there was something more to Jack's death than a simple suicide faded."

"That's understandable when everybody was convinced that it was a simple suicide."

He looked up then, searching her face. "Were you convinced? And it won't offend me to hear it if you were." His lips tilted in a smile so brief it almost wasn't there. "I won't go for your throat again, I promise."

She hesitated, her thoughts going back to that time. She'd felt personal failure when Jack died. And absolute shock. So much so, that she'd searched diligently for some other explanation. Why? Like Cam, had she, in the back of her mind, doubted conventional wisdom? "I don't think I was convinced it was suicide," she said slowly, thoughtfully, "but I wasn't entirely certain it wasn't." She looked into his eyes. "Does that make any sense?"

"Yeah, it does. You had doubts, how could you not? As you just said, everybody thought it was a simple suicide." Then he added with a bitter twist of his mouth, "As if there is ever a simple suicide."

"If I'd truly accepted the cause of death after searching my files and poring over and over the notes of my sessions with Jack, I would have stopped there, wouldn't I? Instead, I bugged Marta, who'd taught him honors English, I interviewed every one of his other teachers—more than once—I questioned his teammates, I grilled Monk Tyson, really pushed him. I just wouldn't let it go."

"So, what did Monk say?"

"The same thing he told you. Stop torturing yourself, get over it. You can't save 'em all." She looked disgusted. "He was his usual sensitive self."

"Gosh, that kind of sensitivity really moves me," Cam said sarcastically.

"Like you," Rachel said with a look of regret, "I finally gave up."

To Rachel's surprise, he suddenly put out a hand and cupped her cheek. "Don't look so sad. It's never too late."

She felt her throat go tight. She was supposed to find words to comfort him, and instead he was having to console her. "I'm going to go back and try again," she told him huskily, resisting the urge to capture the warmth of his hand.

"Me, too." He stood up and handed his empty glass to her. "Thanks for the wine and the…other stuff. I do need to talk to Cara."

"We shrinks are supposed to listen, not advise. But you're welcome."

"I can see myself out," he told her, already going toward the door. But once he had it opened, he turned back. "I think I may have said this before, but here it is again. Ted Forrester is a damn fool."

Thirteen

Monday dawned cold and wet. Overnight, Mother Nature had stirred up a storm that dumped four inches of rain after spawning two tornadoes just north of Rose Hill. Taking the weather as a sign, Cam told himself the visit with his ex-wife would probably be a complete and total washout. He'd then spent all day Sunday thinking up excuses why he shouldn't go, but in the end, he'd known it was the right thing to do. And he owed it to Jack.

His voice, he could tell, had taken Cara completely by surprise. Who could blame her, as it had been five years ago at Jack's funeral since they'd last spoken? After a polite remark or two about her health and the weather, which had been gearing up even then, he'd told her there was something he'd like to discuss with her…at her convenience, of course. He guessed it was sheer curiosity more than anything else that made her agree. He had noted with some surprise that there had been no animosity in her tone.

Cara had moved to Fort Worth after her marriage to Rosetti, and from the directions she'd given Cameron the night before, he'd estimated an hour-and-a-half drive from Rose Hill. The neighborhood, he thought now, looking it over as he went up the sidewalk to her front door, was nice. It was not the most exclusive area of Fort Worth, but it was one of those neighborhoods with character, charm and trees. Cara's house was a cottage that, to Cam's admitted unknowledgeable eye, appeared to date back to the thirties. Quaint, almost a dollhouse, it looked just right in the neighborhood. If there was anything special about it, it was in the landscaping. There was a look that reminded him of Dinah's passion. Someone had an interest in gardening. If it was Cara, he'd never have guessed it, but gardening as a hobby would have been impractical living as they had in a New York apartment. Maybe it was Rosetti. Not that Cameron would know. Rosetti, as an individual, was then and still was an unknown entity. At the time of Cam's divorce from Cara, the division of their assets had been a complex, legal maze that her lawyer had negotiated to her benefit. Cam hadn't objected, knowing she was moving back to Texas and taking Jack with her. Looking at it in a practical sense, he hadn't wanted Jack to lack for anything. Afterward, when Jack was gone, nothing about Cara mattered.

A door with intricately worked leaded panes enhanced the entrance to the house. He'd barely touched the old-fashioned doorbell when he saw movement deep inside. Someone approached, but with the distortion of the glass, it was hard to tell whether it was Cara or not until the door opened.

It was. A very pregnant Cara.

"Hello, Cam."

"Cara. You're looking—"

She smiled. "Fat?"

Happy. She looked awkward and bloated and very happy. He managed to keep the shock off his face and glanced at her enormous belly. "Do we have time for this or are you on your way to the hospital?"

"I'm late—a week, according to the doctor," she said, cradling herself with both hands. "And no such luck that it'll be today, but don't I wish." She hesitated, showing some unease as her smile slipped a bit. "Come in, Cam. Please."

"Thanks." He stepped over the threshold, and while she closed the door behind him, took a look about. Like the outside of the house, inside was very appealing in a homey, eclectic mixture kind of way. He was having trouble fitting the woman he'd been married to into this house and, above all, this situation.

"Let's have coffee in the breakfast room," Cara said. "It's made just the way you like it. I'm betting you haven't changed in that. Dark roast, black and straight, right?"

"Right." From the hall, they went through a dining room and entered a light and airy kitchen, fully modernized. True to its origins, a breakfast nook was nestled in a bay window area looking out on to a stunningly landscaped backyard. She led him there and he took the chair she indicated. Coffee mugs were already in place on two flowery place mats. She took a decanter from a Williams-Sonoma machine and poured coffee into Cam's mug. It was hot and fragrant and—she was right—just the way he liked it.

"Herbal tea for me," she said, wrinkling her nose. "I'm counting the days until I can once again enjoy a decent cup of coffee." With the mug of tea cupped in her hands, she slipped into the chair opposite him. "Coffee okay?"

"It's fine. Perfect."

She smiled. "Good."

Cam was still trying to get his bearings. He didn't know what he'd expected from Cara, but it wasn't this. He'd spent the last five years infuriated with her, bitterly resenting her preoccupation with Rosetti while Jack's mental state deteriorated unnoticed. Now she was remarried, living a normal life in a cute little neighborhood—not quite suburbia—and having another baby to replace Jack.

"Interesting place you've got here," he said, adding, "especially the landscaping."

"Thanks." She beamed. That was the only word to describe her expression when she looked out at yellow, red and orange flowers framing a bubbling fountain in a riot of color. "One of the disadvantages of being at this stage of my pregnancy is that I can't play in the dirt." She paused, patting her stomach. "I suppose I could try, but once on my hands and knees, how would I get upright again?"

"I never knew you were interested in gardening." *Or that you had a sense of humor.*

"I live for gardening, Cam," she said, still smiling. "But

don't look so surprised. I didn't know it myself until I married Anthony. He's a horticulturist, and once he introduced me to the joys of gardening, we began to fight over who gets which part of the property to tend.''

We began to fight. That he could understand, as he and Cara had spent most of their marriage in a tug-of-war. Who was this happily contented woman? ''A horticulturist,'' he said, playing for time to climb out of the rabbit hole.

''He teaches. He's a college professor.''

''I guess I didn't know that,'' Cam said.

''How are things with you?'' she said, her tone and expression gentling.

''Okay, I guess.'' He studied the coffee in his mug before looking up at her. ''I'm living in my parents' house in Rose Hill.''

''I know. And it's a lovely place. I always thought it needed someone who'd love it and restore it.''

He managed a laugh. ''Well, I guess that's me. It was in sad shape at first, but I've been doing some of the repairs myself.''

''You?'' Her eyebrows rose at his nod. ''Well, now you've surprised me.''

''Then we're even.''

''I know. I must seem almost like a stranger,'' she said, and impulsively touched the back of his hand. ''The person I am now is nothing like the person you knew, Cam. I know I hurt you. I wish I could go back, do things differently.''

''Was it losing Jack that changed you?''

She nodded, again tasting her tea with quiet contentment. ''And finding Anthony.''

He leaned back, nursing his coffee and studying her almost as he would a puzzling element in one of the criminal cases he researched. It was difficult to find a hint of the sleek and sophisticated woman he'd met and married in New York in this earthy Cara who contemplated petunias and drank herbal tea. Even when pregnant with Jack, she'd watched her diet so rigidly that by the time she'd given birth, she'd gained only about sixteen pounds.

"What did you want to talk to me about, Cam?"

He hesitated, finding it difficult, in the face of such obvious joy, to broach a subject that was sure to be painful. Somehow, Cara had managed to put together a new life, complete with husband, home and plans for a new baby. He hitched his chin toward the enormous mound of her abdomen. "What's the baby, boy or girl?"

Her expression grew tender. "We don't know," she said, again spreading both hands over her precious cargo, then added, "Our choice. But whatever it is will be just fine since I never expected to be a mother again. After Jack died, I thought that part of me had died, too." Her gaze drifted to the flowers around the fountain. "You should never say never."

"Anthony again?" he guessed.

She gave him a sideways look softened with a smile. "Who else?"

Cameron studied her thoughtfully for a moment, wondering whether or not at this stage of her pregnancy it would be risky to ask her to think back to a time that had to be the darkest in her life. "I came over to ask you some questions about Jack, Cara. But I don't want to do anything that might cause harm at this stage in your pregnancy."

"What kind of questions?"

"I haven't wanted to think about how Jack died or what might have been going on to push him to do what he did. When it happened, I was looking to hang the blame somewhere. I didn't leave any stone unturned trying to get a fix on *why*." He got up and went to the window, keeping his back to her. His next words were spoken not so much to Cara as to himself. "Why would a kid with everything going for him do something like…he did without giving a hint that he was so close to the edge?"

"Oh, Lord, you don't know how many times I've asked myself that question," Cara replied. "There is no answer."

He turned to look at her. "There has to be an answer. I didn't find anything five years ago, but I can't accept that now. That's why I wanted to talk to you. He must have given some indication that something was bothering him."

"Only the usual. He was fifteen. He was moody and irritable. I didn't dream his behavior meant anything more than the teenage ups and downs all kids feel." Her hands spread wide over her abdomen as if protecting this child. "Believe me, I've racked my brain trying to find a clue I might have overlooked. I've agonized over being blind to what was going on with Jack because I was distracted by what was going on with Anthony and me. Still—I swear to God, Cam—I can think of nothing out of the ordinary."

"What was he talking about at the time? That should give us a clue."

"What else? Sports in general. Baseball in particular. He'd poured his heart and soul into making the team, even though I don't think it was as wonderful as he thought it would be after he was in."

"Why do you say that?"

She shrugged. "Just a feeling. When I tried to get him to talk about it, he was evasive and I put it down to a boy's reluctance to talk male stuff with his mom. It was frustrating, but I consoled myself by knowing he had a straight line to you and anything he was hesitant about saying to me, he could say to you. As for admitting to me that anything was wrong, no, he never did." Her brows knitted as she thought back. "I remember thinking that if he was having trouble adjusting, why was it after he'd made it through the hard part. We'd moved from New York, he'd entered a new school, a new world, realistically speaking. Then in a relatively short time, he'd been accepted. Which was not an easy thing, coming to Texas from New York."

"It's never easy being the new kid on the block, even if you move from one part of town to another," Cam said.

She nodded, agreeing. "At the time, I was convinced that

getting involved in sports made the transition somewhat easier.''

Cam remembered how impressed Jack had been with the school's reputation in sports even before he enrolled. It had made the bitter pill of separation a little easier to swallow for both of them, or so Cam had believed at the time. Now he wondered if he'd seen just what he wanted to see to keep from having to disrupt his own life and career.

''It took all of that first year and the entire fall semester of the second before he knew for sure that he was in,'' Cara said. ''We rocked along for a while with him living and breathing baseball. But next thing I knew, he began to talk about quitting. He—''

''Quitting the team?'' Cam said sharply. Jack had never mentioned anything of the kind to him. ''He talked about giving up baseball?''

''Yes, but it was hard for me to take him seriously, considering how much he'd wanted to play. I thought it was more likely that he was getting static from other players, perhaps someone whose position was affected when the coach put him on varsity. Some of those kids had been playing together since they were six years old.'' Still thoughtful, she brought the mug of tea to her lips and took a little sip. ''He was such a super athlete, Cam, and the coach had the good sense to recognize it.''

''That was another question I wanted to ask,'' he told her, grimacing at the taste of cold coffee. ''What did he think of Coach Tyson?''

''Here, let me heat that up for you.'' She started to struggle to her feet, but Cam was already helping himself.

Leaning against the counter, he asked again, ''Was he tight with Tyson?''

''He certainly was at first. All he could talk about was the man's fabulous success rate and the possibility of breaking into the pro ranks if he could just get on the team. And of course, Monk Tyson had all the power there.''

''You said 'at first.' Did he change?''

She frowned. "I'm not sure. Tyson pushed the kids, made them work hard, and if Jack stopped gushing about how great he was, I suppose I assumed that he was reacting to the coach's truly demanding regimen. Sort of like army recruits react to their drill instructors. They 'hate' them—" she used her fingers as quotation marks "—but not really."

"What did you think about Tyson?"

"I only met him once briefly at a ball game. As you know, he was at the funeral, he and a whole cadre of athletes from Rose Hill High. Not that I remember much about that…or about the next few months, to tell the truth. In looking at the register a few months later, I saw their names, which is how I know they came."

"What about—"

"On the other hand—"

They both spoke at once and Cam held back what he was going to say. "On the other hand…what?"

"Now that you mention Monk Tyson, it reminds me of something Anthony said."

"What?"

"Well, being a teacher himself, he has some insight about these things, as you can imagine. I mean, maybe he's a bit more sensitive about the student-teacher relationship—or athletes in this case—than we parents are, so he looks a little deeper, you know?" Her face lit with enthusiasm. "He's such a good teacher, Cam. You should be here some night when his students show up for these impromptu sessions. It's just the most—"

"Cara." He stopped her. "I'm sure Anthony's a sterling fellow and a gifted teacher. I'm also delighted that you seem so happy now, but what did he say about Monk Tyson?"

"Oh. Of course. Sorry." She smiled, then when he blew out an impatient breath, rushed on. "He said that he'd known teachers like Tyson who wielded power and control with a ruthless disregard for any long-term damage that might result. He said that Tyson struck him as a bully and a tyrant. Then he said that Tyson probably needed the adulation of those young athletes as much as some men needed sex.''

Rachel was studying Jason Pate's file and wondering what tactic she could use to persuade the boy to come in and have another talk with her when, with a brief knock and no hesitation, Marta opened the door and stepped into her office.

"Is the doctor in?" she asked, leaning against the door, a can of cola in one hand and a fistful of mail in the other.

"What you see is what you get." Rachel closed the file as Marta moved away from the door and perched gingerly on the edge of a chair. "What's up?"

Marta shuffled through her mail, pretending to look at it. "Pete followed me back to my house Saturday night."

Rachel smiled. "I'm shocked."

"I refused to let him come inside."

"Why?"

"What kind of question is that? Have you forgotten? I broke off our engagement when I caught him having sex with that rookie sexpot, Tammy What's-her-name."

"Tanya was her name."

"Whatever." Marta rolled her eyes and tossed the mail on Rachel's desk. "We had set the date for our wedding. If he was getting cold feet, he should have told me before hopping in the sack with Tootsie."

"Tanya."

"So I told him to buzz off last night." She glared at the label on the cola can. "Maybe not in those exact words."

Rachel could imagine the exact words Marta had used. She had never dealt with her anger over Pete's betrayal, and even now, it took little provocation to flare up. Nor had she ever given him an opportunity to try to explain himself. Deny it, she might, but she was still emotionally vulnerable where Pete was concerned.

"I guess that's that, then," Rachel said, tapping her pen on Jason's file. "So you're rid of him now for another six years. Isn't that about how long it's been since you've seen him?''

''Five and a half. Remember, we bumped into him at the state fair that time.''

''Ah…'' Rachel nodded. It had been only a few months after the breakup and not a moment to remember. Marta's sense of betrayal at the time was still too new and her pride and heart were still wounded. She'd refused Pete's plea for a second chance outright. Rachel doodled a little with her pen. ''He phoned several times after that, as I recall. A less-determined man would have given up, it seems to me.''

''Yeah, you'd think so.'' She toyed with the can and dropped her gaze to her feet, where it remained until Rachel spoke again.

''Are you having second thoughts about closing the door in his face last night?''

''We never got as far as the door. He pulled up behind me in my driveway and that's where we talked.''

''Well, at least you talked, which is more than you did when it happened.''

''Uh-huh.''

Rachel waited and, when Marta still sat thinking, slipped her pen into a cup holding various other things, then took a tube of hand cream from her top drawer and squirted some into her palm. ''I don't know about you,'' she said, working the cream into her skin, ''but my hands have been so dry. I must use this stuff half a dozen times a day.''

''Yeah.'' Marta's gaze strayed to the window.

''It's the humidity,'' Rachel said, recapping the tube. ''Or lack thereof, I can never decide which.''

''Uh-huh.'' Marta's gaze was still fixed thoughtfully somewhere else.

''When it's high, my hair won't do a thing, and when it's low, it turns my skin into alligator hide, just like that TV commercial.'' Closing the drawer, she stole a glance at Marta's face. ''And speaking of pets, I'm considering getting Kendall an alligator. Don't you think she'll love that?''

"Uh-huh."

"Marta, hello-o…"

"What?" Marta blinked, looking at Rachel. "I'm sorry. I missed that."

"And that's because…" Rachel paused, waiting.

"Because I was awake until 4:00 a.m. last night," Marta said, "can you believe it? After I swore I'd never again waste one minute thinking about Pete Singletary. I worked like hell to kill every particle of emotion I ever felt for that man, Rachel, and it took three hours in your garage to stir it all up again." She got up, dodging the corner of the sofa that crowded the small office, then turned back to say, "But here's the craziest part of all. He didn't just get back in his truck and leave when I told him to. No, not Pete. Uh-uh. He's so damn…arrogant. He had the nerve to…to scold me, can you believe that?"

"It seems risky, considering."

"He said if I hadn't been so damn set against hearing him out…" She thumped her chest. "Me, stubborn! As if I was supposed to just let it slide that he'd got the hots for that…that rookie cop and brought her to his apartment and screwed her in the same bed where we—" Pacing now, words failing her, she dashed at the start of tears in her eyes. "Anyway, he said we should have talked it over. I should have let him try to explain. He said if I'd done that, maybe we could have worked it out. Maybe I could have f-forgiven him." Sniffing in disgust, she tossed the can in the trash. "As if all it took were a few sweet words and I'd say, oh, it's okay what you did, Pete, honey. I know men have needs." With a pained sound, she pressed both eyes with a thumb and forefinger. "As if any explanation could excuse what he did."

Rachel pulled open a lower drawer in her desk, plucked out a tissue and handed it over. "I guess you'll never know, will you?"

Marta looked up, blinking. "Know what?"

"Whether or not you would have been persuaded to give your relationship another chance if you'd talked it over."

"I don't see how. He had sex with another woman while he was engaged to me. That's something he could never explain away." When Rachel said nothing, Marta stood for a long moment, searching her face, then she sat down again. "Okay, I know that look. What? You agree with him? You think I overreacted?"

"If it's overreacting to do what most women do when this happens, then yes. We're only human," she added sincerely, recalling her own hurt and humiliation.

"But you think Pete's right, that I should have listened to a bunch of lame excuses."

"This isn't about what I think. You went with your feelings and ended your engagement. You're certainly not the only wronged woman who couldn't get beyond the pain of infidelity."

"You didn't answer my question, Rachel. Do you think Pete's right, that I was so busy feeling sorry for myself that I threw away something precious?"

"Is that what he said?"

Suddenly, Marta's shoulders drooped and she stared at her hands clasped between her knees. "Yeah."

"I've always wondered what he'd say if given the chance."

"Me, too, to tell the truth," Marta said. "Oh, not at first. At first I was so furious that I spent most of my fantasy life killing him or killing her. I made up elaborate scenes where I planned the dialogue with a lot more enthusiasm than I wrote the thesis for my doctorate. But later, when I wasn't so damn furious anymore, I wondered why. Was it retaliation in some way? Was job stress a factor? Was he spooked at the prospect of marriage itself?"

"Those questions and more have certainly been on my mind lately."

Marta looked up. "And—"

"From the way Ted talks about his relationship with Francine, she just makes him feel good, sexually and otherwise. She appeals to his ego." It was Rachel's turn to gaze thoughtfully outside. "Which begs the question. Why did he turn to another woman to make him feel good, or manly, or strong? Did I fail to do that? And doesn't that seem a rather shallow reason for terminating an eighteen-year marriage?" She turned back to Marta with a wry smile. "When I figure out the answer, I'll share it with you."

"When I broke it off with Pete, I know you thought I was too hasty," Marta said. "But was it so wrong of me to be scared of marrying him when I caught him cheating? Wasn't it better to know then rather than after we were married and possibly had children?"

"Well, I can tell you from personal experience that it definitely hurts then, too," Rachel said dryly.

"I'm sorry, Rachel!" she cried, clapping a hand over her mouth. "That was so stupid of me, totally insensitive. My God, here I am whining when you're the one with two children, an eighteen-year marriage down the tubes and a financial debacle to cope with."

"Don't forget, I'm homeless, too."

They both laughed, not entirely without humor. Then with a groan, Marta dropped her face in her hands. "Oh, why did Pete have to show up again? Nobody has ever been able to...to throw me into such a tizzy as that man."

"I wonder why that is," Rachel said, smiling softly.

"I don't love him anymore, Rachel, if that's what you're thinking. I got over that the day I caught him in bed with Tanya."

"If you say so."

"It's true!" After a second, she released a sigh. "But just for the sake of closure—" She wrinkled her nose. "I hate that word. I guess I should take your advice and have that talk with him."

"Talk to him only if you want to, Marta, not because I think you should. No one would argue that you had good reason to end your engagement, or at least to put your relationship on hold. It was a prudent and practical step to take in light of Pete's behavior. But I know how much in love you were—both of you. Maybe your relationship can't be saved, but there's something there still, or you wouldn't be so undone that he's suddenly reappeared in your life."

"He's not in my life and there is no relationship, Rachel. It's over!" Marta sliced the air with one hand. "It's kaput. Done. Finished."

"But you're still willing to have a conversation about it?"

She shrugged without replying, then after a minute, said in a defensive tone, "I know how it'll turn out."

Rachel's eyebrows went up. "Oh?"

"He set the whole thing up because he wanted me to break the engagement and he didn't have the balls to do it himself."

"So he slept with another woman just to make you mad so you'd call off your marriage and then he spends the next weeks—months—trying to explain his behavior and win you back? And he's still trying after six years?" Rachel made no effort to hide her view of that theory.

Marta was again up and pacing. "He was giving me all kinds of signs that he was getting cold feet. I suspected it then, but I just didn't want to deal with it."

"What kind of signs?"

"He knew I wasn't comfortable with him being a cop, but no amount of pleading on my part made any difference. Not only did he refuse to consider another line of work, but he volunteered for undercover duty. Do you know how dangerous that is?"

Rachel clasped her hands on top of Jason's file and waited. Down the hall, the bell signaling the beginning of the first lunch period rang. Both ignored it. Marta moved to the window and stood watching while students poured out of the building.

"My dad was killed on duty when he responded to a domestic crisis," she said quietly, without turning. "It doesn't have to be a robbery in progress or a hostage situation to put a law enforcement officer in peril. You can get killed on the most routine call, as I learned when I was nine years old. Some nutty guy was threatening his wife with a gun and he didn't appreciate a cop trying to talk him out of it. Boom! He shot my dad in the face.''

"I remember," Rachel murmured softly.

"I never planned to fall in love with a cop, but I thought I could handle it. Pete knew my concerns, but he volunteered for undercover duty, anyway, the single most hazardous job on the force.''

"You talked about this at the time?''

"I called it talking, he called it nagging." She turned away from the window, her mouth twisting with bitterness. "That's why this is so ironic, that he wants to talk now. It's about six years too late for that, in my book.''

Rachel toyed with a paperclip on Jason's file. "It's hard to square that kind of passion for law enforcement with his decision to be police chief in a town like Rose Hill.''

"He's probably given us only the tip of the iceberg," Marta said with a skeptical snort.

"Does that mean you think he was forced out of the Dallas PD?''

Again she shrugged. "It works for me.''

"No, it doesn't. He said he lobbied hard for this job. Bottom line is, he wants to be in Rose Hill now, Marta, and if you give him a chance to talk to you, he'll probably explain his change of heart.''

Marta rose from the chair and reached for the mail she'd dropped on Rachel's desk. "I still say there's more to the story than he's telling.''

"Maybe," Rachel said, tucking Jason's file in her top drawer and locking it. "There is one possibility you're overlooking.''

"What's that?''

"Six years ago, if Pete had suggested taking the job of police chief in Rose Hill, you wouldn't have had a problem with it, right?''

She shrugged. "I guess not. You don't dodge bullets working behind a desk."

"Exactly. And he would have been home every night by five-thirty." Rachel took her purse from a lower drawer, dropped her keys inside and stood up, ready for lunch. "Like I said, Marta, he's one very determined man."

Fourteen

Cameron parked his car at the gym and sat for a minute waiting for the ache in his chest to subside. He'd missed a lot of games during the time Jack had played for the Mustangs, but there had been a few—all too few, he admitted now—when he'd managed to work his schedule to coincide with Jack's. He recalled watching Jack execute a double play in the bottom of the ninth one cool April evening. His son had nailed the starting first-base position with that play, edging out another excellent athlete. The victory had been especially sweet, since the boy he'd defeated had been a Rose Hill native. Overcoming competition from kids who'd been playing with one another since grade school was only one of the many hurdles Jack had faced and overcome as the new kid on the block. But there had been something Jack faced that he couldn't handle. Cam got out of his car, determined to find out what it was.

Squinting in the late afternoon sun, he saw a group of athletes busy in a variety of activities on the field. Four batting cages were all occupied, the balls being pitched manually. Apparently Tyson hadn't yet persuaded the administration to spring for electronic machines. Across the field, The Man himself was personally supervising a dozen or so boys in vigorous calisthenics. As Tyson barked commands, Cam recalled Jack grumbling about the intensity of the coach's training regimen, but underneath he'd sensed his son's pride in handling a level of physical challenge that hadn't been present in his sports program in New York.

"No pain, no gain," Jack had said with a cocky grin when Cam commented on the hours he spent working out. That conversation had taken place the first year. In Jack's second year, Cam had been preoccupied with concerns regarding his career. Waning personal satisfaction in his work had driven him to go, as an author, in a different direction. Consequently, he'd changed publishers and hired a new agent, which had forced him to spend most of that year establishing himself. Was that when Jack had started to unravel? Cam wondered now. And why had none of the professionals at Rose Hill High noticed? If, as Cara said, Jack talked about giving up baseball, shouldn't Monk Tyson have noticed? And Rachel. She was obviously very concerned today over one particular boy showing some of the same signs as Jack. Why hadn't she noticed Jack when there was still time for her to do something?

Too many questions. And no answers. Yet.

Crossing the tarmac now, he walked to the chain-link fence that surrounded the practice field and kept at bay onlookers who might distract the athletes. They wore practice jerseys of motley designs, but after a minute, he managed to spot Nick in a group "staying loose" by passing the baseball around the bases. It took him a moment more to find Ward Rivers in a batting cage. Sensing an onlooker, Tyson turned and apparently recognized him. He blew a shrill whistle and yelled orders to one of the seniors to take over, then headed toward Cam.

"Mr. Ford, good to see you." Because of the fence, Tyson was unable to shake Cam's hand, but his expression was friendly. "What do you think of my boys?"

"They're looking good," Cam said, lifting a hand to wave at Nick.

Tyson caught the exchange and his eyes narrowed. "You know Nick Forrester?"

"His grandmother lives next door to me."

"Ah." Tyson nodded slowly. "I heard Rachel and the kids moved in with her. Too bad about the divorce."

"Yeah."

"You here to pick him up?"

"Nick? No. Actually, I'm here to talk to you—" he paused "—that is, if you've got a few minutes after practice. Or if that's not convenient, just tell me when."

"No problem. Today's fine. We're about done, anyway. I like to wrap it up by five. That's a long day for some of these kids, the ones whose parents let 'em stay up till midnight. No supervision. Of course, most of those types wash out of the program beginning of the season, but occasionally I'll get a kid motivated in spite of irresponsible parents." He gave a nod toward the batting cages. "Ferdy Jordan's a good example. Comes from a broken home, Dad's long gone, single mom trying to raise a coupla rug rats way younger than Ferdy with a different dad. Kid sets his own curfew which, you can imagine, isn't what you or I would recommend. But he wants to play ball and as long as he can handle the program, he's on the team."

"Uh-huh."

"Hey, I'm talking too much. Let me break this up and send these guys to the lockers and we'll talk in my office." He glanced at his watch. "I'll meet you there in ten...fifteen minutes."

"Thanks." Cam watched at the fence as, on command from Tyson, the athletes broke apart and headed for the door to the locker room. Nick and Ward fell into step together, but halfway there, Nick broke away and headed in Cam's direction.

"Hi, Cam," he said, wiping sweat from his face and neck with a much-used towel. "I thought I recognized your wheels as you drove up. What's going on?"

"Not too much." Cam lifted a hand, greeting Ward, who'd paused and was watching, but from a distance. "That was some workout Coach put on you guys."

"Yeah, he's tough. We're facing some heavy competition in the game Thursday, and he will not be happy if we screw up."

Cam glanced beyond him where Ward waited. "Do you need a lift home? I shouldn't be too long here. I'll drop Ward off at his house, too."

"No, that's okay. Kristin Gates has her license now and she offered to give us a ride. She got a Series 3 Beamer for her birthday. Man, it's too cool."

Cam raised both hands, palms out. "Whoa, say no more. I am clearly outranked."

"Ward's got the hots for her, bad."

"And is the feeling mutual?"

He shrugged. "Who knows? You can't tell about women."

"Amen to that." Grinning, Cam gave a thumbs-up gesture, ready to head for Tyson's office, but something on Nick's face stopped him. With his fingers gripping the links in the fence, Nick looked at his feet for a moment, then back up into Cam's face.

"You're not gonna say anything to Coach about me not wanting to keep on with his personal training, are you?"

"That's your business, Nick. To be honest, I've got some questions about Jack that I should have asked a long time ago. This isn't about you."

His face cleared and he sighed with relief. "Great. Okay." Backing away, he lifted a hand, then stopped. "Oh, I told Ward about helping with the flooring of the attic. All you gotta do is tell us the day and what time to be there. That is, if you still want to do it."

"I do," Cam said, moving along the fence toward the gym while Nick walked on the opposite side. "I've got the supplies on order. I'll call and get your mom's okay when I get ready to do the job. Plans will change only if she needs you to do something that day for her."

"She'll be cool with it." Both paused at the entrance to the locker room.

"Then, like I said, I'll let you know. And to keep your strength up, I'll stock up on root beer, chips and pizza."

Nick disappeared inside, grinning.

Cam stood stock-still, listening to the rowdy racket. No other place sounded quite like a packed athletic locker room. Laughter mixed with whistles and raucous shouts echoed against walls insulated only by metal lockers and hard floors. And above it all blasted music with a booming beat. Some kind of rap, Cam thought. He endured it—and memories of Jack—for a minute more, then turned abruptly and headed for the double doors another fifty feet or so beyond that led to the front of the gym.

Inside the windowless hall, it was difficult to see much in the fading daylight, but Cam recalled the general layout from the only other visit he'd made to see Tyson and now headed that way. Taking a left turn, he reached the office, gave a couple of raps on the closed door and was invited in. Tyson, who was sitting behind his massive desk like a king on a throne, rose as Cam entered.

Cam thought that if Monk Tyson wanted to convey the power and prestige of his position, then the trappings of his office achieved just that. All were evident, not only in the furnishings, but in the citations and photos on the wall. Cam stepped onto dark green carpet, thick and luxurious. Two leather club chairs—Moroccan leather, Cam guessed—faced the huge desk. A long, deep couch, also upholstered in Moroccan leather, was positioned on the far wall. In one corner stood a huge live plant, and in the opposite one, a glass curio cabinet held sports memorabilia. Impressive sports memorabilia, Cam noted. He didn't recall Tyson's office being as splendid on his last visit, but at that time, he could easily have missed a live elephant in the room. He'd been thinking only of Jack and burning to find someone to blame for the death of his son. Today he was more interested in digging deep to find out why.

"Have a seat," Tyson said, gesturing to one of the club chairs.

"Thanks." Cam sat. "I appreciate this. I'll try to be brief."

"Take as long as you like." Tyson leaned back in his

chair. "It's been, what, five years? By the way, I've read all your books. I'm a big fan."

"You like true crime?"

"It's fascinating to read about the evil in people, but doing the research must make you wonder sometimes what the world's coming to."

"It does sometimes," Cam agreed, "but as long as good triumphs over evil, I finish the books reassured that all's right and God's in his heaven."

"Yeah. Uh, is this about Nick?"

"Nick? No, why? What made you ask?"

Tyson shrugged. "Well, I saw you chatting him up just now, so you must be acquainted since you're neighbors. Guess I made an erroneous assumption." His lips formed a smile. "You know what they say about assuming."

"Yeah."

"Helluva athlete, Nick. I'd managed to arrange my schedule to carve out some one-on-one time for him and he comes to me a few days ago and says he appreciates it, but no thanks. Duties on the home front, he claimed." Another smile. "I thought you might have some insight why."

"Sounds to me as if he told you why," Cam said.

Tyson shrugged. "Okay, I guess I'll have to concentrate on Ward this semester. He's good, too."

"As good as his brother?"

"Jimbo." Tyson's eyebrows lifted and he smiled. "You remember him, eh? Last I heard, he was negotiating with the majors. I like to think I had a little something to do with setting him on that road."

"I'm sure you did," Cam said. "And do you think his little brother has the same talent?"

"As good as, and maybe better. Nick's top caliber, too." He leaned forward, resting his forearms on the desk. "If you have any influence with that kid, now's the time to use it, Mr. Ford. You—"

"Cam."

"Oh, okay. Cam. If you could persuade him to make time

for me to smooth out the rough edges, it would give him a leg up in the game. He's got what it takes and then some. Trust me on that.''

Tyson was saying all the right things, but for some reason, Cam wasn't persuaded to trust him. ''Isn't it a bit unusual for a coach to single out an athlete for one-on-one coaching? Doesn't that do negative things to team morale?''

''Team morale is improved when I can point to an impressive number of boys who've gone on to make it big. I don't expect all of the ones I single out for special treatment to make it in pro sports, but most of them can definitely count on an athletic scholarship to a respectable university.''

''Is that what you saw in my son's future?''

Tyson's features sobered. He leaned back in his chair. ''Jack was as fine an athlete as any I ever coached, Cam. And yes, indeed, he was headed for a brilliant future in sports. He was a helluva baseball player.''

''Then why did he kill himself?''

''I've asked myself that question a thousand times. And like I told you five years ago, I still have no answers for you. Besides, sports is only one aspect of a boy's life.''

''Did you ever question Jimbo about Jack?''

''Jimbo?''

''Yeah, they were best friends,'' Cam said. ''They went everywhere together. Jimbo must have had a clue to what was happening in Jack's head. Did you ever ask him about it?''

Before Cam finished, Tyson was shaking his head. ''Nah, you don't want to go down that road. If Jimbo knew anything, he would have told me.''

''So you never asked, even though they were rooming together the night it happened?''

''Jack was alone when it happened. And it wasn't in the room they shared.''

''I'm trying to get my head around this picture, Coach. You assumed Jimbo knew nothing, the kid who would be most familiar with what might have been going on in Jack's world?''

Tyson shrugged. ''I was his coach, Mr. Ford, not his shrink. I accepted what I was told by the folks whose job it was to investigate these things.''

''And it had nothing to do with the idea that you might have been reluctant to apply any pressure to Jimbo for fear it would distract him from where he was headed—to the University of Texas—on a major baseball scholarship?''

''Wait a minute.'' Tyson was scowling now. ''Maybe you should just say flat-out what you're thinking.''

Cam knew he was pushing, but so far Tyson hadn't yet thrown him out of his office. ''I'm not sure what I think. I had questions five years ago about my son's death, but I backed off then. Now I need to know if you had personal knowledge about Jack that might have led to his suicide, and I apologize up front if my questions seem offensive.''

''I don't know how I can say it plainer. I'm as in the dark as you.''

Cam's gaze went to the trophies displayed on shelves mounted behind Tyson's desk—baseball, football, basketball, track. God, the man was an icon in Rose Hill, maybe in all of Texas. School board members and parents alike genuflected at his name. If he did know anything, how was it going to be possible to pry it out of him when it might embarrass him, or worse? ''Look, Coach Tyson, I've spent five years wondering what I could have done to rescue Jack, but failed to. I'm admitting that I was an absentee dad and when he needed me, I wasn't there. Something drove him to take his own life. As his father, I owe it to him to find out why, even if I'm five years late. And I know in my gut the answers are here.''

''If there was anything here I would have found it,'' Tyson snapped.

''Excuse me, but it would have been vital to you personally to avoid any scandal attached to your sports program.''

''I don't deny that,'' Tyson said, ''if there was any scandal. And contrary to what your gut is telling you, I'm telling you that you're wasting your time. The best advice I can give you is to get on with your life. Concentrate on something else. Write your books.''

It was a trite and condescending attempt to discourage him, and Cam ignored it. ''I was in a state of shock over losing Jack the last time I asked for information,'' he said. ''Now I'm not. Now I have time and the resources to keep going until I have the answers. And, fortunately, I'm good at researching crime.''

''Crime?'' A dull flush rose upward from the collar of Tyson's golf shirt. He got up out of his chair. ''There's no crime to be researched. Face facts, man. The autopsy revealed your boy was stoned out of his mind. And believe me, it gives me no pleasure to say that.''

''Jack did not have a drug problem,'' Cam said stubbornly. He, too, was now on his feet.

''He damn sure had one that night!'' Tyson released a sigh and his manner gentled, as if trying to reason with one of his wayward athletes. ''Look, he was depressed over you and his mom splitting, plus he'd been uprooted from a place he was familiar with and set down cold here in Texas. Talk to any shrink. That's more than enough reason for a kid to use a little junk and think about ending it all.''

''He was here a year and a half,'' Cam argued, struggling to keep the conversation as civil as possible. ''He had more than enough time to adjust. He had adjusted. You said yourself he was a promising athlete and had earned a prime position on the varsity team, he'd made friends, and I know that he didn't expect his mother and me to get back together. She had a new boyfriend and Jack told me he was okay. So he wasn't harboring unrealistic expectations about us.''

''That may be the way you see it, Mr. Ford, but Jack might have been pretty good at concealing his real feelings. Suicidal kids are.''

''And as for drugs,'' Cam went on doggedly, ''nobody

came forward to say Jack was a habitual user. On the contrary, no one ever claimed to have seen him using…ever.''

The phone rang on Tyson's desk. He picked it up and spoke tersely, listened a few seconds, then said, "In a minute." He covered the mouthpiece with one hand. "Nothing changes the basic facts here, Mr. Ford. Jack, and nobody else, did what he did."

"And nobody had a clue?" Cam demanded. "That's what you're saying?"

"Hell, I'm saying I didn't have a clue. I can't speak for anybody else."

Cam clenched his jaw in frustration. He would get nothing more from Tyson, still it was tough to admit defeat. He knew there was more, but he wouldn't find it now. He'd have to try another way. Tyson's stonewalling only made him more determined that there was something. Turning, he went to the door and had his hand on the knob when Tyson spoke.

"I understand your need for closure, Mr. Ford. All Jack's teammates were shocked and saddened when Jack died. And I include myself in that number. He was a special kid and I'm sorry for your loss, believe me."

"Thanks." Cam left, closing the door softly behind him.

The gym appeared deserted as he retraced his steps on the sidewalk along the fence. Only two cars were left in the parking lot beside his own. No sporty little Beamer and, consequently, no sign of Nick or Ward. Smiling to himself, he imagined his own reaction if, when he'd been fifteen, a pretty girl with her own car had offered him a ride home. Then, drawing even with the entrance to the locker room, he heard voices, clearly audible, coming from inside. The music had been shut down and the words bounced eerily off the walls. He found himself slowing down, listening.

"I'm sick of this shit, man. I'm not going there again."

"Yeah, so you'd rather get shit-faced and spend another night in jail? Uh-huh, that's real clever planning for the big time, Jace. Coach is lining up scouts for you and you're AWOL? Man, you're gonna screw up big time if you keep on."

"I know what'll happen and it's never gonna end. Who's turn will it be next?"

"What difference does it make, man!" Angry and impatient, his companion swore. "Just think about something else. Shit, it's over soon enough."

"It's not worth it!"

There was real anguish in that last statement. Cam hesitated, knowing he wasn't meant to overhear the exchange between the two boys. He picked up his pace and was even with the door just as they stepped outside. Spotting Cam, both looked startled and ended their conversation abruptly. He didn't indicate that he'd overheard anything and made his way directly to his SUV. But once behind the wheel, he replayed the conversation in his mind. It could have any number of meanings, he told himself, although nothing good presented itself. AWOL from what, a game or…what? No athlete on Tyson's team who failed to show for a game survived to play another day.

Glancing in his rearview mirror, he saw the two athletes climb into a beat-up Mustang. He did not recognize them as friends of Nick and only one car was left now, a big Chevy Suburban. Tyson's, he guessed, and easily capable of hauling eight boys.

He drove away from the athletic field, but instead of turning left and leaving the school complex, he drove around to faculty parking and saw that Rachel's car was still in there. He'd noticed she was putting in long hours lately and he couldn't shake the feeling that all was not as it appeared at Rose Hill High, so he wasn't quite comfortable with her being there after hours. His conversation with Monk Tyson had done nothing to change that. Impulsively, he wheeled in beside her car and parked.

Rachel tucked the notes she'd made into a folder, slipped the file into the cabinet and closed the drawer. She stood thinking for a moment, gazing out her window where she had a view of the parking lot next to the gym. The only vehicle left was Monk's Suburban. For a second, she toyed with the idea of walking over and having a talk with him, but what would she say? It was like looking for a needle in a haystack when you didn't quite know what you were looking for or where to start.

"I don't even know the location of the haystack," she muttered, turning back to get her purse and keys and coming face-to-face with Cam. "Oh!" Her hand flew to her heart. "You scared the heck out of me!" She closed her eyes. "Don't *do* that."

"Sorry," he said, and took her arm, guiding her to her own sofa. "I'll skip the lecture about keeping your door locked when you're working alone in a huge building where any pervert could be lurking. Anybody could have walked in here, Rachel. Don't you people have rules for this sort of thing? Where's the janitor, for God's sake?"

"That was a lecture," she said, feeling her heartbeat settling back to normal. "And the janitors are somewhere about, just not on this wing at the moment, I assume." She paused. "What are you doing here?"

"Rattling Tyson's cage," he said, and bent to pick up her purse and keys where she'd dropped them.

She glanced out her window. "I didn't see your car."

"Must've just missed it." He placed her purse on the sofa beside her. "Do teachers do the happy-hour thing?"

"Happy hour, as in a bar?"

"There's a nice, quiet little place on the way home. I'm buying."

She checked the time on her watch and stood up. "After the day I've had, why not? Now that I know you talked to Monk, I can't wait to hear what he told you."

"We can go in my car or yours," Cam told her, already hustling her toward the door. "Or you can follow me."

"I'll follow. It'll save having to come back here later."

The bar was actually a spiffy little bistro—the only one

that Rose Hill had—called Flanagan's. Marta had mentioned that it had an interesting menu and that they should try it out sometime. No one was more surprised than Rachel herself that she was trying it out for the first time with Cam.

They ordered, and when the drinks were in front of them, Cam touched his glass to hers. "Cheers."

"And to you." She took a sip of gin and tonic, noting his crisp white shirt and the way it turned his gray eyes a silvery hue. No scruffy pullover and faded jeans today. He'd taken a bit of care for his visit to Tyson. Then it dawned on her. He must have been to see Cara.

"What haystack?" he asked.

"Haystack." She thought a minute, then laughed. "Oh, that haystack. The reason I was still in my office is because I didn't have a chance to begin my search of Monk's athletes until it was time to go home. And I do know the risks of being alone in a building. I knew practice was still going at the gym and the janitors don't leave until around seven."

"Still, you should have locked your door."

"You're right." She leaned forward. "So, did you make that trip to see Cara?"

He tossed a few peanuts into his mouth. "I thought you wanted to hear about my talk with Tyson."

She sat back, deflated. "I'm sorry. It's none of my business, is it? And yes, I want to hear about Tyson."

"I was kidding, Rachel. Yeah, I went to see her. And it was…" He glanced away, still munching, then met her eyes. "Let's just say I wish I hadn't waited so long."

She sighed, smiled and put her hand on her heart. "Now you're talking."

"She's pregnant."

She smiled widely. "No!"

"Yeah, but she didn't have much to offer about Jack. Still, it helped me with—what do they call it?—closure." She saw by the look on his face that he didn't put much store in pop psychology. "She's totally abandoned her career, which was the driving force in her life in New York, and has turned into little miss happy homemaker. All she could talk about was how wonderful her life is with Anthony.''

"Anthony. I recall him being with her that first day I tried to talk to her. He was very protective.''

"Oh, he's a prince.''

She raised her eyebrows at his tone. "He was there when you visited?''

"No, but I'd know him if he appeared. He'd be the guy in the white hat and wings.''

She covered her lips to hide a smile. "I thought you said the trip was helpful.''

"Aw, hell, it was.'' He rattled the ice in his drink, then tasted it. "She literally glowed with happiness at having another child. She told me she thinks of this baby as a gift. After losing Jack she never thought she'd get another chance at motherhood.''

"That's very touching. You should be happy for her.''

"Yeah, I know. And I am. Wait, there's more. She's into gardening, if you can believe that. This is a woman who used to think her nails were for painting and nothing else, certainly no useful purpose. Now they're clipped short so she can scrabble around in her flowers.'' He stared into his glass. "She's a complete stranger. I can only assume that I never knew the real Cara.''

"Maybe the two of you were wrong for each other.''

"I don't know why. We had good sex.''

He shot her a wicked look, then warded off a scolding by lifting a hand, palm out. "But I'll know from now on to look for more meaningful markers if I should ever contemplate marriage again.''

"I'm certainly glad to hear it.'' Letting her smile bloom, she took a sip of her drink. "What did she say about Jack?''

"Only that he'd started talking about quitting the team and getting out of the sports program altogether.''

"Really?'' Rachel frowned. "Didn't she think that was odd? He'd overcome considerable obstacles just to get on the team.''

"She put it down to a kid's natural resistance to a demanding physical schedule, which definitely defines Tyson's methods." He toyed with the bowl of peanuts. "But Jack took pride in being able to take anything Tyson dished out. I don't think that was the cause of him wanting to quit." After a pause, he glanced up at her. "Speaking of Tyson..."

"And—what happened?"

"His story now is the same as then. Jack's death shocked and baffled him. He's still inclined to blame it on the drugs revealed in the autopsy."

She nodded. "Same thing he told me. That's his story and apparently he's sticking to it."

"Yeah." Cam stared into his glass, twirling it round and round. "As I was leaving, I overheard two kids talking, older athletes. Varsity. I caught them off guard, but I got enough to make me suspicious. I only heard one name." He looked up at her. "Do you know anyone in the sports program named Jace? It would be a kid with a future. They discussed what it meant if he dropped out."

"Jason Pate," she said instantly, but with disbelief. "Jason would never drop out. He's the cream of the crop and definitely one of Monk's chosen. He's slated for a major scholarship. Are you certain it was Jason you heard talking about quitting?"

"Positive."

She'd been playing with her napkin, now folded into a tight little accordion. She moved it aside and picked up her drink. "I'm bound by confidentiality, but I'll just say that Jason has some personal problems. I've been working with him, trying to get him to open up to me." She set the glass down without tasting it. "It won't be easy as his problems are deep-seated. Truly serious."

He reached over and squeezed her hand. "I'm sorry, it may have been just idle talk, but I thought you ought to know."

She managed a smile. "Thanks. I think."

"I'm just the messenger." A beat later, he turned her hand,

palm up, as if studying it. It felt so natural, she thought, having her hand in his. He tended to do this, a warm hug, a touch to her cheek, a sympathetic clasp of her hand, but oddly in contrast to his lone-wolf personality. Yet it was so casually done that she was convinced he meant nothing special when he touched her.

"I need to go," she said, and, withdrawing her hand, stood up.

He rose, took money from his pocket and left it on the table to pay the check. "Everything points to Tyson, Rachel. I think I'll pay a visit to Pete. See if I can get him to poke around in the man's background a little. He might refuse, but it's worth a shot."

See? Totally casual. And she'd better start thinking that way, too, and not let herself get too used to it. If it felt so good having him touch her cheek or give her a hug, she could only imagine how it would be to do much more with him.

Nick, meanwhile, was reaping the benefits of backing away from Tyson's personal training. That's how he accounted for the definite disappearance of tension on the field and in the locker room. It was nothing he could actually see or touch or smell, but the guys on the team were suddenly a lot friendlier than they'd been since those special sessions with Coach Monk had started. He'd played ball with some of these guys since grade school and it had been tough when they'd started treating him as if he had a contagious disease. But word had apparently made the rounds that he was, once again, just one of the team.

Proof positive came when Robbie Sims stopped at his locker just to shoot the shit. First off, Robbie played varsity short stop. He was one of Coach Monk's core elite and Nick had never spent more than five minutes in Robbie's company except on the playing field. So he nearly fell over on his face in the act of peeling off his dirty socks when Robbie said, "You doing anything special Friday night?"

"Uh, not yet." Nick straightened up, socks forgotten.

"My folks have a cabin on Lake Ray Hubbard. Some of us guys are getting together Friday after school and spending the night there. I'm driving, in case transportation's a problem."

It would have been. Robbie knew Nick didn't have his license yet, only a permit. And you couldn't drive with a permit unless somebody was in the car who was minimum twenty-one years old. "Yeah, that's great," he said. "Do I need to bring anything?"

Robbie grinned. "Just yourself. There'll be plenty to eat and, oh yeah, there's a pool. It's heated."

Hot damn. "Who all's coming, Robbie?"

"It'll be me and Mack Turner, Leo Smallwood, Kyle Burgess, Jason Pate and Steve Morgan. Maybe a couple others, I'm not sure yet."

All big dogs, all varsity. Nick was blown away.

"Oh, and you and Will Smythe from junior varsity," Robbie added.

But not Ward. Nick felt a pang, regret mixed with guilt. He knew as soon as he told him, Ward would guess why he wasn't included, not that a weekend invitation to Lake Hubbard was enough to make Ward reject special coaching. He was as hell-bent as ever to be right up there with Jimbo eventually. Still, Nick didn't like abandoning Ward for a whole weekend. He was struck with a thought. If Kristin would agree to go out with Ward, he wouldn't even notice Nick wasn't around. Ward had been fantasizing about having a date with her for weeks, but was too shy to ask. Nick vowed to try to talk to her himself. Maybe use a little of his famous Forrester salesmanship. Ward was always telling him how he was full of crap, but maybe he could put his talent to work on Kristin. But he'd have to get with it. Friday night wasn't far off. Then he'd be able to go to Lake Hubbard with a clear conscience.

It was definitely a plan.

Fifteen

Burnt coffee, stale smoke and disinfectant. All police precincts smelled the same, Cam thought, making his way down the corridor toward Pete Singletary's office. He'd been inside more than a few in the years since he'd started writing, but mostly for research relating to his current work in progress. Except for his questions about Jack, this was the only time he'd had a personal reason for going. Be interesting to hear the police chief's take on the coach of Rose Hill High.

He hadn't called first, telling himself that if Singletary was gone for the day, he'd try again. The dispatcher behind the desk, a pretty brunette, directed him to the chief's office after offering him coffee, which he'd refused.

"Good decision," she told him, smiling. "It's about four hours old and the guys think if they hold out long enough, I'll give in and make a fresh pot."

"Wrong?" Cam guessed, admiring her spunk. And her legs.

"Totally wrong. If I start making the coffee, next thing they'll expect me to bring it to them. Pretty soon, I'd be dusting and mopping." She gave him a sassy wink. "Instead, I'm working on an application to the police academy. I can't wait to see their faces when I show them my acceptance."

"No doubt about that happening—" he paused, reading her name plate "—Angela?"

"None."

He found himself grinning. "Good luck."

"Thanks." She made a motion toward the corridor. "Chief Singletary's down the corridor, last door on the left."

The door was open and Singletary was at his desk, squinting at a monitor sitting on the right-hand corner. The office was neat. Everything had a place and everything was in its place. It was so completely opposite to the way Cam worked that he simply stood for a minute, admiring a level of organization that was beyond him. The only area he kept neat and orderly was his garage, and that was mostly for safety's sake. There wasn't even anything in the chief's in and out baskets. That could mean one of two things, Cam thought. Policing a town the size of Rose Hill presented so little challenge that Singletary finished everything as it cropped up, or nothing much happened that the cops on the force couldn't handle and he didn't have anything to do.

He gave a little tap on the open door and Singletary looked up. Pete smiled, recognizing him, and rose from his chair. "Cameron Ford. Hey, what a coincidence. I was just thinking about you." He extended a hand across the desk and they shook. "Sit down. Did Angela offer you some of our famous coffee?"

"Yes, but I passed, remembering your opinion of it."

Pete smiled. "Definitely the best thing, this time of day. It's got to be thick enough for shoe polish right about now. And Angela refuses to make a fresh pot. Ever." He waited until Cam sat down, then reseated himself. "What can I do for you, Cameron?"

"It's Cam. And I'll tell you up front, what I'm asking might put you on the spot. I won't be offended if you tell me flat-out to get lost."

"And I won't be offended if you say the same thing when I explain why I was just thinking about you," Pete said, settling back in his chair. "You go first."

Cam relaxed enough to manage a smile…of sorts. "Okay. Here's the deal. I need information about a prominent citizen. I get the feeling he may not be what he seems, but I'm going on gut instinct alone. However, it's served me well in the past. When word gets out that there's a hint of suspicion about this guy, there are definitely some folks in Rose Hill who'll be ticked off. It may cost you."

Pete grinned. "Goddamn, that was one helluva opening statement. What a teaser. Makes it impossible for me to say no thanks, I don't want to know any more and have a nice day. Were you a lawyer before you started writing true crime?"

Cam's smile was now more genuine. "No, I was a stock-broker."

"Huh." Pete lifted a brow, his eyes shrewdly assessing. "That's interesting. And who is this prominent citizen?"

"Before we go there, I need to explain where I'm coming from." His gaze strayed to the wall behind Singletary. Citations. Commendations. A photo with George Bush when he was governor. Another at the White House with a Christmas tree in the background. Hell, this guy was as connected as Tyson, but Cam hadn't decided yet if he had as much ego as Tyson. "I lived in New York when my wife and I were divorced," he went on. "Afterward, I stayed there. It was her decision to return to Rose Hill and she took our son with her. Jack was just fourteen then and a promising athlete. Making the team at Rose Hill High was important to him. But he did it. After less than two years, he was playing varsity baseball."

Cam paused, looking at a signed photo of Pete and fellow DPD cops standing at the ruins of the WTC towers in New York with Rudy Giuliani. "Then, one night I had a call from Jack. He said he needed to talk to me about 'some trouble with the guys on the team.' His exact words. I was working on a tight deadline and I told him I'd get back with him as soon as the book was done. He hung up and later that same night, Cara—my ex-wife—called to tell me that Jack was dead. He'd killed himself."

"Ah, Jesus," Singletary said quietly. "I'm sorry."

"Yeah." Cam bit at his bottom lip, cleared his throat. "I've relived that phone conversation in my mind until it's etched forever. So—'' his voice firmed ''—that was five years ago. I'm doing now what I should have done then. I made a stab at it then, but I know now I wasn't in any shape to be rational. Now I want to know why. Jack's suicide took everyone by surprise…or at least that's what they all said, the people I spoke to then. But I learned nothing to explain it. Everywhere I turned, I heard the same thing. Everyone assumed he was just a troubled teenager, pointing to the divorce, the move from New York to Texas, the stress of a new school and his ambition to play sports. I rejected that then and I reject it now.''

''No drugs were involved?''

Cam let out a short, unhappy laugh. ''The autopsy revealed that he did have drugs in his system.''

''Drugs can cause bizarre behavior,'' Pete said, using a cautious tone.

''I'm aware of that, and of course, it's the most logical answer.'' Cam's gaze was steady on his face. ''He was not a druggie. I can't explain how he came to be stoned that night, but it was not usual behavior for Jack.''

''What do you need from me, Cam?''

''Two things. First, I'd like to see the file on Jack's suicide. The whole file, everything. I don't know what your rules are, but I'm hoping you'll bend them…under the circumstances when you hear my second reason.'' He shifted in his chair and said, ''Something about the sports program at Rose Hill High just doesn't smell right to me.''

''Something? Can you be more specific?''

''No. And I don't have a scrap of evidence to make that judgment, only a hunch. Jack's statement to me on the phone that last night still haunts me. Something's going on in Monk Tyson's little kingdom, Pete. I can't prove it and I can't identify it, but my suspicion is stronger than ever.''

''Holy smokes, your prominent citizen isn't Monk Tyson, is it?''

''See what I mean about pissing off some of the citizenry?''

"Yeah, shit." Pete straightened and squared himself at his desk. "And don't tell me, let me guess. You're leading up to asking for Tyson's file."

"Is there one?"

Shaking his head, Pete gave a heavy sigh and sat for a minute thinking. "So, why are your suspicions stronger now?"

"Jimbo Rivers was Jack's best friend at school. He's at UT now. I spoke to Jimbo briefly after Jack died, and, of all the people I talked with, I had the strongest impression that Jimbo knew something, or suspected something. But he was up for a major athletic scholarship at UT and he wasn't talking. Now he's being courted by the majors for a ticket to the pros. I don't think he'll want to talk now, either, for fear of screwing that up."

"But you have no proof? You can't even identify the nature of whatever's going on?"

"Right."

"Is it drugs? You think the athletes themselves are using? Are they selling? You think Tyson's running a drug cartel and the kids are the soldiers?"

"Let me put it this way. I don't think it's impossible." Cam got up and strode to the window. "To tell the truth, I don't have a clue what he's doing. Could be drugs, but somehow that doesn't feel right. Tyson has a no-tolerance rule and I haven't seen anything to make me think otherwise. Could he have a substantial business going and keep it away from his boys? I guess, but I don't think so. Could he use the kids in a drug operation and keep all of them clean? Not likely. On the other hand, Rachel says one of Tyson's prime kids is into booze in a big way, not drugs. He's bingeing on the weekends, even bringing a flask to school so that he's drunk by noon. This is a kid who had no hint of an emotional problem last year. I'm thinking the kid's drinking is a symptom."

"Of what?"

"I wish I knew," Cam said, staring straight out. "I haven't

talked to the kid personally. Yet. But he's got a fabulous future and he's hell-bent on destroying it before it ever begins. Why?''

"Problems at home?''

"Could be, I guess. There's trouble there. Then again, my gut tells me—''

"That Tyson's driving the kid to drink?''

"I know it sounds like paranoia.'' Cam had turned from the window and now faced Pete. "Like I said, this could reflect badly on you, Pete, and just when you need to be making friends, not alienating them.''

Pete dismissed that with a look and asked, "Is there anything else?''

"This is more gut feeling,'' Cam said, "but Tyson has singled out Nick, Rachel's son, and his friend, Ward, for special one-on-one coaching time. Ward is Jimbo's younger brother and is intensely focused on getting a leg up from Tyson, hoping it'll propel him into pro sports by way of a college scholarship.''

"Following in his brother's wake?''

"According to Nick, yeah,'' Cam said. "Meanwhile he—Nick—has just decided to back off from Tyson's freebies. He told me it makes him uncomfortable that his teammates think he has an unfair advantage. But I sense there's something else and it has to do with Tyson.''

"Can you get him to tell you more?''

"I'm working on it.''

"Huh.'' Again, Singletary sat thinking. Then he turned to his computer and tapped out a few keys, sat still while information loaded, then stared at the monitor. "Just looking at Tyson's record,'' he said after a few minutes. "Reputation's spotless. You've picked a doozy here, Cam.''

"The man's been here more than five years. Seems if there was anything it would have shown up by now.''

"Yeah, but after nineteen years in this business, I've learned things aren't always as they appear to be.''

"This may be a dry hole," Cam said. "I could be seeing things where there's nothing."

"Maybe. Maybe not," Pete said, and turned away from his computer to gaze out the window in deep thought. He wore the same expression Cam had seen on his face when he'd first appeared at his door when Singletary was studying his computer monitor. He had something in his hand, working it. A stress ball, Cam realized, watching the compulsive squeeze and release, squeeze and release with growing respect. Chief Singletary talked like a homespun son of Texas, but Cam sensed that behind the mask was a man with shrewd and effective law enforcement skills. Cam had interviewed similar types in his research. How, he wondered, had Rose Hill managed to snare a lawman of Pete's caliber?

"I have a rich uncle," Pete said in a reflective tone. "He's a wildcatter, almost eighty years old now. Started out drilling for oil in West Texas. Had his share of dry holes, too. Made and lost his fortune several times. There're no guarantees when you drill for oil, but that doesn't mean you don't drill."

"You don't think I'm a grieving father looking to pin my son's death on something vague and shadowy when it was mostly my own failings that drove him to take his life?"

Pete was now studying the stress ball in his hand. "I've seen a lot of grieving parents, some who were eager to blame anything, anybody. You're saying you never felt that?"

"I felt it and worse, I've carried it around for almost five years. It's just lately that I've begun taking a more honest look at myself." Honesty meant he'd have to take his place in the lineup now.

When Pete remained silent, Cam decided to shoot for the moon. "You don't need me to tell you how to do your job, but for starters, I wonder whether or not Tyson has more income than might be expected for a high school coach. We both know that if word of an official investigation leaked out, you'd have Tyson's fan club on you, big time."

"On the other hand, thanks to the politicians, we've now got the Patriot Act," Pete said, tossing the ball into a side drawer. "What you suggest would have been a lot trickier before nine-eleven, but in today's suspicious climate, Tyson's secrets are my secrets, so to speak. It's still dicey, but doable. And it's the logical place to start. Good suggestion."

"One more thing," Cam said, going back to his chair. "While Nick has backed off from Tyson, Ward hasn't. He's still too hungry for what it could mean to his future to tell Tyson to kiss off."

Pete waited, sensing Cam hadn't reached where he was headed.

"Nick told me Ward is depressed lately. He's up and down, whereas he's always been a level kind of guy. Doesn't laugh as much anymore."

"He's a teenage boy with raging hormones, Cam. Or it could be girl trouble."

"He's interested in a girl—Kristin—but so far no luck with her, so it's not like they've been a couple and she's dumped him. No, this is deeper than that." He was squinting at Singletary's trophy wall, but his thoughts were focused on that last conversation with Nick. "All the books tell us to watch for changes in behavior. It's a basic danger sign."

"You think he's going down the same road as your boy?"

"Not really, but how about this? The other kid I mentioned who's poised for the big time seems troubled to the extent of drinking to excess, which could jeopardize the future Tyson's set him up for. Now here's Ward, who's also getting special treatment from Tyson that'll set him up, too. And he's also showing signs that he's unhappy, depressed…whatever. Is there a connection?"

"I'll be honest, Cam. It's a stretch." Both men were again silent, thinking. "Nick may know something even if he doesn't know he knows it, if you get my drift," Pete said.

Cam nodded. "Like I said, I'm working on it. I don't want to spook him."

"He doesn't seem affected?"

"No, not that I can tell. Nick's strong enough to reject

Tyson's one-on-one instruction, in spite of the fact that he might be jeopardizing his chance at a terrific scholarship.''

"I don't mean to suggest anything negative about your boy," Pete said, speaking cautiously again, "but do you think it's possible that Jack wasn't strong enough to cope with whatever might be going on in Tyson's house?''

"That's just it," Cam said, rubbing at the six-o'clock stubble on his chin. "Jack was strong and he was street smart. He wasn't the kind of kid likely to be goaded into doing something against his will. That's why it doesn't make sense that he would have just killed himself rather than face a challenge.''

Pete opened the center drawer of his desk, took out a pen and a small notebook. "Let me do some nosing around," he said, making a few notes. He scribbled in silence for a minute or two, then closed the flap on the notebook and slipped it into his breast pocket. "You must have spoken to Tyson when it happened. What did he say?''

"Yeah, I did. Same thing he said yesterday. He claimed to be shocked and baffled.''

"Yesterday?''

"Yeah, I spoke to him as practice was winding down. Except for the trappings of his office being substantially improved, there was no change. Again, he didn't have a clue. But if he had to guess, he'd say it was drugs. Which is what he said then. But no one else admits having been aware of Jack getting into drugs, Pete. No one.''

"Okay. Give me a few days. I'll let you know something either way. Now—'' Singletary leaned forward, both forearms on his desk "—my turn.''

Saying nothing, Cam waited, reading the look on Pete's face warily and gearing up internally for a skirmish.

"I noticed when we were putting in those shelves that you weren't exactly a stranger to Rachel. I was wondering if you might have noticed what a fine woman she is.''

"Only a dead man wouldn't notice," Cam said, still cautious.

Pete was nodding, not quite smiling. "Then I guess it wouldn't exactly be a hardship to spend an evening with her. Am I right?"

"Are you trying to fix me up with a date, Chief?"

"No, I'm trying to fix *me* up with a date." Pete glanced at his computer monitor, reached over to his mouse and clicked something. To Cam, it appeared to be simply a way to buy time as he figured out what he wanted to say. "You met Marta Saturday afternoon when we were installing those shelves for Rachel, right?"

"Yeah."

"She's my ex-fiancée, and because of a stupid mistake I made, that was the first opportunity I've had to actually talk to her for five years. She's flatly refused any contact with me since the day she returned my ring."

"She seemed talkative enough Saturday."

"Yeah, but it was mostly zingers and sarcasm. The only reason she spoke then is that I caught her off guard. I stopped at Rachel's house when I was driving by and saw Marta in the garage, otherwise I'd still be wishing. I know she wanted to split, but Rachel managed to keep her from bolting. Rachel tried to intervene when Marta broke our engagement."

"Yeah, she can be like that."

Pete's eyebrows rose. "I won't ask how she's 'intervened' in your affairs."

"Good."

"Anyway, she thought Marta should at least give me a chance to explain, but it was no use. Marta was hurt, pissed off and bent on punishing me." He had the stress ball in his hand again. "And with good reason."

"Not that it's any of my business," Cam said, still in the dark as to where this was going, "but, just for the sake of the conversation, what did you do?"

"Marta had some serious hang-ups about me being a cop and we fought about it. I mean, we really disagreed. I was ambitious to a fault in those days and resented like hell what I saw as her blind prejudice about everything to do with law enforcement. I knew where she was coming from—her dad was a cop and he was killed on duty by some crazed jerk. It was a domestic disturbance. You never know what you're stepping into on a 10:16. So, Marta was paranoid about my line of work. She kept nagging me to apply to law school.'' His lips twisted into something like a smile. ''I felt it was…not so much a rejection of my job as a rejection of me, you know what I mean?''

''And so you retaliated…how?''

He gave a short laugh. ''Sounds like a passel of excuses, doesn't it? Long story short, there was this gung ho rookie cop, cute, sexy and so goddamned approving of everything I did and said. I got drunk one night and brought her back to my apartment and we had sex. Mindless, comforting sex. Marta walked in and found us.''

''Whoa.'' Cam recalled his own unbridled rage when he discovered Cara's infidelity and found it difficult to work up much sympathy for Singletary.

''She didn't just return my ring,'' Pete said, ''she flushed it down the toilet. Right then and there.''

''I'm not surprised, and from the way she handled the tools required to put those shelves together, you should be grateful there was no power drill handy.''

''Yeah, don't think I wasn't. Then I found out the man she'd married had died of cancer. And ever since, I've been working on a plan for a lifestyle that Marta might not reject outright.'' Pete glanced at the window where Rose Hill's rush-hour traffic moved leisurely. ''I think I've found it.''

Cam's gaze went to the array of photos and commendations on the wall behind Singletary. ''You left a successful career at Dallas PD to be police chief here in Rose Hill because of a woman?''

''Because of Marta. She married Jorge Ruiz six months after we split. On the rebound, damn it. Then, after I got over being royally pissed, I realized how I'd screwed up and what it meant. It looked like I was going to spend the rest of my life without her.'' He studied the stress ball in his hand. ''I'm sorry about Jorge dying. Honest to God. But he did die, and because of that, I have a second chance.''

"And I'm hearing all this because—"

"What's your relationship with Rachel?"

"No relationship. She lives next door. We're neighbors." Cam was beginning to get an idea of where this was going and wasn't ready to share the way Pete obviously was.

"I'm thinking of having a housewarming," Pete said. "Saturday night. Just a few people."

"I'll send a gift," Cam said.

"I was thinking of you more in the way of an escort," Pete said.

"Don't tell me, let me guess. I'll be escorting Rachel, who will try to persuade Marta to join us."

"Exactly what I had in mind," Pete said, then quickly scooted his chair closer to the desk. "Wait, just hear me out. I know if you and Rachel come to the party, there's at least a chance Marta can be persuaded to come, too. No way she'd come on her own. And no way she'd agree to anything resembling a date with me."

"You mentioned a few people."

"Counting myself, four. That's a few." He dropped his head for a second before looking up into Cam's face and admitting, "I don't know anybody else yet."

"What about the city council?" Cam asked sarcastically. "You clearly have friends there."

"Come on. You like Rachel. I saw the way you looked at her Saturday."

"As you say, she's a beautiful woman."

"Is that what I said?" He was smiling.

Cam didn't bother to deny that he liked Rachel. He liked her too much. He hadn't been involved with a woman since his divorce, and he found himself thinking about her more and more. He liked talking to her, being with her. Touching her. If he thought she was ready, he'd like to do a lot more than that.

"You'll be doing me a favor, man." Pete paused, and Cam

gave him credit for not stating the obvious. But what Cam needed from Pete was far more than a social favor. If he started an investigation of Tyson's affairs and it was somehow discovered, Pete might find his carefully planned new life in Rose Hill over before it ever started.

Cam found himself on his feet again. "I'll give it a shot, but if you'd asked a month ago, there would have been no chance Rachel would let me escort her anywhere. And not because I wouldn't like her company," he said slowly, "but she wouldn't like mine. We were barely speaking then."

"That's hard to believe, considering how tight the two of you were when we were putting up those shelves. What's the problem?"

Cam's hand was clamped to the back of his neck. He was going to have to share, after all. "We have some unfortunate history. Rachel was the school's guidance counselor when Jack transferred from New York. She had him in her office several times before it happened. Afterward—" He knew pain showed on his face and he looked away. "After it happened, I was all hung up in looking to blame someone for failing to do something. Rachel was handy. Shrinks are supposed to know this stuff, right? So I was pretty unpleasant. Had an ugly scene in her office. Of course, there was plenty of blame to go around, starting with Cara and me, and I'm coming to terms with that now. But at the time—"

"You showed your ass."

Cam nodded ruefully.

"Looks to me as if you're on the way to making amends for that," Pete said. "But even if Rachel was the type to hold a grudge—and she isn't—she'll do this just to throw Marta and me together for an evening. She's a romantic at heart...Rachel, not Marta. The three of you can come together, then after, I'll drive Marta home. That is, if she'll let me."

Cam headed for the door, knowing he'd been outflanked. "How long will I have to wait to see Jack's file?"

"Got it right here." Pete immediately faced his computer terminal, pressed the print button and settled back in his chair, grinning. "Social hour begins at six-thirty. What's your beer preference?"

Sixteen

"**W**ho was that on the phone?" Dinah looked into the den where Rachel stood holding the cordless in her hand with a peculiar expression on her face. "Rachel? Is it bad news? Is it Ted? What has he done now?"

Rachel turned her head, realized she still held the telephone and laid it on the table. "What? Oh, no, it wasn't Ted. It was Cam." She still gazed thoughtfully at the phone.

"Cam? Well, did he have bad news? Has his book been panned?"

Rachel gave her mother a distracted look. "No. I mean, he certainly wouldn't want to discuss that with me if it was..." Her words trailed off.

"What? What! You're looking a lot like you did when Stephanie called to tell you that Ted had cashed in your CDs." Dinah made her way across the den, picked up the cordless and put it back on its base. "So what did he want?"

"He asked me to come over."

After a startled moment, Dinah walked to the television set and turned down the volume. "Well, now things are getting interesting. I had hope when the two of you had drinks together, but I thought I'd have to wait a lot longer before you got together again. You can be cautious to a fault, Rachel."

She gave Dinah an exasperated look. "For heaven's sake, Mother. It's nothing like that. It's probably something about Monk Tyson. Or Jack. He was going to see Pete and try to get access to the police report, if possible. Or it could be the kids are bugging him and rather than speak to them directly, he'll tell me. He needs his privacy, and in spite of me trying to head them off, they're both over there a lot, especially Nick.''

"Cam's capable of protecting his privacy. He doesn't need you to do it for him.''

"Hmm, that's what he told me, but—'' Rachel picked up a Game Boy lying on the floor and put it on the table beside the phone, then scooped up a couple of cushions and tossed them on the sofa where they belonged. "Or it could be Kendall. She showed me her latest pictures yesterday and Cam and his house were in a lot of them. She's fascinated with his tale of a ghostly ancestor. I told her she wasn't to be bugging him, but she said he told her the ghost had been prowling lately and maybe if she took some pictures, he might show up in them. Can you believe that?''

"He was teasing her, Rachel.'' Dinah leaned against the chair, smiling. "Could be he recognizes someone with an imagination on a par with his own. And as for Nick, Cam's just about the only male influence in the boy's life at the moment with the exception of that smarmy Monk Tyson.''

"I don't want either of them becoming a nuisance.''

"I repeat, he's perfectly capable of getting rid of children who are annoying him, Rachel. He doesn't have to ask you over for that.''

"Then why in the world did he?''

"Because he likes you?''

"Mother, be serious.'' Rachel headed for her bedroom to change out of the clothes she'd worn to school that day. It would not be possible to hide the traces of black eyeliner and purple mascara on the front of her white blouse where Tamika Jessup, a ninth grader, had wept inconsolably in Rachel's arms after failing to make the cheerleading squad for next year. No amount of sympathy had brought a letup of the girl's tears, and since it was nearing the end of the day, Rachel had finally resorted to driving her home herself. By the time they'd reached Tamika's neighborhood, she had not calmed down. Then, when Rachel explained to the girl's mother why she was upset, Mrs. Jessup was almost as disappointed as her daughter. And she made no secret of it. Which told Rachel a lot about the values of the Jessup family.

"Wear something sexy."

Dinah stood in the doorway watching Rachel remove her blouse. Rachel sighed, tossed it in a hamper and went to her closet. "How about this?" She pulled out a slinky black sequined top that she'd worn once on New Year's Eve. Backless, too.

Dinah laughed. "It's only when you're my age and have my eccentricities that you can get away with sequins before eight, dear." She crossed the room and took a seat on the side of Rachel's bed. "But better sequins than the oversize sweats I'll bet you were going to wear."

Rachel stopped rummaging through her closet and looked at her mother. "Why are you so determined to pretend that there's a chance in hell of Cameron Ford as a possible replacement for Ted? That is, *if* I were looking for a replacement, which I'm not."

Dinah put a forefinger to her temple and pretended to think hard. "Beats me, except, as I've pointed out before, he's interesting, sexy, successful and right next door."

Ignoring that, Rachel held up an outfit. "How's this?"

"Excellent choice." Her mother eyed with surprised approval the smart little T-shirt and classic jeans Rachel had purchased last weekend. Now that she'd skinnyed down, she actually had precious few items in her closet that fit. Besides, if Cam was going to issue a complaint about her kids, she didn't want to look…matronly.

"I wish I had time for a snack before I go over," she said, wriggling into the snug jeans. "I skipped lunch. What are the chances there's an apple left? I meant to do some grocery shopping on my way home, but by the time I left Tamika's house, it was time to pick Kendall up from her piano lesson."

Dinah got up, seeing something on the T-shirt. "I don't have to look," she said, peeling off a stick-on size tag beneath Rachel's left breast. "The cupboard's bare. But don't worry, Kendy and I will make a run to Kroger's, and by the time you get back, the pantry will be replenished."

Rachel sighed. "Mother, I'm going to owe you half my share of the settlement when Ted's lawsuit is resolved. Not only for groceries. I can easily repay you for that, but for all the hassle. We've moved in and invaded your privacy, you're often stuck chauffeuring the kids, your house is a wreck because they never pick anything up, and they're always tying up your phone. I don't know how you can ever make a call these days." She dropped both hands to her sides. "How can you stand it?"

"Oh, hush! We've discussed everything you're moaning about a dozen times." Dinah stepped back and gave Rachel a critical once-over. "But if it were a problem, I'd probably die of old age waiting for that rascal Ted to settle up with you."

Rachel studied herself in the mirror and decided to change her earrings. "He called me today at school and said Walter was playing hardball with Francine over the divorce. She was very upset, he told me."

"Francine." Dinah gave a snort of disgust. "What did the silly twit expect, a generous cash settlement and warm wishes for continued happiness after she betrayed him with his business partner?" Leaning against the dresser, she watched Rachel sort through her jewelry box. "I can't find much to admire in your ex, honeybun, but I wouldn't wish a future with Francine on any man, not even Ted. Which reminds me, why was he calling you to whine about it? You should charge him for an hour of psychological counseling."

Rachel laughed. "Maybe, but we shrinks never counsel family. I know, I know," she said quickly. "Ted is no longer family."

"Damn right."

She finished fastening small gold circlets on her ears and faced her mother. "How do I look?"

"Very foxy."

"Oh, please."

Dinah put both hands on her hips. "Listen to me, Rachel Rene. You've proved in the past six months that you're strong, resilient and, in spite of Ted's stupidity, far less embittered than I think I would have been. And on top of that, you're lovelier than you've ever been in your life."

Rachel grinned. "And you're oh so unbiased, Mom." But she reached for her mother and hugged her. "But thanks, anyway."

Dinah gave her a little swat on the behind. "Now, go and dazzle that sexy Cameron Ford."

Rachel didn't bother with a reply to that. "Since I'm not sure how long I'll be, I need to check that Nick's working on that biology project. It's due Friday, and as usual, he's left it to the last minute."

When she opened the door, Nick was sprawled on his bed, staring at the ceiling. She heard the muffled bass of a rap CD going in the earphones he wore on his head. He glanced at her, gave a resigned sigh and rolled up to a sitting position. Clearly bracing for a lecture, he made no move to shut down the music.

"Turn it off, Nick."

Another resigned sigh, but he complied. "What's up?"

"Just what I was about to ask." She glanced around the room. "Did you finish the biology project?"

He dropped the earphones on the table beside his bed. "Today's Wednesday. I've still got another day."

"Nick, it's an important project. Your grade will depend on the quality of the work. James Morton won't cut you any slack. Sloppy work will get you a bad grade...and you don't need another bad grade in biology."

"It's a piece of cake, Mom. Don't worry, I won't embarrass you."

"I'm concerned that you'll embarrass yourself, not me. You haven't even started it. You know—" She stopped. After being accused of lecturing from both Nick and Ted, Rachel knew she was wasting her breath. "Instead of a lecture, here's a promise, Nick. If you don't get that report in on time and get a decent grade, there will be consequences.''

"Like what?''

"Like no driving, no getting that watch your dad promised you, no new CDs for a whole year, no dates.''

"For a year?'' He looked outraged.

"Oh, I'm kidding, you dopey kid.'' She leaned against his chest of drawers and folded her arms. "Why are you making me think up threats, Nick? Just do the report, get it behind you and then you'll have the whole weekend in front of you to enjoy. I know you don't want to spend Saturday finishing it and getting a letter grade less than if you'd turned it in on time.''

"I'll do it, I'll do it.'' He drew his knees up and wrapped his arms around them. "Speaking of the weekend, I've got plans.''

"Such as?''

A hint of excitement showed in his eyes. "Robbie Sims invited me to go to his folks' cabin on Lake Ray Hubbard with some of the team. It's an overnight thing. It's really cool. They've got a pool and I've seen pictures of his dad's party boat. We're leaving Friday after practice. And I know you're gonna ask about adults being there. Robbie said his dad's coming.''

She frowned. "Who else besides Robbie?''

He shrugged. "Mack Turner, Leo Smallwood, Kyle Burgess, Jason Pate and Steve Morgan. Maybe others, but that's who Robbie said.''

"That's most of the varsity baseball team,'' she said with surprise. "Anyone else who isn't varsity?''

"Will Smythe.''

"Oh, Nick, I don't know…''

"Mom!'' Ticked off, he got up and stood facing her from across the bed. "Do you realize what a cool thing this is? The place isn't like our chintzy lake house, it's like a…a sportsman's paradise or something. I've heard the guys talking about it. I can't believe I'm getting a chance to see it.'' He set his jaw stubbornly. "I'm going, Mom.''

"I know about it, Nick. What I don't know is why you're being invited with a bunch of ball players who are two years older than you. I really don't think—''

"I know how you think. You're so cautious you'd probably still hold my hand when I cross the street if I let you. I'm not a baby anymore. I'll have my cell phone if I get in trouble.''

And from the look on his face, it would have to be something just short of a murder on the scene to make him call. "You mentioned Will Smythe, but not Ward. Since he's your best friend, surely they invited Ward?''

"No, they didn't. And it's because Coach is still putting in extra time with him.'' Nick bent and popped out the CD he'd been listening to. "And I wouldn't be asked if I hadn't quit.''

"Why is that, do you think?''

A slight lift of his shoulders. "To the rest of the team, it looks like sucking up to Coach,'' he said, bending to select another CD.

"But neither one of you asked for special coaching. It was Monk's idea.''

"Yeah, well, I had enough of it, but Ward's still hung up on beating Jimbo at his own game.''

She nodded, reluctant to push anymore. Having Nick open up this much was heartening. "Let me discuss this overnight thing with your dad, okay?''

"No, Mom.'' He tossed the CD case on the bed and looked at her with defiance in his dark eyes. "I'll talk to Dad. And if he says I can go, it'll be settled. Right?''

She hesitated, knowing that to hold out would push Nick's anger to another level, which would drive yet another wedge into her relationship with her son. Better to save that battle for another day. "Right, Nick.''

Her hand was on the doorknob when he stopped her. Turning back, she saw he was waving a notebook he'd fished out from under the bed.

"The biology thing," he said. "It's done. I finished it an hour ago."

It was almost dark when she finally started across the lawn to see what Cam wanted. Light spilled from the windows of his house and she was reminded again how much she liked it. Secretly, she understood Kendy's fascination with its nooks and crannies, as well as the possibility of an ancestral ghost. Climbing the stairs now to the porch, she admired the richly glowing colors in the fanlight above the door. As an example of Cam's handiwork, it was really impressive. She was reaching to push the old-fashioned doorbell when the door suddenly opened.

"Oh, hi," she said, caught off guard. She stared at his face, its masculine planes and angles exaggerated by distant light from the street lamps. Interesting and sexy, she thought, echoing her mother's assessment. Her own heart, she realized, was beating too fast and she forced herself down to earth. Next thing, she'd be buying into her mother's ridiculous fantasies.

"I was just admiring the beautiful fanlight," she said. She could hardly tell him she was admiring him. "Nick tells me you're doing the stained glass work yourself."

"Yeah, it's fun. Come on in." He reached for her hand and pulled her across the threshold. As soon as she was in the foyer's full overhead light, his eyes swept her from the top of her head to her toes and he gave her one of his rare smiles. "You do nice things to those jeans." And she was suddenly flushed and breathless again.

"Have you had dinner?" he asked.

"No, but—"

"Great. A chance to redeem myself. How does this sound? Gazpacho to start and portobello risotto with crab cakes for the main course."

Rachel stared at him. "You're kidding. The last time I was here, you told me you weren't much of a cook."

He grinned. "Actually, I'm not. And yeah, I'm kidding." With his hand at the small of her back, he ushered her through the house to the big country kitchen that she'd always admired. "I have two dishes besides steak—spaghetti and lasagne. Tonight, it's lasagne. I hope you don't dislike pasta. And please don't say no. You've already refused my spaghetti and another rejection will have me thinking it's not my cooking you dislike, it's me."

"I thought you wanted to talk to me about…something," she said, giving the table a confused look. He'd set it for two, complete with a centerpiece of Dinah's camellias and candles. Now she wondered if her mother had been in on this and if that snack she'd mentioned had really been unavailable. "You didn't mention having dinner."

"I didn't?" He gave himself a bump to his head with the heel of his hand. "Well, I should have. So, now that you're here, how about some wine?"

"Will I need it?"

"I'm no world-class chef, but my lasagne's not that bad." He held up two bottles. "White or red? I recommend the red."

"I wasn't talking about food," she told him. "Are you softening me up to make a complaint about Nick or Kendall?"

He stopped, set both bottles down. "What gave you that idea? How else am I gonna get cheap labor when I begin reroofing my house and Kendy's set to perform an even more important favor for me?"

"Like what?" Rachel asked faintly.

"She's boning up on how to exorcise the ghost of my cheatin' ancestor."

Rachel lowered her head, pinched the bridge of her nose with two fingers and fought the urge to laugh. When Cam set out to charm, he didn't do it halfway. "Red," she said.

"Excellent choice." Opener at the ready, he bent to the

task of uncorking the bottle of—she glanced at the label—a really good cabernet.

"We've finished off the Chianti, have we?"

"I'm told by the same guy who recommended it that we won't be disappointed in this one, either. But if you are, there's more Chianti in my wine cellar."

"You have a wine cellar?" He certainly had been busy turning this old house into something special.

"Sure, on the shelf above the washer and dryer." He worked the cork free, then pointed in that direction. "There's a special place between the detergent and the Spray 'n Wash. Have a look."

She propped her hands on her hips. "What is going on, Cam?"

He'd poured the wine, which he now offered her. She took it and let him guide her over to the cushioned seat in the bow window. He waited until she was sitting down to take a seat himself. "I'm on a mission of mercy."

Sipping wine, she glanced over the glass at the beautifully set table. "Whatever it is, it wasn't necessary to go to such elaborate extremes just to ask. What do you need from me?"

"A very big favor, but not for myself. It's for Pete and Marta."

"Pete and Marta? You're on a mission for Pete and Marta?"

"You knew I was going to see our new police chief. I did—a couple of days ago. But he's a shrewd operator. Seized the opportunity to grab a favor in return. He's having a housewarming. He'd like Marta to come and he figured there'd be no chance if he asked her outright." He set his wine on the floor and crossed an ankle over one knee. "You and I are invited and he's hoping you'll be able to talk Marta into joining us."

"Oh. Well, I'll try," she said with some disappointment that he'd been more or less forced into escorting her. In spite of her effort not to, it looked as if she was buying into her mother's fantasies. Time to stop it. "When is this important event?"

"Friday night, around seven."

"Okay, but only if Dinah's willing to stay with Kendy. Nick is going to be out Friday night," she told him. "An overnight thing on Lake Ray Hubbard."

"Understood," he said, nodding. "So, I'll pick you up, then we'll swing by for Marta and the three of us can go together," Cam told her. "That way, when the evening's over, you and I will leave and Pete will drive Marta home."

"Ah." Indeed, Pete was a shrewd operator. Still, it wouldn't hurt to keep from him the fact that Marta had already decided to have that dialogue with Pete, although she wasn't yet ready to say she would—or could—forgive him.

"So, what do you think?"

"It's a plan," she said. "But I wouldn't presume success just yet if I were Pete. Marta's very bitter and rightly so. What he did was beyond the pale."

"He told me she caught him in bed with another woman. He was pretty frank about it. Said it was a stupid thing to do."

"And hurtful beyond anything he could have done. I don't know if Marta can ever get beyond it enough to risk trusting him again."

"But you still think he deserves a second chance? It surprised me when Pete said you'd tried to get Marta to reconsider."

"Not exactly to reconsider. I just thought they should talk about what happened before deciding their relationship was over."

"You're the one who said infidelity is one of the most difficult problems to overcome in a relationship. Have you changed your mind?"

"No, but Pete and Marta weren't yet married, and the purpose of the engagement period is to work out problems before they cause major catastrophes. They skipped that step, and then when Marta rushed into marriage with Jorge Ruiz, it was too late.''

"What was he like?''

"Jorge? A nice guy, quiet and shy. There wasn't a kinder, gentler man in the state of Texas.''

"Safe, was he?''

She gave him a chiding look. "He was a very nice man.''

"Boring. And Marta hasn't had a significant other since ol' Jorge died?''

"No.''

Cam bent over to pick up his wine. "And now, looking back after all this time and water under the bridge, you still believe there's a chance this marriage can be saved?''

"Relationship. Not marriage. And I don't have a crystal ball,'' she said, sensing something more in his questions than friendly interest in Pete and Marta's situation. "But what do they have to lose just by talking?''

"I don't know. No damn way it could have saved my marriage,'' he added.

Or mine, she thought, studying the etched pattern on her wineglass. She guessed it had belonged to his mother, as did many of the things that were placed about in the house. She looked up into his face. "And since we've agreed to do this small thing for Pete and Marta, the rest is up to them and we're out of it, okay?''

"Hey.'' He put up both hands. "I wouldn't be doing this much if he didn't have me over a barrel.''

"You haven't told me what you're getting in return for escorting Marta and me, if anything.''

"The pleasure of your company, for one thing,'' he said. "And I'm not sure whether the other is helpful, but I did get copies of the initial report of the first cops on the scene at the hotel where Jack…died, and the medical examiner's report. Not here in Rose Hill. It happened in Angelina County.''

"Both must have been pretty painful,'' she murmured.

"Yeah.'' He cleared his throat and drank some wine. "I

couldn't have taken it five years ago when I was making such a big push to get that stuff. I don't know if it's a good thing or not that I've read so many autopsy reports in doing the research of past crimes, but when it's someone you care about—''

With only a moment's hesitancy, Rachel reached out and touched his hand. He breathed in a long, fortifying breath, turned his hand and grasped hers. Without actually thinking about her words, and knowing he was probably hungry for any scrap of positive information about Jack, she simply began talking. "Marta considered Jack a gifted student, which, as his father, you already know. She's tough, too. Her Honors English class is the best and when she says a student is gifted, you can believe it. His father's son, wouldn't you say?'' She gave him a small smile. "In fact, she shared a couple of Jack's assignments with me during the first semester. It was unusual, a gifted athlete with an equally impressive talent for writing. That's why I was so puzzled when he seemed to get off track that second semester.''

Cam was staring at her. "You have something written by my son?''

"No, no. Marta never left anything with me. We just…enjoyed it. We're often amused by the stuff kids write, but Jack was in a category beyond that.'' She paused, aware of something on his face. "You knew he had a flair for writing, didn't you?''

He released her hand, stood up and moved to the window so that she was looking at his back. "Where are those writings now?''

"It's possible that Marta kept them.'' Lord, he didn't know. She felt a flash of terrible sympathy. "We can ask, Cam. I hate to tell you, but it wouldn't be unusual if they've been shredded. It was five years ago, and ordinarily, no teacher keeps her students' papers that long.''

"Not even the gifted ones?'' Cam swung about. "Not even if he's contemplating suicide?''

"We've talked about this, Cam,'' she said gently. "There

was nothing to suggest that Jack was contemplating suicide. That's why it was such a shock. What he wrote was sometimes offbeat, but such thoughts can stem from any number of emotional issues.''

"My son wasn't screwed up!"

"I'm not saying he was screwed up, just that something was on his mind." She sighed wearily. "As a counselor, I can try to show a troubled student a door, but it's up to him to open it." She could see the fingers of his hands flexing and knew he was struggling with fierce pain. "But sometimes trying just isn't enough."

She watched him consider that, his face still dark with the memory of losing his son. "Can you tell me anything about what Jack wrote?" he asked.

He appeared ready to ease off, so she made an effort to recall. "As I said, in the beginning, it was quite beautiful, a view of life through the eyes of a boy just on the verge of manhood. It was funny and touching, creative. He missed you," she said. Risking a glance at his face, she found it stony and his eyes bleak. "But that was normal. There was nothing to signal more than the natural need of a boy to be with his father. But later..." she was frowning, "I remember Marta remarking that his writing had taken a turn that troubled her."

"And that didn't send up a red flag?"

She managed a wry smile. "To be a teenager is to be riddled with angst," she said, "so that in itself wasn't so unusual. But it caused Marta some concern and when she showed it to me, I agreed. That's when I first called Jack into my office. I got the feeling that he felt he didn't need a shrink, that whatever was bugging him, he could handle."

"That sounds more like the Jack I believed him to be."

She spread her hands. "You know the rest." She got up, took a deep breath, set her wineglass on the counter and pulled the hem of the T-shirt down neatly. "Well, thanks for the wine."

"What?"

"Thank you for the wine," she repeated, and took a step, intending to go around him, but he moved in front of her, stopping her with just a look from his eyes, silver-gray and intense with the emotion stirred up by talk of Jack. The breath caught in her throat, and she realized suddenly that her attraction to Cam was inching beyond anything she'd reckoned on. As a newly single person, she thought a flirtation with someone as interesting as Cam had been deliciously appealing…in the abstract. She'd been telling herself it could never come to anything. The problem was, she'd forgotten the risks.

"Dinah should be back from Kroger's now," she said shakily, looking at his chin. "So—"

"Look, I'm sorry if I seemed a little intense just now," he said, rubbing the back of his neck, "but you caught me cold saying there was something Jack wrote floating around, if we could just find it. That's more than I ever hoped for." He picked up her wineglass from the counter and put it back in her hand. "Add to that the fact that it may offer a clue to his state of mind and…well, I know I came on strong. I apologize." His laugh had an ironic ring. "It must seem I'm always apologizing to you."

"It's okay. I understand. And if Jack's writings are still intact, we'll find them," she told him, pushing wayward thoughts deep down and out of reach. "But please don't get your hopes up too high. Marta may have kept them, but she may not."

"Yeah." Taking her hand, he gently urged her back onto the window seat, reached for the wine and refilled her glass, then dropped down beside her. "Okay, it's your turn to share about your ex. Could a nice dialogue between you and Ted bring you two together again?"

She had to smile. "First of all, Ted doesn't want us to be together. Nor do I now. He's told me why he wanted out and he's blabbed on ad nauseam about Francine and her superiority as a lover and mate until I know far more than I care to. So, the answer is definitely no."

"Good. Because he's not worth recycling." He stood up and reached for her hand. "Will you stay for dinner…such as it is?"

She let him pull her to her feet, wondering at how often he expressed his dislike of Ted. Did it matter to him whether or not she'd washed her hands of her ex? "I really should get back and help Dinah fix dinner."

"Not necessary. She's bringing home a pizza," he said, nudging her toward the table.

She gave him a startled look. "She is?"

"She called as you were walking over. Said to take your time."

Lips pursed, Rachel stopped in her tracks. "Why do I get the feeling that my mother is as chummy with you as my kids? It's your own fault. I can't lecture her as I do them— remember, I'm the One Who Lectures—but I can't keep them from bugging you if you keep on acting like their kindly old bachelor uncle."

"No objection to being their kindly bachelor uncle," Cam said, seating her at the table, "although strictly speaking I'm no bachelor. But I resent being called old. Hold on a minute." He went to the kitchen, donned two oven mitts and lifted the dish of piping-hot lasagne from a warming tray. When he set it on the table and inserted a serving piece, the aroma, a blend of basil, oregano, fragrant tomato sauce and cheese, made her empty stomach growl in anticipation. At least, she told herself, it was the anticipation of a tasty meal stirring her up and not Cam himself. She sat with her hands in her lap as he plucked a huge bowl filled with garden greens and other salad ingredients out of the fridge and sat down, not across from her, but at the end of the table, within touching distance. "Let's toast," he said, lifting his wineglass.

"Why not?" she said, deciding to enjoy herself and damn the risks.

"To the success of Pete's plan."

"I thought we'd done with that subject for the night."

"We are, but just in case…" He took a sip, watching her

over the rim of his glass as she did the same, then added, "And to Ted and Francine. May they get all they deserve."

She burst out laughing and took a big drink of the excellent cabernet.

"Now…" Cam said, rubbing his hands together, "how hungry are you?"

Seventeen

The Sims's place on the lake was no cabin, Nick thought, staring at the low, sprawling structure materializing at the end of a long lane. Sitting in the back seat of Robbie's Expedition beside Will Smythe, he decided that since it was made of Texas hardwood logs, that had to be the reason Robbie called it a cabin. Tucked in a setting of tall pines on the shores of Lake Ray Hubbard, the place was awesome and screamed money, money, money.

The wraparound porch was outfitted with Adirondack chairs and tables to match, and hanging at both corners were a couple of swings. Really neat. Flower baskets swung from the eaves all around the porch, and on the grounds, in keeping with a Texas theme, were a lot of rocks and cacti. He could imagine hanging out on the porch early in the morning when nothing but birds and squirrels stirred, and he thought longingly for a moment of his family's lake house. Unfortunately, with his dad hanging out there now with Francine, it was generally inaccessible to the rest of the family. But he didn't want to think about that. He was here for a party. Hot damn!

All passengers piled out of the Expedition and waited as Robbie signaled a second SUV, driven by Mack Turner, to an area around the side of the cabin. Mack, another varsity player, parked beside a Chevy Suburban, but as the daylight was fading, Nick was not able to identify the vehicle. Whoever it belonged to must have already gone inside.

"Wow, this is some place," Will said, looking as dazzled as Nick. "What kind of job does Mr. Sims have?"

The two had dropped back, following at some distance behind Robbie and Kyle Burgess, who'd been in the front seat. "Something in politics," Nick said. "Mom told me he's big in Austin."

Will dropped his voice. "Why's he living in Rose Hill? Why doesn't he live in Austin?"

"He does, but he and Robbie's mom are divorced. They came back to Rose Hill 'cause her folks live here. C'mon, let's catch up with the others."

Some of Nick's pleasure faded when he saw that Ferdy Jordan and B. J. Folsom were passengers in Mack's SUV. By his tally, there were about ten guys on hand for the party, not counting whoever drove the Suburban. That was a big enough crowd to make it easy to avoid two assholes.

Inside, they entered a huge great room with exposed beams of rough-hewn wood. Suspended from the roof peak was a light fixture made of a ton of deer antlers. Somebody was a hunter, big time, Nick thought, looking around. Trophy animals had been mounted and placed here and there on the walls. He ventured closer to the vast mantel where a big spotted cat lay with one paw dangling over the edge. Jeez, a leopard.

Then, straight through the back glass wall was a view of the pool that Robbie had mentioned. It looked to be Olympic-size. Nick had his swimsuit in his duffel and was itching to hit the water. But it looked as if most of the guys were heading first for the bar. Robbie was already stationed there, setting out long-neck beers. Plenty of takers, too, Nick thought, as music blasted from the surround-sound system. Mack, Kyle and Leo Smallwood all snagged a bottle each. He looked around, wondering where the adults were, expecting if not both Robbie's parents, then at least his dad, but there was nobody but Robbie's guests. Adults were probably in another part of the house.

Will scooped out a handful of peanuts from a dish set on a low table. "You gonna have a beer?"

"Later," Nick said, helping himself to pretzels. He wasn't comfortable with this group yet. He still hadn't quite figured out why he'd been invited. These players were the coach's core elite. Was he here because he'd kissed off Coach Monk's special treatment? If not that, then why?

"Nick, my man." Robbie's arm went around his shoulders and a beer was shoved in his hand. "Time to party! Ferdy!" He yelled across the room where Ferdy Jordan stood sorting through CDs. "Man the bar for a while. I'm gonna show Nick around." Ferdy didn't appear pleased, but he did as Robbie asked.

Now that the beer was in his hand, Nick thought he'd probably look like a wuss if he didn't drink it. "You've got a nice place here," he told Robbie.

"Yeah, but don't be too impressed. My old man's company owns it. They use it for sucking up to politicians and VIPs. Actually, a couple of presidents have been wined and dined here."

The beer was good, cold and crisp on his tongue. He glanced back and saw that Will had bellied up to the bar and was drinking like everyone else. What the hell. It wasn't as if they needed to stay sober to drive. Nobody was going anywhere tonight.

"Want to check out the pool? It's heated." Robbie pushed a glass door open and went outside. "There's a cabana with towels and stuff."

"Great, I brought a suit in my duffel."

"Well, it's not a problem if you don't want to use it. Mostly, the guys just go in buck naked. Do whatever you like."

"I was hoping to maybe shoot a lion first," Nick said.

Robbie laughed. "Cool, Nick. But you have to prove your manhood in a different way here."

"Yeah? What way would that be?"

Robbie opened another gate and waited for Nick to pass

through. "It'll be a surprise, but it can wait. Let's go check out the Jet Skis."

Nick fell into step with him as they made their way past the pool and onto a path that led to the boathouse on the lake. "Did your dad get here yet?"

"He canceled. Had to go to D.C., I think. Or maybe L.A. His company has offices in both places. But even if he was in Austin, he'd think of a reason not to be here." Robbie picked up a stone and sailed it out over the water with the kind of force he used on the mound. "He's too busy fuckin' around with his assistant to remember his own family."

"He's having an affair?"

"He's always having an affair."

They'd walked out on the pier past the boathouse to the end and now stood looking out over the water. Nick turned back, looking at the boathouse, which was as elaborate in its design as the cabin. Robbie told him it housed a couple of boats and two Jet Skis, which they'd launch into the water tomorrow.

"If you're wondering about it still being a little chilly, we have wet suits."

Wet suits. Of course. Couldn't heat the lake. Something caught his eye and he turned, thinking he saw movement. "Did you see that?"

"What?" Bending to tie his shoe, Robbie had missed it.

"Is there anybody in the boathouse? I thought I saw somebody."

"There's plenty of wildlife moving around the lake at night. You wouldn't want to look too close."

Nick laughed. "Just tell me that leopard on the mantel was shot in Africa and not out here."

"On a genuine safari," Robbie said, adding sarcastically, "an excursion with some bigwigs in Austin and D.C., plus Dad's current squeeze."

Nick heard and understood. Coach might be right, he thought, swigging more beer. According to him, half the kids at Rose Hill High knew about divorce firsthand. Made him wonder at the way grown-ups got married before being certain they had the right partner for the long haul.

"Hey, I'm ready for a refill," Robbie said, finishing off his beer. At the end of the pier, he tossed the empty into a conveniently placed trash barrel. "I just wanted to mention one thing." He turned to head back. "There'll be a couple older guys at the party. They usually drop in when word gets around we're having a party out here."

"Are they driving the Suburban?"

"Yeah. There's a workout room and stuff in another wing of the cabin. A sauna and hot tub, the whole works. They probably headed there when they arrived."

"Or the boathouse," Nick suggested.

"Could be. Like I said, they show up and we're nice to 'em. Doesn't hurt to be nice, right?"

"Right. Sure."

He glanced at Nick's bottle. "You about done?"

Nick quickly finished off his beer and tossed the empty. Then he turned and followed Robbie back the way they'd come.

Hours later, he'd lost count of the number of beers he'd drunk. The party was rowdy and loud and, except for peanuts, popcorn and pretzels, had no real food. Robbie and his buddies were a lot of fun, and the more beer Nick drank, the more relaxed he felt. He'd even stopped caring that Ferdy and B.J. were still assholes. And even though the older guys Robbie had mentioned were kinda weird, Nick made it a point to avoid them the same way he dodged Ferdy and B.J. There was only one thing missing at the party and that was girls.

He didn't count the cheesy females in the porn video that was now playing on the big-screen TV, which had been tuned to ESPN earlier. Jeez, he'd seen some porn before, but this stuff was in a class by itself. A couple times, he'd been…like, embarrassed. But nobody else seemed to be.

Sex made him think of Ward. Slouched deep in the cushy sofa in front of the fireplace with his beer resting on his middle, he wondered how Ward was making out with Kristin. If there was a God, Ward was a happy man right about now and Nick had definitely done his part to help the cause along. Yes sir, he sure hoped ol' Ward was taking advantage of a golden opportunity.

As he stared blearily at the fireplace, someone moved into his line of vision. One of the old guys. Robbie had introduced a couple of them, this one and somebody named Malcolm. No last names.

"Hello, I'm Joseph."

What was it with these weirdos not telling their last names? Nick lifted a finger of the hand that held his beer. "Hi. Nick."

Joseph smiled, letting his gaze linger somewhere in the vicinity of Nick's beer. "What's your position, Nick?"

"I'm a conservative Republican," Nick said, deadpan.

"No, no, I mean, what position do you play as an athlete?"

"First base. Junior varsity."

"Junior varsity," Joseph repeated, standing with one hip cocked. "You must be very good."

"I try." Remembering Robbie's admonition to be "nice," Nick resisted an urge to get up and head for anyplace else. Instead, he drew in a long breath and asked politely, "What is your line of work…ah, Joseph?"

"I'm a cinematographer. I make videos," Joseph said. "And I would just love to put you in a video. Your cheekbones are marvelous. And those exquisite amber eyes." He put a hand over his heart. "Have you ever done any modeling?"

Modeling? Doing a swift body curl, Nick got off the sofa, feeling a sudden craving for fresh air. At the door, he stood swaying as the effects of too much beer kicked in. He swallowed hard when it threatened to roll up in the back of his throat.

He didn't know Joseph had followed him until a heavy

arm settled around his shoulder. "Are you okay, Nick? You look pale. Let me—"

"I'm fine. I'm good," Nick said. Stunned and sickened, he shrugged off the man's hand. Joseph had made a move on him! He imagined one of his teammates being cornered and having to fend off the other creep's advances, Malcolm No-Last-Name. Worse yet was the realization that Robbie must know what these guys were. That's what he'd meant when he told Nick to be nice to them.

His head spinning, he looked around to see if he was the only one freaked out. The room was crowded with people. A heated game of darts occupied half a dozen athletes, and far in the back, others were playing pool. More were clustered near the bar. Outside, a bunch were horsing around in the water, all buck naked. Music pouring out of the surround sound was deafening. It seemed to magnify the effect of the alcohol and he wished fervently that he'd stayed sober. Worse, he wished he'd stayed home.

Gulping fresh air as he stumbled outside, his mind raced, thinking what he should do. No way was he going to stay the night in that house. He thought he could find his way out of the area, but it was a hell of a long walk. He couldn't call his mom, either. All he needed after this was to have her say I told you so. Even if she had been right to be suspicious. Maybe Marta…but no, she'd tell Mom in a heartbeat and they'd both head out here and it was already way past midnight.

Shit!

He lifted his head suddenly at faint sounds of people talking and he made out two people coming from the boathouse. Most likely one of the guys from the team. The other, tall and muscular, was a big guy. Nick didn't make much of an effort to stay out of sight, but they wouldn't have noticed, anyway. They were too busy arguing. In easy earshot now, Nick dropped his jaw as he suddenly realized who it was.

Jason Pate and Coach Monk.

"I mean it!" Jason exploded, facing Monk with his arms

straight at his sides, fists clenched. "I'm quitting. I'm getting out of your whole stupid sports program. It's not worth it."

"Aw, Jace, not that again…" Tyson put out a hand to comfort him, but Jason flinched and avoided his touch. "You know you don't mean it."

Suddenly Jason was crying. To Nick's astonishment, he saw the Mustangs' star athlete cover his face with both hands and dissolve into hard, gut-wrenching sobs. Jeez, he'd never seen anybody cry like that. Coach's reaction was almost as surprising to Nick as Jason's sobs. Monk just rolled his eyes and looked off in the distance as if bored to death. After a minute, he said, "Knock it off, for God's sake! You want the guys to see you sniveling like a baby?"

It took a while, but Jason somehow stopped and drew in a long, shuddering breath.

"You do this every time," Tyson said in disgust.

"I hate you," Jason said fiercely, facing Tyson head-on. "One day I'm gonna kill you."

Nick, watching spellbound, could see Jason's face as a whole host of emotions, mostly anger, contorted his features. Then Jason cleared his throat and wiped his face on the sleeve of his shirt. "I'm going out to the lake," he told Tyson. "I'll be in later."

"Damn right you will. And knock it off talking about quitting. You know it's not happening." With that, Tyson stepped to the door and, to Nick's amazement, laughed. "I guess I'd better get inside before Joseph puts the make on somebody he shouldn't."

Eighteen

It was not late when Rachel settled in the front seat of Cam's SUV, sated with barbecue ribs done to perfection by Pete and the excellent red wine provided, she learned later, by Cam. The man professed not to know much about vintage wines, but she was quickly coming to know better. What she now had to be cautious about was letting him ply her with enough wine to impair her judgment when she was with him. And she was not thinking about her ability to drive.

"Well, that went...not too bad, don't you think?" he said, giving her a sly smile as he pulled away from Pete's house.

"I'm reserving my opinion," she said, watching him load a CD. "Anyone would have smelled a rat when you made that flimsy excuse about expecting an important call from your agent so we could leave early. It'll be on your head if we hear tomorrow morning that they've killed each other."

"I'm in contract negotiations at the moment," he told her, the smile still lurking at the corner of his mouth. "An important call could come any minute. Technically, it wasn't a lie."

"Your answering machine would pick up a call...or your cell phone, which I note is on your person." But she was fighting a smile, too. Cam's bogus excuse had been so obvious that she and Marta had laughed about it while the men talked on the opposite side of the car as they were getting ready to leave.

"The important thing is that Pete's plan was successful,"

he said. "And we're driving away, leaving the two star-crossed lovers to fish or cut bait."

"I didn't know you were such a romantic."

"I like to do my part for true love."

She smiled. "I have a confession to make. Marta was already questioning whether or not she was hasty in breaking her engagement without giving Pete a chance to explain. She was ready to listen."

"You mean Pete's big plan was unnecessary?"

"Well, it probably speeded things up a bit," she said, recognizing the song on the CD he'd chosen as one of Rod Stewart's bluesy, sexy ballads. Oh, Lord, and after spending the evening watching Pete and Marta in provocative, former-lover give-and-take, both clearly feeling sexual hunger, she herself was feeling restless and a little overstimulated. Her mother's fantasies about Cam were rapidly becoming her own.

Time to get a grip, Rachel.

"Anyway, it was nice of you to help out," she told him, then added, "I wouldn't have thought you'd want to get involved in something that could get sticky. You're so—"

"Reclusive? Rude? Outspoken?"

"Well…" She thought of his courtesy as a neighbor, of his patience with Kendy and the time he managed to spend with Nick. "No, not really. But I do think, as a writer, you need a certain amount of solitude and you make no apologies about demanding it. When you want to be, you're really…nice."

He glanced over and met her too-bland look. "Isn't that how you described Jorge Ruiz?"

Her smile broke. "Yes, and it was a compliment."

He looked over at her, smiled slowly, devastatingly. "Watch out, Rachel. Tossing me a compliment might give me ideas."

Don't I wish…

But they were almost home now. The distance between Pete's house and their neighborhood was less than a ten-minute drive. As Cam made the turn onto their street, Rachel felt a pang of disappointment that the evening that was, essentially, just beginning for Pete and Marta, was over for Cam and her. As he came around to her side of the car, she opened the door herself and climbed out. "I think that was the quickest barbecue I've ever been to, but it was fun. I had a good time." Tying the sleeves of her sweater around her shoulders, she stuck out her hand. "Thank you, even though I know Pete coerced you to help him pull it off. It was for a good cause."

He took her hand, but instead of the friendly shake she expected, he turned it over and laced her fingers through his. "Just because we left Pete's place early doesn't mean we have to end the evening for ourselves. Is Dinah at home with Kendy?"

"Ah...yes." She stood there with her hand in his, her senses still humming from Rod Stewart's sexy song.

"And Nick's some place with his friends on Lake Ray Hubbard?"

"Uh-huh."

Still holding her hand, he stood with his profile in shadow, backlit by the streetlight. "So, you really have no reason to rush right home?"

"I suppose not."

"What if I told you I know of a place that's quiet, where the music's good, the drinks aren't watered down and they won't throw us out no matter what time it gets? Would you be interested in going there?"

"It can't be Flanagan's as they don't have music. And I can't get too far from home. If Nick calls, I—"

He put a finger to her lips. "It's close. In fact, we're here." Now he was gently stroking her cheek. She felt the pull of attraction and the beguiling danger of it, as well.

With her heart beating fast, she looked up at his house. "Here? Your place?"

"Yeah. You said yourself it's early. And I have wine—"

"No." With a shaky laugh, she caught his wrist firmly.

"No more wine. You're certain to have some fabulous vintage that you'll claim was recommended by that fellow at the liquor store, when if the truth is known, you're probably giving him tips as to what's good and what isn't. And it's too late for coffee."

"Then how about dessert?"

She looked at him skeptically. "Was this the plan all along? We'd leave early and you'd have a fabulous dessert waiting?"

"Define *fabulous*." His smile was truly devastating. It was probably a good thing he didn't use it much.

"Let's see…bananas Foster would be fabulous."

"No bananas Foster, but how about ice cream?"

"Ice cream."

"That all-time favorite."

She stared into his eyes, knowing it was a risky thing to go inside his house at this hour, mellowed out as she was with good wine and her senses heated and thrumming with music that turned her on. Standing in a pool of reflected light from the street lamp, his smile was too enticing and his hand linked with hers felt…right, oddly right. Somehow, their evening, which had started out as a favor for Pete and Marta, seemed about to turn into something more.

"C'mon, you can decide after we check out what flavor Kendy picked out."

"Kendy went with you to grocery shop?" She tried, but failed to visualize Cam and Kendy shopping together at the corner supermarket.

"Yeah, she keeps me from buying dopey stuff. That's her word for canned sardines and potted meat."

"Then she's right," Rachel said dryly, going along as he tugged her toward his front porch steps. Mention of her kids had brought her down to earth fast and her thoughts now seemed silly. She wasn't a date he'd chosen for the usual reasons a man asks a woman out. She was an almost forty-year-old divorcée and he was, basically, a neighbor. In that capacity, he was friendly to her children. What they were doing tonight was ending the evening on a friendly note.

But still…

She couldn't restrain a little shiver of delight. Because just being alone with Cam even if only for sharing ice cream made it deliciously exciting, she admitted. As a man, he was enough to excite even a forty-ish, feet-on-the-ground woman such as herself. And, he was totally out of her realm. It was indeed risky to fool around with Cam like this, but it was hard to resist it. He'd been so *there* for her kids and her mother, even for Pete and Marta, all of which made him dangerously appealing.

"You're cold," he said, his keys jingling in his hand.

"Just a little." She should have put her sweater on instead of tying it around her shoulders, but then it wasn't necessary. Cam's arm went around her. Stayed there, warm and strong, as he used his key to open the door. It seemed so unusual and strange, standing in the circle of a man's arm this way, a man who wasn't Ted.

Once inside, she was struck again by the interesting mix of…things in his house. He'd kept many of his mother's antiques, but he'd added other pieces obviously picked up on his travels. Exotic travels, she thought, examining an odd-looking statue. Since he'd been a single man for the past few years, it must have made it easy to hop a flight and go anywhere, at any time.

She thought suddenly of Ted. Was the idea of being without the restrictions of a wife and kids simply irresistible? Francine had stated once to Rachel at a party that she had no desire for children, and since Ted's affair with her, he'd definitely backed away from any meaningful time with Nick and Kendy. Was his life with Francine going to be more appealing without the demands that had tied him down in his marriage?

Suddenly, Cam was in front of her, untying her sweater and lifting it from her shoulders. "That's a very serious look on your face. What's it about?"

"Oh, nothing much. I was just wondering about this statue and where it came from."

"I picked it up at an estate auction in Chicago when I was there at a signing for one of my books."

She picked it up. "It looks African or...something."

"It's from Ethiopia."

"Really?" She set it back where she got it, carefully.

"Does a fertility goddess really make you feel so sad?"

"I was thinking of your freedom to travel and wondering if Ted is seeking something like that with Francine. She's opposed to the idea of having children and they'll definitely enjoy more freedom than we did."

"You think Ted left to 'be free'?"

"He left for some reason, and I keep trying to find one that's more intelligent than having sex with Francine."

He moved to his really impressive bank of electronic gadgets and slipped in a CD. Sarah Brightman's sweet voice filled the room. He turned the volume down and moved back to where Rachel stood. "I want to say this just once and then we won't ever have to discuss it again, okay?"

"Depends what it is."

"It's about Ted and his incredible stupidity in leaving you, Nick and Kendy for a life with Francine Dalton."

She almost smiled. "Okay...I think."

He led her to the kitchen and seated her at the bay window. "Ice cream's coming up, but first..." He sat down beside her and took both her hands in his. "We can analyze and wonder until hell freezes over what motivated Ted to screw up his life and yours and his kids without ever understanding why. He probably has a list of grievances, just as you could make a list of things you didn't particularly like about him. That's the way marriage is, plain and simple. Most folks suck it up and keep on keeping on. But, in my opinion, his grievances aren't really what motivated Ted, which lets you off the hook, sugar."

He studied the back of one of her hands. "I think it's more likely this—that he's well aware of the gray showing up in his beard and his pubic hair and he's desperate to deny both. Francine's young and hot-blooded and he probably feels the same way when he's with her. It won't last, but he's not thinking that far ahead, I can promise you.'' He looked into her eyes. ''I shouldn't have to tell you, a bona fide psychologist, something so basic.''

''It's hard to be objective with something so basic.''

''Uh-huh. Now, in his panic, he's done something that wipes out everything he's worked for for almost twenty years. He's lost his practice, his wife, his children, his home, probably most of his friends, his good name and his retirement IRA because you and the kids are going to get the lion's share of what's left over when the dust settles, since he will have used his in trying to reestablish a practice. The truth is, he's selfish and self-centered and in his vanity, he's tossed away what really matters in life.''

''Gosh, now I feel sorry for him.''

He laughed. ''Don't, sugar. He's a man without integrity. And now he's a man without you, and if there's anything that might make me feel a tiny bit of sympathy for him, it's that.''

She smiled and reclaimed her hands, otherwise she might have given in to temptation and kissed him out of sheer gratitude. Or maybe half gratitude and half lust. ''I don't know why I ever thought you were moody, unapproachable and testy,'' she told him.

''I am, but only when I'm on deadline.'' He stood up and went to the freezer. ''If you'll get us a couple of dishes from that cabinet, I'll check out Kendy's selections. Okay, here's what we have flavor-wise, Choco Malt Whopper, Macadamia Mania and Phish Food. Name your poison.''

It was so easy to laugh with Cam. ''And Kendy told you sardines were dopey?''

''She assured me that there was no hamburger meat in Choco Malt Whopper. But as for Phish Food…I don't know.''

"Macadamia Mania," she told him, setting two bowls on the counter.

"Good choice. I think I've got a thing to dip—" The phone rang as he rummaged through a drawer. When the answering machine picked up and he heard the voice, he swore and shoved the drawer shut.

"Cam, you're gonna like this, buddy. I just left the—"

"My agent," he told Rachel, hurriedly picking up. "I'll only be a minute."

She took a step, intending to leave, but he stopped her with a hand on her arm. "Ben, what's up? Uh, huh…no kidding. Yeah, well, maybe. Just what I said, Ben, maybe." He gave Rachel a gentle shove back to the kitchen. "Look, I'll call you in the morning, okay? What? Yeah, I have and— I know it's important, but it can wait until morning. I'll call you." He hung up, gave Rachel a wry smile and went back to the freezer. "Ben tends to overreact."

"Oh, really? But I thought you were expecting his call." With a bowl in each hand, she blinked innocently at him. "Wasn't that the reason we left early?"

"You're not going to let me forget just one little white lie, are you?"

"Probably not."

He crossed the kitchen, bearing down on her with a wicked gleam in his eye. "You keep looking at me like that and—"

"And what?" she asked, feeling a laugh bubbling up.

"What do you think, sugar?" He was flirting with her. It slipped into her mind like sunshine after rain. And it was fun. Ted had never flirted because he didn't have much of a sense of humor. He'd courted her in a way that was totally unoriginal, a means to an end. Oh, he'd let her know she pleased him and he'd compliment her when the occasion called for it, but their relationship had developed mainly because they shared similar backgrounds, career aspirations and some sexual attraction.

Cam took her face in his hands and her urge to laugh changed to something more exhilarating. "I just may forget the ice cream and do something else instead," he said, looking at her lips. And before she could say stop or not, he was kissing her. It was so unexpected that her lips parted in surprise, which gave him instant opportunity to take the kiss deeper. And he did.

Clutching at his shirt, she had vague thoughts of his taste, rich and male and...absolutely wonderful. It was a turn-on more potent than sexy music or any nighttime fantasy, which was all she'd had to satisfy her needs since months before Ted left. She'd lived so long, it seemed, with logic and reason, the weight of responsibility, and restraint, but all that went up now like dry grass in a wildfire. She arched against him, wanting and willing and wishing what was happening would never end.

Seeking to prolong the pleasure, she slid her hands around and up his back and moved her body against his greedily. Kissing like this was an intimacy that had been missing so long in her marriage that she'd almost forgotten how good it was. How necessary. Swamped with need after months of deprivation, she was lost in the sheer delight of it.

Her response made what Cam had intended as a light, teasing kiss into something more, and for a few heady moments, he was as lost as Rachel. But then, with a low sound, he broke the kiss and pressed his mouth against her throat, holding her while trying to catch his breath. "Jesus," he said, his arms strong about her as she swayed dreamily, all her defenses down and her senses scattered.

Going on sheer instinct, she kissed the hollow in his throat and breathed in the masculine scent of him. "That was so nice," she murmured. "Thank you."

He managed a strangled laugh. "Another minute and you'd have something to really thank me for."

"It's been so long," she said softly, her head nestled beneath his chin while her body nestled snugly against his arousal. "I'd almost forgotten how it feels to be so...turned on."

"I was pretty turned on myself."

Yes, and it thrilled her to know that. Then she raised her eyes to his. "Why did you stop? You must have known I was...beyond thinking straight." Then, when he didn't reply right away, she added dryly, "I suppose I just proved that tired old saying about divorcées, didn't I?"

"It was a kiss, Rachel. You're entitled."

Embarrassment was beginning to set in now. She moved away from him. "I really need to be going." Glancing around, she spotted her sweater on the back of a chair in the dining room and headed that way. Cam followed, making no effort to persuade her to stay, which did nothing to ease her embarrassment. She grabbed the sweater and, without taking time to put it on, headed for the front door.

Cam was close behind. "Rachel." He caught her arm as she reached for the door handle and gently took her sweater from her. "I meant it when I said I was close to taking you, right there on the kitchen floor." He draped the sweater over her shoulders and added, "although I'd like to think I would have managed some finesse."

"Okay." She again groped for the door handle, but he put a hand on hers.

"Listen. I want you, Rachel. I have for...I don't know how long. Maybe about ten minutes after I realized you were moving in next door."

"That's crazy," she murmured.

"Yeah. And I thought it would be good between us. I just didn't know how good." With her eyes on the floor, she heard the smile in his voice. "But if you stay any longer tonight, we're going to wind up in bed. Are you sure you're ready for that?"

She found she couldn't look at him. "No, of course not. I'm not the type of person who can manage casual sex, as you wisely guessed. Thank you." She wasn't the kind of person who could have a casual sexual encounter...ever.

"It won't be casual sex with us, Rachel."

Since he had his hand on the door handle and she couldn't open it, anyway, she put her hands to her cheeks—which must be burning!—and finally looked up at him. "I'm so embarrassed. I didn't realize I was so...so..."

He smiled. "Ready?"

"At least you didn't say the *H* word."

"Horny?"

"Oh, God." She rolled her eyes. "Please open the door and let me go home and try to convince myself that living day and night with a teenager hasn't turned me into one."

Chuckling, he did as she asked, but to her dismay, as she darted out onto the porch, he was right behind her. "We had a date," he reminded her, slowing her by catching her hand. "I'm walking you to your door just as you would expect Nick to escort his date to her front door."

She could see there was no point in trying to talk him out of doing it, so she didn't bother trying. And she was becoming accustomed to him taking her hand. So, instead of fighting fate, she breathed in the chilly night air and fell into step beside him, thankful that it cooled her cheeks and hid from his amused eyes how she was blushing. As they crossed the lawn between his house and Dinah's, a car pulled up to the curb and stopped. Her spirits dropped as she recognized it.

"Ted's Lexus, right?" Cam said.

"Yes." And absolutely the last person she wanted to see tonight. Unless it would be Francine. And Rachel admitted that would be worse.

"Pretty late for a social visit."

Thankfully, it appeared that he was alone. "It's probably something else his lawyer has come up with that he wants me to sign," she said.

"Keeps on trying to screw you, does he?"

"Yes."

"And you'll demand that he take it to your lawyer, right?"

"Of course. And why he keeps trying to do these silly end runs beats me. He knows Stephanie and I are on to him now, but he's in such a financial bind that I guess he hopes I'll take pity on him." She glanced up at him. "You don't want to be a party to the scene, I'm sure. So, thanks again and—"

"You can thank me when we reach your front door," he said, keeping a firm hold on her hand.

By the time they reached Dinah's sidewalk, Ted was out of his car, but he hadn't yet noticed them. Rachel saw with surprise that his clothes were wrinkled and he seemed flustered. He dropped his keys and fumbled around on the ground for them. Up again and walking, he ran a hand over his hair and made a hasty effort to tuck in his shirt. Clearly, something was wrong.

"He looks like he's been rode hard and put up wet," Cam murmured.

"Yes, and it's very unlike him," she said, frowning. He was usually neat to the point of fastidiousness.

"Is he drunk?"

"If so, it would be very unusual. He's not much of a drinker. Ted," she said, finally catching his attention. "Is something wrong?"

"Rachel, I need to see—" He stopped when he realized that she wasn't alone. "I didn't expect—"

"You remember Cameron Ford?"

With a distracted look, he nodded curtly at Cam. "Sure, hello."

"Ted." Cam greeted him with a lift of his chin. "Been a long time."

Ted eyed their clasped hands with a frown. "Yeah. How are you?"

"Never better." Cam released Rachel, but only to draw her a little closer with a palm at the small of her back. It was a small intimacy, but a telling one.

Ted didn't often look disconcerted, but he did now. "Ah, am I interrupting something?" he asked Rachel.

"We were about to call it a night," Cam said, nudging her up the walk. Ignoring Ted, who lagged a few paces behind, he reached around her to open the door. Then, just as he'd done in his kitchen moments ago, he took her face in his hands and kissed her. It was a slow, deliberate melding of his mouth to hers and she felt the same wild leap of her senses as before. And again, it was over too soon.

Stepping back, he grinned at her. "G'night, sugar."

He went down the steps and, as he passed Ted, lifted his hand in a casual gesture, then headed across the lawn to his house, whistling.

A little dazed, Rachel thought longingly of going inside while she still had the taste of him on her lips, then falling into bed and going to sleep. Where, if she was lucky, her subconscious would finish what Cam had started in his kitchen. But her ex-husband was standing on the steps with a look on his face that warned her he was about to say something to ruin the happy glow she was feeling.

"How long have you been fooling around with Ford?"

She sighed and resisted an urge to close the door in his face. "What brings you here at this hour, Ted?"

"It didn't take him long to start sniffing around, did it?"

She made to close the door, but he was too quick. He caught it before she could slam it in his face. "What do the kids think about you acting like a teenager?"

She managed not to wince at that. "If you could carve out fifteen minutes to be with them, you might ask. And besides, what I do now is none of your damn business."

"I see Dinah's hand in this, Rachel. As soon as she realized her neighbor was a famous author, she got a plan."

She sighed with impatience. "Why are you here, Ted? It's after eleven. Kendy's in bed and Nick is at an overnight party with friends. If you want to talk to me, make it about something besides my personal life." She paused, studying his face and disheveled appearance. "What's wrong? You look like hell."

His hostility suddenly seemed to dissolve as he rubbed the back of his neck. "I don't want Dinah to hear. Where can we talk?"

"In the den." She let him in then and started down the hall. "And keep your voice down. I don't want to wake

Kendy. She's getting up early tomorrow morning to go to the zoo in Dallas with her friends.''

"I'd like a drink. Please."

As if he cared what Kendy had going tomorrow. Without a word, she went to the cabinet where Dinah kept a modest stock of liquor. "Whiskey?"

"Yeah, but make it a double."

"You look like you've already had a few drinks and I'm not in a mood to drive you home."

"I'm not drunk." He gave a short laugh, then muttered, "Maybe I'm just sobering up."

She frowned, looking at him for a moment, then poured a small drink. "Here, take it or leave it. And sit down over there on the sofa."

"Bossy as ever," he grumbled, taking the glass.

There was less likelihood of waking Kendy if they sat on that side of the room, but she didn't bother explaining. "I need to let Mother know I'm home and then we can talk."

With a grunt, he tossed half the whiskey back in one gulp, then went to the sofa. Rachel hesitated, thinking he really looked strange. Maybe he'd had another run-in with Walter. "Where's Francine?" she asked curiously.

"I'm not sure."

One of Rachel's eyebrows rose in surprise, but she said nothing before turning and heading for her mother's room. The door was not quite closed and she could see Dinah's reading lamp was still on. With a soft knock, she pushed the door open and looked in, but before she spoke, Dinah said, "I heard. What's up, do you think?"

"I have no idea, but something's wrong. He looks like he's been sleeping in his clothes."

"Francine's probably not as willing to do his laundry as you were."

"Mother…"

"I know, that wasn't very nice. But I swear, Ted brings out my bitchy side." She marked a place in her book and put it aside. "How was your date with Cam?"

"Nice."

"Just nice?"

Rachel couldn't stop the smile that suddenly bloomed over her whole face. "It was very nice, if you must know."

"Then I'll try not to say I told you so. But—" she smiled wickedly "—I told you so."

"He's sexy, interesting and he really knows how to—" she paused and Dinah's face brightened in anticipation "—choose wine."

With a snort, Dinah picked up her book, opened it and said, "Hopefully, Ted's problem will be quickly resolved and you can send him on his way. But…" she said as she tapped the bookmark against her lips, "isn't it odd that when he's in trouble, he heads straight to you?"

"I don't know why. He thinks I'm bossy. He just told me so."

"Not the best way to get you to solve his problems, is it? And he thinks you're bossy because he's such a weakling. Cam, on the other hand, is a real man. He—"

"Don't stay up too late," Rachel said hastily, and closed the door on her mother's laughter.

Back in the den, Ted sat with his elbows on his knees, studying his drink. The whiskey bottle sat on the floor beside him and she realized he'd helped himself to another drink. He'd always made it a point to drink in moderation. She could count on the fingers of a single hand the times in their eighteen-year marriage when he'd been drunk.

She picked up the bottle and took it back to the cabinet. "That's your limit tonight as long as you're here, Ted. Now, tell me what's happened. Why are you here?"

"Francine's having dinner with Walter."

"And—"

"I'm afraid she's having second thoughts about leaving him."

"Oh." Rachel stood for a moment, then moved to the ottoman and sat down facing him. "Did she say so specifically?"

"More or less."

"You'll have to do better than that for me to get a clear picture."

He jiggled the ice in his whiskey. "It's complicated."

"You said yourself I have a better-than-average IQ."

He gave a short, totally humorless laugh. "Strange as it seems, I've missed that."

"Missed what?"

"Your sarcasm. Hard to believe, but it's true."

She sat back at that. First she was bossy, then she lectured, and now she was sarcastic. He had a whole litany of complaints. But did she often resort to sarcasm? Instead of finding it funny, had he seen it as ridicule? Or a mockery of him?

"I'll try to be serious," she said. "What complicated reason does Francine have for changing her mind?"

"She hasn't done it yet, but I'm worried she's getting there." He took another taste of whiskey. "I think it's the money."

Now, there's a real surprise. Oops, sarcasm. "Do you mean the division of assets in her marriage to Walter or the financial problems you're having? Which is it?"

"Both. All. Everything." He blew out a long, whiskey-laden breath and she reeled backward, waving away the smell. He might give the impression that he was mostly unaffected that Francine wasn't proving as constant as he'd claimed she would be in the beginning, but something was bothering him.

"I don't think she anticipated Walter being such a hard-ass," Ted said. "She thought she could bring him around, get him to split things evenly with her. You know what he told her?"

"I don't know, kiss off? In your dreams, Franny? Get real?"

"He said why should he, as long as she was sleeping with me."

"Well, he is the injured party, Ted," she said.

"Bottom line," he said, brushing that aside, "is that the

amount his lawyer's talking is piddling compared to what Francine wants.''

''And your finances are going to be tied up indefinitely.''

''Yeah—again—thanks to Walter. Anything to stick it to me,'' he said with a shrug, as if it didn't matter. ''So, like I said, it's made Francine start rethinking everything, which is his sole purpose. Of course, I told her that. He thinks if he holds out, she'll decide it's not worth it and come back to him.'' His gaze drifted to the piano and the gallery of family photos there, many of them taken by Kendall. ''She's having second thoughts about being a stepmother, too.''

Now I'm really shocked. But she managed to be silent and show little on her face. ''What did she expect? That you'd walk away from your children? Banish them from your life?'' Actually, he'd almost done exactly that.

''I don't think she thought much about it.''

''Did you?''

''Not really.'' He met her eyes, and for a moment, she saw the man she'd once thought him to be.

Rachel got up and moved to the window, where there was a clear view of Cam's house. The lights in his kitchen were still on and she could see him moving around. Had he helped himself to ice cream after she left? she wondered. As if sensing her, he stopped and they stood looking at each other across the way.

''What do you want from me, Ted?'' she asked without turning.

''I'm not sure.'' He drew in a long breath. ''It's like I'm sort of waking up from some kind of—I won't call it a nightmare, but a state of suspended consciousness...or something.''

''Do you still love her?''

Another short laugh. ''The question is, did I ever? And what does it matter now that she's probably going back to Walter. She's not like you, Rachel. You'd be more understanding if you were in a relationship that hit a rocky patch. You'd have more...more thought for the feelings of the other partner. For working it out." He studied his empty glass with a frown. "Francine's more focused on herself and what she needs. What she wants."

"You mean, I'm a doormat and she's not."

He gave her a quick look. "No, no. I meant you're a kinder human being."

"But you fell for a bitchy human being, Ted. I don't see anything about what's happened that surprises me, and if you're honest, you must admit that." She thought he looked as if he wanted to argue and whether it would be to justify having gotten involved in an affair at all or whether he was toying with the idea of patching things up in their marriage, she didn't know. She found she didn't care. "I'm still not sure why you decided to tell me about all this, but it's late and I'm tired. You look as if you could use a good night's sleep, too. Go home and go to bed. Sleep on it."

"You forget. I don't have a home."

And whose fault is that? But being "a kinder human being," she left the words unspoken. "You have the lake house, Ted. You forget, it's the children and I who don't have a home."

For a long moment, his gaze stayed on the empty glass, and then he raised his eyes to hers. "I've really screwed up there, haven't I? With the kids, I mean. I was thinking about that tonight, too. I put them through those visits with Francine and they thought I'd be with her forever, that she'd be their stepmother. I don't know if I've done so much damage that they'll ever want me to be a part of their lives again. I wouldn't be surprised if it turns out like that."

"That's up to you, too, Ted. Nick and Kendy have only one father and they love you. That'll never change. But they've been hurt and disappointed by what you've done. They don't understand how one day they were part of a traditional family and the next, you left. Just…left. And because of that, their lives were turned upside down."

"I never meant to hurt them."

It took remarkable restraint not to lash out at him. If he

hadn't meant to hurt them, why had he? No one forced him to leave. It had been a choice made of his desire to have his cake and eat it, too. And it was a little late to be discovering that the price he'd paid was too dear.

"Unfortunately, they were hurt. You're right in thinking that it won't be easy to mend fences. Like other kids with divorced parents, they've coped. But, like I said, you're still their father and children are remarkably forgiving."

"You could help…if you were willing to."

"I've said all along that Nick and Kendy's welfare comes first with me. I won't do anything to sabotage your campaign to win them back. But don't expect forgiveness on my part. I'm only human."

"I guess I can't ask for more than that."

"No," she said dryly. "You can't."

He stood up. "So, I guess it's not a good time to ask to stay the night, huh?"

She gave him an incredulous look. "Not even if the lake house burned to the ground and every motel in town was full."

"I guess I deserve that," he said with a chagrined look.

"I guess you do." She watched him get to his feet, moving without his usual confident purpose. Or arrogance. He wouldn't come out of the affair with Francine unscathed. She'd done a number on him. Or, if what Cam thought was true, Ted had done a number on himself.

"It's okay if I go to the bathroom, isn't it?" He handed her the empty glass.

"You know where it is."

Midway across the den, he stumbled over Kendy's sneakers. In spite of Rachel's nagging, she'd left them lying in the middle of the floor. It was an indication of Ted's distracted state that he barely noticed. Had this happened when they were married, he would have cursed and demanded to know why Rachel couldn't manage to teach the kids not to leave their things lying around.

A few minutes later, she heard him come out of the bathroom, but didn't bother to see him out. He knew the way.

Nineteen

The phone call had come sometime in the wee hours of the morning, interrupting Cam's very good dream featuring hot sex with Rachel, whose long, lithe limbs were wrapped around him and whose lush and delectable mouth was doing things that left him breathing hard and tangled in his sheets. It took a minute before he was awake enough to realize that it was only a dream. And to recognize the voice on the answering machine as Nick's. His heart thundered in his chest as he fumbled to pick it up. One horrendous call five years ago and for the rest of his life, he reacted with sick panic when the phone rang after midnight.

"Cam?" Nick's voice had been pitched at so low a level that Cam strained to hear him. "I guess I woke you up, huh? I'm sorry."

"Ah…yeah. I mean, it's okay." Up on one elbow and groping for his reading glasses, he blinked to clear his eyes and focused on his bedside clock. It was 2:00 a.m. "What's the matter, Nick? Is it Dinah?"

"No, sir. It's me. I'm at Lake Ray Hubbard."

Lake— Nick sat up in bed. "Are you hurt?"

"No, sir. I'm drunk."

Cam rubbed a hand over his whole face, dropped his head low and conquered an urge to laugh. "Ah, the sleepover party with Mustangs' finest, right?"

"I guess Mom told you."

"She did. And you wanted to call and tell me about it in the middle of the night…why?"

"It's not what Robbie made it out to be, Cam." If possible, his voice dropped even lower. "There are some men here."

Cam frowned. "I take it you don't mean Robbie's father?"

"No, sir. I guess he knows 'em, but…they're gay."

"Gay men." Cam threw off the sheet and now sat on the side of the bed.

"Uh-huh. And I think they want us to, you know, make out."

The drive to Lake Ray Hubbard would normally take two hours, but Cam cut it almost in half. Hunched forward behind the wheel, he squinted at each mile marker as it passed, but it was a moonless night, so he wasn't certain he hadn't taken a wrong turn. So far, the bridge Nick gave as a landmark hadn't appeared. Couple miles beyond that was supposed to be a turnoff onto a secondary road.

The bridge suddenly materialized out of nowhere and next, a sharp curve. In negotiating it, he almost missed the turnoff. The road, narrow and bordered on each side with deep drainage ditches, was peppered with Private Property and Posted signs. Winding through heavy-wooded acreage, it was also as dark as a whore's heart.

He drove only a couple of hundred feet when Nick stepped out into the glare of the SUV's headlights. Standing foursquare in the road, Nick had his duffel in one hand and shaded his eyes from the brightness with the other. Cam swore and jammed on his brakes, wrenching the steering wheel to avoid running him down. Tires scrabbled for traction, churning up road dust and loose gravel before finally skidding to a stop.

With his heart pounding like the SUV's pistons, he got out on shaky legs and headed around the front, ready to take the boy's head off. "Goddamn it, Nick! I nearly ran you down. What the hell's the matter with you? You told me you'd wait a mile or so down the road."

"I'm sorry. I—"

But that was all he managed before he turned aside abruptly. Dropping his duffel to the ground, he bent over, made a couple of choking sounds and threw up.

"Aw, shit." Cam went back to his vehicle and grabbed a towel that he'd thrown in the back after a workout at the gym the day before. He always had a water bottle handy and he grabbed it now, opened it and soaked the towel. He winced in sympathy, hearing Nick's violent retching and, when he got back, was unsurprised to find him down in the grass, weak and miserable. But he'd heaved himself dry. For the moment.

"Here, let me help you up, son." Shoving the towel in the boy's hands, he put an arm around his waist and guided him back to the car. He'd left the back door open and now eased him onto the seat, facing out, just in case. "Breathe deep," he told him. "Take a minute."

Nick did as told, holding the wet towel against his face with shaky hands. In fact, he was shaking all over. Cam shrugged out of his jacket and draped it around his shoulders. As he waited for Nick to recover, he studied the dark road that he assumed led to the Sims's cabin. No sound or sign of life that he could hear or see, but it was likely they'd start looking for Nick as soon as they discovered him gone. The main road was more or less deserted at this hour, too, with few highway patrol sweeps. He didn't want to be spotted, as he did not have a good feeling about any of this.

"We need to move on as soon as you think you can travel, Nick. Let's hope they haven't noticed you're missing."

"Yes, sir." Weaving slightly as he sat, Nick glanced down the road, just as Cam had done. "But I think they're mostly too drunk to notice."

Maybe, Cam thought, but he would have assumed Nick was too drunk to navigate the distance from the Sims's place to the main road, but he had. It wasn't wise to underestimate a bunch of athletes in prime condition if they were marshaled up to search for Nick. "You think you're about finished?" he asked.

"You mean am I dead yet?" Nick took the bottled water Cam offered, got shakily to his feet and rinsed out his mouth. "No, I only wish I was."

Cam chuckled, knowing Nick's world was probably still moving in sickening whirls. "I know the feeling. And I'd wait a while before drinking much of that water."

"Yes, sir."

"Cut that out. This isn't the army."

"No." Still unsteady on his feet and clutching Cam's jacket, which dwarfed him, he stood with his legs spread for better balance. "And I appreciate you coming out here, makin' this drive and all, in the middle of the night."

"I'm glad to do it."

"I tried calling my dad, but I could only get his voice mail."

"Huh."

He made a valiant effort to stand tall and look decisive. "And I appreciate you not calling my mom about this. She didn't want me to go, but I talked her into it. Well, Dad overruled her, I guess, when I called him."

Good ol' Teddy. "She has to know, Nick. First thing tomorrow."

"Okay," he said, blinking owlishly.

"So, you about ready to go now?"

Pleased at having put off a hairy scene with his mom, Nick nodded. But the movement made him dizzy. He would have gone down, but Cam sprang forward, catching him before he tumbled backward into the ditch. He placed the boy's arm around his own neck, hauled him back to the SUV and buckled him in.

By the time Cam reached the driver's side, Nick had already flipped the lever that reclined the seat and was sinking fast. Stretched out flat now, he threw an arm over his eyes in a maneuver Cam recognized as an effort to shut out an unstable world and went down for the count. His thoughts, as he headed back to Rose Hill, were grim. Nick hadn't given many details yet, but Cam got the gist of it. Nick, among other young athletes, had been set up as targets for sexual predators.

Rachel rose early Saturday morning because Kendy was going to the zoo in Dallas with her friends. After coaxing her to eat some breakfast, Rachel had drifted out onto the patio to savor her coffee in sweet solitude while Kendy waited inside watching TV until Madison's mom arrived in the van. The day was full of promise, bright and sunny, crisp without being cold. Sitting down in the swing, she gave it a gentle shove, wrapped her hands around the warm mug and heaved a satisfied sigh. Her mother was in the shower, getting ready to go to Moody Gardens in Galveston overnight with three of her friends who were gardening enthusiasts. Nick probably wouldn't be home until nearly dark, as Lake Ray Hubbard was a two-hour drive, and if she knew teenage boys, they wouldn't want to leave until they had to. It gave Rachel a rare chance to simply do nothing but admire the day and think about last night.

She had tossed and turned for hours, and not because of Ted's unexpected appearance or his troubles. Perhaps that is what should have occupied her mind, but after those kisses in Cam's kitchen, Ted's self-pitying whining made barely a blip on her sympathy meter. It would take more than a few mealymouthed regrets and halfhearted resolutions to make amends before she'd take him seriously ever again. No, her restlessness came from her own conflicted feelings about Cam and his restraint last night.

She watched a spirited hummingbird, one of the first of the season, zoom into Dinah's hanging feeder. It was impossible, now, to pretend that she was indifferent to Cam. For a while lately, she had let herself wonder what it would be like to have him as a lover, even though such a thing was unlikely. A man with Cam's sophistication would hardly want a fling with a small-town high school counselor who was also a single mom bogged down with a recent divorce and all the problems that came with it. Too sticky, from his perspective. And even if he were interested, it would be brief.

She knew now it would be dangerous.

She meant it when she told him she was not casual-sex material. The kiss hadn't changed her character, but what it had done was destroy her notion that she could continue seeing Cam and involving him in her personal life without falling in love with him. She could do that so, so easily, she'd learned last night. Ted's treachery had hurt and humiliated her, but the same treatment from Cam would be far more devastating.

Which, if she stopped and thought about it, didn't make much sense. She had eighteen years of marriage, two children and many shared experiences with Ted and just a few months of tentative friendship with Cam. Lucky she had a taste now of just how lethal he could be when he set out to charm her. Forewarned was forearmed.

The squeak of his back door had her looking across the way to his house. He stood on his back porch holding a coffee mug, wearing nothing but faded jeans and a killer tan. He didn't look like a man who made his living writing books, she thought, admiring the smooth symmetry of line in the breadth of his shoulders and flat tummy. He must have a workout room somewhere in that house to be so fit. Realizing suddenly that she was staring, she took a quick gulp of coffee and promptly choked.

When she looked up again, Cam was heading her way. He'd pulled on a T-shirt, something old and soft with age. His feet were shoved into shoes that looked as if he'd picked them up at the Goodwill store, and did he ever comb that unruly dark hair? He looked rumpled and a little rough around the edges, sleep deprived and supremely sexy. He might have stepped right out of her best dream.

"You're up mighty early," he told her, zinging her with that half smile as he approached the patio.

"Kendy's having a day at the zoo with friends, so we're

up early." She wondered if he could see that she was flustered, remembering last night.

"Taking along her trusty digital cam, I assume."

Rachel smiled and sipped her coffee. "She might forget her shoes, but never her camera."

"Gorgeous day for a road trip." Leaning against an old chest, he asked casually, "She's coming home tonight?"

"Actually, she's spending the night with Carly, her best bud."

"And it's this weekend that Dinah and her buddies are heading for Galveston to check out Moody Gardens, isn't it?"

She looked at him. "Is it?"

"Hmm." Sipping coffee. "So, what are your plans for the day?"

She was shaking her head, but before she decided whether or not to be honest about having no plans, the door flew open and Kendy dashed out. "Mom, my camera's gone! I had it yesterday when I was taking pictures of a hummingbird drinking out of a flower. I put it on the shelf in the kitchen with Gran's cookbooks where you told me to always keep it and it's gone, Mom. And I know where."

"Wait, wait." Rachel was already up off the swing and heading for the door. "Are you certain you didn't put it in your backpack when you packed last night?"

"I looked already! But you don't need to check anything, because Nick took it."

"Nick? Nick wouldn't take your camera without asking, Kendy. Have you looked in your room?"

She stamped one small foot. "I don't have to. He wanted to use it and I told him no, I had to take it to the zoo. So he just *stole* it, Mom!"

"If it's truly gone," Rachel said, straightening the collar of Kendy's shirt, "I'll give you some money and tell Madison's mom to pick up a disposable camera to use just for today." She started toward the door. "But first, let me just make a quick search to see if I can find it."

Kendy ignored that and instead looked over at Cam. "Will you take me to that stupid lake where he is, Cam? I bet it's in Nick's stupid duffel bag. He's so stupid all the time now. He can't even make good grades anymore."

"Kendy." Rachel's tone was stern. "Cam can't take you anywhere. You'll have to make do with a disposable today. I'm sorry, and if Nick truly does have your digital, he will be in serious trouble."

Cam, who'd been listening, said to Kendy, "Are you positive your camera's in Nick's duffel?"

She nodded vigorously. "He wanted to take pictures of girls at the party," she said with disgust.

"I might be able to resolve this problem," he told Rachel. "Nick is asleep in my guest room. I think his duffel is in my truck." He reached for Kendy's hand. "Let's go check it before your ride gets here."

Rachel was rooted in place. "Nick's asleep in your house? Why? What—" She caught sight of something in Cam's expression and her eyes narrowed. "Are you serious?"

"I'm serious. And I'll explain. In fact, I came over to tell you but decided it could wait until you'd finished your coffee. Let me check out the duffel and as soon as Kendy's on her way, we'll talk."

Kendy, looking from one adult's face to the other, said in a gleeful tone, "Nick's in trouble, isn't he, Mom?"

In spite of the fact that Nick had been doing some troubling things lately, Rachel was shocked to find that he had taken Kendy's camera. It was in his duffel, which was on the floor of Cam's SUV, just as he'd said. When Cam handed it over, Kendy shot them both a triumphant look and said, "See, I told you. He's gonna be grounded, isn't he, Mom?" Fortunately, Madison Snow's mom pulled into Dinah's driveway just then and there was no time to discuss what was in store for Nick. As soon as Rachel waved her daughter off, she marched back to Cam's house.

"He's upstairs," Cam told her before she had a chance to

ask, "in the shower. And if you have any compassion in your soul, you'll cut him some slack until he can focus. Nothing you can say will make him feel worse, anyway, considering his condition. He's hungover."

She sat down wordlessly in the chair he nudged in her direction. On her way back from seeing Kendy off, she'd thought about what to say to Nick for sneaking off with Kendy's camera, but that transgression was almost forgotten now that she knew he'd been drinking once again. She braced herself for who knew what else he might have been doing. "How did he happen to wind up at your house?" she asked Cam. She had so many questions that it was a toss-up where to start.

"He called me from Robbie's party. He said he tried to reach Ted but couldn't. And he didn't want you driving alone out there in the middle of the night. I give him credit for that."

"So he was at the party."

"Yeah." Cam took a mug from a cabinet and poured her a cup of coffee. "I don't have all the details myself as he was pretty wiped out when I got there. He fell asleep in the car, but I did get this much. There was some questionable goings-on, and nothing like what he expected. He had the good sense to leave."

"Kendy said he took the camera to take pictures of girls. There weren't supposed to be any girls. It was supposed to be all boys, mostly athletes and, of course, Robbie's father was to be there."

"No girls and Robbie's dad wasn't there. Robbie probably lied about that for obvious reasons. There were adults, but hardly the type you'd want as chaperones for Nick. You can get the details firsthand," he said, glancing at the stairs. "He's coming down now."

Nick was pale and moving gingerly, but he made his way gamely into the kitchen and eased himself down on the chair across from Rachel. Bright morning sun poured in the bay window, and with something like a whimper, he turned away from it. Cam sat down beside him.

"You want some juice or something?" he asked, then smiled when Nick closed his eyes, putting up one hand in mute refusal. "Still a little queasy, huh?"

Nick looked across the table at Rachel. "I'm sorry, Mom. I know I'm grounded for all time, but I swear I didn't know what was going down at that party. And you're probably mad 'cause I woke Cam in the middle of the night and made him drive all the way out there to pick me up. So, just give the lecture."

His eyes were bloodshot and his hands weren't quite steady, but she firmly quelled a spurt of sympathy. "Why don't I save the lecture until I know exactly what I'm to lecture you about? Just tell me what was going on at the party."

"Before I get into that—" he looked at Cam "—I just want to say that you don't have to pay me anything to help you with flooring the attic or working on the roof when you get ready to do the job. I owe you big time."

"We covered that last night. You don't owe me. And I'm glad you felt you could call me. Next time, don't hesitate."

"There won't be a next time," Nick said fervently. "Believe me, that kind of party is not my thing. And it wasn't that I was just upset over what was going down. I was disgusted and pissed off at being so damn dumb to think a bunch of senior varsities were inviting me because they liked my smile." He rubbed his finger over a small scar on the table. "Well, actually one person liked my smile and also my exquisite amber eyes and my fabulous cheekbones. Called himself Joseph, no last name. None of them had last names." He added with a twist of his mouth, "Joseph was a cinematographer and would love to put me in a video."

"I think I'm beginning to get the picture," Rachel said, frowning. "So what did you do when you realized what kind of party it was?"

Nick drew his knees up close to his chest. "I went outside

on the back porch where it was pretty dark and deserted. I'd had a lot of beer…'' He chanced a quick look at Rachel. "I know it was stupid, Mom, and it was just about then that I wished I'd been drinking Pepsi. So I needed a minute to calm down and to figure out how to get home. No way was I gonna sleep there.

"About that time, I saw these two people coming up from the lake, one of 'em a big, burly guy, but I didn't know then who it was. So they get real close and I hear them plain as anything, and even if I couldn't see them properly, I hear the big guy use Jace's name."

"Jason Pate," Rachel said. This, at least, was no surprise.

"Yeah, that's when I knew it was Jace and Coach Monk was the other guy. It was just so…out of sight, you know? I was, like, shocked. And here's the real shocker, Mom. I could tell by what Coach said. They'd been having sex."

Half an hour later, Rachel sent Nick back upstairs to bed, promising him she'd deal with the consequences of his behavior later. As Cam said, he was in no shape to be chastised, but he was clearly aware of the implications of what he'd seen. And he had done the smart thing in leaving, even though she chided him for not calling her instead of Cam.

"I'm with Nick on that one," Cam said. After pouring himself more coffee, he carried the pot over and refilled her mug. "I had a few uneasy moments myself. That area's pretty deserted and especially for a lone woman." His fingers brushed hers as he passed the sugar bowl to her. "I'm betting you wouldn't have even thought about calling me to go with you."

"No, of course not. He's my son and he's my responsibility."

"Yeah. And neither one of you can depend on Ted, as Nick discovered last night."

"Don't worry, I plan to clue him in on what he missed," she said dryly. "But for now, what do you think of all this, Cam?"

"You did the right thing in telling Nick to play it cool, keep his mouth shut about what happened and tell us if he gets wind of anything else." Cam didn't sit back down but settled against the counter, nursing his coffee. "You know him better than I do, but can we trust him to do that?"

"I'm not sure. He's shaken over the whole mess. At any rate, I don't want to wait around and see what Monk intends to do. I'm not sure why he risked letting Nick see what's really going on."

"Unless Tyson never intended for Nick to see it. Could be that Joseph making a move on him was an unscripted moment, so to speak. But now that the cat's out of the bag, Tyson will have to do something."

"I want to go to Pete with this," Rachel said. "I think he should know what's going on. My concern now is for Nick, but I can't help wondering about other athletes."

"I can't help wondering why some other kid hasn't blown the whistle on Tyson before now," Cam said, folding his arms. "There's never been any talk about Tyson at school?"

"About that? No, not a word."

"Without breaching confidentiality, can I ask if Jason gave you any hint of his involvement with Tyson when you spoke with him in your office? He's clearly a favorite of Tyson's, but that doesn't mean he's happy 'enjoying' Tyson's attentions."

"He's definitely conflicted about his sexuality. I see other boys who are dealing with sexual identity and Jason didn't seem such a textbook case." She gave a quick shake of her head. "Oh, but now that I know what Nick saw, I can better understand Jason's dilemma. No wonder that boy is in agony. Monk Tyson is a…a monster! How dare he? How *dare* he! He's entrusted with those boys' welfare by their parents and the school board. He's paid to coach them in sports, not…not…"

Cam squeezed her shoulder gently. "I know it's upsetting, but I don't think you should let your outrage over Monk push you into jumping the gun before Pete has a chance to work things from a law-enforcement angle."

"I won't. It's just so…distressing." She toyed with a spoon, turning it over and over. "When you came to my office Friday afternoon, I was scanning the records searching for students—athletes—who may have transferred out of Rose Hill High but who didn't move out of this school district. It's a time-consuming task, but I'm getting back to it first thing Monday morning. There has to be a paper trail if nothing else."

"Yeah." He turned and poured the dregs of his coffee down the sink. "But for today, what do you say to taking a drive with me to Austin? We'll give Pete a heads-up on what happened and let him do his thing on his end. And now that we've got something concrete to go on, I'd like to try to fit it into what happened to Jack."

"Why Austin?" she asked, trying not to be seduced by the idea of a whole day in Cam's company. After last night, there was little else that she'd like more even if it was an invitation to heartbreak. "I assume it's not a tour of the state capital you have in mind?"

"No, I've done that and so have you," he said, clearing the table. "I was thinking of a visit to the UT campus."

"Jimbo Rivers is a student at UT," she guessed, watching him put their mugs in the dishwasher.

"Uh-huh. While you were seeing Kendy off, I called his dad and was told Jimbo has practice today, so he'll be on campus."

"I'm sure you know most kids don't hang around, especially on a Saturday."

"Let's give it a shot, anyway. We could be there by noon if we leave in an hour or so." Done with the cleanup, he slid his palms in the back pockets of his jeans. "But if I don't see him today, I'll keep trying until I do."

"You could call him directly. Wouldn't that be more logical than driving all the way to Austin on the off chance of finding him?"

"I'm afraid he'll say no if I call. He was polite five years ago, but I suspect—no, I know—he was withholding information. I didn't push him then, but I'm ready to push now."

She studied his face, knowing what they were discovering about Monk Tyson's organization was feeding into his fierce belief that Jack had not committed suicide. He was driven to uncover the truth of his son's death by the same kind of relentless determination that pushed him to analyze past crimes in real life when he wrote a book. She knew it would be a waste of time to tell him he could be setting himself up for more pain. If Jack had been murdered, the loss was just as great and the pain maybe even more so.

"Are you sure you want someone along when you talk to Jimbo?" she asked. "You might have a better chance of getting him to tell you what he knows if there's just the two of you."

He smiled. "Does this mean you'll go with me?"

"Was there ever any doubt?" she asked him.

"All right. I'll pick you up in an hour," he told her, hustling her to the door. Then, just before seeing her out, he bent and gave her a quick kiss on her surprised mouth. "Better pack your toothbrush. Just in case."

If there was one thing Monk Tyson despised, it was having to alter his plans because somebody screwed up. And he especially despised having a weekend at Sims's lake cabin screwed up. Sims offered the use of the cabin whenever he wanted it and was always conveniently elsewhere. He also made it a point to lay in the food Monk preferred with a chef to prepare it—one who was deaf, dumb and blind. The place was big enough for the kind of privacy Monk required and the bar was amply stocked with quality liquor.

Best of all, Sims didn't question the guest list. If Monk wanted to spend a weekend with Jack the Ripper, he didn't think his host would object. Whatever it took to get Robbie into pro sports was Sims's focus. Apparently, he didn't suspect Monk's sexual preferences, but even if he did, to guarantee Robbie an eventual draft by the majors, Sims would probably hand over the kid himself for Monk's pleasure. Only one problem. Robbie wasn't to Monk's taste, never had been even when he was four years younger. Big, thick-necked kid, bulked up with steroids and dull as dirt, he just didn't ring Monk's bell.

Another kid did, which is how the weekend got screwed. How the hell Nick Forrester had managed to disappear in the middle of the night was a point he'd take up with Ferdy and B.J. on Monday, but for today, Monk was forced to do damage control. Twice now Nick had pissed him off. He was a problem that would have to be handled. Later. Otherwise, Nick was to his liking in every way. Dark-eyed, intelligent and lean-limbed, sleek and graceful as an antelope on the ball field. Just thinking about him made Monk's mouth water. But thanks to that idiot Joseph making a move on him, it might never be possible to get a taste of him now.

The house party was supposed to dazzle Nick, bring him around so he'd want to belong to the group. Most tenth-graders would have been awed to be invited to join the elite of Monk's varsity for a weekend. He'd issued orders that Nick wasn't supposed to see—or suspect—anything that would put him off until Monk had a chance to soften him up. It took real confidence and a badass attitude to walk out of the compound in the middle of the night with no access to a vehicle. Rejecting Monk's special coaching had taken guts, too. With his folks' divorce breaking up his home and his prick of a father flaunting his mistress, Monk had figured Nick for an easy mark. It was bullshit that the reason he backed off the special coaching was because of his mother. Sharp as he was, he'd sensed danger, Monk realized now, even though he hadn't yet made his move. It would be particularly satisfying to break him.

What irritated him, too, was that he'd handled the kid as carefully as he'd handled Jack Ford a few years back. That, of course, had proved to be a major miscalculation, one of the very few he'd made while at Rose Hill. He still broke

out in a sweat at how close everything had come to meltdown
when Jack wound up dead.

The link, however, between Nick and Cameron Ford was
troubling. Monk hoped he'd seen the last of that son of a
bitch. He'd been suspicious about his boy's suicide, but
Monk had been extremely careful with damage control then.
When Ford visited his office last week, he'd been a different
man from the shocked and grieving father who'd begged for
information five years ago. It would be a major complication
now if Nick had confided his suspicions. Or, maybe Nick
had talked to his mother. Which might be even worse. Rachel
was one tight-assed bitch who, if she picked up the scent of
what Monk had spent years carefully concealing, would take
him down, even if it meant sacrificing her own job to do it.
She had that kind of zeal as far as those kids she counseled
were concerned. With Nick thrown in the mix, she'd be twice
as zealous.

So, between Nick, Rachel and Cameron Ford, there could
be big trouble brewing. Up to now, he'd relied on discretion,
caution and ruthless control to survive, but nothing lasted
forever. He'd felt for a while now that it might be time to
move on. One thing first, though. He still had a powerful itch
for Nick and he wasn't leaving without scratching it.

Twenty

They arrived at the UT campus in time to watch the last hour of practice in the covered stands at UT's famed Disch-Falk Field. Cam had seen Jimbo play five years ago in Rose Hill when he and Jack were both coached by Monk Tyson. The raw talent Jimbo had displayed on the mound then had been honed to near perfection now. As they watched, he'd thrown one stinging pitch after another, his talent shining as bright as the Texas sun at high noon.

"Well, even I can see why he's being courted by the majors," Rachel said. "He's beautiful."

"He is that." Cam knew she was no sports expert, but she could still appreciate sheer grace and flawless form in a male athlete. "And if his little brother wants to outshine him one day, he's got his work cut out."

"I just wish they'd stay off his back until he's finished his education," she said wistfully.

She would. She was first and foremost an educator. It was nice that the ballplayer in question might turn out to be the next Roger Clemens, but there were more important things to Rachel's way of thinking. "I bet you say that about all the promising athletes whose files cross your desk."

"Sports doesn't last, education does," she said, paraphrasing some anonymous sage.

"But if he makes a gazillion bucks on the mound, who cares if he can't read? Ouch!" Chuckling, he rubbed his side where Rachel's elbow connected sharply. "Just kidding, I swear."

"You're a sports nut. Your kind doesn't kid about that."

He couldn't deny how much he would have loved seeing Jack where Jimbo was right now, and watching him, Cam felt again the sting of his own loss. It was impossible not to think how Jack might have blossomed as an athlete, had he made it to a university.

After Jack's death, Cam had been told that Jack and Jimbo had been the most promising athletes Rose Hill High had produced in a generation. He had to accept that it just wasn't meant to be. As if she sensed his thoughts were of Jack, Rachel leaned against him and patted his knee, effectively closing his throat and killing the smart-ass retort he'd been ready to make.

Damn. He wasn't here in Austin today to brood over losing Jack. "If it's any comfort," he said, "Ward tells me Jimbo's struggling with the decision whether to play his senior year or to sign with St. Louis."

"Well, at least he's giving his education serious thought. That's something." Lifting her drink, she sipped cola through a straw before adding dryly, "Which is not the advice he would have gotten from Monk Tyson."

They sat for a moment watching the game. Rachel's gaze stayed on the playing field, but her mind was obviously elsewhere. "Cam, do you think Nick stopped those special coaching sessions because Tyson was coming on to him?"

"No," he said firmly. "It's the first thing I thought, too. Nick talked with me about opting out, and I think if Tyson had made a move, he would have mentioned it. Or hinted at it. What I do think is that Nick sensed the way the wind was blowing, as far as Tyson's concerned. He didn't completely connect the dots, but he was getting there. Plus, Nick genuinely wanted to make it on his own, and not have it said that Tyson had given him special treatment to get there. So he quit."

Seeing her distress, he wished they weren't in such a public place. He'd like to give her a hug. "He's one helluva kid,

Rachel. He's got guts and scruples. He's smart and he has a good heart. You can trust him to make good decisions.''

She made a sound of disbelief. ''You've obviously forgotten that his grades are tanking, he's surly and uncooperative, he swiped Kendy's camera when she expressly told him no and he got drunk last night.''

''He's temporarily off track, but he'll be okay, Rachel.'' He had her hand now and brought it up to kiss, then added, ''As for taking Kendy's camera, that one may require some drastic response. Kendy's out for blood, I think.''

''He's going to have to give her a choice of ten CDs from his collection and never have to return them...ever.''

He winced. ''Ever?''

''Ever.''

On the field, the players were beginning to break up. Cam stood and extended his hand and she rose with him. ''You're one tough cookie, Mom,'' he said as they started down.

''Yes, well, in the absence of a father, it appears that I've got to wear the pants.''

''And you look fantastic in them, too.'' And grinned when she brushed past him looking pink and flustered.

''I've been thinking about Ward,'' she said a few minutes later as they waited for Jimbo across from the entrance to the practice field. ''Do you think Jimbo might know what Tyson is and has kept it to himself?''

''If he thought blowing the whistle might jeopardize his future in the majors, it's possible. After all, without Tyson's coaching and his contacts, Jimbo might not be where he is today. So, I do think it's possible.''

''But Ward...'' Rachel put a hand to her cheek in distress. ''If that's true, wouldn't he be concerned that his younger brother might be victimized?''

''I don't know, but if he hasn't thought about it, I have. Nick says Ward has his heart set on competing with Jimbo as an athlete. Tyson would pick up on that, you can bet. And if he had a yen for Ward, he'd have leverage to pressure the boy into acts that Ward wouldn't ordinarily dream of doing.''

"I can't believe this!" In her agitation, Rachel paced back and forth, then stopped and looked at Cam. "Actually, I do, but I'm appalled that I didn't suspect something before now. My God, how many boys—"

Cam gripped her shoulder. "Listen to me. Tyson is one shrewd operator, and I bet we'll find he's been doing this long enough to perfect his technique. We've told Pete what Nick saw and the fat's in the fire. The man's days are numbered. But you're not to blame in any way, Rachel. Tyson fooled a lot of people." Then, instead of turning her loose, he pulled her closer and stood holding her, understanding how a threat to the students she counseled—and to her son—struck at her heart.

Rachel allowed the embrace, anchoring her hands at his waist. "This is so bizarre, Cam. Just when you think things might begin to make sense in the world, something like this jumps out of the woodwork."

"If anything came out of the woodwork, it was Tyson." He was swaying a little, enjoying the way she fit in his arms, soft and womanly, a little fragile at the moment, but Rachel had a core of steel. He turned his face into her hair, breathing in the scent of flowers and silk. "I wish we were here for something more enjoyable than trying to dig up Tyson's secrets." He pressed his lips to her temple. "After last night, I wanted to be with you today. I'm glad I had an excuse to finagle you into making the trip with me."

"It didn't take much finagling."

He smiled and said in her ear, "I promise the next date we have will be dinner and a movie. Or something better." He didn't think she was ready to hear the "something better" he had in mind.

She sighed, her gaze focused beyond him on the gate of the practice field. "Look, isn't that Jimbo now?"

Cam released her and, using the bill of his ball cap to shade his eyes, watched Jimbo come through the gate with two other athletes. All appeared to be headed to the parking lot. Cam saw the other two peel off, then he touched Rachel, murmuring, "Stay here, I'll be back in a minute." Cutting diagonally across the tarmac, he was almost on top of Jimbo when he was recognized.

"Mr. Ford, hey." A grin, quick and pleased. "It's been a while. How are you?"

"I'm good. And it's Cam. How you doin', Jimbo?"

"Okay. I'm okay." He'd stopped now, glancing once curiously over at Rachel, standing beside Cam's SUV. "Isn't that Ms. Forrester, the guidance counselor?"

"Yeah. Rachel. She made the drive with me."

"Very nice lady. I heard about the divorce. Ward was really shocked. Me, too." He was shaking his head. "You never know, I guess."

"It looks that way."

Jimbo focused on Cam again. "I thought you'd move back to New York, but Ward tells me you're living in your folks' old house."

"It suits me. And I only get back to New York when I need to deliver a manuscript."

"Man, I don't think I'd want to hang around Rose Hill if I had a chance to go somewhere else, especially some place interesting."

Cam smiled. "Like St. Louis?"

Jimbo grinned. "Ward's got a big mouth."

"He's proud of his big brother."

"Ward's got what it takes, too. And so does Nick. I've watched them both and they're good. By the time they're seniors, Coach Tyson will probably have them whipped into shape and lined up for scholarships." He shook his head. "That guy's phenomenal."

With a glance at Jimbo's duffel, Cam asked, "You headed anywhere in particular right now?"

"Not especially." Jimbo flicked a glance in Rachel's direction. "You have something in mind?"

"Food, you name the place. Maybe somewhere on Sixth Street? Best I recall, they have some interesting places to eat." With his keys out now, Cam looked about, checking for a girlfriend, but saw no one. "Practicing the way you do must work up an appetite."

"Yeah, I could eat. And Sixth Street's cool. Thanks." He reached for the cell phone riding at his waist. "Just let me make a quick call and we'll head out." Another glance at Rachel. "Ms. Forrester's coming, too?"

"If it's okay by you."

"Sure, like I said…"

Cam smiled and they said it together. "She's a nice lady."

Jimbo suggested a small bar and grill on Sixth where he promised the food was good and the noise level wouldn't quite drown out conversation. "My girlfriend and I like it here," he told them after their food arrived at their table near the back. "A lot of places where students hang out have really loud music and stuff, but sometimes…" He shrugged. "Sometimes you want to just talk and be able to hear yourself, you know? Gail's kinda quiet, anyway. She doesn't like a lot of noise."

"That wouldn't be Gail Maddox, would it?" Rachel asked with surprise.

He looked up, a French fry suspended midway to his mouth. "Yeah, it would."

Rachel smiled broadly. "You and Gail were dating in the tenth grade. My word, Jimbo, not many teen romances survive that long."

"Ours didn't, either," he told her. "Two months here at UT and we broke up. All those girls…" He was shaking his head, grinning.

"And all those guys…" Rachel said, still smiling.

"Uh-huh. So, for the next three years, we both dated other people. And then about six months ago I was at this party, and suddenly there she was."

"And there you were," Rachel said, her voice going soft and her smile gentling. "Ah, that's really nice."

He shrugged, looking a little embarrassed. "I guess you could say we rediscovered each other. I gave her a ring at

Christmas, although I don't know when for sure we're getting married. It'll have to be after I graduate or...whatever.''

Cam sat with a beer between his palms. "It's a tough decision, whether to stay in school or go with the majors."

"Tell me about it."

"I'm happy for you, Jimbo," he said softly, and lifted the beer in a salute.

"Yeah, thanks." Jimbo toyed with a French fry, drenching it in ketchup. "But sometimes when I'm lying in bed and thinking about the...just the wonderfulness of it, then I want to tell somebody how lucky I feel. Gail...she's really happy about it, but she's pretty...girly, if you know what I mean. She knows from nothing about baseball. Or sports, either, to tell the truth." He chewed the fry, swallowed and added, "Don't get me wrong. She turns me on, so I wouldn't want to change her, but like I said, I wish I could tell somebody who'd really get it." He looked up from his plate into Cam's eyes. "Somebody like Jack."

Cam nodded, barely. "Yeah."

"He was somebody special, Mr. F—Cam. The best friend I've ever had."

"That's good to hear," Cam said, managing a smile. "Like most dads, I like hearing good things about my son. Jack thought a lot of you, too."

"It took me forever to believe he was gone. I mean, it was so wrong, so crazy." He looked up quickly, apologetically. "I didn't mean that the way it sounded, 'cause Jack was the least crazy person I knew. But it was so...not like him to suddenly up and...do that." He shoved his plate aside. "If he was so close to meltdown as that, why wouldn't he say something? We were close. He could have told me any-thing...*anything*. I mean it."

Cam studied his face for a minute. "Could he, Jimbo? Could he tell you anything?"

Jimbo frowned, picking up on something in Cam's question he didn't quite get. "Yeah, he could." He looked at Rachel, whose eyes were on a paper napkin, folding and refolding it. He shifted back to Cam. "Why? What's this about?"

"First, I need to ask you to keep what we talk about here in confidence. Are you okay with that?"

"Yeah," Jimbo said, but only after a serious study of Cam's face. "I didn't think you drove all the way to Austin just to watch me throw a few balls at practice. This is about Jack, isn't it?"

"It has to do with Jack, yes."

"So, what's the question?"

"I have your word?"

"Yeah. Damn right, if it'll shed some light on why he did what he did."

Cam, who hadn't ordered anything to eat, pushed his beer aside. "You're not the only one who found Jack's death hard to understand," he began, and tried to stifle the sudden rush of emotion that rose in him. Finding it difficult to sit still, he wanted to get up and walk it off, but he could hardly do that now that he was finally beginning to get somewhere. He took in a deep breath. "I wanted to think it couldn't be true. My son wouldn't do that. Like you said, he could have talked to me, told me what was on his mind. No matter what it was, I would have understood, been there for him, prevented it."

Rachel put her hand over his and he found he needed that touch to say the rest. He gave a bitter smile and forced himself to look at Jimbo. "Jack did call. He did talk to me. Briefly. He said something bad was going on in Monk Tyson's organization. But I was too busy with a deadline to get details then, so I put him off. I told him we'd talk about it in a week or two, when I was done. He didn't wait a week or two. Instead, he killed himself that night."

Jimbo's eyes went bright with tears. "That must have been tough," he managed finally.

"Yeah," Cam said, then cleared his throat. "I only bring it up now to ask this, Jimbo. Do you know what Jack meant? Was there anything going on in the sports program that you thought was not right?"

"Nothing that I think had anything to do with Jack doing what he did," he said, choosing his words carefully, almost as if picking his way through a minefield.

"Okay, but that sounds like you thought something wasn't right. So, even if you don't think it relates to Jack's death, I wish you'd tell me what it is."

Now Jimbo seemed to be the one who wanted to get up. His plate sat half finished, the burger and fries gone cold. "It was only rumors," he said finally.

"Rumors about what? About somebody?"

Jimbo moved back in his chair. "Man, I don't know if I should be talking about this. It's just rumors and if it got out, it'd be—well, it could do majorly big damage."

How to get him to say the words without putting them in his mouth? Cam wondered. "Damage to the school? Or to an individual?"

"Both. Look, I wouldn't be where I am today but for the breaks I got at Rose Hill High. I'd feel like shit—" He gave Rachel an apologetic look. "Sorry, Ms. Forrester. But I'd feel rotten stirring up stuff that turned out to be total crap."

Cam realized he was going to have to prime the pump. "Is it Coach Tyson whose reputation is at stake here?"

Jimbo's gaze locked with Cam's. "I guess," he said carefully.

"I can't say the words for you, Jimbo. Just say it straight out. If it's what I suspect, I'll take it from there and your name will never—and I repeat—never come up."

Jimbo's hands were on his thighs, rubbing hard and fast, the same as his thoughts were racing, Cam guessed. And then he seemed to come to a decision. "Look, it's not my name coming up that worries me. I'm thinking of Ward. If Tyson gets wind of it, he'll retaliate by benching Ward and putting an end to his ambition before it ever gets off the ground, man. He's ruthless. I've kept quiet about him for one reason only and that's Ward."

"Before we deal with Ward's situation," Cam said, "I

need to know what you're taking such pains to avoid saying.''

Jimbo blew out a breath. "Rumor was he liked boys."

Bingo. But Cam simply nodded.

Rachel made a sound of distress.

"I never actually saw anything," Jimbo said, "but there were a couple of guys who were…special to him. I guess that's the word. We all knew there was something…you know, weird, but we were careful what we said. Coach ran a tight ship, I mean, a really tight ship, man. Best way to find yourself blacklisted from the whole sports program at Rose Hill was to get on his mean side."

"But surely there were boys who did that," Rachel said, "boys who made a misstep, even if it was unintentional. What happened to them?"

"Mostly they transferred to other schools. I know of a couple that I suspected left because Monk was…too friendly. But like I said, he ran a tight ship. It was like *The Sopranos,* you know? He had enforcers, some of the big guys who played tackle or guard for the Mustangs. Big as gorillas, some of them. A word from Ziggy or Jay—worse yet, a visit—and all dissent disappeared."

"You have any idea where Ziggy and Jay are today?" Cam asked.

"No, but their folks still live in Rose Hill. They'd be easy enough to locate."

"Enforcers," Rachel repeated faintly.

"I don't think they'd kill anybody," Jimbo said dryly, "but they were definitely effective in keeping the lid on gossip and rumors."

"And every year he had new recruits to victimize," Cam said softly.

"Yeah, so if you wanted to play ball for Monk Tyson, you 'played ball,'" Jimbo said, using his fingers as quotes.

"Do you think he made a move on Jack?" Cam asked. He spoke quietly because a sick rage simmered inside him, and if he gave into it, he might take somebody's head off since the object of his rage wasn't here in Austin.

"No, I honestly don't," Jimbo said. "That's why, when he committed suicide, it was such a shock."

"You and Jack never talked about Tyson's…tastes?"

"Sure we did. Jack was big-time disgusted because he said Monk had these guys he particularly liked over a barrel. He didn't think they were necessarily gay, you know? But he had the power to make or break them as athletes, so play along or be cut from the team. Jack said it was rape, pure and simple."

Cam's look was incredulous. "And when he suddenly killed himself, you thought what, Jimbo?" He was amazed that the boy hadn't made a connection between Jack's sudden death and his frank criticism of Tyson's methods and the fallout if Jack blew the whistle.

"I didn't know what to think, but I knew Jack wouldn't let Tyson get within a mile of him, so that couldn't be the reason he wanted to end it all." He gave Cam a contrite look. "To tell the truth, I thought it was because he missed you and wanted to be with you, Cam. I mean, he said it often enough. He loved his mom, but she was kinda…flighty, you know? And she was all nuts about this new guy and Jack really missed you. He talked all the time about how he wished you were here and not way off in New York, but he knew that would never happen. Your books were suddenly best-sellers and the Big Apple was where the action was, not back in Rose Hill, Texas. Plus, he knew you didn't have the kind of lifestyle where he'd fit in." Jimbo leaned back with a shrug of his shoulders. "When it happened, I thought he'd just rather be dead than settle for what he had."

What Cam felt was so terrible that he had to grip the edge of the table to stay put. He wanted to run. Or give an agonized scream of denial. He wanted to leap up out of his chair and take to his heels to escape the guilt and pain and regret. How had it happened that he'd been so preoccupied, so *selfishly* focused on himself that he'd been blind to his son's needs? While he'd been lost in spinning his take on an old crime, Jack had been lost in a real present-day hell.

Rachel's hand sought his. She laced her fingers through his in a silent gesture of sympathy and understanding. But it was to Jimbo that she spoke.

"How can you be certain, Jimbo, that Ward isn't Tyson's newest victim?"

Twenty-One

"I can guess what you're thinking, Rachel, but I don't think we should move on what we heard today from Jimbo. Not yet." Cam pulled into his driveway and stopped, then looking at her with his arm draped over the steering wheel, he added, "Everything he said is hearsay. First thing Pete will ask for is evidence. And we can't go to Preston Ramsey and demand Tyson be removed as coach on the grounds that he's a sexual predator. Like Pete said, first thing he'll want is evidence."

Rachel opened the door, flooding the interior of the SUV with overhead light. "I see your point, but I just can't sit back and do nothing while he still is free to—" she shuddered "—do whatever." She climbed out and found Cam at her elbow as she closed the door. "What I can do is try to talk to Ward. Now that I know he's at risk, I'm going to figure out an excuse to bring him into my office. Maybe he'll trust me enough to talk. I've known him since he and Nick were in pre-K."

"Which might make it even more difficult to tell you." Cam reached past her for the purse lying on the seat and handed it to her. "You might have better luck with Jason. At least he broached the subject when he was in your office, whereas we don't know that Ward's recent moods have any connection to Tyson."

"The possibility certainly shook Jimbo up, didn't it? Did you see his face when I asked if he'd thought about that?"

"Yeah, I think he was under the impression that Tyson wouldn't fool around with Ward for fear he might say something to Jimbo, who could possibly blow the whistle."

"The sad thing is," Rachel said, "if Tyson has made Ward one of his boys, Ward is probably too ashamed to mention it to his brother."

"Probably. Just as he might be too ashamed for you to know it. Fear and shame are the weapons that predators like Tyson rely on to keep the abuse ongoing." Cam chirped the remote in his hand and locked his SUV. "Come inside for a while. We can't do anything about any of this tonight, and frankly I'd like to change the subject." When she hesitated, he added, "I have wine."

"I think I guessed that," she said, but her attention was on Dinah's house and whether or not Nick was in for the night. She'd given orders that he wasn't to leave, but lately she couldn't be sure what he would do. Or not do. "Nick's confined to quarters, but I'll just walk over and check on him to be sure."

"I'll open the wine so it can breathe," he told her.

She smiled. "Is there something I can bring? Cheese, fruit? Do you need anything?"

She'd taken a couple of steps, but he closed the gap between them and, without warning, pulled her into his arms. "This is all I need." His mouth came down on hers, fierce and demanding. Taking her completely by surprise. The kiss exploded through her senses, giving her such a rush that she wanted nothing but to move closer, put her arms around his neck and sink into delicious sensation.

But he had other ideas. Breaking the kiss, he closed his hands on her waist, gently lifting her aside, and said, "Hold that thought."

She had a little trouble sticking her key into the lock, but after taking a calming breath, she finally was able to get inside. Wow, she was way out of her league with Cameron

Ford, she thought, making her way down the hall. But in spite of the danger, she was drawn to him in a way that was nothing short of amazing. She was suddenly struck by a thought. Had Ted's attraction to Francine started like this? Had it made him feel like this? If so, she could almost understand him going off the deep end. The difference was, the only person in jeopardy if she and Cam did have an affair would be herself.

She paused at Nick's door, then opened it, being careful to make no sound although he was notorious for being able to sleep through anything short of a major earthquake. In the pale moon glow, she could see that he was out like a light. Sprawled out and tangled in his sheets, he slept untroubled by the mess he'd landed himself in. Looking at him, she felt her heart swell. She thought about Cam, who would never again have the pleasure of seeing his son home safe after a party, and her heart caught with a terrible ache.

With a sigh, she resisted the urge to straighten the covers and tuck Nick in as she'd once done. Her boy was a child no more, especially after Robbie's party, but he wasn't a man yet, either, and she was swept by a fierce determination to guard his innocence. As she backed out and closed his door softly, she prayed he wouldn't be touched any more than he already had been by the evil pervading Rose Hill High.

She didn't bother with more lights as she made her way to the kitchen. There, she took two apples from a fruit bowl on the center island and turned to the fridge to get a wedge of Brie. But as she rummaged, she paused, thinking she heard something outside. Moving to the window, she stood for a minute searching the shadows around her mother's greenhouse and beyond, but the yard now seemed quiet and still. And then she heard a sound she couldn't mistake. Graham.

Cats liked to prowl at night, she thought, opening the door to let him inside. He instantly wound himself around her ankles, purring and meowing. Missing Kendy. Snapping on a light now, she filled his food dish and set out fresh water.

She then scribbled a note to Nick that she was next door with Cam—in the absurdly unlikely event that he would wake up and even notice she wasn't in the house—jotted down the time she'd be back and left the note on the island. Dropping the two apples and the wedge of Brie in a bag, she snapped off the light.

However, on her way across the lawn, she found herself glancing back over her shoulder at Dinah's backyard with an eerie feeling that someone was watching. But after a moment, she put it down to the weirdness of the day. She told herself she was imagining things and briskly picked up her pace. She was eager to get back to Cam.

She was a little breathless when he let her in. "Apples and cheese," she said, holding up the bag. To go with the wine."

"Sounds good." But as he took her offerings, he noticed something in her face. "What's wrong? What happened?"

"It's nothing. I—" She shook her head. "All this talk of intrigue has me spooked a little, I guess."

He picked up her hand. "Scared of the dark?" She thought for a minute that he was going to kiss her again, but he just gave her a quick hug and, keeping his arm about her waist, walked with her to the kitchen, where he put the bag on the counter. "So, is Nick okay?"

"Dead to the world. Sleeping like a man without a guilty conscience."

"One of the few advantages of being fifteen."

She watched him remove the Brie and apples from the bag, then took the cheese from him to unwrap it. "I've been thinking about the Sims's place on the lake, Cam. Doesn't it strike you as odd that Monk felt comfortable including people like Joseph to a gathering of teenage boys? It makes you wonder if Robbie's father knows what's going on."

Cam watched her peel away the wrapping on the Brie. "Maybe he knows it and turns a blind eye."

"Do you have a serving dish for this?"

He produced a dish that appeared to be pewter. "Will this do?"

"Uh-huh, but I bet you don't have a spreader." At his blank look, she added, "For spreading the cheese."

"You'd be wrong." He reached up on top of his refrigerator and took down a box with four small knives, never opened. He broke the seal and handed over one of the knives, which had a mouse for a handle. "That adds a touch, don't you think?"

"Very cute." Setting the Brie aside, she reached for the apples and washed them at the sink. "If Sims knows and is turning a blind eye, you know what that means, don't you?"

"His kid gets a leg up for a scholarship." Cam took a paring knife out of a drawer and handed it over. "Or am I being too cynical?"

"Unfortunately, no. Robbie has one nailed down, but it's not what his father wants. Mr. Sims was in my office a few weeks ago telling me he was confident something better would materialize soon. It was a not-so-subtle hint, but I'm no miracle worker and I told him Robbie's chances of getting a better offer were unfavorable considering his GPA."

"Maybe he should offer to outfit Tyson's office with new furniture, although what I saw when I was there didn't look as if it needed replacing."

"He'd have to get in line," Rachel said dryly, thinking of the ratty couch in her office. "Tyson has numerous local VIPs ready to ante up for the sports program. I just wish they'd spread some of that largesse around. I could certainly use some new furniture. That couch in my office gets a lot of traffic, as you can imagine, and I don't see money in the budget to replace it anytime soon." She arranged the apples and Brie on the platter and, with a damp sponge, gave a swipe to the island counter where she'd worked. "I'll just go to the powder room and freshen up if you'll tell me where," she said, dropping the sponge in the sink.

"Second door on the left, but I'll show you." She went

with him and waited as he pushed the door open, crossed an arm in front of her to flip the light on. "I'll take the platter in the den, then run upstairs and check the answering machine. Be right back."

In the bathroom, she stood before the mirror after washing her hands and applied fresh lipstick. With a small brush from her purse, she gave a few swipes to her hair, and then, as she dropped the articles back into her purse, she took out the small perfume bottle she always carried but seldom used. Removing the cap, she dabbed a bit in the cleft between her breasts and caught a glimpse of herself as she recapped the bottle. She'd just spent a full day with Cam, and in spite of the purpose of the trip, she had loved every minute of it. She loved being with Cam. When, before her marriage failed, had she last spent a day with Ted and loved it? When was the last time she'd put on perfume with Ted in mind? When had the joy of being together faded for them?

Caught up in her thoughts, she started at a quick tap on the door and Cam's voice. "Everything okay in there?"

She closed her purse with a snap and opened the door, smiling at him. "Yes, everything's fine." He was a bit closer than she expected and she again went a little breathless when he reached behind her to pull the door shut.

"Just a second," he said, leaning in even closer as if to give her another soul-shattering kiss. "Hmm, whatever you put on in there smells good. What is it?"

"Eternity. It's nothing special."

"On you, it's special." He slipped an arm around her waist and fell into step with her, heading for the den. But no kiss. He had some technique, she thought, kissing her when she least expected it and not kissing her when she did. "I was thinking," he said, "why don't I donate some stuff for your office?"

It took her a moment to recover. "What a good idea," she said, thinking he was joking. "And I'd also like a new carpet.

Oh, how about a piece of original art, too? Something like that fantastic watercolor you have in your foyer.''

"Go pick everything out and I'll have it delivered."

She looked at him. "Are you serious? They wouldn't even let me accept a bouquet of flowers, let alone furniture and a new carpet."

"Sounds like a double standard. Tyson can take whatever's offered in the name of sports, but you can't have a new couch?"

"I know it makes no sense, but that's pretty much the way it is."

"You said you needed it and I'd like to do something for the school. In Jack's name. As for school bureaucracy, let me handle that."

In Jack's name. A gift to the school. Cam's first outward gesture in coming to terms with his terrible loss. At last, Rachel thought with joy bubbling up inside her. He'd been moving in the right direction, but such a gesture was indeed a giant step emotionally. And that he would choose to outfit her office, of all places, in Jack's name warmed her heart. She hoped it meant he was letting go of the bitterness he'd felt toward her for failing to save his son. She wanted to hug him as he bent to turn on a lamp near the sofa.

The glow threw into relief the austere look of his features, shadowed now with dark beard. She liked looking at him, she admitted. Too much. Turning, she headed for a big, man-size chair and a half that, combined with the matching ottoman, looked big enough for a bed. Curling up in it, she watched him go to the bar and take down two wine stems. Being with Cam all day was making her too aware of him as a man.

"Still prefer red, I hope?"

"What?" He held up the bottle. "Oh, the wine. Yes, red. Thanks."

She realized that what she felt was more than being pleased to see a friend coming out of a long, dark winter of grief. Cam wasn't merely a friend now, and her reaction meant much more than that, but she shied away from defining just then exactly what he had become to her.

My God, she really was falling in love with him.

He crossed the room carrying the wine he'd poured for them. "What was Ted's problem last night?" He handed hers over and put napkins for each of them within reach on a table beside the chair.

Glad to turn her thoughts elsewhere, she took a taste of the wine.

"He wanted to tell me that Francine is thinking of breaking off their affair and going back to Walter."

"I'm shocked. Walter's playing hardball with Francine as far as splitting the marital assets. He's also got Ted by the short hairs splitting the assets of the practice." Cam sat on the huge ottoman facing her. "Which puts the lovers in financial straits and takes some of the fun out of life."

She sputtered out a startled laugh and quickly sat up, blotting her lips. "What are you, psychic or something? That's exactly it. And you were pretty psychic in your observations about what he stood to lose in all this. Seems he's waking up and might be thinking he's made some mistakes."

Cam got up and came back with a fresh napkin. "Why come and cry on your shoulder about it?"

She set the wineglass on the table. "The same thing my mother asked. But I think it was more force of habit than anything else. He had no one else to talk to, is my guess."

Cam said nothing, but pretended to draw a bow across an imaginary violin. Rachel gave him a chiding look, resisting the urge to laugh, and shoved at his knee, very close to hers. This was awful, laughing when Ted might genuinely be in a midlife crisis.

"I remember when it first happened I reminded him that Francine was married when she met Walter, who was better off financially than her husband, whom she dumped without a qualm. Well, Ted told me then that the love they shared was special, implying whatever we'd shared was chopped liver, I guess." She reached for her wine again and took a long swallow. "It hurt at the time."

"And now?" He was studying her face, his eyes intent.

"I'm sorry that Ted has made some disastrous decisions, but whatever bit of sympathy I feel isn't based on any special concern for him. I'd feel bad for anybody whose life was in shambles. But I was pretty distraught myself when this first happened and he hardly noticed. Nick and Kendy were both shocked and scared, plus, we were forced out of our house and we were suddenly in financial straits. Ted, meanwhile, seemed oblivious to the havoc he'd caused. His basic responsibilities were last on his list of priorities."

"What exactly did he want from you last night?"

"You mean besides permission to stay the night?" She cut her eyes in his direction, curious to see how he'd react to that.

She said it to be funny, but Cam wasn't amused. Far from laughing, his gray eyes were as sharp as cut glass and a scowl darkened his face more than his beard. "You didn't let him?"

She shook her head. "No, of course I didn't let him. I cut off the whiskey to be sure he was sober enough to drive, gave him a pep talk and sent him on his way." She kept to herself that she'd been less interested in listening to Ted than in wanting to be alone to savor the memory of the first real kiss she'd had in longer than she cared to count. "Ted's always needed a little propping up when stressed."

He gave a disgruntled "Huh." Then after a brief silence, he added, "She'll probably dump him and he'll probably be back wanting sympathy and a second chance. He's relied on you for years and he'll revert to form. It'll be for the children's sake, he'll say. He made a mistake and he'll swear never to do it again."

"He's already asked me to help him rebuild his relationship with the kids. I said I would."

Cam stood up suddenly, put his wine on the bar, barely tasted, and reached for a bottle of Scotch. "Yeah, well, it's the right thing to do," he said, pouring himself a stiff drink. "Nick and Kendy...they need to know he's there for them. You won't be the first woman to forgive and forget in this situation."

Rachel got up and went over to the bookcase that covered a whole wall of his den. He had very eclectic taste. "Did you build these yourself?"

"Yeah, my first carpentry project. Don't look too close." He was beside her then, preparing to refill her wineglass.

"No, no more," she said, covering it with her hand. Actually, it looked like a very professional job, she thought, but she was hardly qualified to judge cabinetmaking. She ran a finger over some of the titles and found none of his own books and decided he must keep them upstairs. She wondered what his office looked like. And, as she imagined a writer's workplace was extremely personal, she wondered if she'd ever see it.

"That's all I promised Ted I'd do for him," she said, examining a framed picture of Cam and Jack when the boy was about ten. It was tucked in among Cam's mother's well-read collection of Agatha Christie novels. With the picture in her hand, she turned to look at him and added, "Nothing else."

He put his glass down and walked over to her. "Because you can't forgive him for cheating?"

She thought for a minute. "Well, I guess I can forgive him, but I sure wouldn't ever be able to forget it. I don't think I could forgive his callous disregard for the kids, either. I'd never be able to trust him not to run out on us again. So, what's a relationship without trust?"

"A very rocky one."

"I don't love him anymore, Cam," she said, frowning. It was troubling to admit, but true. "I don't think I have for a long time, and I think Ted sensed it before I did, and in admitting that, I have to assume some of the responsibility for the death of our marriage. Maybe, because Nick and Kendy are such a major part of my life, I didn't feel the void as soon as he did. You get caught up in the everyday things of family life, kids' activities, keeping house, shopping, social obligations, career demands…'' She stroked a finger over the face of his son in the photo. ''Counseling is fulfilling. Oh, it's thankless at times and I tend to take kids' problems home with me, but at a deep emotional level, I love helping when I can. So, if my marriage was somewhat disappointing, there was much in my life to compensate.''

''It's pretty obvious that Ted compensated by finding an extramarital sex partner,'' Cam said dryly. ''Besides, the man's a physician. If you want to talk about fulfilling work and helping people, isn't medicine the ultimate?''

''I think Ted went into medicine primarily for the money. I know that's a harsh assessment, but I've had to face several harsh truths lately.'' Unconsciously, she held the photo against her chest. ''I think one of the reasons I found it so difficult to accept that Ted was serious about Francine was just that, his emphasis on making money. His practice was so lucrative that I doubted he'd do anything to jeopardize it. Stealing Walter's wife was bound to do just that. The consequences would be dire.''

She looked over at Cam. ''Then again, there are two sides to every story. You said it last night. Francine was probably hot in bed. Apparently, Ted was hungry for that, so much so that he risked everything to have what he wasn't getting at home.'' She shrugged. ''I'm just not the hot-and-sexy type.''

''You could have fooled me,'' Cam said. Gently taking the photo from her hands, he set it back in its place. ''Want me to prove it again?''

He really was going to kiss her now and knowing it sent a warm thrill over her. Slipping his fingers into her hair, he tipped her face up and lightly touched his mouth to hers. It was feather-light and tantalizing, a mere whisper of a kiss.

Her lashes fluttered and she closed her eyes for what was to come. But instead of following through, he rested his forehead against hers, his thumbs caressing her lips, and said, "Be sure, Rachel."

She was sure she wanted more. She was sure she wanted to feel the thrill and pleasure the way she'd felt it Friday night. She was sure she wanted him to go even further. She wanted to be touched, she wanted to lose herself in mindless, sexual sensation. She was sure she wanted it to be with Cam. And she was sure it would not be casual sex. For her, sex with Cam could never be casual.

She drew in a shaky breath. "I haven't ever been with any other man," she told him. "Just Ted. So, I don't have much sexual experience. And since I didn't really know what was missing in our sex life, maybe I'm just a lost cause. What I mean is, how could I have been that preoccupied with other stuff and not missed it? So, if we make love tonight, I want to be honest with you. I don't think I'm using you to prove something to myself, but it's a possibility." She looked into his eyes. "Will that make you change your mind?"

"Maybe...if I could make any sense of it." He smiled, his thumbs still stroking. "But I think I understand. And I'm willing to take a chance that you're wrong about yourself."

She gave a shaky laugh, and then he was trailing those little kisses over her face again. "I guess you do have a lot of experience?" she managed.

"Enough to know that when a woman responds the way you did Friday night, there's not a chance anything's missing in her." He was nibbling the long line of her throat now and she dropped her head back, closed her eyes at the sheer pleasure of it. He was barely started and she was breathless already, her skin tingling everywhere he touched and her blood singing. She never even thought of stopping his fingers as he worked to undo the buttons on her shirt or when he pushed it off her shoulders.

"Oh, look at this," he said, smiling. Her bra was a frothy

scrap of lace, pretty and provocative. "But it has to go." Cam popped the front clip and made a satisfied sound as her breasts spilled out into his hands. "Pretty, very pretty," he told her in a voice going thick with desire. And, watching his face, Rachel suddenly felt appealing and feminine and she exulted in it.

All it took was just the tip of his tongue touching her nipple and she shuddered, nearly coming apart in his hands. And he hadn't even kissed her yet, came her disjointed thought. With his mouth at her breasts, he caressed the slope of her shoulders, played the length of her backbone and sought the flare of her hips. Then he opened the fastener of her jeans and found the zipper tab, eased it down and slid his hand inside beneath the lace of her panties to palm the warm skin of her belly. And beyond.

"I want to kiss you there," he told her, his breath warm on her skin. "But first..." This time his mouth took hers in a deep, lush kiss. Rachel's mind reeled. All worry that she was somehow missing the ability to respond sexually went in the hot, hard branding of that kiss. With her palms flat, she slipped her hands under his shirt, then sank her fingers into hard muscle and warm flesh. He tore his mouth from hers when she flicked the tiny bud of a nipple and she heard him suck in a quick, harsh breath. Turning her loose, he grabbed his shirt, pulled it over his head and tossed it to the floor. Then he helped her take off her jeans, and when she stood naked before him, he suddenly stopped.

She was appalled. The lamp that he'd turned on earlier cast a soft glow in the room, but it seemed a thousand watts now, spotlighting her body. In the dizzying heat of arousal, she'd forgotten how she must look. She was almost forty, she'd had two babies. She had stretch marks! She wanted to move to him, to fit herself against him, and keep him from seeing that she wasn't young anymore.

She moved to cover herself, but he stopped her, capturing her hands. "Don't. You're beautiful, Rachel."

"Oh, Lord, I'm not. I've had two pregnancies. I'll be forty in September!"

"And I'll be forty-four." He trailed a finger over the swell of one breast and gently cupped it. He sighed and gave her a wicked look while his thumb moved tantalizingly over her nipple. "So in that case, I guess we have to stop now."

She managed to laugh…shakily. The idea of stopping was preposterous.

"Or do it in the dark," he added.

Her body was tingling. She was breathless with wanting him, and although he still wore his jeans, she could see that he was fully and no doubt painfully aroused, too. And if they turned out the light, she wouldn't be able to see him and she realized she had a powerful need to do just that.

"Don't stop," she said, and moved close to him, but not with the intention of hiding herself. Her hands went to his jeans and she popped the snap. "Leave the light. I want to see you, too."

"Ah, that's my girl."

He unzipped his jeans and kicked them off, taking in a sharp breath when she slipped her hands inside his shorts and ran them over his firm, tight buttocks and then around to the front to find his hot, heavy erection. As she stroked him, he held her head with one hand spread wide, pressing her to his chest. She could hear the thunderous beat of his heart and smell the heat of his body, the hint of soap from that morning's shower, a whisper of the Scotch he'd just drunk. She was drowning in a cascade of sensation and it was glorious.

Then, with a stifled groan, Cam lifted her and turned to lay her down in the cavernous depths of the huge chair. She'd been right about it being almost as wide as a bed, and she lifted her arms to welcome him to her, but he was busy touching her. While his hands moved everywhere, his lips skated over the swell of her breasts and her belly. He nipped at the inside of her thighs and then used his tongue as a wicked and wild thing, until she was in an agony of need. She came then and it was so intense that it stole her breath away, catapulting her into pleasure so exquisite that she thought nothing could ever be so good again. But when he entered her and they fell into perfect, pulsing accord and the two of them were together in climax, she found she was wrong. It could be as good again. Even better. Perfect.

Cam had never before truly experienced the deep satisfaction to be found in the aftermath of lovemaking. But now, with Rachel curled up beside him, her body warm, scented and soft, he knew a sense of completeness that took him by surprise. He lay for a moment, considering. What he was feeling went far beyond the pleasure and release of having sex, as good as that could be. If he was any judge, he'd finally found the woman who'd been meant for him above all others and he hadn't even known that he was searching. It was something for which he was unprepared and he didn't quite know what to do about it.

With his face turned into the soft curve of her throat, he inhaled the scent that had tantalized him earlier when she'd stepped out of the bathroom. He'd known in that moment that he hadn't wanted to wait any longer to coax Rachel into bed. Somehow—he wasn't sure how it had happened—but somehow, instead of beginning an affair that he'd hoped would be simply satisfying and enjoyable to them both, he found himself in much deeper waters. Floating now on a river of deep contentment, it came as a surprise to discover that he was in love with Rachel.

One hand rested near the curve of her breast, idly stroking the satiny smooth skin. What he'd really like now, he realized, was to persuade her to come with him upstairs to his bed, where they would make love again and possibly again, then go to sleep together. Wake up together. He hadn't been even remotely tempted to invite a woman to his bed—to stay—in more years than he was willing to count. That it should be Rachel should have surprised him, but instead, it felt…right.

It was something that he'd told himself was not going to happen. She had a new divorce, a truckload of financial problems, she had two kids—great kids, he admitted that—who'd gotten under his skin even before he suspected their mom was just as serious a threat to his solitary lifestyle as they were. And she had a very real distrust of men after her husband's betrayal. His job, if he went with his heart, would be to convince her to put all that behind her. After all, she'd persuaded him to take the first step that took him beyond his pain.

"What are you thinking?" she murmured.

"That I wish we were upstairs in my bed and you didn't have to go home in a few minutes."

He felt her smile against his temple. "That would be nice."

He lifted his head to look into her eyes. "No regrets?"

"None. I laid a few ghosts."

"So to speak," he said, chuckling. Then, frankly curious, he asked, "What ghosts would that be?"

She shifted, made herself a little more comfortable. "First of all, making love isn't something you do occasionally just because you're married and you're supposed to, which is what happened with Ted and me. Second, I know that I'm not missing any female parts, and that if the right things happen, I can have an orgasm. Making love is about spontaneity and feeling sexual and feminine, but how can you if your partner sees you only as the manager of the house and a sounding board for *his* problems, but not yours?"

"Wait, wait." He was up on one elbow now and frowning. "What was that about an orgasm? You aren't saying you seldom reached orgasm, are you?"

She moved and reached over on the floor to pick up her shirt. "No."

"Good, because it's one thing to stay in a marriage—or a

relationship if you can call it that—that's turned into an emotional wasteland even for the sake of the children, but to be deprived of good sex to boot would really be unforgivable.''

"Men seem to be able to separate the two." On her feet now, she shoved her arms into the shirt and looked around for her panties.

She sounded a little testy and he didn't yet have a clue what he'd said. Interrupting her as she buttoned up, he took her face in his hands, forcing her to look at him. "That didn't happen, did it?"

"What didn't happen?" Her eyes slid away from his. "I need to finish getting dressed."

He saw her panties underneath the ottoman and bent to pick them up. "Your marriage wasn't exactly idyllic, but you did have sex occasionally—just quoting here—and it was okay, wasn't it? Not earth-shattering, such as we just had—" he waggled his eyebrows to tease her into a smile "—but he brought you to orgasm, didn't he?"

"No." She snatched the panties out of his hand. Unsmiling.

"No? As in you didn't come?"

"Is that so awful?"

"Ever?"

She sat on the edge of the big chair and took a deep breath. "It's no big deal, Cam. I'm sorry I mentioned it. And don't you think you should put some pants on?"

He was unconcerned with modesty, but he glanced around to find his jeans if it would make her more comfortable. Now that he knew the truth about her marriage, he could better understand her shyness when he'd undressed her and her uncertainty as she'd tried to analyze why Ted left. Occasionally? Christ.

"You know what I think, Rachel?" Not spotting his shorts, he simply put his pants on without them. "I think it's a goddamned miracle that you didn't find somebody to have an affair with before Ted. What just happened between us was not just good sex, sugar. It was way beyond that. It was out of this world.''

She looked at him. ''Really?''

His pants were on, but nothing else. He sat down beside her on the ottoman and, using his forefinger, marked an *X* on his chest. ''Cross my heart.''

She smiled and he took her hand, brought it to his lips and kissed it. ''Now we have another major problem,'' he told her.

''I know. My mother definitely will know at a glance. Nick, too, probably. I'm afraid it'll be written all over my face. I told you I wasn't the casual-sex type.''

''That is not our problem, sugar,'' he told her patiently. ''And what we just had together wasn't casual.'' He kissed her hair. ''Our problem is how soon and where can we do this again? I'd take you somewhere really special for a few days, but now that we have something definite to go on about Tyson, I need to follow through on that right away. But, trust me, we're just at the beginning of something big, you and me.''

''You're talking about having an affair,'' she said, although her eyes kept dropping to his chest and to the pattern of hair that narrowed and disappeared into his unfastened jeans. ''I can't, Cam. Think about it. If word got out at school, I'd probably be asked to resign.''

''In this day and age?'' He was ready to laugh, but he saw by the look on her face that she was serious. ''Come on, Rachel. Some of those kids could probably teach you a thing or two about sex. Make that definitely.''

''That's beside the point, and if I were accused and tried that argument, Preston would be the first to tell me so.''

''Okay, how long is long enough after a marriage breakup before an affair will be considered acceptable?''

''I can't have an affair at all.''

''What about Marta?''

''What about her? Marta isn't having an affair.''

He dropped his chin, giving her an are-you-kidding look. "I'll bet any amount of money that she and Pete are in the sack as we speak."

"Besides, Marta doesn't have any children. Think about the example it gives Nick and Kendy. I don't want to go down the same road as Ted with Francine. Look what resulted when that happened."

Cam stood up suddenly and pulled her to her feet. "Okay, I see we can't settle this now, so the subject is tabled for tonight." He had both her hands now, and he did a little number that brought her up against him, then he buried his face in her hair. "What I'm counting on is that since it was so good—" he chuckled while keeping a firm grip on her hands to stop her from hitting him "—that you'll compromise your scruples."

"You are so bad, you know that?"

He pressed a quick, hard kiss on her smiling mouth. "I give it about three days."

Twenty-Two

"**O**kay, Mom, I know I'm grounded and I know I've got to sacrifice ten CDs to Kendy even though they'll be wasted on her." Pacing restlessly, Nick swiped an apple from the fruit bowl in passing. "But you can't confine me to quarters, too. I'll croak." He bit into the apple. "It's child abuse."

"Sorry, but that's what *grounded* means, Nick. You're benched, all movement is restricted." Rachel stirred an egg into the batter for banana muffins. "You've broken so many rules that you'll be lucky to ever see the light of day again, except for school."

"I said I'm sorry, Mom. I screwed up and I admit it." He drove the fingers of one hand through his dark hair in frustration while munching his apple. "What'll I do with myself all day? It's only eight o'clock and I'm bored out of my skull."

"Too bad." Rachel carefully measured out batter into a muffin tin. "Marta mentioned coming over sometime today. You can keep us company." She pretended not to hear the sound he made at that. "Or, here's an idea. You can straighten up the mess you made in the garage when you and Ward mounted that new basketball hoop."

"Mom…"

"Oh, darn! I thought I had a nice fresh cantaloupe in the fridge," she said, rummaging around in the veggie drawer.

"I ate it last night."

"Oh. Well, I guess I'll just have the strawberries." After

a minute, she straightened up and looked over at Nick. "Did you eat the strawberries, too?"

"I was hungry, Mom."

She threw up her hands. "Nick, I swear you've got a tapeworm or something. I wanted fruit to go with the muffins. Now I'll have to go to Kroger's."

"Hey, let me go. I know, I know, I can't use the car. I won't even ask. But for just a couple of pieces of fruit, I'll go on my bike."

"Well…" She did need the fruit. And Marta was coming. Pete would probably be with her. Rachel's gaze drifted to the window where just the corner of Cam's house was visible. And Cam might drop in, too. If she went herself, she'd have to drop everything and get dressed. She hadn't yet had a shower and—

"Where's your purse?" In the scant half a minute since the possibility was mentioned, Nick had changed shirts, put on his sneakers and brushed his teeth.

She handed over five dollars. "If you aren't back with that fruit when Marta gets here, your present punishment will seem like a walk in the park."

He tossed the apple core and was gone before she could say anything more.

The supermarket wasn't Nick's primary destination, although he did dash inside and buy the cantaloupe and strawberries, as he'd promised. Then, he pedaled hell-bent for leather to Ward's house. He hated disobeying his mom again, considering the numerous times he'd screwed up lately. Seemed like he was batting a thousand in the bad behavior department lately. He felt like shit for taking Kendy's camera and a jackass for getting drunk. He'd been sassing his mom a lot and generally taking it out on her that his life sucked just now when it was his dad who'd dogged out on them. So, whatever his mom doled out in the way of punishment, he deserved it.

Problem was, he needed to talk to Ward in the worst way. Yesterday, after he'd recovered enough to want to live, he'd called Ward to see how the date with Kristin went. And boy, he'd opened a door to disaster-ville with that call. Ward hadn't sounded like a man who'd scored big with his woman. He'd seemed more like a man who'd struck out.

"So, where'd you wind up going?" he'd asked, hearing something in Ward's tone.

"A movie. Then Pizza Hut."

"Yeah, yeah. And then—"

"I took her home. Hey, Nick, I'm in the middle of something here. I gotta go, okay? I'll talk to you later."

"Wait! Ward, what—" But he'd found himself talking to a dead line. Definitely something wrong, somewhere. Ward, he'd decided, was having another of his freakin' moody-blue days.

Standing with the phone in his hand, he'd given it three more minutes of intense thought and then dialed Kristin's number. That had been the second puzzler. As soon as she recognized his voice, she'd been one cold and hostile lady, but he'd decided to overlook that, in the interest of solving the puzzle. "So, how was your evening with Mr. Rivers, Kristin? You gonna thank me for facilitating?"

"No, Nick, I'm going to ask instead why you and Ward thought I'd be that kind of person?"

Nick was instantly concerned. And baffled. "What happened, Kristin?"

"I was really wrong about you both, Nick. I bet your mom would be shocked."

Not as much as he was when he finally dragged it out of her. Ward had lost control, she told him. Came on too strong. Scared her. Really made her afraid for a minute that she was going to be raped. Talk about stunned. Nick was. Big time.

Which is why he was going to see Ward. He felt responsible in a way, since he'd kinda set the two of them up, knowing how Ward really had this thing for Kristin. Now, zooming along on his bike, he knew he was under the gun, time-wise. But, as his friend, Ward deserved a chance to explain himself. And it had better be good.

He had planned to be the concerned friend, show understanding and all that until he got an explanation, but instead he dragged Ward out of his bedroom where he'd been holed up listening to country music and lit into him. "Are you crazy? Are you nuts? What did you think you were doing, Ward? Kristin's a nice girl." He kicked at an old tennis ball on the grass as he paced back and forth. "Kristin's the kind of girl that you open doors for, man. You hold her hand and maybe, just maybe, you only kiss her after about three dates. You don't—hear me, Ward—you don't jump her bones and try to prove your manhood, you moron."

Ward sat on the grass with his arms draped over his bent knees. "My mom's gonna hear you," he said, but he sounded as if he didn't care. No excuses. No denial.

Nick stood over him in a challenging stance. "Kristin's a friend of mine. She thinks we made up some kind of scheme together for you to get her in the sack."

"I don't know where she got that idea."

"You didn't try to put the make on her? You didn't try to jump her bones? You didn't scare the bejesus out of her and make her cry?"

"I mean I don't know where she got the idea you had anything to do with it."

Still standing, Nick studied him hard. He'd been best friends with Ward since grade school. If he'd been told yesterday that Ward was even capable of scaring a girl, he would have defended him to his last breath. He didn't—couldn't—understand it.

"Help me out here, Ward. I'm trying to make some sense of this."

"If it matters," Ward said, looking utterly miserable, "I feel like crap."

"You should! She's a nice girl. The nicest."

Ward turned his head. "I know," he said in a thick voice.

Nick saw he was close to tears. With a sigh, he squatted down beside him. "She said you weren't drunk, so…what, Ward? Talk to me."

Ward wiped his eyes on the sleeve of his shirt. "Did she...uh, did I...hurt her?"

"She was more scared than hurt, I think. She didn't let her mom see how upset she was. She knew it would freak her out."

"She should have," Ward said with sudden feeling. "She should have called the police. It'd serve me right."

Totally baffled now, Nick dropped his head back and looked skyward. A bird was singing its lungs out in the tree overhead. It seemed a ludicrous thing, birdsong while they were talking about this stuff. "This is getting more nutty by the minute, Ward. First, you're all over Kristin like a caveman, I call you on it and you act like a...like...you don't much care. Now you're suggesting prison might be the answer. I don't know you anymore, Ward."

"You got that right."

Nick gave him a sharp look. "You want to explain that?"

Ward drew in a breath and looked squarely at Nick. "Tell me something, Nick. Why did you stop those special sessions with Coach Tyson?"

"We're changing the subject here? What, are you bored?"

"Just answer me."

Frowning, Nick lifted a shoulder. "I told you. I didn't like the rest of the team thinking I was getting special treatment. If I made the team on my own, fine. Otherwise, I wasn't sure it was worth it."

"And that's it? That's all? There wasn't anything else?"

Nick looked at him and suddenly it dawned on him. "Like what, Ward?"

Ward's eyes slid away, fixed on his feet. "I don't know," he mumbled. "Just...anything else."

"Like maybe Coach wanted to feel me up?"

"Did he?" Ward asked, meeting his eyes again. "Was that why you quit?"

"He didn't—but not because he didn't want to. I think he did, but he didn't get around to that kind of stuff before I quit." Beside Ward on the grass now, Nick picked up the tennis ball, examining it. "He made me uncomfortable. There was just something about him, about the way he insisted on demonstrating a handhold or a grip or a stance, whatever, but he'd have to touch me to do it. It gave me the creeps."

"You never said anything."

"Because it never came to anything. It didn't crystallize in my mind until—" He stopped, remembering his promise not to tell. He shrugged. "It was just a feeling."

Ward was coming alive now, eyeing him hard. "Was Coach Monk at that party?"

"If so, we never saw each other." It wasn't quite a lie, but he didn't break his word to Cam and his mom, either. "Why, Ward? Are you thinking there's something rotten in the locker room besides Ferdy's sneakers?"

Ward dropped his eyes. And Nick knew then. "Okay," Nick said, after a long study of his friend's face. "For what it's worth, if you want to talk about this, Cam's the man. Or my mom." He tossed the ball aside. "But for right now, you tell me what's going on. After what you did last night, Kristin has put me in the same box with you, and I need to know where you're coming from before I go back and try to make things right with her."

"I've gotta go see her and apologize," Ward said, getting to his feet.

"Forget it, man. She gets one look at you within a block of her door, she's gonna call a cop."

"Like I said, maybe that's what I deserve."

Marta reached over and helped herself to a warm muffin. "We spent the day laying tile in Pete's kitchen and then we ordered pizza because we were both too pooped to even make a sandwich." Breaking it open, she took a bite and closed her eyes. "Hmm, it was so romantic."

"It could be if you're with the one you love," Rachel said. Resting her chin on her fist, she looked across the way where Cam and Pete collaborated in an effort to repair Dinah's riding lawn mower. Earlier, Cam had called to say he was going to pick up a Sunday *New York Times* and was there anything she needed. Since Nick had been gone an hour on a trip that should have taken thirty minutes, she suspected there would be no cantaloupe or strawberries to go with her muffins unless she took Cam up on his offer. And when he came back, Pete and Marta were with him.

"If I wasn't such a nice guy," Cam had told her in a low voice as he handed over the fruit, "I'd make you pay up on that bet we made last night."

"They were at Kroger's," she'd whispered, sending a surreptitious glance outside to the patio where Pete and Marta sat close together on the swing. "You don't know they spent the night together."

Cam had tipped up her chin and given her a slow kiss. "Keep up that naiveté, sugar. It turns me on."

Flustered, she'd sent him out with the muffins in a basket and busied herself putting the coffee tray together. If he could tell what Pete and Marta had been up to this weekend, they'd probably be able to tell what she and Cam had been up to. And probably the only person shocked by what they'd been up to was Rachel herself.

"Speaking of being with the one you love," Marta said, reaching for a dewy strawberry, "what's up with you and Cam?"

So much for fooling Marta. "I don't get the connection," Rachel said.

Marta shot her an amused look. "Hello? This is your old friend, Rachel. The connection is, you were looking at Cam the way my female students look at Ben Affleck. Like he's a buffet and you've been on a diet."

Rachel groaned and put her hand to her forehead. "Is it that obvious?"

Marta chuckled. "Yeah, and I think it's great. For what it's worth, he can't keep his eyes off you, either. What have the two of you been up to this weekend, for heaven's sake? Dinah and I leave you unchaperoned for two days and you hop in the sack with the second sexiest man in Rose Hill."

"You don't know that!"

"I know Pete's the sexiest."

"I mean," Rachel said patiently, "that you don't know we were...you know."

"What I don't know is this," Marta said, licking powdered sugar off one finger. Graham, the cat, walked over and she gave him a piece of muffin. "How the heck can you blush like that over sex when you deal with teenagers five days a week who constantly discuss—and practice—every aspect of human sexuality and especially how to do the nasty?"

"Can we change the subject?"

"If you haven't done it yet, it won't be long." Marta grinned wickedly. "And I can't wait until Ted finds out."

"He's already suspicious. In fact, he accused me of fooling around with Cam. Can you believe that? He actually seemed outraged. If I hadn't been so irritated, I would have laughed."

"When was this?"

"Friday night. After we left Pete's house. Francine, it seems, is getting cold feet. She and Walter are reconciling."

"What goes around comes around."

"He wants me to help him make amends to Nick and Kendy. Seems he woke up and noticed he has two kids and wants to be a father again."

"Sure. You'll do that. For their sake, not his."

"Yes." Rachel rose and poured herself fresh coffee from the thermos carafe. "He was upset, but I couldn't tell if it was because she was dumping him or it's dawned on him he's tossed away his family, his career and his reputation in this town for a—"

"Slut."

"A temporary infatuation is what I was going to say."

"Oh, please. She's a slut." After a bit, Marta said, "It's one thing to patch things up with the kids, but I hope you aren't tempted to let him back into your life again, are you?"

Rachel's gaze strayed to Cam and Pete across the way. "When it first happened, I thought he was having a midlife crisis and that he'd come to his senses. I thought perhaps we'd be able to work through the problems that had driven him away. Which was reasonable since I'm a counselor by profession.''

"And your middle name is reasonable," Marta said dryly.

"But as time passed, I found myself hoping he wouldn't come to his senses. What kind of father would do what he did and then show so little concern for its effect on his children? And while we were struggling financially and emotionally as a result of what he did, Ted was utterly focused on how it messed up his life. You have to wonder what kind of man is that?'' She put up a hand as Marta opened her mouth. "That was a rhetorical question, Marta."

"So, no second chances for Teddy?"

"No." Rachel tasted her coffee and made a face when it was cold. "Not even for the sake of the children."

"This is so crazy," Marta said, pushing a few crumbs around with her finger. "Do you notice the similarity here? Both of us totally trusting of our men and so unprepared when we discovered they were cheating. Now you're saying no way Ted is going to get a second chance and I'm saying the opposite." After a pause, she looked up at Rachel. "Pete's scheme to get me back in bed worked. I spent the whole damn weekend with him."

Rachel smiled. "I'm shocked."

"After you and Cam left, he drove me home, just as he planned." She brushed the crumbs into a neat little pile. "Only this time, when we got to my door, I let him come inside. The rest, as they say, is history."

"You look happy, Marta."

"Go figure. I think I knew if I ever let my guard down, I wouldn't be able to resist him. I even think the reason I married Jorge so quickly was to avoid dealing with Pete, which is a little different from hastily marrying on the rebound, as you suspected." Her fidgeting stopped. "Jorge Ruiz was the sweetest, kindest, most dependable man who ever lived on this earth, Rachel. And I knew he'd be as constant as the stars in the heavens. What I felt for him was so safe compared to what I feel for Pete.'' Frowning, she swept the crumbs into a napkin and folded it up. ''With Pete, I don't know if I'm coming or going. I love the way he looks, I love the way he smells. I love that macho manner of his. I love to hear him singing in the shower and cussing when he can't find his keys. Nobody can make me so mad or so happy. Or so turned on. When we made love, it was so wonderful I cried.''

''But did you talk?''

''Yes, Doctor, we talked. He really didn't have an affair with Tanya. He never went out with her after we split up, so I guess he didn't have a thing for her after all. And he hasn't had a significant relationship since we broke up.'' Her gaze wandered over to Pete, tinkering with the mower. ''The big bone of contention between us was his job and how I hated it. So when we got around to talking about that, he said something that really made me stop and think. He said what if he had demanded that I give up teaching. I would have been insulted. I love what I do. Nothing's as satisfying to me as those moments—rare, but they happen—when I see a student suddenly get it, the beauty of literature, I mean. And eagerly wants to know more, to read more. I have opened the door to the world for that student. It's a heady thing. What if Pete had said you don't make much money teaching and why don't you get a job in the corporate world? You could write technical manuals. Or give seminars on how to write technical manuals. Don't laugh, I'm serious,'' she said when Rachel pressed her fingers to her mouth.

''Because that's exactly what I was doing to Pete. Not only was I pushing him to give up a profession he loved, but I went even further and told him what I thought he should do instead. He'd hate being a lawyer, Rachel. Lawyers are the bane of any cop's existence and I knew that. What was I thinking?'' She pushed her coffee cup toward Rachel.

Rachel collected their cups and stacked them on the tray. ''There's often a difference in the way men and women think of their work. For some men, the job defines who they are.

Women are less likely to invest so much of their personal identity in a career.'' She picked up the tray. ''They give it time and energy, because there are some career choices that demand it, but there's also kids and their activities, the home and church, social commitments.''

Marta again looked over to where the two men were now in the process of reassembling the lawn mower, knowing her feelings for Pete showed on her face. ''I'd love all that if Pete and I were together, but most of all, I'd love to have his babies.''

''Marta,'' Rachel said gently, touched by the look on her face, ''you can.''

''If I'm lucky. It has taken only two days to make me admit that I never stopped loving Pete. When I caught him in bed with Tanya, it gave me a legitimate reason to wimp out before I became the wife of a cop, because I knew that if he got killed, I wouldn't be able to survive it.'' She brought her gaze around to meet Rachel's. ''That may sound like psycho-babble, but I honestly think it's true.''

''So you cut off your nose to spite your face.''

Marta laughed shortly. ''You shrinks are so profound.''

''Then here's another thought or two from this shrink, after which I won't say another word.'' Rachel held the loaded tray, ready to go inside. ''I think the way Pete has gone about making amends for his mistake shows real character. He's been single-minded in winning you back, paying a price careerwise that many men would not have considered. And, for what it's worth, I also think he's every bit as dependable and constant a man as Jorge Ruiz.''

Marta's eyes were still focused across the way. ''But he's not safe, Rachel.''

Rachel stood holding the tray, her eyes also on the men. No, but she'd felt safe in her marriage with Ted and it had been anything but. As she watched, Cam reached over and hit the starter on the mower. The motor fired up instantly. He looked up, saw her looking and gave a thumbs-up. Marta must make her own decision, but for herself, she would never again settle for safe.

Twenty-Three

After it happened, Nick felt like a dope for getting himself into a situation where two goons could bushwhack him. He was pedaling along with the cantaloupe and strawberries, congratulating himself on playing the role of peacemaker by talking Ward out of a lost cause—going over to beg Kristin's forgiveness—when he looked over his shoulder and saw the pickup.

Whoa, he thought, way too close. And he hadn't worn a helmet, getting out of the garage too fast to take time to put it on. He turned back for another quick look, but the sun was reflected on its windshield, almost blinding him. Without a doubt the driver was crowding him. Dumb ass, was his fragmented thought as he made a wild maneuver off the shoulder, skirting a ditch that was pretty steep. Another look and his eyes went wide with shock as he realized the pickup meant to use him as a hood ornament. It was either jump or be mowed over, so he leaped from his bike, flying over the handlebars just as the truck's bumper struck. He tucked instinctively into a body roll, but he hit the ground hard, anyway, bouncing his head off something that rang his bell, big time.

He lay for a minute with the wind knocked out of him, seeing stars and thinking he was maybe dying. While he struggled to breathe, he thought about the cantaloupe and strawberries and figured they were history. As he'd nearly been. Then, as his breath returned and his head cleared, he realized he was flat on the ground and two men were standing over him. Two really big dudes.

But he must have got a serious knock on the head because he couldn't make out their faces, only that they looked strange, like aliens. Then he figured out why. Although they each wore baseball caps, they had stockings pulled over their heads mashing their faces flat. Okay, he was hallucinating because when you were in an accident, people were supposed to help you. Instead, these two stood there as if lending him a hand was going to be a committee decision, like not happening.

"He's coming around," the biggest of the pair said. "Guess he coulda broke something."

"We were told not to mark him," the other said, sounding ticked off. He wore a Harley Hog T-shirt and looked mean. "You can be the one to explain when he asks what happened. And we gotta hurry before anybody drives up. Just because it's Sunday doesn't mean somebody won't come along."

Big Guy ran his hands over Nick's arms and legs. Still dazed, Nick wasn't able to object. "He's all right. Gettin' his wind back now."

Harley Hog peered over in the ditch where the remains of Nick's bike lay. "Get the fuckin' bike," he ordered his partner. "Throw it in the truck and let's get this little prick back home to his mommy before somebody shows up and wants to help."

"You gonna deliver the message?" Big Guy asked, making no move to get the bike.

"Yeah, I'm gonna deliver the message," Harley said sarcastically, "but not until he's able to listen. He's still groggy. Plenty of time since we're gonna drop him near his house on account of you catapulting him into the ditch."

"What's…" Nick, up on one elbow now, spat out a mouthful of grass and grit. "What's going on? Who are you?"

"Bitchin' already," Harley said with disgust. He grabbed

Nick's elbow and jerked him up on his feet. "You've been a pain in the ass, Forrester. Get in the truck."

In spite of the whirling landscape, Nick preferred taking a chance on making it back on his own to hitching a ride with these two. "Thanks, but I think I can make it."

"How? Ridin' this?" Big Guy emerged from the ditch carrying the bike. The back wheel was bent at a crooked angle and the broken chain dangled from the crank set like a dead snake. "I don't think so." He tossed it into the truck.

"Get in the truck," Harley repeated in an "or else" tone.

Limping and truly scared now, Nick did as told. A hand at his butt boosted him and he found himself crunched between the two men. So far, he had no idea who they were or what was going down. Or why. He had a wild thought that he was being kidnapped, but these two didn't seem like kidnappers. Besides, there was no reason to kidnap him. His mom hardly had enough money to pay their bills. But what was that about giving him a message? From who? About what?

Harley, now driving, said, "We're two minutes from your house, asshole. So, listen up. You went to the party at Sims's place this weekend. You had a good time. You did not see anything that you didn't love. You gettin' the picture?"

"Aah…"

Big Guy gave his shoulder a hard shake. "You get the picture?"

Wincing, Nick managed to nod.

"You recognized no one," Harley said, eyes straight ahead on the road. "You could not name the guests if asked, because if you did, you would never be able to play baseball again."

He wasn't going to play baseball anymore, anyway, Nick thought. Not after what he saw Coach doing. "Okay," he said. "Not a problem."

"No, I don't think you get it, asshole," Big Guy said, as if talking to a nitwit. "You couldn't play baseball or football or even qualify for the swim team because of a terrible accident where you broke all your fingers and toes."

Nick gulped hard. "I—okay."

"Let's hear some enthusiasm in that answer, boy."

"I understand. I g-get the picture."

"Because if you don't get it," Harley said, continuing in a softly menacing tone, "there's no telling what might happen."

As the pickup turned on to Gran's street, Nick licked his lips and tasted blood from a cut inside the corner of his mouth. "You don't have to say any more," he said. "I understand."

"Could be," Harley continued as if Nick hadn't spoken, "that your little sister—what's her name? Kendall, yeah, that's it, Kendall. Could be Kendall might have an accident, too. Sort of like you did tonight."

Nick's heart was banging and he needed to pee. He had a brief flash of Kendy, bloody and broken in the road…all because of him. "I promise. I don't know what else to tell you to convince you," he told Harley earnestly. "I understand. Don't hurt Kendy. I had a great time at that party and I don't remember anybody who was there. If I'm asked, I—I…I have amnesia."

"You especially will not talk to your friend, Mr. Ford."

Oh, shit. "Okay."

"See, the health of everybody you care about rests on your shoulders, boy."

Big Guy turned and caught his face in his hand and squeezed it hard. "That includes your mom and your grandmother, but you guessed that already, didn't you?"

"Yeah." It was hard to talk with his jaw in a vise grip.

"Smart. Very smart, Nicky." Harley stopped the pickup two houses up from Gran's house.

"I think he's got it," Harley told his pal. "Let him out."

"You better pay attention, kid," Big Guy said, reluctantly turning him loose. "Bad things can happen. You don't want to wind up like Jack Ford."

"Let…him…out!" Harley shouted, shooting a killing look at Big Guy.

And Nick was abruptly hauled across the seat by the tail of his shirt and shoved out of the pickup. He stood, unsteady on his feet, scared to believe they were truly done with him, but unable to make a run for it. Cussing, Big Guy lifted the bike out of the truck bed and tossed it at Nick's feet. Then he climbed back inside and Harley made a quick three-point turnaround, gunned the pickup and left Nick standing in the dust, squinting to read the license plate.

Rachel passed a basket of muffins and bagels across the table to Cam and Pete. "Our strawberries and cantaloupe are courtesy of Cam. Nick was supposed to pick them up but," she said dryly, "apparently he rode his bike to Dallas and not the local Kroger store."

Cam frowned. "Has he called?"

"No, but that doesn't surprise me, either. He's bored. He did his best to talk me into letting him out of the house this morning and frankly I was almost relieved to find a legitimate reason to send him to Kroger's."

"Couldn't resist making a little side trip, huh?" Pete rooted through the basket before looking at Marta. "Where are those sausage biscuits we brought?"

"Here." Rolling her eyes, Marta shoved a covered casserole dish over. "Your cholesterol is probably off the stick, Pete. Don't you know that white carbohydrates make you lethargic?"

He bit into a sausage biscuit and said, "Have I seemed lethargic to you?"

Everyone laughed as Marta actually blushed. But she recovered quickly. "Make me even happier by eating an orange, too." She took one out of the fruit bowl.

"Making you happy is my life, darlin'," he said, winking at her.

"Did Nick take his cell phone?" Cam asked as he poured himself a cup of coffee.

"He never leaves home without it," Rachel said. "I called him a few minutes ago and got his voice mail. He probably detoured to see Ward and find out how the date with Kristin went. I'll check again in a few minutes."

Cam patted the chair beside him. "Come and sit down. Pete's done some digging into Tyson's background. Now that we know what the coach is about, you won't be surprised at what he found."

Pete reached for another sausage biscuit. "The first job he had out of college was at an exclusive school for boys in Virginia. He resigned abruptly just before the end of the second semester two years later. There was nothing negative in the file as to why he would have cut out a month short of year's end, so I called the school. Spoke to the headmaster, who's still concerned for the reputation of the school. According to him, Tyson was a damn good coach. Had those boys winning everything in their division, but after due consideration, they decided not to renew his contract."

Marta, peeling the orange, looked up. "Why? What was on his termination papers?"

"Budget constraints."

"Uh-huh." She broke the orange in half and put it on Pete's plate.

"He had no arrest record," Pete said, "and his career is a carbon copy of other sexual predators. Every job he took was rich with juveniles and opportunities to abuse them."

"When was this?" Rachel asked.

"Twelve years ago." Pete reached for a third biscuit, but Marta slapped his hand and he settled back to enjoy his coffee. "He went from there to a parochial school in St. Louis. Stayed only a year, then moved to the East Coast, where he coached briefly. That's been his MO—one, maybe two years in a smallish school, then move on. Never stayed anywhere longer than two years."

"Until he got to Rose Hill."

"That's right." Pete flicked at a crumb on his shirt. "The only thing I can figure is that after that first abrupt termination in Virginia, he decided to minimize the risk of exposure by moving on before being outed by the boys he was abusing. At least, that's the only reason I see that he escaped detection for twelve years.''

Cam laid his arm across the back of Rachel's chair. ''You're thinking that his management style—strict discipline, swift punishment—kept kids from ratting him out?''

Pete shrugged. ''It's possible. But he's been here in Rose Hill awhile. There's bound to be a couple of boys he couldn't hush up.'' He hitched his chin toward Rachel. ''How about doing a quick search of school records? Look for athletes who left abruptly.''

''I'm already doing that,'' Rachel said. ''It's time-consuming and I haven't found anything yet that appears suspicious.''

''If what we suspect is true,'' Marta said, ''Monk settled in at Rose Hill after perfecting his technique and began a cold-blooded, systematic pattern of sexual abuse.''

''Yeah. And he kept it within his own organization where he had complete control,'' Pete said.

''Only athletes need apply,'' Cam said.

Rachel pushed her coffee aside in disgust. ''He kept them cooperative by showing them special treatment. A boy got star status in the school when he was singled out by Coach Monk. That's very seductive among peers. Then, if an athlete had enough talent, there was always the promise of an athletic scholarship.''

''And if they acted reluctant about cooperating,'' Marta said, ''his power alone made it easy to intimidate them.''

''Or shame them,'' Rachel said. ''That's another effective weapon in a sexual predator's arsenal. I know it sounds incredible that he could get away with this for so long, but Texas has a strong sports tradition. Teachers learn quickly what the philosophy is at Rose Hill—it's not how you play the game, but winning it. Monk happened to land in a town that was tailor-made for him.''

She gazed into her coffee cup, thinking of the young athletes Monk had undoubtedly placed on a road to fame and fortune, but it didn't begin to excuse his fiendish behavior for the ones he abused. It was difficult to come up with a sentence severe enough for the pain and suffering he'd caused.

"What can we do to stop him?" Marta asked.

"Now that I've been told he used some of his bigger boys to enforce discipline," Pete said, "I'll be nosing around to find out who they are. See if I can get anything out of them. We'd be home free if a boy he's abused would step forward."

"Two thugs Tyson used to strong-arm kids still live in Rose Hill," Cam said. He'd promised Jimbo he wouldn't use his name, but there was nothing to keep him from passing on Jimbo's information.

Pete nodded, but looked skeptical. "I wouldn't count too much on them ratting out the coach if it implicates them."

Rachel got up and walked to the door of the kitchen. "I need to call Nick's cell again," she said. "He really should be back by now."

Inside, she picked up the phone and punched the programmed number for Nick's cell. As she stood holding the cordless, she realized she was actually hearing the in-coming call jingle on Nick's phone and the sound was coming from somewhere down the hall. Still holding her own receiver, she followed the sound.

The cordless was lying on Nick's bed. She disconnected and saw his sneakers lying on the floor. Looking puzzled, she left his room, and when she heard the shower running, paused by the closed bathroom door.

"Nick?" she called after knocking. "Are you in there?"

Muffled sound of something dropped in the shower stall. "Yeah, Mom. I'm taking a shower."

She stared in surprise at the closed door. "When did you get back? Did you bring the fruit?" When all she got was a mumble, she stepped closer. "Where are the things you were supposed to get at the store?"

"I forgot."

"Nick." She pressed fingers to her forehead. "You forgot?"

"Sorry, Mom. Actually, I didn't forget. I had a little accident and the stuff didn't survive."

She frowned. "What kind of accident?"

"Took a tumble on my bike."

She heard the water being shut off. "Are you hurt?"

"Just scratched up a little. I'm gonna crash for a while, okay?"

She rattled the door. "Nick, let me see where you're hurt."

He opened the door and stuck his arm through the crack, giving her a brief look at his elbow. "I'm gonna put stuff on it, don't worry."

"There's antibiotic cream in the medicine cabinet above the sink," she told him, after looking at the nasty scrape. "Was there anything—" But she was talking to the closed door, a frank signal that he no longer needed his mom to kiss his boo-boos and make them well.

When she returned to the patio, Marta had the table cleared and was sitting beside Pete in the swing. Cam saw her face and asked, "Were you able to reach Nick?"

"He was in the shower, if you can believe that." She settled in the chair next to him, still puzzled. "Apparently, he crashed his bike somewhere between Kroger's and here. I got a very brief glance at his skinned elbow and now he's holed up in his room, probably with his headphones going full blast. The cantaloupe and strawberries were casualties of his accident, he claims."

Cam again laid his arm across the back of her chair. "I'm glad he's back, and frankly, it's probably a good thing he's grounded. I don't like the idea of him being out just now. Stop and think about it. From Tyson's point of view, Nick is a loose cannon. Tyson's public image is vital to holding his position as a coach. If Nick says anything to screw that up, it would mean dire consequences to Tyson."

"I think you're right," Pete said. "And I don't know how

far Tyson might go to do damage control.'' He pushed the swing into gentle motion and said to Rachel, ''To be on the safe side, I'd keep Nick's activity restricted, just for a couple of days until I can get my ducks lined up. When we go public with this, it'll go a long way to safeguarding Nick and other boys.''

She looked worried. ''Do you think it's okay for him to go to school?''

''Yeah, I think he's safe enough there. Tyson will probably be nervous, but Nick should be cautioned not to do anything to spook him. I don't want to show my hand until I have more evidence.''

''Be sure you don't pull any punches when you tell Nick,'' Cam cautioned Rachel. ''Like Pete says, we don't know what Tyson might do if he feels cornered.'' He paused a moment, then withdrew his hand and said to the group, ''So, if we've got that settled, I'd like to throw something else out. I have been told that my son despised the way Tyson abused his power. In Jack's opinion, it was nothing short of rape. The same person who told me that said Jack was very frank in criticizing Monk Tyson.''

''I can believe that,'' Marta murmured. ''Jack had very strong convictions and he knew how to express them. He was a gutsy kid.''

''Exactly,'' Cam said. ''And that's the reason I could never believe in my heart that he committed suicide.'' He looked from one adult to the other.

Pete was nodding. ''I bet I know where you're going, Cam, but I'll let you say it.''

''I think Tyson knew Jack was going to blow the whistle and so he had to silence him. The only way to do that was to kill him.''

Twenty-Four

"**M**om, Graham's missing!" Kendall burst through the back door, panting and out of breath. "I've looked everywhere. I looked in Gran's greenhouse and behind all the bushes and I even went to Cam's yard and looked there. He's gone, Mom," she wailed.

It was Monday morning and Rachel had a thousand things on her mind. Glancing over at Kendall while buttering toast for breakfast, she gave an irritated click of her tongue. "Kendall, your sneakers are filthy. You know better than to go outside to play before school, especially when it's wet. Now you'll have to change. And hurry or you won't have time for breakfast."

"But I can't find Graham. He's always waiting for me, but not today. We have to find him." She dashed into the den where the cat spent a large part of his day curled up on a chair. "He's not *anywhere!*"

"Kendy, you want to hand me that OJ?" Nick sat hunched over a bowl of cereal, eyes glued to the TV screen.

"Please," Rachel prompted.

"Please," Nick said.

"Somebody, listen to me!" Kendall cried. In her hand, she held the cat's collar, a strip of red nylon with a tiny bell attached. "See, here's his collar and he's *gone!*"

Nick looked at her, finally noticing her distress. "How'd that happen?"

"Maybe you took his collar off and forgot to put it back

on," Rachel said, setting a pot of honey on the table. "I'm sure he'll turn up, Kendy."

"I would never take his collar off and forget to put it back on," Kendall said, her brown eyes filling. "That way, if he got lost nobody would know where to call to bring him home."

"Ah, honey, he's not lost." Rachel slipped an arm around her. "He's a male cat. They sometimes wander quite a ways from home, but they always come back."

Kendall turned worried eyes up to Rachel. "Did you remember to feed him yesterday? Did you even see him yesterday?"

Rachel frowned. "Let me think. I definitely remember feeding him Sunday morning. He was on the patio with Marta and me, but as for Sunday night—" She glanced at Nick. "Nick, do you remember seeing him last night after you got home?"

"I don't think so, but I wasn't really looking, either." Nick got up and went to the back door. He'd had stuff a lot more important than Kendy's cat on his mind last night.

"I'm going over to ask Cam if he saw him," Kendall said.

"I'll go," Nick volunteered. "You go change shoes like Mom said."

"No, he's my cat and I'll do it."

"Nobody should do it," Rachel said firmly. "Cam might not even be up at this hour. You can't go knocking on his door at—"

"He's up. I see him all the time sitting on his porch real early having his coffee," Kendall said. "He makes me a fruit smoothie. And Graham's always with us." Kendall darted past Nick and out the door before Rachel could stop her.

"Nick, put a couple of those breakfast bars in a plastic bag," Rachel instructed. "She can eat them in the car on the way to school." She went toward her room to get her purse and a stack of files. "If she's not back in five minutes, you'll have to walk over and bring her back."

"Right." Nick did as told and left the breakfast bars on

the table, then he pushed the door open and stepped out onto
the patio. He guessed Graham could have wandered off, but
the fact that the collar was left behind bothered him. He made
his way around the property, alert for…he didn't know what.
But in the back of his mind now was his family's safety.
He'd spent the day and half the night worrying over what
had happened yesterday and what to do about it. But so far,
he was totally at a dead end. Which meant he could be
spooked by almost anything this morning, even a missing
cat.

Glancing at his watch, he saw that Kendy's five minutes
was up. When she was with Cam, she never knew when to
leave. Room to talk, Forrester, he told himself as he headed
over to get her. He spent a lot of time with Cam, too. Gran
did, too. And now, his mom. That was really interesting.
First, they did the road trip together Saturday and then yesterday with Pete and Marta, and last night when he managed
to drag himself up to go to the bathroom, he found both of
them in the den sitting on the couch pretty close together
eating popcorn. He wondered what his dad would think if he
knew that.

The kitchen door at Cam's house was open and he went
inside. Cam and Kendy were sitting in the window seat. Cam
had his arm around her and her face was turned into his chest.
She was crying. "Jeez, Kendy," he said, going over to them.
"Graham's okay. Like Mom said, he'll turn up, don't
worry."

"No, he w-won't. He—he's gone forever," she said, hic-
cuping. "I know it. He w-wouldn't have lost his collar if he
was okay."

"Mom sent me to get her," he told Cam. "She has to go
to school."

"C'mon, sweetheart." Cam turned her face up and wiped
it with a paper towel. "Let's get you back to your mom so
she can fix you all up. And while you're gone, I'll look for
Graham. Hopefully, by the time you're home, he'll be back,
safe and sound."

"Do I have to? I'd rather s-stay and look for him."

He ruffled her hair. "Aren't you working on that perfect-attendance award? All it takes is one absence to ruin it. You wouldn't want that, would you?"

"I guess."

Watching, Nick wondered how Cam knew about Kendy's obsession with that goofy award. He knew their dad didn't have a clue about anything he or his little sister did in school. "We gotta go, Kendy."

"Okay." With a sniff, she took the paper towel from Cam and wiped her eyes, but she was still distressed. Her mouth was all wobbly and she looked pitiful. But she stuck her hand in Cam's when he offered his.

"Where did you find the collar, Kendy?" he asked, falling into step with them.

"It was all the way around at the front door. I always let him in at the back and when he wasn't there, I went to the front."

"Was it buckled or unbuckled?" He saw Cam's narrow-eyed look and wished he'd waited until they got in the car to ask.

"Unbuckled."

"There you are! I was just coming to get you both." His mom, looking flustered and pretty, flashed a smile at Cam. "Good morning. Sorry to disturb you so early, but Kendy—"

"Is very worried about Graham," Cam said, giving Rachel a slow smile. "You look good enough to...hug."

Nick flicked a glance at them, then looked quickly away. If that scene on the couch hadn't given him a hint, the way Cam was looking at his mom now definitely did.

Rachel's smile died when she saw that Kendall had been crying. "Oh, honey, don't cry. I've told Gran to be on the lookout for Graham. We'll find him."

Another sniff, but Kendy's face was still sad as anything. It made Nick wish he could stick around and try to find that stupid cat for her.

"Cam's gonna look while I'm at school," she said.

Rachel gave him a soft look. "Thank you. We appreciate it. If I didn't have such a packed calendar, I'd stay home myself to search for him. My mother is calling the Animal Rescue people."

"No! They'll put him to sleep," Kendy cried.

Cam squatted on the ground and put his hand on her back. "No, they won't. Even if they do pick him up today, they never put animals to sleep so soon. And that's another place I'll check for you."

"Come inside and let's change your shoes, honey," Rachel said. "Nick, be ready to leave in three minutes." And with another flushed and flustered look at Cam, she mouthed a silent thank-you and took Kendall inside.

"She looked like she wanted to kiss you," Nick said to Cam after they were gone.

"Kendy? Well, Graham means a lot to her."

"No, I meant my mom looked like she wanted to kiss you," Nick said with a grin, and got a kick out of the fact that Cam definitely turned red, pretty much the same way as his mom had a minute ago.

"Would you have a problem with that, Nick?"

Nick gave him a sideways look as if considering it, but he'd already decided. He grinned. "No, so long as you respect her in the morning."

Cam dropped his head, laughed softly. Then, after a beat, he reached out and grabbed Nick's neck in a choke hold, but stopped short when he let out a yelp. "What? That hurt?" Cam said, looking concerned. "Where?"

Nick gave an offhand laugh. "Nothing, just a twinge in my shoulder. Took a dive on my bike yesterday."

"Your mom mentioned it," Cam said, giving him a shrewd look. When his gaze settled on the bruise at Nick's temple, his frown deepened. "That's a pretty nasty bump on your head. Sure you didn't tangle with a bus?" He watched as Nick raked a hand through his hair, forgetting it would expose the scrapes on his palms. And before Nick had a

chance to react, Cam had a grip on both his wrists, turning
his hands palm up.

"Jesus, Nick. That was a joke about the bus. Are you hurt
anywhere else?"

"Hey, it's nothing. It looks worse than it is. I'm okay. I
didn't just crash the bike, I went ass-end over the handlebars
down into a ditch that was almost a ravine. Got pretty banged
up. I didn't show Mom all this stuff. She'd just worry."

It was a half lie, but Nick hadn't figured out what to do
or who to tell about what really happened. He didn't see how
he could without harm coming to Kendy or somebody else
in his family. But Cam didn't seem to be buying his story a
hundred percent. He was giving Nick that cool study that he
did real well. "Did your mom talk to you about keeping low
for a couple of days, Nick? Hang close to home. And don't
quit the team, if you're thinking about doing that. Pete needs
a little time to strengthen his case against Tyson."

"I'm cool, okay? It's not a problem 'cause, except for
school and sports, I'm grounded, so I wasn't gonna be having
much of a social life, anyway. And we've got a game tonight
and I'm starting at first base for junior varsity. I wouldn't
want to let the team down. Plus if I made noises about quitting, it's bound to make Coach suspicious, don't you think?"

"Probably. But your mom and I will be in the stands keeping an eye on you, anyway. Just be careful, Nick. Don't put
yourself in a position where there's nobody else around. Remember that." Cam tilted his head, giving Nick another
sharp once-over, as if he might read something more in his
face than Nick had told. "Nothing you want to tell me,
Nick?"

There was plenty he wanted to tell, such as what Big Guy
said just before he shoved Nick out of the pickup yesterday.
*"Bad things can happen. You don't want to wind up like
Jack Ford."* At the time he said it, Nick was still dazed and
didn't remember it, but later it came back to him. You didn't
have to be a rocket scientist to figure out what it meant. Cam
was right all along in not believing his son committed sui-

cide. But would he feel any better about it knowing he was killed to keep him quiet?

Just then, to his relief, his mom honked the horn as she backed out of the drive. "Look, I've gotta go, Cam. I'll see you later." And by the time the day was done, he hoped he would have formulated some kind of plan about how to handle this situation. The way it stood now, nothing short of Coach dropping dead could fix it.

It was while he was sitting in Biology that the idea came to him. It was all he could do to sit through the rest of that period, then when the bell rang he was the first one out the door. He found a place beneath the stairs and whipped out his cell phone. Thanks to Ward, he had the number. He needed to call Jimbo Rivers.

Twenty-Five

Rachel arrived at her office that morning distracted and uneasy. The disappearance of Kendy's cat bothered her in a way that she couldn't quite pin down. Cats disappeared all the time, as she'd told Kendy, especially tomcats. Graham, although neutered, might simply have had the urge to prowl and he'd come home in a day or two. She was grateful that Cam offered to look for him, which was just one more mark in his favor to endear him to Kendy.

And to Rachel. There were several reasons she could name that had made her fall in love with Cam, and his thoughtfulness to her children and her mother were at the top. She wasn't certain when her feelings for Cam had changed. Only a few months ago, she'd been certain that Cam could never get beyond his bitterness over her failure to recognize that something was pushing Jack to the breaking point. Rachel herself had trouble coming to terms with the fact that she'd failed to save Jack. Now it seemed they'd come full circle, both of them. It was hard to believe where they were today. Incredible, really.

At her desk now, she put thoughts of Cam and Kendy and Graham out of her mind and booted up her computer. In minutes, she was scanning files. It was impossible to believe that Tyson could have been abusing boys for five years and leave no trail. There had to be one or two red flags, maybe more. Her search was confined to athletes—especially the gifted ones—going back to the time Monk Tyson first arrived at Rose Hill.

Two hours later, she sat back and rubbed her eyes. There were some athletes whose grades had slipped or who had dropped out of school. Several had gotten involved in drugs. But over a five-year period, there didn't appear to be an alarming increase in troubling behavior, at least, no more than was in the general enrollment. She glanced at the print-out of the dozen or so student files she'd pulled. They were athletes who were still in school and she planned to call them in, one by one. It might be a waste of time, but it was worth a try. The most troubled student appeared to be Jason Pate, or rather, Jason was the only one who had revealed his angst.

There were no other suicides, only Jack Ford's.

She admitted with disappointment that she'd really wanted to find something specific, a pattern of troubled behavior or excessive dropouts—just something—that she could take back to Cam to prove that Jack's death was more than just a simple depression-induced teen tragedy.

It was there. She just had to find it.

Nick managed to make it through most of Monday without a personal encounter with anybody who'd been at the house party on the lake. He wasn't sure how it would go down when he came face-to-face with any of those guys. But, heck, what could they do, kill him? Somebody already tried that and it wasn't even anybody he knew.

He should have known it would be Ferdy Jordan who took the first shot. Nick was at his locker when he looked up into Ferdy's face on one side of him and B. J. Folsom on the other. A stream of students milled around them, but nobody seemed to notice he was being strong-armed except a couple more players who'd been at the party. No help there. "What the hell happened to you Friday night, Forrester? You get lost in the woods?"

"Yeah, something like that." Nick tossed in his math text and, with his head deep in the locker, pretended to look for a biology notebook. That way, he wouldn't even see what weapon they used to kill him, he thought with dark humor.

"We thought you drowned or something." Ferdy again.

Out of the locker now, Nick shrugged and kept his mouth shut.

B.J. moved in front of him, so that anybody watching wouldn't see his face. "That was a friggin' stupid thing to do, you know that?"

"It seemed a good idea at the time," he said cautiously.

Ferdy crossed his big arms and nudged him, so that Nick was pinned against the locker. "That was a very select group, Forrester. You won't get a second chance."

He didn't want a second chance. In fact, he'd already primed himself to drop sports altogether, but that might screw up the official investigation. Meanwhile, there were two games tonight. He'd have to show up. Junior varsity played first, and then the team was required to sit on the bench when the seniors played. After talking to Jimbo, he'd come up with a plan. It bothered him to go against what his mom and Cam had warned, but they didn't know they were in jeopardy. What the heck was he supposed to do?

Nick held up his notebook in a valiant attempt not to appear scared shitless. "Gotta go, guys."

"Not yet, you don't." Ferdy again.

Together, Ferdy and B.J. made four-hundred-plus pounds of muscle. They could crush him like a bug, but they could hardly do it now. And even without Cam and his mom's warnings, he wouldn't be dumb enough to be caught alone again like he was Saturday. Nick took a deep breath. "Look, the party wasn't what I expected. So I decided to split. No, problem, right?"

Ferdy stood looking at him long enough for Nick to start sweating. "What's going on with your mom?"

"Huh?" He blinked.

"Your old lady," B.J. said. "She's been calling us in all day."

Nick was genuinely baffled. "I don't know what you're talking about. She called all who in today?"

Ferdy leaned one beefy shoulder against the lockers. "Me

and B.J., Robbie, Kyle. We're not sure who all else. And the day's not over. We each go in and have a chat with her and you say you didn't know anything about it? Nothing happened at the party that you wanted to share with your mama?''

''No. Not a word. And I don't have a clue what she's doing.'' He shrugged, but inside he was chilled to the bone. ''It must be something—''

''Forrester,'' Ferdy said softly, ''let me give you a little piece of advice to pass on to your mama. And this is coming not just from me and B.J. here, but from the team. She needs to stay out of Coach Tyson's house. You got that?''

He got it.

It was midafternoon when Rachel stood up, rubbing her aching back, and thought of going to the break room to get a cold drink. The interviews had been a bust. If there was anything going on and the players were aware of it, they were not going to tell it to her. Maybe when Pete's investigation began to heat up, he'd have more luck getting them to talk. So, all she'd managed to do today was to put off work that would have to be sandwiched into tomorrow's schedule. Somehow.

''I know a great massage technique to fix that.''

It was Cam. She smiled in surprise. ''Hi, what are you doing here?''

''Couple of things.'' He came inside, closing the door behind him, and headed for her desk. Or so she thought. Instead, he came around it. ''First this…'' He caught her up and kissed her. Caught off guard, it took a moment before she grabbed hold of his shirtfront and kissed him back. It would have been nice to do more than simply enjoy such a new and heady feeling, but she was in her workplace and had a famous open-door policy. A student might walk in at any moment.

Pushing at him gently, she moved out of his arms. ''As

nice as that was, I don't think it would do me any good professionally if a student walked in."

"I know." He touched her face and then moved back to the front of her desk. "I'm on my way to see Pete and I thought you'd probably want to go with me when you hear what happened."

She glanced around at the files strewn over her desk, on the credenza behind her and at her feet on the floor. "I can't go anywhere. I've spent the day scanning files and being stonewalled by jocks. If I don't want to have a horrendous day tomorrow, I need to stay here and catch up." She gestured to a chair. "But tell me what happened."

He didn't sit down. "Jimbo Rivers told me he had a call from Nick. Apparently, after he got to school, he used his cell phone. Nick didn't just have an accident on his bike yesterday, Rachel. He was deliberately run off the road by two thugs who threatened his family, you, Kendy and Dinah."

Before he'd finished, Rachel had sunk back into her chair, her face pale.

"That's the reason he slipped into the house after going to the grocery store," Cam added. "He knew after one look at him we'd guess it was more than just a tumble on his bike.

"There's more, Rachel." Cam rubbed the side of his neck. "We're not the only ones suspicious about Jack's death now. Nick has it in his head that Jack was murdered."

Rachel sat trying to take it in. "Why did he call Jimbo about this?"

"He thought Jimbo might be able to shed light on who Tyson would send to do the deed, I presume."

She put a hand on her throat. "We told him we'd take care of it. He has to stay out of this, Cam. He promised he'd let us—and Pete—handle it."

"I think he believes a threat to his family trumps that promise."

"He has a game tonight. I don't want him playing."

"I'm on my way to talk to Pete right now. I want to hear what he thinks we should do, but I don't see how Nick can be harmed playing baseball with the stands full of people watching him. You and I will be there. I told him that this morning."

She was on her feet again, pulling her purse out of a desk drawer. "You're right. I want to go with you. Just let me check if Marta can drive Nick home after school. I don't want him hitching a ride with Kristin or anybody else. I would speak to him directly, but this is the hour he's at the gym. He'll be dressed out on the field. If I pull him out to talk to him, Monk might get suspicious."

"He might." Cam went to the door and opened it. "Let's go. Pete's expecting us."

Pete ushered Cam and Rachel into his office and waited for Angela to distribute coffee all around. She politely served Rachel and the chief, then finally Cam, bestowing a brilliant smile on him as she did so. Ignoring Pete's amused look and Rachel's more interested one, Cam thanked her and launched into the reason he came.

The chief listened intently until Cam got to the part where Nick's suspicions coincided with his own regarding Jack's death. Pete sputtered in his coffee. "How in hell did he figure it out?"

"I'll find out more when I get a chance to talk to him, but here's what Jimbo told me. Nick asked for names of athletes who were in Tyson's program five years ago when Jimbo and Jack were there. When asked why, Nick told him he'd been threatened after getting run down on his bike."

Pete looked thoughtful. "We knew he'd stumbled into some mean territory, but I'm trying to figure how he was led to suspect Jack was murdered."

Rachel spoke up. "Nick told Jimbo that Tyson set the thugs on him to keep him from talking. He wanted to know which of Monk's former athletes that might be."

"Jimbo was in the sports program a full four years, three

years after Jack died," Cam said, "so Nick was right in thinking he was a good source of information. It was only after Jimbo had given him the names, thinking that Nick would come to me for help, that Nick revealed his theory about how Jack died."

"Are these names the same thugs I'm checking out now?" Pete asked.

"Yeah." Cam shoved pages torn from the notebook across the desk. "And after I told Jimbo you were taking a look at a few people he'd mentioned, he said he'd done some more serious thinking. After giving me the names, he said he'd be happy to answer any questions you might have now."

"I think in hindsight, he's worried about Ward," Rachel said. "We probably planted that seed in our visit to him, don't you think so, Cam?"

"Probably. But whatever the reason, we've got names now. He's narrowed it down to six players he thinks might have been persuaded to do Tyson's bidding back then."

Cam pushed up out of his chair. "Nick asked a lot of questions about Jack. That, plus what he's learned from Rachel and Marta—and from me, I guess—has led him to suspect that Jack might have been ready to blow the whistle. If Tyson suspected the same thing, he would have had to stop Jack. That's Nick's theory."

"Well, we can't fault his reasoning, can we? Basically, that's your theory, too, Cam."

Rachel's hands were unsteady as she set her coffee aside. "Pete, Nick is now every bit as much a threat as Jack was. What's to keep Tyson from removing the threat the same way?"

"This may not be much reassurance," Pete said, "but Tyson has to assume we're suspicious, which ties his hands somewhat. He knows Nick's a spunky kid and that his thugs didn't deliver their threats until Sunday morning, time for Nick to have already told what happened at the party. If I were Tyson, I'd be making plans to get out of town right about now, not trying to figure how to silence a kid who may have told another kid who may have told another." He waved a hand with a shrug. "My take, for what it's worth."

Cam was still pacing. "Why didn't Nick come to me first? As soon as he told me what went down on the lake, I promised him I'd see to it personally that Tyson was stopped. He knows you're involved now. He knows something like that can't happen overnight. Why go to Jimbo and not me?"

"I think I can guess one good reason why," Rachel said. "The threat was not only to me, Kendy and my mother. It probably included you."

She stood up suddenly. "I need to visit the ladies' room," she said, wiping at her sleeve with a napkin.

"Are you okay?" Cam asked, scanning her face with concern.

"Yes, I splashed a little coffee on this blazer." She headed to the door. "I'll just be a minute. Don't make any decisions without me."

When the door closed behind her, Pete got up and came around to the front of his desk. "Let's hope Nick doesn't come up with some wild-and-crazy plan to handle things on his own."

"I've been worrying about that and I know Rachel has, too." Cam fought down a sense of déjà vu. He hadn't been available when Jack needed him, but he'd be damned if he'd let Nick down. And Rachel. "Everything's on the line for Monk Tyson, Pete. In spite of the fact that we think he won't do anything stupid, I'm concerned that he might make a move on Nick." He was at the window now, scowling. "I found his bike this morning while I was searching for Kendy's cat. He'd stashed it in an old shed behind my garage. It was a total loss. He was lucky to walk away." He paused, then turned back to face Pete. "I can't let anything happen to him, Pete. I'm not letting Monk Tyson hurt another boy."

"I know you feel a special bond with Nick, but I don't like seeing you take the full burden of responsibility. He has a dad. You think he knows anything about this?"

"Doubtful. Nick called Ted for help Friday night but couldn't reach him. There's a disconnect between Ted and his kids since he and Rachel filed for divorce and Nick's aware of it. He's bitter about it. He thinks Ted cares more about Francine than his own kids. He thinks Ted just isn't there for him." Cam shook his head sadly. "Jesus, I don't have any room to talk about absentee fathers. When Jack needed me, I damn sure wasn't connected. He might be here today if I had been."

"That's a heavy load to carry around, buddy."

"Tell me. But I'm not on deadline now or too busy. Nick has wandered into the same mean territory that got Jack killed. He's a boy and he doesn't realize just how mean things can get. Jack apparently underestimated the danger and there was no one to caution him or to keep an eye on him. It'll be different for Nick. I'm not letting another boy be sacrificed for Tyson's sick obsession. I'll do for Nick what I didn't do for Jack."

He glanced up and found Pete giving him a knowing look. "What?"

"Searching for Kendy's cat, looking out for Rachel's mom, rescuing Nick…" Pete was back behind his desk now, getting ready to feed the names into his computer. "This sounds serious, my man."

"It is."

Twenty-Six

Rachel stood at the fridge, distracted from preparing Kendy's dinner by worry over Nick. She'd talked to Marta a few minutes ago and been assured that Nick was safe in her car and they were on the way home. She was thinking of calling again when suddenly he stormed in from the garage and slammed his books on the counter. He was red in the face and breathing hard. Kendy sat at the table with Dinah, her homework spread out before her. She jumped up. "Did you find Graham?" she asked eagerly.

"I need to talk to you, Mom."

Rachel frowned. "What's wrong? Where's Marta? I just—"

"She's fine. She dropped me off and went to meet Pete for dinner. Mom, can we go somewhere private?"

"You didn't, did you?" Kendy said angrily, hands on her hips.

Rachel put a bag of salad greens on the counter and said to Kendy, "Nick hasn't had time to look for your cat, sweetie. Now, finish your math and Gran will check it for you." She looked at her mother, who nodded.

Kendy threw her pencil across the table, glaring at Nick. "You didn't even look for him, I bet. He promised, Mom."

Irritated, Nick said, "Didn't you hear Mom? I haven't had time to look for your damn cat, Kendall!"

"Nick! No swearing."

Nick visibly tried to calm himself. "Mom, it's getting late

and we need to leave for the ball field soon, but first, we need to talk. Please?''

Rachel nudged him out of the kitchen and down the hall to his bedroom. She and Cam had decided not to question him before the game about his call to Jimbo. But from his agitated state, he might be ready to talk to her, anyway. Closing the door, she faced him. ''What's wrong?''

''Why did you call the varsity athletes into your office today, Mom?''

''I can't discuss what happens in my office, Nick. You know that.''

''Mom! Just answer me. It's important.''

She moved toward him slowly. ''Why is it important? Why do you want to know?''

''Don't start that question-with-a-question psychology stuff, Mom! This is serious. Did you have a real excuse for bugging them or was it a bogus reason, like you were hoping they'd say stuff about Coach?''

''You know I can't discuss what I talk to a student about, Nick. Or why.''

''I was nearly creamed in the halls today because of it.''

Rachel stared at him in shock and sank down on the bed. ''By whom?''

''Just don't ask. All I want to know is why were you doing it?''

''Tell me their names, Nick. You know that questionable things are going on. It wouldn't be ratting out anybody.'' She saw by the look on his face that he wasn't talking.

''Is that what you said to them? It'll be a service to mankind if you tell me what you think Coach is up to?'' He raked a hand over his hair. ''Mom, you don't know what you're fooling around with. Are you finished? Are you gonna drag other players in and keep on tomorrow?''

''No. I saw it was useless. I didn't get any more information from the boys I talked to than I'm getting from you now.''

''If you start meddling in Coach Tyson's business, Mom,

bad things can happen. I thought we were gonna let the chief take care of this,'' he said, his tone rising.

"We are. What I was doing—'' She broke off, startled by a piercing scream. "That's Kendall!'' she cried, looking around wildly. She turned and raced out of the room with Nick on her heels. Dinah and Kendall were both gone from the kitchen, but the door was open. Dashing out onto the patio, she almost crashed into Cam, who must have heard the commotion and come on the run.

"Here,'' Dinah called out from the direction of the utility shed near the greenhouse. "Somebody bring a flashlight.'' Her outline was barely visible through a thick growth of azalea bushes. She appeared to be bending over Kendall, who was on her knees on the ground.

"Nick,'' Rachel ordered, not taking her eyes from Dinah and the little girl. "There's a flashlight at my bedside table. Go get it.''

Nick hesitated, but she gave him a shove. "Go, Nick!''

"Rachel, let me.'' Cam caught her by the arm, but she was already pushing through the azaleas to get to Kendall, heedless of low branches lashing her face and arms. As she rushed forward, the little girl looked up.

"Mom, Graham's hurt.'' Only then did Rachel realize that Kendall was cradling Graham in her lap. The cat stirred feebly but appeared too weak to move much. Rachel crouched down beside Kendall, more concerned about her daughter than the cat. "Are you okay, Kendy?''

"It's Graham, not me. Somebody did something terrible to him, Mom.''

Cam was on one knee beside Kendall. "Let me see, sweetheart.''

Nick appeared, breathing hard. "I've got the flashlight,'' he said. There was shocked silence when he turned the beam on the cat. A large splotch of paint in the shape of a crude bull's-eye had been sprayed on Graham's side.

"Jeez,'' Nick breathed.

"Mo-o-om,'' Kendall wailed. "Is he gonna die?''

"He's hurt, honey, but let's take a look," she managed in a tone that belied the outrage simmering inside her. Who would do this to a helpless animal? And why?

"We need a vet," Cam said, his face grim. "Let's get him back in his carrier."

Nick bent to examine the crate. "This isn't ours. It's too big, for one thing. And it's black. Ours is gray."

"Was he inside the carrier when you found him, Kendy?" Cam asked. He sounded calm, but he had a fierce look on his face.

"Uh-huh. I heard him meowing and me and Gran came out to look and this is where he was. Will he die?" she asked in a voice that trembled.

"We hope not, sweetheart. Cats are pretty tough."

"I didn't hear a thing," Dinah said, handing over a towel she'd fetched from the greenhouse. "But Kendy insisted that we go outside and look. I see now he was too weak to make much noise."

"What's that all over him?" Kendy asked.

"It looks like paint," Rachel said, taking her hand. "It'll have to be removed with some kind of chemical that's safe for cats, so Cam's right. The place for him tonight is at the animal hospital." She didn't mention that there seemed to be more wrong with him than a mere spray-paint job. She was no expert, but it looked as if Graham had been poisoned.

Cam took the cat from Kendy, who handed him over with an anxious look. "C'mon, we'll go straight to the clinic. The vet'll need to check him out and maybe keep an eye on him overnight."

"How will I get to the game?" Nick asked. "By the time you get home from the vet, it'll be half over."

Rachel, following Cam and Kendy, headed to the garage where Graham's cat carrier was stored. "Maybe you shouldn't play tonight, Nick. I can call Monk and—"

"Mom, I can't just dog out! I'm playing first base. C'mon…jeez."

"I'll take him, Rachel," Dinah said. "I had no plans for

tonight. I'll drive him and sit in the stands while he plays, then when you and Cam get back from the vet, the two of you can relieve me at the game and I'll take Kendy back home.''

''Well…'' She studied his face worriedly. ''Promise me you won't even think of getting out of Mother's sight, Nick.''

''I've gotta go in the locker room and get my gear,'' he said.

''Except for that.''

He held up his right hand. ''Not a problem.''

''He'll be fine,'' Dinah assured her. ''What can happen in full sight of the stands?''

Nick was wound pretty tight when he got to the locker room. For a few minutes after the problem with Kendall's cat, he'd been afraid that his mom would keep him from playing tonight. And if it hadn't been for Gran, that probably would have happened. He had a plan, of sorts, but to carry it out he had to get to the game. He was cutting it close, thanks to the cat emergency, because almost everybody was already in the dugout and he still had to get his cleats and glove out of his locker before he was ready to roll. With less than ten minutes before play started, he hit the ground running as soon as Gran stopped the car.

He jerked the door of his locker open and was on the point of reaching for his glove when he saw the note. A big sheet of paper with large letters, which he knew at a glance somebody had done at a computer. Snatching it down, he stared at it.

IT WAS EASY TO GET THE CAT.
IT'LL BE EVEN EASIER TO GET YOUR FAMILY.

''What's going on, Nick? You've been in la-la land since the game started.'' Ward turned a bottle of water up and drank half of it, then in an undertone, added, "Coach is getting suspicious. He's already been over and asked me what's bugging you."

"What'd you tell him?"

"I'm clueless, what do you think I told him!" He leaned over and put his water bottle beneath the bench. "And guess who else has been asking questions about you?"

"J.Lo?"

Ward snorted. "This is serious, Nick. Jimbo. He called me and chewed me a new one. He said you were getting into some heavy shit and for me to tell you to lie low, that he had taken care of it."

"How'd he do that?"

"He didn't say and even if I'd asked, he wouldn't tell me. He still treats me like I'm six years old," Ward said bitterly.

Looking straight ahead, Nick was thinking about the note. He knew it came from Coach Monk, but he'd put somebody else up to do his dirty work. Somebody too stupid to do it well. It had to be Ferdy—or B.J., his alter ego. Those two were just foul enough to half kill a helpless animal and then use it to try to spook him. But Nick didn't intend to be spooked by anybody, including The Man himself.

On the field, the pitcher zinged one wide to Will Smythe. As they sat in the dugout, Nick continued their conversation. "Ward, can I ask you something?"

"Way to go *Will!*" Ward leaped up at Will's base hit and whistled when he slid safe at first. "About what?" he asked, settling back on the bench.

"If the chief needed you to testify in court, would you?"

Ward waited a little too long, his gaze fixed on the ball field. "I don't know. It's…embarrassing."

"What about the fact that he killed Jack Ford?"

"We don't know that for sure!" Ward hissed.

"Yeah, but what if he did?"

Ward watched as the next Rose Hill batter up struck out,

ending the inning. "You're hero material, Nick. Not me. And I think you ought to do like Jimbo says and lie low for a while."

Both of them rose with the rest of the team to go out on the field. "I think it's too late to lie low, Ward."

Nick's chance to get to Ferdy came just before the game ended. He rose to follow the creep to the john, waving casually to his grandmother, hoping she wouldn't freak out over losing sight of him for two minutes. Nick knew he had to be armed to get Ferdy's attention, so he grabbed a bat on his way out of the dugout.

This was meant to be, Nick thought, spotting Ferdy with his back to him taking a leak. Karma and all that. What goes around comes around. Using the bat, he poked Ferdy hard in a kidney, midstream.

"Yow!" Ferdy yelled, and looked at Nick in total astonishment. But with the bat swinging in a threatening arc and his hands otherwise occupied, he was caught with his pants down, literally. "What the hell are you doing, you little piss-ant?"

"I'm answering your note, Ferdy," Nick said, waving the bat in front of his nose. "I know you wrote it, which means you tried to kill my sister's cat."

"What note? What the fuck you talkin' about?" He looked genuinely baffled. Grabbing the note, he scanned it and shoved it back at Nick. "I never saw that before."

"It's about as low-down a stunt as I ever knew, but then you're so low-down yourself it's the only way your mind can work. Hold it!" He brought the bat up in a threatening stance when Ferdy would have charged him. "This is just to warn you, Ferdy. I'm on to you and to the whole bunch of jocks in cahoots with Coach Monk. You do anything else that touches my family or anybody who's a friend of mine and I'll bring this whole stinking mess down. You got that?"

"What whole stinking mess?"

"Sex stuff. Parties with old gay men. Payback in scholarships to keep quiet."

Ferdy was shaking his head slowly. "You are so diggin' your own grave, Forrester. You don't have a clue what you've stepped in."

"I think I do."

"Okay, but I don't know nothing about your cat or that note. And look, for your own good, you gotta back off about Coach Monk. You don't want to fool around like that, dude, I'm not shittin' you. You could wind up very dead."

"Dead like Jack Ford?" Nick stood his ground, daring Ferdy to deny it. After a long minute, Ferdy turned away, zipped up and walked out of the john.

Neither of them realized they'd been overheard. After a minute, Jason Pate came out of a stall and stood in the door watching both ball players heading back to the dugout. A base hit by the visiting team brought cheers from the crowd, drowned out by boos from Rose Hill. In the bright lights of the floods, the grass on the ball field was so green it hurt his eyes, and the smell of popcorn and sawdust teased his nose. From the time he was four years old and had first picked up a bat, Jason had dreamed of a future in baseball. He had done whatever it took to make it happen, hating himself sometimes, but doing it, anyway. And now he was close. So close.

Damn Nick and his Dudley Do Right act. From what Jason knew of him, he figured there was a slim-to-none chance he'd heed any warning from Ferdy Jordan, who, without a doubt, would rat to Tyson. And once Tyson knew, he would be forced finally to cut and run. Or to deal with Nick the way he'd dealt with Jack Ford. Jason squeezed his eyes shut, not going there tonight. Doing nothing now meant that his dream might still be possible. Doing otherwise would destroy it. He stood another minute or two, conflicted and miserable, then walked to the dugout and sat down.

Twenty-Seven

After the encounter between him and Ferdy in the john, Nick knew the fat was in the fire. He wasn't certain when Ferdy would rat to Coach, only that he would. What Tyson would do, Nick didn't even begin to guess, but he was sure to retaliate, and "shock and awe" would probably be the best way to describe it. His plan was pretty desperate, and he knew he would be in hot water big time by leaving after being told in no uncertain terms by Cam and his mom not to, but he couldn't sit back and wait for Tyson to hurt anybody in his family. The cat was a message and Nick got it.

If Ferdy was telling the truth and knew nothing about the note and Kendy's cat, then there was only one other possibility as to who'd done it: Harley or Big Guy. But no matter who did it, the source of the threat was Coach Tyson. Nick wasn't giving Tyson the opportunity to rig his "suicide" like he'd done with Jack Ford.

As the junior varsity game ended, the team broke out of the dugout. There was about thirty minutes to kill until the second game. The Mustangs had won and there would be some celebrating in the locker room, but Nick had other plans. He'd scoped out the stands looking for Kristin at the beginning of the first game. With a muttered "Yes!" he'd spotted her, as she was necessary to his plan since she had a car.

Seeking to reassure his Gran, Nick waved to her, sitting up high, and then instead of falling in with the rest of the team, he cut away and headed for a spot that would take him within speaking distance of Kristin. He was peering up, trying to catch her eye when somebody touched him on the shoulder.

"Hi, Nick."

He started and turned. "Dad!"

Ted's smile was tentative. "Surprised to see me, I guess."

"Well, yeah. I mean—" He turned, swept the stands with a panicked gaze and saw Kristin rising to leave with her friends. If she left, he was screwed. "It's been a while," he said, turning back to his dad while his mind raced to figure out plan B.

"Too long, son." Ted was studying Nick's face as if he had sort of forgotten what he looked like. "Can I buy you a drink?"

"Got some," he said, holding up a bottle. "Thanks, anyway."

"Take a short walk, then?" Putting out his hand, he didn't quite touch Nick but urged him with a look that was uncertain. Nick couldn't remember ever seeing his dad looking uncertain. "We won't go far."

"Sure." Nick glanced around, looking for the Lexus. "Is Francine here?"

"I don't think she does sports. I know you don't have much time between games," Ted said, "but I wanted you to know that I was here. I saw you play. You're turning into a fine baseball player, Nick."

Nick guessed it wasn't the right time to tell him that as of tonight, it was iffy whether he'd be playing anymore. And if his dad hadn't walked out on them, he might be able to tell him the world of shit he was in and get some help to do something about it. It was a bitter thought, and suddenly he didn't care if his dad knew of his resentment. "How do you know what kind of player I am, Dad? You don't have much of a base to compare with since I don't think you've hardly ever been around to watch me play."

"That's true. But it doesn't mean I can't start coming more often."

"When? Between setting up a new practice and keeping Francine happy, how will you work it into your schedule?" Nick knew bullshit when he heard it. "You never had time before and Mom wasn't nearly so high maintenance as Francine, right?"

"I know you're bitter. I can see— Well, all I can say is that I'm going to make it up to you, Nick."

"Yeah, sure." Nick kicked at a cigarette butt on the ground.

Ted stopped and faced him. "I mean it, son. I've made some huge mistakes. I know you and Kendy are hurt. I know it'll take some time to get over that. But I—"

Nick spotted Kristin heading back from the concession stand. Which meant she hadn't left. Maybe he wasn't screwed. "Sorry, Dad, but I've got to see someone about something that's pretty important." He lifted his hand to get Kristin's attention.

Ted frowned at the distraction. "I'm going to call you about this weekend, Nick," he said.

"I don't know, Dad. I've made plans already." Not exactly the truth, but he wasn't sure he wanted his dad to decide to drop back into their lives now, with him and Kendy just rolling over and letting him. Except for rare occasions like holidays and stuff, his dad had hardly ever been around for him or Kendy. He'd maybe show up for a Little League game or go out with them sometimes for a pizza. Most of the time, he was up real early and off to the hospital, then on to his practice. Home too late to hear about anything his kids had done. Nick had only started to wonder lately whether or not his dad had even spent much time with his mom.

"Cam wants me to help him floor his attic this weekend," he added. Cam hadn't exactly set the time, but it could be this weekend, he told himself.

Ted was momentarily speechless. "I didn't know you knew how to do that kind of work."

"I'm learning a lot from Cam." The kind of things he'd never have learned from his dad. Ted probably didn't even know the right end of a hammer. And if he'd had an old house like Cam's, he would have hired someone to get the work done without even thinking about doing any of it himself.

"How about a pizza or something when you're done?" Ted asked.

"That's the thing when you're doing manual labor, Dad," he said, looking anywhere but at him, "who knows how long it'll take to do a job. So I guess I'll have to take a rain check. See what happens." Nick couldn't ever recall blowing it off when his dad had suggested spending time with him, but it was surprisingly easy.

"You spend a lot of time with him?"

"Cam? Yeah, me and Kendy both. She's really nuts about him, takes pictures of his house, kills a lot of time over there. Lately, she's been trying to exorcise the ghost in his attic."

"What?"

"He's got her thinking one of his ancestors haunts the place."

"I see." Ted was nodding slowly. "And how does your mother feel about him?"

Nick looked directly into his dad's eyes then. "Maybe you should ask her. A good time would be when you drop by to give her the money you owe that's past due."

Ted raked a hand over his hair. "There are things you don't understand, Nick."

"Yeah, shit happens. Isn't that the excuse most deadbeat dads give?"

"Is that how you think of me, son? As a deadbeat dad?" His dad looked really...like, sick.

"You want the truth, Dad? I'm not sure how I think of you. Or what I think of you. What you did was pretty rotten. It caused a world of hurt to Kendy and Mom. And, you know what? It was embarrassing, too. Your old man steals the wife of his partner, that's not something you're proud for your friends to know."

"If it's any comfort," Ted said, looking strained and

shaken, "I've been thinking the same thing lately when I look in the mirror. But it's a thousand times worse hearing you say the words, Nick."

Nick wasn't so mad now, just kind of sad. There hadn't been a lot of time in the past when he'd had his dad's full attention. When it came, he'd lapped it up like a puppy dog, but that was when he'd worshiped his dad and looked forward to any crumb he might toss him. He didn't worship him anymore. He just felt sorry for him.

Looking away, he saw Kristin watching him. "Look, Dad, I've gotta go."

"Francine and I are not together anymore, Nick. That should make the time we're together, you and Kendy and I, more enjoyable."

"She go back to Dr. Walt?"

"It looks like she might. I really don't know."

With a shrug, Nick began a backward getaway. What did his dad expect? Women like Francine weren't faithful and true like his mom. And he'd walked away from her.

"Bye, Dad."

Turning, he jogged toward the stands and Kristin without looking back. Ted was left looking somber and shaken.

It took him a few precious minutes to maneuver Kristin to an area at the edge of the stands where he could make his pitch. She held a soft drink in a paper cup. She took a sip through a straw and indicated his dad still standing where Nick had left him. "Wasn't that Dr. Forrester talking to you?"

"Yeah, he just dropped by, I guess."

"I don't think I've ever seen your dad at a game," Kristin said, still watching him.

"That's because he's never been."

"Oh."

"Kristin, I don't have much time. This is an emergency."

"Again?" She gave a huff of exasperation. With her hip

cocked and her eyes fixed on the ball field, she said, "Just tell it to me without all the hyperbole."

"Hyperbole?" He almost smiled. That Kristin was something else.

"Ms. Ruiz is very big on expanding our vocabulary. We have a list of unusual words that she encourages us to use. *Hyperbole* means—"

"I know, exaggeration. But I'm not exaggerating, Kristin. But since you're clued in to what's going on, sort of, I'm hoping you're gonna save the day. I don't know anybody else who has a car and I need a car in the worst kinda way."

"Where do we have to go and why?"

He thought a moment, looking away. He didn't think he was putting her in harm's way by doing this, but this whole situation was getting dicier by the minute. If anything happened to her, it would kill him. He was beginning to like Kristin. A lot.

"Don't even think of spinning me a line of baloney, Nick. Just tell me straight where we're going and why."

"You'll do it?"

"Depends. Maybe. After you told me Sunday what was going on with Ward, I thought about telling my mom and going to the police, but—" She shook her head. "Don't freak out, I didn't do it. Yet."

He'd like to go to Chief Singletary himself, dump everything in his lap. He would, too, if his mission tonight was a success. "I need to make a road trip tonight to check out where a couple of Coach's former athletes live. And I don't have wheels."

"Why?"

"I really think I shouldn't tell you that." When she instantly opened her mouth to argue, he said, "I got some names from Ward's brother, Jimbo. There was a guy named Ziegler. I looked him up. I used the Internet at the library," he said before she could ask. He glanced over his shoulder at the field house. Yeah, like he figured, the team was beginning to head to the dugout. Play would begin in a minute.

"There's neat stuff that cross-matches names with addresses and phone numbers, too. Besides Ziegler, only two of the people he named still live in Rose Hill. I want to take a ride and see if anybody drives a pickup that I recognize."

"What if it's parked inside a garage and you can't see it?"

He blew out a breath. "Kristin, why do you always have to come up with a negative argument?"

"It's logic, not negativity."

"If it's closed up in a garage, then we're cooked," he said. "Now, listen. I need to locate the vehicle before I can tell Chief Singletary what happened. There's stuff I didn't tell you about, but it's bad. The chief needs facts to pump up his investigation. I think identifying the driver of that pickup will do it."

"Ward could do that right now," Kristin said. "I mean, he could give facts to pump up the investigation. His statement alone would be enough to bring Tyson down."

"I don't think he's ready just yet," Nick said.

"Because he's not as brave as you are."

Nick felt himself turning red. "C'mon, I'm not brave."

"Yes, you are. And that's the reason I'm willing to help you. Otherwise, I wouldn't get mixed up in this, no way. Because when it's all finished and Coach Monk is brought down, you're going to be able to say you did the right thing. It's scary, but that's the way it is, Nick. Some of us have guts and charisma and some of us don't."

Nick found himself grinning. "Is it okay to tell a girl that she's got guts?"

She tossed her drink in the trash. "As long as you add the 'charisma' part."

"You've definitely got it all, Kristin."

To his amazement, she went up on her tiptoes and, with her hands on his shoulders, kissed him. "I'll pick you up at this gate as soon as the game's over, okay?"

Now he was really red. "Okay. And thanks. I owe you one."

"No, you owe me two. But just for the sake of argument,

suppose the thugs all have a garage?'' When he rolled his eyes, she laughed. ''Just kidding. You'd better get to the dugout. The Man's looking.''

The varsity game was almost over when Rachel and Cam finally arrived at the ball field with Kendy. They quickly located Nick sitting in the dugout and then Dinah high up in the stands. When she caught Rachel's eye, she made her way down to the ground. ''How's Graham?'' she asked Kendy, ruffling the little girl's hair.

''He's sick as anything, Gran, but the vet says he'll be all right.''

Dinah questioned Rachel with a look. ''It was touch-and-go for a while,'' Rachel said in a tone meant to convey reassurance to Kendy. ''The vet is keeping him for a few days. The paint can be removed, but he'll have to have some other treatment to help him overcome whatever it was that made him sick. It was a close call. Thanks to Kendy, he'll pull through.''

She didn't say in front of Kendy that Graham had been poisoned. Another hour and it would have been too late to save him. The paint could be construed as a juvenile prank—mean but not lethal—but giving Graham poison was a vicious act. If it was meant as a message to Nick—or his family—it worked. And now that she was here and saw that Nick was okay, she'd prefer taking him off the bench and bringing him home, but again, they didn't want to arouse suspicion in Tyson. Once he felt the net drawing in around him, who knew what he might do?

''Was that Ted's car I saw just now?'' she asked Dinah. Over in the parking lot, the Lexus was just pulling away.

''Yes, he and Nick had a long conversation at the break after the juniors played.''

Rachel's gaze moved to Nick, who lifted a hand to acknowledge her. ''Did he seem upset?''

''Nick or Ted?''

''Either one, Mother. Both.''

"No, not upset, but neither one of them looked particularly happy."

Rachel sighed and decided she could ask Nick what was up when he got home. She glanced up and found Cam watching her. "It just surprised me to see him here." Cam's only response was a noncommittal grunt. Ted would probably never be redeemed in Cam's estimation, she thought.

They turned Kendy over to Dinah then and stood watching while both got into Dinah's car and drove off. "At least Kendy's safe," Rachel murmured. "And the sooner we get Nick home, the better I'll feel."

Nick had been tardy getting back to the dugout after the break and he'd fully expected Coach to blow a gasket, but he didn't. Winning this game was vital, as it was a final match between Rose Hill and a chief rival, so discipline was usually as tight as it ever got when the stakes were high. Instead of being relieved that Coach gave him a pass, Nick thought it was a little weird.

"You are trying to get your ass benched for the next season," Ward muttered when Nick eased onto the bench beside him. "Where were you?"

"I had business to take care of," Nick said, wiping sweat off his face with a towel.

"What? Your mom sent you to the grocery store?"

"Funny, Ward."

Ward sat looking out at the playing field, his face set. "What's going on between you and Kristin?"

"Who said anything was going on?"

"I saw you talking to her and it looked like something to me."

"It's not what you're thinking." His friendship with Ward meant a lot to Nick, and if he did have any ideas about Kristin, he'd have to think about the fallout between him and Ward before acting on it. But he'd think about it tomorrow. Or next week. Tonight, he couldn't afford to be distracted. His dad popping up on the scene had been stressful enough. Now he had to figure a way to slip away with Kristin, which

he knew would freak out his mom and Cam. He just prayed
they'd get over it if his mission was a success.

"Forrester!"

Jeez. "Yes, sir!" Nick jumped up. Coach Monk was
standing at the end of the dugout.

"Over here. On the double!"

"Told you," Ward muttered.

Nick scrambled past the knees of the juniors to get to the
front, where Tyson waited. He'd expected to get his ass
chewed, but not in the middle of a game. Usually, Coach was
so focused on the action on the ball field that he seldom
spared a glance for the juniors during senior play.

Tyson shoved a glove in his hand. "Sims got his glove
wet. There's another one in his locker. Go get it."

Nick hesitated, looking at Tyson. "You want me to open
Sims's locker?"

"You heard me," Tyson growled. "Number 416. And see
if you can do it without detouring through the stands again."

Nick stood for a second looking Tyson straight in the eye.
So okay, he wasn't going to get his ass chewed in front of
the team, instead he was gonna be the team gofer. That was
the kind of stuff Coach did when he wanted to humiliate
somebody.

"Not a problem," he said, and set off at a jog. Remembering at the last minute that his mom would be watching,
he turned and waved.

"Where is Nick going?" Rachel's voice rose a little, drawing a look from the couple sitting in front of her and Cam.
She lowered her tone. "We told him not to go anywhere by
himself."

"He's probably going to the john," Cam said, glancing at
his watch. "If he's not back in five minutes, I'll go check on
him."

"They all look alike from this distance," Rachel complained. "For a second, I wasn't sure it was Nick, since we

were so definite in warning him about not putting himself at risk. But that's his number.''

"Fifteen-year-old boys don't think of themselves as ever being at risk," Cam said. "Which is why they often wind up in trouble."

Rachel heard her cell phone ringing and reached down at her feet for her purse. Digging into it, she glanced at the number displayed before clicking the talk button. "It's my home phone," she told Cam. "Hello?"

"Rachel." Dinah's voice caught, making Rachel's heart jump into her throat.

"What it is, Mother? What's wrong?"

"It's Kendall. Rachel, she's not in her room. She's gone."

Robbie's locker, Nick discovered as he scanned the numbers, was in the last section where most of the seniors stored their stuff. When they were dressing out before the game, all the lights were on, but now the whole area was dimly lit, and by the time he reached 416, he could barely make out the numbers.

He jerked it open and dug around the junk inside, looking for Sims's spare glove. Plenty of stuff in the locker, plus it smelled like dirty socks and Nick made a face, actually holding his breath while he searched. No glove.

He backed away, slammed the door, which made a loud metal clang, and with one hand resting on the surface of the door, his head down, he wondered what he was supposed to do now. Go out there without the glove, get his ass chewed again, but what the heck. He was used to public humiliation now.

He turned then and almost pissed himself when he saw Coach Monk standing in the shadows. Just standing there. Silent. Scary as shit. Nick's heart dropped to the ground. His first thought was to run, but when he saw what was dangling from one of Tyson's fingers, he froze.

Kendy's sneakers.

"Nicky. You have caused me a lot of grief, you know that?"

Nick tried out a smile he knew looked sick. "No glove, Coach. I looked everywhere."

"Forget the glove. You're coming with me."

Nick looked at the little pink sneakers. "Where did you get those?"

The laces were knotted together and Tyson held them up as if surprised to find them in his hand. "These? Oh, from Kendy's feet. Where else would I get them?"

Nick had never been so scared. "What are you gonna do? What do you want?"

Tyson smiled. "I think you know what I want and nothing will happen to your sister if you cooperate."

"Is she okay? Have you hurt her?"

"Not yet."

"I want to see her." Nick felt sick to his stomach, but he knew Tyson had the power. At the moment. "Coach Monk, I don't know what you want from me, but we can't even talk about it until I see Kendy and know she's okay."

"Big talk," Tyson grunted, reaching for a roll of duct tape.

"How did you get to her, anyway? Did you hurt my grandmother?"

"She was taken from her bedroom with your grandma sitting in the TV room watching reruns of *Murder, She Wrote.*" As he talked, he was wrapping Nick's wrists with the duct tape. "Piece o' cake, Nicky."

Then, with a shove, he walked him to the exit at the side of the gym where the lighting had been turned off. A corner of the playing field could be seen, but with a game going, Nick knew no one was likely to notice anything.

"What about the game?" Nick asked. "It's the top of the ninth. You're walking out on the team?"

"I'm walking out on this whole stinking town, Nick. And you're coming with me. Make a sound and you'll never see Kendall again."

Twenty-Eight

While Rachel placed a frantic call to Pete reporting Kendy's disappearance, Cam went to the locker room to get Nick. The game was just ending with Rose Hill eking out a tight win. As Cam hurried past the field, the players still on the diamond tossed gloves and hats skyward in victory at the same time junior varsity and others poured out of the dugout. Cam hardly noticed, but jerked the door open and stood for a moment to get his bearings. He'd been at the gym and in Tyson's office not too many days ago, but hadn't ventured here where athletes dressed out, showered and celebrated or decried a game, depending on the results on the scoreboard. None of that mattered at the moment. He was frantically searching for Nick, but he was nowhere to be found.

With a deep sense of dread, he made his way through the athletes, who were now converging on the locker room as he headed, in the opposite direction, for the door. But before he reached it, he realized from the look on the kids' faces that there was something wrong. "Anybody seen Coach?" one of the boys said.

"He came in here just before the game ended. Gotta be somewhere."

"Really weird."

"Yeah, 'cause he would have had something to say to Jace for that error that almost cost the game. Where's he at, I wonder?"

Cam slowed his pace, listening with a fatalistic calm. Tyson had left in the final moments of a crucial game. And

Kendy had been snatched from her bedroom less than an hour ago. Now Nick had disappeared? Forcing back a red tide of rage, he elbowed past two big, sweaty ball players and went out into the still brightly lit confines of the ball field.

The same general confusion and bewilderment was everywhere. The game had been won and Coach Tyson had disappeared. He spotted Rachel searching the crowd, her face panicked. He wanted nothing more than to banish that look from her face, but he was only going to make it worse.

"Did you find him?" she asked anxiously.

"He's not in there, Rachel."

She pressed her fingers to her lips, shaking her head in denial. "No, he must be. He has to be. Where—" She stopped, reading the look on his face. "Oh, Cam, they're both gone. What can we do?"

"Did you call Pete?"

"Yes, he's on his way over. He sent a car to my mother's house, but he said we should wait for him here." Her hands were clasped together, held close to her chest as if praying. "He said no matter how you did it, you should keep Monk Tyson from leaving."

Cam sighed, rubbing at the five-o'clock shadow on his cheek. "Too late, Rachel. He's gone, too."

Kendy thought she was having a really bad dream. It was like she was floating and she was very thirsty, so she was going to have to get up and get a drink of water. But when she tried to move, nothing worked. Her whole self was just stuck on the bed. And then came the voices from somewhere. It was a lot of trouble, but she finally managed to open her eyes.

"It's wearin' off. See, I told you I didn't give her too much."

"Monk'll be here any minute so we need to have her on her feet by then."

A short laugh. "Why? She's not his type."

"Tell you what, dude. I don't like getting mixed up in

this. It's one thing roughing up the kid on his bike, but this shit—''

"Yeah, what's he gonna do with her once he's got his hands on Nick?"

Kendy finally managed to stir a little, then she rose up on her elbows, looking at the two men. "Are you talking about my brother?"

"Yeah, Nick, right? He'll be here in a few minutes." The man with a Harley Hog T-shirt folded his arms across his chest and looked down at her. "You be a good girl and everything will be fine."

"Are you the person who hurt my cat?"

"Who, me? Nah, no way."

She stared hard at him. "I have to go to the bathroom."

Both men looked at each other nervously. "Oh, okay," said Harley Hog. "It's that door right there."

Kendy slipped off the bed and stood for a minute, a little dizzy. Looking around, she saw that the room was like the cabins where her Girl Scout troop camped out. "Where is this place? Is it at the lake where we camp?"

"No lake, honey. Just trees and sky."

"Is that my backpack?" she pointed to the floor where it lay.

"Yeah." Harley scooped it up and handed it over. "Jay here saw it in your room, honey, and he thought you might need it."

There was something yucky about Harley Hog when he tried to be nice, Kendy thought. But she was glad the other man, Jay, had picked up her backpack. She did need it. It had her camera in it, and if she had a chance to take some pictures, she would.

"There's Kristin," Rachel said, spotting her coming toward them with Shelly Reynolds, one of her friends. "Maybe she knows something."

"Hi, Ms. Forrester." Kristin sent Cam a polite smile.

"Hi, Kristin. Shelly. I don't mean to be abrupt, but have

either of you seen Nick? He went to the locker room just before the game ended and never came out."

"I was going to ask you the same question," Kristin said. Biting her lip, she gazed around the ball field and over to the parking lot, which was quickly emptying. "I think he must have left."

"There's Pete now," Cam said. Although no siren was going, blue lights flashed from the chief's vehicle as he nosed through the traffic in the opposite direction from fans exiting the ballpark. Cam touched Rachel's arm. "If you want to stay here for a minute, I'll go over and see what Pete says."

With a nod at Cam, Rachel turned to the girls. "We're trying to find out why Nick left the dugout so close to the end of the game. Was he upset?"

"I talked to him during the break between games," Kristin said, "and that was right after he talked to his dad." She bit her lip. "He didn't seem upset."

"So it was nothing Ted said," Rachel murmured, trying to find an explanation that wasn't so fraught with menace. And it certainly wasn't Ted who had taken Kendy.

The lights suddenly flashed on and off, signaling all activity at the ball field was shutting down. Rachel glanced over and caught Cam's eye. He started toward her. Turning to the girls, she said, "Well, thank you both. If you see or hear of anything—"

Suddenly she noticed something in Kristin's face. "What is it, Kristin?" Rachel touched the girl's arm. "Tell me."

Anxiety darkened her pretty blue eyes and she was chewing her lip again. "Well, the reason I noticed he didn't come back...maybe you should know. I promised not to, but—"

"But what?" Rachel glanced from Kristin to Cam, whose face was unreadable. "What is it?"

"Nick asked if I could drive him somewhere after the game." Her gaze fell to her hands. "I told him I would."

"Are you serious? He had strict orders to stay here," Rachel said, wondering at Nick going against what he'd been told after they'd cautioned him about the danger. ''Where did he want to go?''

''It's kind of a long story,'' the girl said, looking more and more worried. ''He thinks Coach Tyson is involved in some pretty awful stuff and he's on a mission to prove it. He doesn't think Chief Singletary has enough evidence to stop Coach, so he found out the names of some people who he believes do know stuff that will help the chief put him behind bars.''

''Oh, my God,'' Rachel murmured, and reached out blindly for Cam, who'd returned while Kristin was talking. He slipped an arm about her waist and she leaned into him gratefully as Pete walked up.

''The main thing now is to find Tyson,'' Cam said. ''The fact that he simply walked away from a game with just minutes of play remaining tells me he's ready to cut his losses and make a run for it.''

''Showing up to coach tonight,'' Pete said, shaking his head ruefully, ''that was clever. Lulled us into thinking we had more time to make a move on him than we did.''

''Monk Tyson has kidnapped my children,'' Rachel murmured in disbelief, her lips white with fear.

''Nick would have gone with him willingly if Tyson convinced him that Kendall's safety depended on it,'' Cam said, his face grim.

''I'm thinking the same thing,'' Pete said, ''which means he had help. Somebody had to get Kendall while he snatched Nick.''

''The two thugs who tried to wipe Nick out on his bike,'' Cam guessed. ''To them, taking a nine-year-old girl would be a walk in the park.''

''What do you think, Cam?'' Pete said, gazing thoughtfully toward the now-empty stands. ''He sent Nick on a bogus errand to the locker room, waited a few minutes and followed, cornering him in there?''

''Seems logical. It would have been deserted at that point in the game, giving him time to persuade Nick to go with him…somehow. Everybody's attention was riveted on the action on the ball field. Including mine," he added bitterly.

Rachel had visions of a terrified Kendy in the hands of men who had no qualms about using a large vehicle to run a fifteen-year-old boy on a bike off the road. What would they do to a little girl?

Moments later, she slipped into the seat of Cam's SUV, dazed and shaken. Pete had received a report from the men he'd dispatched to Dinah's house that the screen in Kendy's room had been sliced and the glass cut with a professional tool so that the lock was easily accessible. In the opinion of the cop, the window had been tampered with earlier to make entry quick and efficient when the time was right.

"You mean, when Tyson gave the word," Cam said, looking ready to tear somebody's head off.

"I know when they did it," Rachel said, wondering now how she could have been so careless. Cam looked at her sharply. "The night you and I were…together and I went home to check that Nick was okay, remember? I heard something outside in the backyard, but I decided it was just my imagination…or Graham. He meowed at the door after a minute or two and I let him in. Then, as I walked back to your house, I felt as if somebody was watching."

"They would have had ample time that weekend," Cam said. "Dinah was gone, you were with me and Nick and Kendy were doing their thing. The house was just sitting there waiting to be compromised."

Rachel suddenly buried her face in her hands. "If anything happens to them, I don't think I can bear it, Cam."

"We'll find them," Cam said, praying he could make good his promise. "There hasn't been time for him to get very far. Don't lose hope." He knew well what she was feeling and he cursed Tyson for putting her through this kind of torture. It was torture for him, too, Cam realized suddenly. If something happened to Nick and Kendall, he knew it would be almost as hard for him as losing Jack. Which is why he couldn't let it happen. There had to be a way to keep

Tyson from succeeding. He leaned over and took her in his arms, pressing her close to his heart.

"We'll find them," he repeated fiercely.

Kendall was confined to a chair in the cabin. Harley Hog had not restrained her in any physical way, but he wouldn't allow her to walk around, either. "I'm thirsty," she told him. "Can I have a drink of water, please?"

With a pained sigh, he put aside the electronic game he'd been playing and went over to the small kitchenette. First, she had to go to the bathroom. Then she complained that the bathroom was dirty. Next, she wanted the chair examined for bugs before she'd sit in it. Now she was thirsty. Taking down a glass, he turned on the water.

"Do you have bottled water?" she asked.

He turned to look at her. "No, we don't have bottled water, Princess. Just this kind."

"It isn't safe," she said, wrinkling her nose. "This cabin is like the place where we go for Girl Scout overnights. We never drink the water because it has a lot of stuff in it that might give you a tummyache."

"Trust me," he said, offering her the glass. "I drink it. It's fine."

"No, thank you." She folded her arms and turned her face slightly away. "And you're going to be in trouble—" she glanced at Jay, who stood at the window with his back to them "—both of you."

"Is that so?" Harley Hog drank the water himself and put the glass in the sink. "And how do you know that, Princess?"

"Because my godmother is going to marry a policeman. And when he finds out you've kidnapped me, he'll hunt you down and you'll be in big trouble."

He wiped his mouth with the back of his hand. "And who is this policeman your godmother is gonna marry?"

"Chief Singletary."

"Shit!" Jay turned around and looked at Harley Hog.

"I'm telling you, Zig, we're gonna get our asses fried over this. Monk's digging his own grave, but that don't mean we gotta jump in it with him."

Kendall watched them, knowing the one who was named Jay wasn't in charge, so it didn't matter what he thought.

"We walk out now, we don't get paid. We gotta wait for Monk."

"We're gonna wind up having to go to Mexico, Zig. We shouldn't of got mixed up with him again."

"Yeah," Zig returned sarcastically. "And if we didn't do what he wanted, just sit back and wait for the cops to come down on us for what happened to Jack Ford? Use your head, dude. We're stuck. Monk's got us by the short hairs."

Kendall stood up. "I've gotta go to the bathroom again."

Pete Singletary moved from behind his desk with a notebook in his hand. "I sent a unit to Tyson's house," he told Rachel and Cam. "There's some furniture, but clothes, personal items, his car—all gone. Looks like we were right. He was ready to cut and run. Not even somebody with his survival instincts could have cleared out, lock, stock and barrel, so fast. I'm thinking he's probably known for a while that his time in Rose Hill was running out."

"He can't just walk away from a house with furniture in it, can he?" Rachel asked incredulously. "And what about all that stuff in his office, the mementos and awards? Won't he need credentials to set up somewhere else?"

"Not in Mexico," Cam said, standing behind her chair. "Or some other place where nobody asks too many questions."

Rachel's eyes widened. "He wouldn't take Nick and Kendall to—" She turned and looked up at Cam with dawning horror. "He wants Nick, but not Kendall. He won't saddle himself with a nine-year-old girl, will he? So what will he do with Kendy?"

Cam went down on his haunches beside her chair. "I don't think he'll hurt her, Rachel. What's the point? He needed her for leverage to use on Nick, but harming her will bring the wrath of law enforcement down on him. And don't forget, Nick's a resourceful kid. He'll look out for his sister.''

''If Monk ever lets him see her,'' Rachel said bitterly. But she touched Cam's face, warmed by his concern. Inside, she was chilled by thoughts of what could happen to her children.

Cam stood up, squeezing her shoulder. ''Let's wait until we pick up his trail before thinking the worst.''

''I've posted a statewide APB on Tyson's Suburban,'' Pete said, ''but so far there's no sign of it. And we're following up on your suggestion to try questioning Jason Pate,'' he said to Cam. ''He wasn't in the locker room after the game, and somebody said it looked as if he cut out even before the game ended, but we're not sure. We're on the lookout for his vehicle. It's a beat-up Toyota Celica. As one of the athletes Monk favored, he may be our best bet.''

Pete glanced at the notebook in his hand. ''Three names were mentioned by Jimbo Rivers, as people Tyson uses when he needs muscle. These are probably the same people Nick was going to check out on his own. I showed them to Kristin and she recognized two as Nick's suspects in his search for the white pickup.'' He passed the notebook to Cam. ''A unit's checking both now.''

Rachel jumped up from her chair, unable to sit a minute longer. ''I can't believe Nick planned to do something so dangerous on his own after what we told him.''

Cam studied the licenses on the list. ''Any of these a white pickup?''

''One. Owner, Carl Ziegler. Lives over on Ashmont.'' Pete flicked a forefinger at another name. ''Jay Dunne and Ziggy work construction together. Both were Jimbo's teammates.''

Rachel frowned. ''I remember them. They were always in trouble at school, but Monk managed to get them both into a second-rate college in Arkansas, anyway. I heard they washed out before a second season.'' She closed her eyes, remembering the bruise on Nick's temple and his scraped palms. "If they tried to hurt Nick, they have grown even more inhuman as adults."

"Don't forget, Monk Tyson's the real villain here," Cam said quietly. "Ziggy and Jay are following orders."

"But they're the ones who have Kendall." She saw in both male faces what she found so hard to believe. "It's just that after working with Monk for more than five years, I don't want to believe he's so heartless. Maybe that's the reason people like Monk get away with such monstrous behavior for so many years. People just can't see them as...as monsters!"

"At this point, Tyson's fighting for survival," Cam said, trying to find something to ease her fear. "I believe he'll think twice about harming Nick or Kendall."

"Then why take them at all!" she cried.

"I think he's obsessed with Nick," Cam said quietly. "And that's probably our best hope that he won't hurt him."

Rachel stood looking at them both for a minute, trying to take it all in. Then, braced against the wall, she ran a shaky hand through her hair. "I need to call Ted and let him know. May I use your phone?" she asked Pete, who handed the cordless over.

Cam followed her out of the office, then watched as she dialed the number. Her mouth was unsteady, waiting for a pickup. "Ted? Yes, how are you? Actually, I'm at the police station in Rose Hill and I have some bad news...ah, yes, bad news. Nick and Kendall are...we think they've been kidnapped. Yes, yes, that's right. Nick was taken from the ball field. Not too long after you left." She pinched the bridge of her nose. "And Kendall was taken from her bedroom."

Rachel paused and listened for a minute. "Mother was in the den and heard nothing." She looked around, met Cam's eyes and waited through the crackle of Ted's voice rising and falling. Finally, she just interrupted him to say, "I'm at the police station, where Pete Singletary is in charge of the search, Ted. We're fairly certain Monk Tyson is responsible. Yes, he..." She pressed two fingers to a spot between her eyes. "Ted, just come on down here if you want and you can get answers...what few there are."

She clicked the off button and looked at Cam. "Well, that's done. He'll be right over."

Cam wanted nothing more than to take away the fear and despair in her eyes, but nothing except the return of her children could do that. "Let me get you something to drink," he said.

"Chief." Angela stood in the doorway. "Tyson's Suburban was spotted at the shopping center by unit 5. We know he's not shopping. It looks as if he's abandoned the Suburban."

"Damn." Pete moved to the window, thinking. "What about the pickup?"

"No sign of it yet," Angela said. "And word's out that the children are missing." She sent Rachel a sympathetic look. "It won't hurt to have the eyes and ears of the town looking." With a fleeting smile at Cam, she headed back to the front.

"The Suburban is school property. Monk doesn't own it." Rachel was rubbing her forehead. "I don't know if he owns a car personally." She went with Cam down the hall to the break room.

"How's Dinah holding up?" Cam said, filling a paper cup with coffee.

"She's distraught, of course, blaming herself. Marta's with her, thank goodness."

"This was a well-planned abduction, Rachel. We were all set up."

"I know, but it's hard not to see in hindsight how easy it was for Monk to pull it off." She took the coffee. She'd probably need a lot of it before this night was done.

"Rachel!"

Breathing in deeply, Rachel turned to face Ted, striding down the hall toward them. "What is happening?" he demanded. "What is this all about? You didn't make any sense on the phone."

"I'm sorry if the message didn't get through, Ted," she said. "Nick and Kendall are missing. Nick disappeared from the ball field and Kendall from my mother's house."

Pete moved forward and put out a hand. "Ted, sorry we meet again under these circumstances. Come into my office and I'll fill you in. The details are sketchy, as yet, but it looks as if Nick has landed himself in a world of mean and Kendall's being made a part of the scheme."

Ted shot a look at Cam, then back to Pete. "I just saw Nick at the ball field. There has to be a mistake. He's probably with some girl. He was waving at her when I was trying to talk to him."

"He's not with a girl," Rachel said, her head aching now. "And didn't you hear what I said? Kendall's gone, too."

"Let's take this into my office," Pete repeated firmly.

Ted hesitated, then did as asked. At the door, he turned and said to Rachel, "Are you coming?"

"Yes." She slipped past Cam and went with Ted.

Twenty-Nine

The cabin suddenly popped up out of nowhere after about thirty minutes on a winding road through backwoods Nick had never seen before. He sat looking straight ahead as Monk Tyson got out and walked around to the passenger side of the Jeep.

"Home, sweet home," he said, jerking the door open. Nick had no chance to get his bearings before Monk yanked him out and shoved him hard toward the steps of the cabin.

Nick had spent most of the trip wondering if he'd been stupid to let himself be blackmailed into cooperating with Monk. With nothing but Kendy's sneakers to prove he even had her, Nick worried about what might happen if Kendy wasn't around. Hopefully, she'd been missed by now. If so, all of Rose Hill would be out looking, just like those searches on TV for missing children. He bet Cam and the chief were kicking themselves over what was happening, but his mom would be frantic. He didn't like thinking what shape his mom was in right about now. Nick just hoped they all got their stuff together in time for a rescue.

Monk kicked at the cabin door and it flew open. With another hard shove, he sent Nick stumbling inside, nearly making him fall flat on his face. He recognized Harley Hog immediately by his T-shirt and thought the stocking he'd worn when he bushwhacked him Sunday was an improvement over his natural face. Same for his sidekick, but that dude had changed into a clean shirt, Nick noticed.

"Hi, guys," he said. And then he saw Kendy. She was

sitting in a chair, her feet not quite touching the floor. She had shoes on, too. How'd they get the sneakers Monk had used for bait? Kendy looked okay, no marks like they'd hit her or anything. And she had her freakin' camera around her neck! Jeez, if they'd let her take pictures, did that mean they weren't worried about who might see them, because they knew she'd never get out of this cabin alive enough to put them in the one-hour photo mart? It was a scary thought. "Kendy, you okay?"

"They make me sit here, Nick," she said in her I'm-telling voice. "They won't let me walk around. I told them I couldn't do anything walking around this stupid cabin, but they're mean. And there's no bottled water."

Harley rolled his eyes in disgust. "I gave you water, I let you go to the bathroom, I even let you play with my Game Boy, Princess. Quit complaining."

"You didn't let me play with your Game Boy. You didn't know how to do it and I had to show you. I could take you down in about two minutes, but you won't share."

Harley looked at Tyson. "She's a pain in the ass, Coach. You can have her. Where's our money?"

Before Tyson answered, Kendall said, "I have to go to the bathroom."

"Again?" Harley snarled.

Kendall looked at Nick. "Nick, make them let me go to the bathroom."

Nick, his hands still taped together in front of him, said, "I'll take her. Where is it?"

"It's that door right there," Kendall said, pointing.

"Shut up!" Tyson bellowed. "The whole fuckin' bunch of you are enough to make me crazy."

"We want our money," Harley repeated.

Tyson ignored him. "Take the kid to the bathroom and leave her there. The two of you…" he sliced the air in disgust "—go out on the porch and wait for me. You, Nick, sit down."

"Like I said, I'll take my sister to the bathroom," Nick

told him stubbornly. "She's scared. I'll do what you want, but after I check she's okay."

Tyson looked as if he might throttle Nick, but the moment passed, and with a hitch of his chin, he indicated the bathroom. "Go with her and make it fast." Then he gave a sly wink to Nick. "You and your little sister must be closer than I thought."

Nick didn't dignify that with a word. He moved toward Kendy, not bothering to ask Tyson to remove the tape on his wrists. Not a chance of that. She hopped down off the chair and scooted in front of him so she could open the bathroom door, which had no inside lock.

"Are you okay, Kendy?" he asked.

"Yes. When are we going to be rescued?" She made no move to use the toilet, he was relieved to see. Instead, she dropped the lid down and climbed up on top of it. Standing on tiptoes, she looked out of the tiny window.

"I don't know, so we have to figure out a way to get out ourselves. What are you doing?"

"Trying to open the window, silly." She had a ballpoint pen in her hand and was trying to work it into the crack between the window and the sill. "I've about got it, only they don't let me stay in here long enough."

Nick studied the window. Even if they managed to get it open, he couldn't get through, but Kendy could. "Where'd you get the pen?"

"In my backpack. They brought it with me when they kidnapped me. They're not very smart."

"Let me try." He took the pen after she climbed down and gouged at the crack. It had been painted shut, but he was surprised to see that she'd made a good dent in it.

Both jumped two minutes later when Monk hit the door with his fist. "Get out here, Nick."

Nick quickly flushed as if Kendy had used the toilet, slipped the pen inside the tank, then both stood looking at him innocently when he pushed the door open. "Stay, kid," he ordered Kendy, then yanked Nick out and shut the door in her face.

"Sit down. We need to talk."

Nick sat, watching Monk cautiously. He had a ferocious temper and Nick didn't want to do anything to set it off. At school, he was forced to keep it under control, pretty much. Here, who knows?

Tyson pulled a chair for himself up close and sat down. "First thing I want to know, Nick, is where you got the idea that I killed Jack Ford?"

After Rachel went into Pete's office with Ted, Cam was left to pace with frustration and a growing sense of dread. At the front desk, Angela and two other uniformed cops fielded calls as word spread of Coach Tyson's involvement in the disappearance of two children. Cam moved to the door in time to see a boy dashing up the steps. As soon as he saw his face, Cam pushed the door open to let him in. "Ward, what—"

"Cam, is it true? Has Kendy been kidnapped?"

"We're not sure yet, Ward. You—"

"And Nick, too, right? I know he was supposed to go with Kristin after the game, but he never showed." Ward's face was pale and he was out of breath. "Nick wouldn't dog out on Kristin like that, so I think I know why."

Behind the desk, Angela and the two cops tried to cope with numerous incoming calls. The lights on the base flashed constantly. A reporter from the local paper was trying to get into Pete's office. With a hand on Ward's shoulder, Cam guided him back the way he'd come. "Let's take a walk. It's chaos in here."

"What are the cops doing to find him?" Ward asked as soon as they were outside.

"There's a be-on-the-lookout bulletin and they found his Suburban, but no sign of Tyson. They're looking for a couple of former athletes who might be helpful."

"Cam, if Nick's gone—and Kendy, too—I know why."
He stuck his hands deep in his pockets. "And it's my fault."

"It's Tyson's fault, Ward, not yours."

"Yeah, but Nick's been trying to get me to tell what Tyson's been up to and I wouldn't listen. So, if I had done the right thing, this wouldn't have happened. Problem is, Coach knows Nick does have the balls to tell everything, and if he does and the shit hits the fan, he'll be kicked out of Rose Hill. That's the reason he took him, to shut him up."

"You're not the only one who could have told about Tyson over the past five years, Ward. There's plenty of blame to go around." They stopped at a crosswalk and waited for the signal to change. "What we need to do is find where Tyson is and whether or not he has Nick with him. Chief Singletary doesn't have much in the way of leads so far."

Ward lifted a hand and waved to a couple of teens riding by in a Mustang. "Has anybody talked to Jason Pate? He might know something."

"The problem is finding Jason," Cam said dryly. "But we're looking."

Ward walked along with his eyes on his feet. "There're a couple of places he likes to hang out. It'd be worth a try to check them out." He glanced at the clock on the front of the bank building. "He's had a couple of hours' start, so we'll probably have to sober him up if we find him."

"You think he's somewhere getting drunk?"

Ward shrugged. "Drunk or high."

Cam and Ward rounded the corner, heading back just as Rachel came out of the station house. He watched her scan the street, looking anxious, then lifted his hand to catch her eye. Seeing him, she hurried down the steps. Her hands, when he caught them in his, were ice cold. Saying nothing, she simply rested her forehead against his chest. They stood together, Cam's arms around her, silently comforting.

Ted emerged from the building, saw them and stood watching for a moment with a somber expression. Then he came down the steps much slower than Rachel had seconds before, heading for his Lexus parked in a reserved slot in front.

"Bad scene?" Cam asked, searching her face.

She shrugged. "Just…difficult. He's shocked, and like the rest of us, helpless to do anything but wait."

"Did he give you a hard time?" Over her head, Cam frowned at the departing car.

"He wanted to. Started to, but I wasn't in the mood to hear what I'd done wrong that resulted in the kidnapping of my children." She let him turn her then with an arm at her waist. "I thought you'd gone. I was afraid you'd think with Ted around that I wouldn't need you."

He gave a soft half laugh. "You thought I'd take my SUV and go home? I don't think so." With Ward standing close, watching and listening, he could only give her waist a loving squeeze.

"I'm sorry about this, Ms. Forrester," Ward said.

Rachel gave a small sniff and managed a nod. "Thank you, Ward."

"Ward thinks he might know of a couple of places where Jason hangs out," Cam said. "I don't think there's much we can do here. Pete's running down those leads of Tyson's enforcers and he has people organizing searchers. I think Ward and I will head out to look for Jason. Who knows, we might get lucky."

Rachel wiped briskly at a tear in the corner of one eye, then settled the strap of her purse on her shoulder. "Good idea. I'll go with you."

"Jack Ford?" Nick gave Tyson what he hoped was a purely innocent look. "Gosh, Coach, I was only ten years old when that happened."

"That wasn't the answer I needed, Nick." Tyson had dragged him over and slapped him down in a chair. Now he reached out and dug his fingers painfully into Nick's thigh. "Ferdy said you knew. I'm asking who told you."

It was hard to think with his thigh burning. "Nobody,

Coach. I said what I said to Ferdy just to get him to back off. He tried to kill my sister's cat.'' Nick couldn't help a small wince of pain. The Man had a killer grip. "You know me and Ferdy have always been kinda...not close.''

Taking his time, Tyson released his grip on Nick's thigh, then folded his big arms over his chest and studied Nick's face. "I think you've been talking to Cameron Ford. And I think he's on a mission to pin his boy's suicide on me. And I think it's too late to lie your way out of it.''

Panic spiraled high in Nick, but he fought it. With his hands taped, he was pretty helpless to do anything to protect Kendy or himself, but they'd never get out of here if he lost it. Too terrified to pretend to be cool another second, Nick got up from the chair and rubbed at the pain in his thigh with his locked hands. "Coach Monk, you've got to know the whole town of Rose Hill is probably looking for Kendy and me. You're gonna have the whole state of Texas looking for you. Why don't you just get in your Jeep and—''

"You'd like that, I bet.'' Tyson's eyes had a flat, cold look. He walked over to Nick, crowding him until his back was against the wall. With one hand, he stroked the side of Nick's face. "You're something else, you know that? You're your mama's boy, all right. Here you are up to your sweet ass in shit and negotiating like a seasoned shrink.'' He dropped his hand and went to the window. It was black as pitch out there and he couldn't see a thing, Nick thought, but he stood looking out as if he was seeing something. "I'm no psycho, Nick. I had a really sweet setup here and I owe you for screwing it up.'' He turned back. "I wasn't ready to pack up and leave, but because of you and your nosy mother and that bastard Ford, I've got no choice.''

While Tyson was rambling on, Nick was studying the layout of the room. A single door, two windows and the tiny bathroom where Kendy was hopefully unsealing the window. It worried him that Monk made no effort to keep Nick from seeing where they were going as they'd made the drive out here. Was he going to take two kids with him when he left? If not, he didn't like thinking what plan B was.

"So, Nick, I'm going to ask once more," Tyson said, his eyes narrowing. "Who told you what happened to Jack Ford?"

"Moe and Curly?"

The blow landed on the side of his head, sudden and savage. Nick didn't even see it coming, but his ears were ringing and he tasted blood. With Monk standing over him, however, he did not make the mistake of licking at it. Weird stuff turned this dude on.

"Once more and no smart-ass answers. Now. Who?"

"That wasn't smart-ass, Coach," Nick said, shaking his head to try to clear it. "After your…friends ran over me on my bike, they put me in the pickup between them and I heard one of them say Jack Ford was killed."

Tyson stared at him a long moment. Then, with his eyes still locked on Nick's, he yelled, "Zig!" More silence, then he yelled again, this time for both men. But there was still only silence from the other side of the door. Then, as Nick held his breath, he heard the pickup start and a loud revving of the engine before it was rammed into gear as Ziggy and his cohort got the hell out of Dodge.

Cam had tried to talk Rachel out of going with them, and as he pulled up at the Lone Star Lounge, he cursed the fact that she was so stubborn. The place was a dive located five miles out of town just past the county line. As such, it didn't fall in Pete Singletary's jurisdiction, which might explain the lax attitude of the proprietors about underage drinking. The parking lot was crowded with motorcycles. Cam was torn between leaving Rachel in the car where she was clearly unsafe, or taking her inside a hangout for bikers.

The interior was dark and smelled of beer and barbecue. The clientele, big and hairy for the most part, looked as mean as their machines. Cam remembered Jason as blond, with a slight frame and sensitive features, and thought he'd stick out here like a sore thumb.

Rachel spotted him through the smoky haze, sitting alone at a booth near the back, nursing a beer. "I think Ward was right," she said. "We may have to sober him up before he can tell us anything useful."

Jason glanced up as they approached without much reaction. When he spoke, it was to Ward. "If Jimbo knew you were here, he'd kick your ass."

"I'm with Cam and Ms. Forrester. We need to talk to you, Jason," Ward said.

Jason peered up at them. "What do you want to talk about?"

"Monk Tyson." Cam nudged Ward into the booth beside Jason, then he and Rachel sat down facing them. "And we don't have a lot of time to waste. Nick disappeared from the ball field tonight just before the game ended. We think Tyson's responsible, but he's nowhere to be found. Can you help us?"

"Oh, shit." Jason dropped his face in his hands.

"You don't sound surprised," Rachel said.

Jason raised his eyes. "Monk sometimes gets obsessed with different guys. He's hot for Nick, but I knew he wasn't gonna be as easy pickings as some."

"Like me?" Ward asked.

"And me." Jason lifted the bottle to take another drink, but Cam stopped him with a hand on his wrist.

"Jason. If you have any idea where Monk could have taken Nick, we need you to tell us."

"Every minute counts, Jason," Rachel said. "He may have my daughter, too. She's only nine."

Head down, Jason rubbed his eyes with the heels of his hands. He gave no indication if he was truly trying to think where Nick or Kendy could be or if he was undecided about revealing whatever he knew. "There's a hunting lodge," he said finally. "It's a few miles from here down an old ranch road. It's pretty isolated, which is why Monk likes it for certain things." He turned his face, looking at a light fixture of deer antlers. "He took me there pretty often at first."

Breaking him in, Cam thought. "You think you can find it?" It was a long shot, but without any other leads, it made sense to check it out.

"Yeah, I can find it."

Outside the Lone Star, Cam placed a call to Pete before they got on the road while Jason went to get something from his car. The cabin was nearly an hour from Rose Hill, which meant they would be at the lodge before any help from Pete's cops had time to make the trip. Pete, however, put more credence in a report that two people, both unidentified males, had left the Rose Hill airstrip in a chartered light plane. The mechanic at the airstrip assumed they were father and son. He overheard the pilot say their destination was Monterrey.

Rachel was already belted in the SUV, but Cam stood outside debating whether the trip to the lodge was worth making in light of Pete's suspicion that Tyson was already airborne. Rachel wanted to press on. "There was no mention of Kendy," she said, strain beginning to tell on her. "We're here now. If we turned around, what would we do, just sit at home and do nothing? Let's check it out, Cam."

"You're right. Where's Jason?" Cam peered over the top of the SUV and a tangle of parked motorcycles, searching. Finally, he saw Jason making his way through a sea of mean machines carrying a shotgun.

"What the hell!" Rounding the front of the SUV in long strides, he reached for the gun. "Is that thing loaded?"

Jason handed it over. "Coach is one mean bastard. His back's to the wall and he wouldn't hesitate to do whatever it takes to get out of Texas. You may not think you'll need it, but if you do and you don't have it, we'll be up shit creek."

"We don't have time to waste, Cam," Rachel said quietly.

With a grunt, Cam stowed the shotgun on the floor behind the driver's seat as Jason climbed in the back beside Ward.

Before buckling up, he leaned forward to drop six shells in the console tray. Then, without a word, Cam pulled away from the Lone Star and, after a few minutes, felt the urge to smile in spite of the urgency of his mission. His life had taken turns so unexpected lately that if he'd written it in one of his books, his editor would have hooted.

It was almost midnight when Jason directed them to a turn off the highway onto the ranch road. Not much of a road, Cam thought, more like a wagon trail through what had once been a pasture. It might still be a pasture, although there was no sign of any living thing except swarms of night insects caught in the glow of his headlights.

"You still with us, Jason?" he asked, checking via the rearview mirror as Jason's head lolled on his chest. "Ward, wake him up."

"Huh? Oh, yeah." Rubbing his eyes, Jason sat up a little straighter, then almost instantly began to sink again.

"Keep him awake, Ward." This was the second time in less than four days that he'd chauffeured a drunk teenager, Cam thought, bracing as the SUV bounced along the rutted cow track. And both times in the middle of the night on deserted country roads. He thought of the shotgun on the floor and simply shook his head.

Rachel, alert in the front seat, suddenly leaned forward. "I thought I saw lights through those trees."

Cam had seen the same thing. Then, without warning, bright headlights were rushing at them. With no time for thought, Cam could only wrench the wheel to the right to avoid colliding head-on and ride it out. The rogue vehicle charged past them, shaking the SUV like a flag in a windstorm and throwing up a blinding cloud of dust that forced Cam to stop.

"Mercy," Rachel murmured, bracing herself on the front dash.

"Jeez!" Ward was turned around in his seat squinting through dust and darkness, trying to get a fix on the vehicle. "It's a pickup, but—"

"That was Ziggy's truck," Jason said, wide awake now. He was turned in his seat, too, with a troubled look on his face.

Cam reversed and got back on the road. But instead of heading on toward the lodge, he sat with the SUV idling. "Why would anyone leave the lodge in the middle of the night?"

"Why would Ziggy even be at the lodge tonight?" Jason asked.

"If he's the one who took Kendy, maybe she's at the lodge." Rachel wasn't sure whether that was a good sign or not.

Ward settled back in the seat. "Maybe it's a good thing we've got that shotgun."

Cam passed his cell phone to Rachel. "Call Pete and tell him what happened. Tell him to send a unit to apprehend Ziegler."

"Don't go to that lodge," Pete ordered when she told him. "Tell Cam to wait for backup. You don't know who's there. I'm sending another unit."

"What if Kendy's there, Pete?" Holding the cell phone, Rachel stared anxiously into the night. "What would those men be doing out here if not following Monk's orders? Maybe both my children are there. It'll take your people almost an hour to get out here. That much time could make all the difference between…" She paused, unable to say it. "We can't wait, Pete."

Pete was silent, then gave a sigh. "Tell Cam to be careful."

Shock and disbelief had gripped Tyson for a beat or two after Ziggy and Jay turned tail and ran. Then, enraged, he grabbed Nick and dragged him across the room, jerked open the bathroom door and shoved him inside with Kendall. "Both of you, stay in there!"

Little choice, Nick thought, putting out a hand and squeezing Kendy's shoulder. It was pitch black now. She must have turned off the light in case they looked in and found her prying the window open. "You still okay?" he asked.

"Uh-huh. And I've almost got the window open." Without wasting a second, he began feeling around the edges to see how much needed to be done to get her out of here. "Kendy, we don't have much time, so I'll make it quick. When we get this thing open, I'll boost you up and you drop to the ground outside. But don't go too deep into the woods, otherwise, it'll be hard to find you when the rescuers arrive."

"I already thought of that," she said. "And I need to use this pen to try to break that tape so your hands will be free."

"After we get the window open," he said. "We better leave the light off in case he comes around the back and sees we've been monkeying with it." Then, feeling his way, he picked up where she'd left off.

As he worked, he heard bumping and thumping and cussing coming from the outer room. Apparently, having Ziggy and Jay cut out on Tyson had really pissed him off. Why it made him so mad, Nick didn't have a clue, unless he had in mind setting up another scheme to snuff Nick out the way he'd done to get rid of Jack Ford. Maybe the reason he was so ticked was that he'd have to do it himself this time.

But while Tyson was busy being mad and breaking things, Nick used the time to finish freeing up the window. He didn't like being locked in a matchbox, but it beat being out there with The Man and possibly become the target for Tyson's ferocious temper. Or his sick sexual preferences.

"Got it!" he said. Then he fumbled in the dark to give the pen back to Kendy. "Poke a few holes in this duct tape if you can," he told her, and stuck out his bound wrists. "Ow!"

"I'm sorry, Nick." The first stab almost put a hole in his artery, but he stoically stood still while she got the hang of it, and after she'd pierced the tape enough that he thought he could work the rest of it loose, he told her to climb up on the toilet seat, then he boosted her up until she could get her upper body into the space.

"You okay?" he whispered.

"Uh-huh."

"And remember, don't go too far. I don't want the whole city of Rose Hill out canvassing these woods looking for you, Kendy."

"Bye." And with that, she dropped out of sight.

A half mile before reaching the hunting lodge, Cam cut the lights on the SUV, then a quarter of a mile later, he stopped and told his passengers to stay put. "I'll try to get close enough to see if there's anybody inside."

"And then what?" Rachel asked.

"I'm not sure," Cam said honestly. "I don't know what the place looks like, how it's situated, how many there are, or even if anybody's in it at all. There may be a perfectly innocent reason somebody was out here tonight."

"And they just decided to leave like they were being chased by the hounds of hell?" Rachel chewed on her lower lip. "I don't think so."

Jason pulled on his baseball cap. "I know what the place looks like, inside and out. I know where Coach parks his Jeep when he's out here, Cam. Besides, you may need help."

Rachel looked concerned. "I don't think—"

"Jason," Cam interrupted her. With his hand on the handle ready to climb out, he spoke quietly and firmly. "You've been drinking. You have to stay here."

"I haven't," Ward said, "so I can go with you."

"And have Jimbo kick my ass, too?" Cam cracked the door slightly. "I don't think so."

"Exactly," Rachel said in a severe tone.

"Nick's my best friend," Ward pleaded. "I owe him. If I was in trouble, no way would he sit in the car and let somebody else do all the work."

"We're wasting time," Cam said abruptly. "Everyone's staying put while I check the area. This isn't a ball game. And when I get out, no talking. Voices carry in the woods, especially on a still night."

"Take the shotgun," Jason said.

"I plan to." Mouth set, Cam quietly climbed down out of the SUV, reached behind the seat for the shotgun and slipped extra shells in his pocket as Jason handed them over. He took a minute while the light was on to check what kind of weapon he held.

"It's a Remington twelve-gauge," Jason told him.

"Please be careful, Cam," Rachel said.

"Yeah." Cam then closed the car door softly, tapped the roof of the vehicle twice, then slipped into the dark woods and disappeared from sight instantly.

For about three minutes, the car was silent as a tomb. Rachel wanted nothing more than to leave the boys and go with Cam, but it was simply too risky. She glanced back at Jason and Ward just in time to see a look—something—pass between them, and as if they'd planned it, both quickly opened the doors on their respective sides and were out of the SUV before she had a chance to stop them.

She swore silently and did the same.

She caught up with them about twenty feet from the SUV. "If I gave you two a direct order to return to the car, you wouldn't hear it, would you?"

"No, ma'am," Jason said in a whisper. "And we can't talk anymore or Cam might hear us. He just might do something like quit the plan, so no talking."

"Also," Ward said, "I don't want to be mistaken for a bear."

Nick figured he'd been locked in the bathroom about twenty minutes, ten of which he'd spent freeing up Kendy to get away. Another couple to finish tearing the tape off his hands. Sounds inside the cabin had ceased a while ago and he wondered what Tyson was doing. If he was outside checking whether or not Ziggy and Jay had really cut out on him, Nick hoped Kendy would stay out of sight.

Standing on the toilet tank, he peered out. He frowned, stared harder, thinking he saw movement in the clearing. And too big to be Kendy. He was ready to make some signal when he heard Tyson come back into the room.

Almost sick with disappointment, he quickly dropped back, stepped off the toilet and was propped against the wall when Tyson jerked it open. He stood with his belt in his hands, letting it slither across his palms slowly.

"Take off your clothes."

It took Nick a moment to react. Not a lot of romance to this creep's technique, he thought. He was still in his baseball uniform and he wondered if that was a turn-on, too. Nick knew girls thought guys in military uniform were really sexy. He supposed if your taste ran along the lines of Monk Tyson's, maybe the same stuff kicked in with a baseball uniform. Go figure.

"I guess we're finished talking," he said, stepping from the dark bathroom into the full light in the cabin. It was then that Tyson realized Kendy had escaped.

"Where's the brat?" But no reply was necessary. In one glance, Tyson took in the jimmied window and Nick's free hands. He let fly a string of profanity that was truly impressive. Nick, seizing the moment, dashed for the door, praying Tyson had failed to lock it when he came back in.

No such luck. Without any rules now to keep him in check, Tyson was like a volcano erupting. He caught Nick from behind, ripping his shirt and locking his arm across his windpipe. Nick, struggling wildly to breathe, thought he was going to die. His vision was fading and he felt himself beginning to go...

Tyson suddenly turned him loose and tossed him on the bed. Then, using his belt, he made a slipknot around the steel headboard and wrapped both Nick's wrists, then pulled the slack out of it and gave it a jerk. Now his hands were trussed together again and bound to the bedframe. If this was some kind of sex game, Nick didn't see how it could be any fun, no matter what turned you on.

It surprised Nick then that what he felt most was rage. Tyson wanted to play his victims like fish on a line and it was sick. He probably got half his perverted kicks knowing they were scared out of their minds and couldn't do a thing to escape. Nick vowed not to show he was scared, although he definitely was in spite of the fact that help might be on its way.

"Stay here and keep quiet," Tyson ordered. "You got your sister out, but you still belong to me, you little bastard. There's someone out there, but he isn't doing you any good."

And that was when Nick realized Monk had a rifle.

Cam was within sight of the hunting lodge when he found the Jeep parked in a dense growth of scrubby bushes. And if he'd had any doubt that it was Tyson's, he suddenly caught sight of him prowling around the grounds of the lodge. Cam quickly retreated and waited a full fifteen minutes to give him time to get back inside. Then, as he decided it was safe to move in, he heard voices. First Tyson's, then Nick's. He felt a deep rush of relief and breathed heartfelt thanks. Nick was okay, but there was still Kendy to worry about. Then, all he had to do was get them out. No way to know if Tyson had a weapon, but seeing the kind of lifestyle he chose, it was more than likely. Jason's assessment that Tyson, under stress, was dangerous, add desperate to that, and there was no telling what he might do.

The fact that Jason carried a firearm in his car troubled Cam. He knew it wasn't unusual in Texas for boys to begin hunting as a sport at a very young age, but having the shotgun as handy as a cell phone was something else. Cam couldn't help but think it had more to do with the abuse he'd had to endure from Tyson than hunting as a hobby. But at this particular moment, Cam was damn glad to have it.

He began to work his way to the front of the cabin, moving cautiously. It might be best to simply retreat and wait for Pete or the unit he'd sent, but knowing what Tyson was capable of now and that he had Nick as a captive—if he hadn't already assaulted the boy—Cam didn't want to give him added opportunity to harm Nick.

It was while he stood planning his next move that he heard the crunch of a footstep behind him, but before he had made half a turn, he felt the sudden, sharp prod of a gun barrel in his back.

"Lay your weapon on the ground," Tyson growled from behind him. "And do it easy."

Cam hesitated, and Tyson rammed the steel up against his right kidney viciously. "Do it now. Thanks to you, Ford, I don't have a damn thing to lose by killing you here and now, but I bet you wouldn't want to leave Nicky in my hands afterward, would you?"

"Where's Kendall?"

"In the woods making the bears a tasty treat."

Cam felt a rush of rage. Not having any more use for her, had he murdered Kendall? But at another vicious prod to his kidney, he bent at the knees and lay the shotgun just out of Tyson's reach. To pick it up, he'd have to take a long, sideways step. "Is Nick okay?"

"Why don't we go inside to see for ourselves? Hands up."

Cam obediently raised his hands while scanning the woods and straining for a sound that Pete's unit was nearing. But all he heard were night sounds and the far-off wail of a train.

Tyson nudged him into a walk. "It was stupid to come out here alone, Ford. I figured you for being smarter than that."

"I'm not alone. Singletary's got a unit parked on the road waiting for backup."

Tyson laughed. "I don't think so. The chief wouldn't have let a civilian venture up here alone while his boys waited safe in their cars. And if there was anybody else with you, I'd have flushed him out. So, looks like me and you and Nicky can have us a party." They were at the steps now. "Actually, it'll be Nicky and me having the party and you'll get to watch."

"Coach!" It was Jason's voice. "Drop that rifle."

Tyson froze. He didn't turn, but froze with the rifle in his hands. "Who's that? Jason? What the hell are you doing out here, you little shit?"

Oh, Jesus, Cam thought.

"You should have picked up the shotgun when you made Cam lay it down, Coach. Big mistake. If I did something stupid like that, you'd have me running a hundred laps."

"Are you drunk, Jason?"

"I'm not too drunk to miss, you son of a bitch. Cam, move so you don't get hurt."

"He moves," Tyson hissed, pointing the rifle threateningly, "and I'll blow his spine apart."

Cam kept his hands raised but turned his head to see Jason. "Don't do anything you'll regret, Jason. Singletary is on the way. This is police business."

"Yeah, Jace," Tyson said in a placating tone, "you hear that? Calm down now and let's talk this over."

"Talking's good, Coach," Jason said. "Let's start with Jack Ford."

"That's ancient history, Jace," Tyson said. "Water under the bridge, boy."

"Not to Mr. Ford there and not to all of us who know what you did."

"What I did was give him a choice spot on the team," Tyson said with impatience. "He got into drugs and came to a bad end. And you know what, Jason, you better watch it with the booze. You could wind up like Jack."

"Only if you figure out a way to rig it like a suicide," Jason said bitterly. "That's what happened and now the world knows it, Monk. You told Ziggy and Jay to do it and they did. They put something in his drink that knocked him out and then they hung him. And as soon as this is done, I'm going after them, too." He wiped his eyes on his sleeve, making the shotgun waver a little. But he quickly realigned it. "You have messed up enough people, Monk, and I'm gonna see you dead now, tonight."

"I love you, Jace," Monk said plaintively. "You know that."

"Jason, give me the gun."

The quiet words stopped Cam's heart. Rachel. Why the hell hadn't she stayed in the car?

"Kill him, Jace. Pull the trigger and kill him."

It was Ward. His voice bitter, egging him on. Cam looked up at the sky, praying Pete's men would soon arrive.

"Who's that?" Monk said, almost smiling now. "Ward, baby, is that you?"

"Don't you move, you bastard!" Jason said. "I mean it."

"Jason." Rachel again. "Please don't do this. Don't give him the satisfaction of destroying your life. That's what killing him will mean. Your life for his. He isn't worth it."

"You don't know what he's done, Ms. Forrester." Jason's voice shook. "You don't know how he hurts people and messes with their heads. He's garbage, he doesn't deserve to live. The world will be a better place if he's dead."

Good, Rachel, keep him talking, Cam thought, straining to hear the sound of a police siren. A few more minutes might be too late.

Rachel wasn't close enough to touch Jason. She moved a small step toward him, not wanting to push him too far, too fast. She could feel the emotion that gripped him and her heart ached for him. He was a sensitive, caring boy and he was struggling with hatred of a man devoid of both traits.

"Jason, think of your mother. Your sister." She took another small step closer. "They need you. They love you."

Now tears were streaming down his face. "They wouldn't if they knew what I've done," he said.

"You aren't the guilty one here, Jason. Please, let me have the gun. If you do, Coach Monk will get the punishment he deserves."

Tentatively, she touched his elbow and felt the tension thrumming in him like an electric charge. And then Tyson was laughing, a low, sneering sound. "Can't do it, can you, Jace? Don't have the balls, eh, Jace?"

And suddenly Jason opened his mouth and wailed out his rage in a long, agonizing howl. It echoed through the trees and high into the night sky. It was despair and misery and woe. Shaken, Rachel reached out with a trembling hand to take the gun, but he suddenly swung it wide to the side and she cried out, ''No-o-o...''

Boom! The shotgun blast struck the wall just to the right of Tyson, who dived in terror off the steps, stumbling and scrabbling to get away. Cam, realizing Jason had not intended the blast to hit anyone, leaped off the porch and jerked the gun out of the boy's hands. In the shock of the blast, Tyson had dropped his rifle, but he now raced to pick it up again. As he reached down for it, Cam spoke.

''Don't...do...it. Don't make me kill you,'' Cam said, sighting Tyson down the double barrel. ''I didn't want this boy to be the one to give you what you deserve, but I swear to God, I won't hesitate. Move a muscle before Pete's men get here and you can kiss this world goodbye.''

And at that moment, faintly in the distance, he heard police sirens.

Thirty

Cam trained the shotgun on Tyson who was down on his knees, and waited for police reinforcements, now just seconds away. As headlights flashed through the trees, Rachel kept an arm around Jason's shoulders. Fine tremors coursed through him, the aftermath of his emotional outburst, she guessed. But he was calm, staring dead-eyed at Monk. Maybe he'd exorcised a demon with that soul-wrenching cry, she thought as the police unit pulled up and stopped. Ward stood quietly beside her, too, showing no more emotion than Jason.

One look at the situation and the two cops were out with weapons drawn. One of them moved cautiously to Cam's side while the other covered him. "Okay, Mr. Ford," the older of the two said. "We've got him. Just step back easy-like and lay your weapon on the ground."

Cam did as told, without haste, his gaze never leaving Tyson's face. Rachel waited with impatience as one cop patted him down and handcuffed him before looking him in the eye. "Where are my children?" she demanded.

"Here I am, Mommy." Kendall darted out from the corner of the cabin and hurled herself into Rachel's arms. With a choked cry, Rachel caught her up tight, weak with relief that her baby was safe. For a minute, she simply held the little girl, breathing in the sweet smell of her and the feel of her small bones. Now, if only Nick—

"Nick's in the cabin all tied up," Kendy said. "We need to go get him."

* * *

But Cam was already inside fumbling with the belt that bound Nick to the bed. "What kept you?" Nick asked, shaking both his hands to restore circulation.

Cam stared at him long enough to assure himself that he was okay, then with a muffled oath, he pulled him into his arms and hugged him fiercely and long. Nick, laughing a little shakily, hugged him back and then had to blink back tears. "Don't tell anybody," he said with his face in Cam's shirt, "but I have been one scared dude."

Cam turned him loose and couldn't resist ruffling his hair, then grabbing him around the neck in their famous choke hold. "It'll be our secret. But at least you didn't have to dodge a shotgun blast."

"I heard everything and for a while there I was holding my breath. I mean, when Jason was gonna shoot him, I thought, don't do it, dude, even if it is the fastest way to solve Rose Hill's coaching problem. And then Mom was doing her talking-him-out-of-it thing." He shook his head, smiling with admiration. "She was one cool lady out there, wasn't she?"

"Yeah."

"Nick." Rachel, with Kendall beside her, stood at the door, drinking in the sight of her near-grown son, beautiful and safe. "Are you okay?"

He spread out both hands, letting her see for herself. "Except for a destroyed jersey, I'm good." He saw her eyes fill and knew tears were next. She rushed over and threw her arms around him, hugging him the way he hadn't been hugged since he was maybe six years old. And it felt fine.

"Did he hurt you, Nick?" Cam asked.

"Nah, he had a plan, but Moe and Curly screwed it up."

"Yeah, they passed us on the way in here—traveling fast."

Kendall stood looking up at them. "They're Ziggy and Jay," she said, making a face. "That's their names." Then she touched her camera, tucked in a fanny pouch around her waist. "I took their picture and they didn't even know. They say bad words and they're not very smart."

Cam ruffled her hair. "I think you're right, sweetheart."

"They talked about Jack," Kendy said ingenuously.

Cam looked at her. "Did they? Do you recall what they said?"

She nodded confidently. "They were afraid they'd get in trouble with the cops because of what happened to Jack."

"I bet that was Jay talking," Nick said, "right, Kendy?" When she nodded, he added, "He's the stupid one. He dropped Jack's name when they were trying to convince me to keep quiet. I wouldn't want to wind up like Jack Ford, he said."

Rachel, seeing the bleak look on Cam's face, touched his arm in mute sympathy. He'd been right in stubbornly insisting that his son hadn't taken his own life, but it was hardly comforting to know he'd been murdered instead.

Hearing more commotion outside, she saw more flashing blue lights as two more police units arrived. Pete Singletary got out of one. Ted was his passenger.

"Your dad is outside with the chief," she told Nick. "You should go out and see him. He'll want to know you're okay." She touched Kendy's hair. "You, too, sweetie."

"Dad's here? No kidding?" Nick moved to the door.

"Of course, Nick. He came to the station house as soon as he found out what had happened."

"That's cool. Two family moments in one day. Maybe his midlife crisis is winding down."

With Cam by her side, Rachel watched Ted sweep Kendy up in a big hug, then after a moment, he put out a hand to Nick—a bit hesitantly—then gave him a hug and a slap on the back. It was light years' different from the heartfelt emotion shared by Nick and Cam a few minutes before. And in spite of the fact that Ted had caused so much emotional pain to her children—and herself—Rachel found herself feeling sorry for him.

Cam was thinking the same thing. But he wasn't sorry

enough for Forrester to step aside and let him have Rachel and her children back if it was within his power. Ted had a lot of work in front of him to repair just some of the damage he'd done to his family. It would take some time, and Cam hoped, for the sake of both kids, that Forrester was man enough to do it. But Rachel belonged to him now.

Pete caught his eye then and went up the steps of the porch. "I'll want a formal statement, of course, but what the hell went on here?"

"Jason saved the day, simple as that. Tyson got the drop on me as I was trying to get the lay of the land. There was no way he could let me leave alive. Fortunately, he didn't pick up the shotgun after making me put it down, assuming, I guess, that I was alone." He gave a wry smile. "Actually, I thought I was alone. I'd told Rachel and the boys to stay in the car, but lucky for me, the minute I was out of sight, they decided to be my backup."

Pete gave Rachel a look with one raised eyebrow, but said nothing.

"Which was a good thing," Cam continued, pulling Rachel close with an arm around her waist, "because Jason had Monk in his sights, Pete. He was ready to kill him. He was itching to pull that trigger."

"Not really," Rachel said. "He's just a confused, anguished boy. I don't believe he would have done it."

"We'll never know that," Cam said, "because Rachel managed to talk him down."

"I understand he did fire the weapon," Pete said, adding dryly, "A whole corner of the cabin is destroyed."

"Jason deliberately aimed it high," Rachel said. "He's been hunting since he was eight years old. If he'd wanted to kill Tyson, he wouldn't have missed."

"How could he with a double-barrel twelve-gauge?" Pete said. Then searching her face, he said, "How're you holding up, Rachel?"

"I'm fine…now," she said, her gaze on her children, who were still talking with their dad. "But that reminds me that

I need to call my mother. She's almost sick with anxiety and a completely false burden of guilt because Kendy was taken on her watch." Touching Cam's arm, she stepped out onto the porch to make the call from her cell phone.

"It was close there for a minute, Pete," Cam said as Rachel made her call. "We were lucky. If Jason hadn't led us to this cabin, Nick might be on his way to Mexico with Tyson or worse. And I don't want to think what he planned to do with Kendall. We underestimated him. His obsession with boys is the driving force in his life. He was willing to risk everything rather than to give it up. He's already killed once."

"I think you're right," Pete said. "And as soon as we pick up Ziegler and Dunne we'll learn a lot more about how Jack died."

"Jason will be a big help there." Cam's gaze was still on Rachel. "When he had him in his sights, he accused Tyson of setting up the plan to get rid of Jack and sending Ziegler and Dunne to do it. I think we'll find he had football scholarships lined up for them. He probably planted visions of pro careers in their minds. And if that was what it took, they were willing."

"You think he told Jason what he did?" Pete was shaking his head. "How risky is that? And stupid."

"Maybe he didn't tell him outright, but he sure made no effort to hide his methods or what he did from Jason. I think he felt confident of absolute loyalty from Jason. He knew how much a career in sports meant to him and he played to that."

Pete grunted and looked over at Jason and Ward, both sitting on the steps now. "Looks like he'll survive to play," he said, "since he didn't pull that trigger. But when I spoke to him a few minutes ago, he was a little too calm. I've seen seasoned cops get like that, and then, when you least expect it, they just completely unravel."

"I'm going to see that he gets treatment," Cam said. "Ward, too. Without a doubt, Jason saved my life tonight and Ward led me to him. I hate that Jason was put through such a scene. If you could have heard that howl…'' Cam shuddered, recalling it. ''He's got some problems, drinking and possibly drugs now. But with the right kind of therapy and his career in sports to focus on, he can be saved.''

''Hopefully, you're right. And Rachel can be helpful in pointing him in the right direction.'' He moved toward the steps. ''I need to wrap it here tonight, Cam. Tomorrow morning sometime, you and Rachel need to come in and make a statement.''

''Yeah, first thing.''

Rachel quietly closed the door to Kendall's bedroom, peeked in on Nick and walked to the den, where Cam waited. ''Both are all tucked in and sleeping, if you can believe that.''

He glanced at the clock on the mantel. ''Since it'll be daylight in another couple of hours, yes, I can believe it.'' He'd been standing at the window looking out, waiting for her to reassure herself that her children were safe and that all was nearly right in her world. Now he held out his arms and she walked into them as easily and naturally as if they'd been lovers forever.

''This has been the longest, worst night of my life,'' she whispered, ''and, thank God, it has a happy ending.''

For a few blissful moments, Cam held her close, sharing in her elation. It still surprised him how right it was knowing Rachel and her children were in his life. How vital they were to his happiness now. It had been just a couple of weeks ago that he'd toyed with the idea of asking her to move in with him. Which would have been a nonstarter, anyway. Rachel wasn't a live-in lover kind of woman. She was the marrying kind. ''I had a few bad moments myself,'' he told her, holding her close to his heart.

''It's scary that he was so callous and calculating in taking Nick and Kendy from me. Doesn't he have any concept of how people are devastated by a threat to their children?

Didn't he see your anguish when you lost Jack?'' Her hands tightened at his waist and she buried her face in his shirt. ''For them to come so close—''

''They're okay now, sweetheart.'' His hands stroked her back, giving her a moment to banish the fear of what might have been.

After a moment, she reached up and kissed him on the side of his mouth. ''I know this has been hard for you, Cam. My children have been returned safely and I can only begin to imagine how it must have been for you when it didn't…have a happy ending.''

''There's some consolation in knowing that Tyson will be punished for taking Jack's life. But there's not much consolation for me knowing I wasn't there for Jack when he needed me. There are times,'' he said, still holding her close, ''when I wish with everything in me that I could have just that one moment to live over again. That night, when he called, if I'd been listening instead of giving my son half an ear when he needed his dad, maybe it wouldn't have happened. Maybe he would have revealed enough that I would have sensed danger and could have intervened. Maybe—''

Rachel touched his lips to stop him. ''You can never know that, Cam. You're traveling a road to nowhere. You loved Jack. Accept in your heart that he knows that—that he knew that—and you'll keep his memory alive forever. That will be the best tribute to his life. And it's not too late for that.''

He said nothing for a long moment, then he gave her an affectionate squeeze. ''You're right, sweetheart. In fact, you were right when you tried to give me that advice five years ago when I was ranting and raving at you in your office.''

She smiled. ''Yes, well, we won't travel down that memory lane again, either, okay?''

''Lucky me.'' He simply held her for a minute, swaying back and forth. Then, ''You were the real hero tonight, Rachel. If Jason had pulled that trigger, we would have had another tragedy to add to Monk's long list. And in spite of you thinking Jason probably wouldn't have done it, we don't know that. But you talked him down, good little shrink that you are," he said, kissing her nose. "I don't know when I first realized I was in love with you, but I knew it for certain when you were working your magic with that boy tonight."

She put a hand on his cheek, searching his face. "Oh, Cam. What are you saying?"

He smiled, his hands now at her waist. "I thought I said it. I love you. Is that such a bulletin?"

She was simply staring at him in stunned surprise.

"I've been falling in love with you since the day you moved in next door, sugar."

"Oh, come on. You were barely civil."

"Purely a defensive strategy."

She gave him a suspicious look. "We're not talking about an affair here, are we?"

"Would you consider it?" Then as her eyes lit dangerously, he laughed and kissed her eyebrow. "I know your opinion about affairs. And I'll be honest, since we can't get married yet, but if I thought I could talk you into that, I would."

"You certainly can't," she said primly.

His smiled faded then. "Here's another thing I learned tonight, Rachel. When it looked as if Nick and Kendy might be in real danger, I couldn't have been more afraid than if they'd been my own. And close on that thought was my fear that you might suffer the way I did when I lost Jack." He brought her hands up and kissed them. "It doesn't take much to figure out that what I was feeling was love—not just for you, but for Nick and Kendy, too."

Joy and hope were now filling up her heart and showing in her eyes. "Cam—"

"Wait." He couldn't say everything until everything was on the table. "Ted's come to his senses, I think. He might want to try to rebuild his life. Win back what he lost. Nick and Kendy need him, I won't deny that. Some would say it's the right thing for you and Ted to be together again. If you—"

She put her fingers to his lips again. "Haven't we gone through all this once? I will never be able to trust Ted again, which in itself kills any possibility of a reconciliation, if that's what you're getting at. But more important than that, I don't love him. I haven't for a long time. I don't want a reconciliation, even for the sake of Nick and Kendy." Then she framed his face with her hands. "Besides, I've been so dazzled by you that I can't even think about going back to the life I used to have."

"Dazzled?" He smiled and dropped his forehead to hers, breathing deep in relief. From the moment he'd realized that her children were gone, his insides had been in a knot. "Then how would you feel about spending a lot more time with me, like say, the next fifty or so years?"

"Cam—"

"I know I'm no prize. You said yourself I'm moody and I tend to close up when I'm on deadline. I'm opinionated. I'm—"

"Intelligent, interesting and sexy."

He grinned and reached out to push a strand of her hair back from her cheek. Then his face gentled and he gathered her close, just held her for a minute. A wave of peacefulness rolled through him and settled. She had found herself on her own with two kids and a mountain of debt and difficulty to overcome and she'd accepted it with grace, style and sheer grit. It would be his pleasure to see that nothing like that ever happened to her again. She probably wouldn't like it that he felt protective about her, but that's the way it was. She was his now and he protected his own.

She tucked her head beneath his chin and let him hold her. "Say it again, Cam."

He smiled. "I love you, Rachel."

Epilogue

"I hope nobody has a heart attack," Marta said, casting a wary eye over at Cam's driveway where a raucous basketball game was in play. Kendy, her camera busy, was on the sidelines recording the event. "They're trying to keep up with those kids. First thing you know, we'll have to call the paramedics."

Rachel set a bowl of salsa on the table and ripped open a huge bag of tortilla chips. "I don't think they're quite that out of shape," she said dryly. She could speak from personal experience that Cam was in great shape. He would not be physically challenged by a few rounds of backyard basketball with Nick and Ward.

"Pete didn't get to bed until midnight last night." Marta pulled paper plates out of a plastic bag. "He's been working long hours with the D.A.'s office putting together the indictments for Tyson and those two creeps, Ziegler and Dunne."

"How is the case shaping up?" Rachel's gaze wandered across the way to the game, going hot and heavy. Cam and Pete had been challenged by Nick and Ward. Pete looked reasonably neat, although out of breath. Cam wore a T-shirt with no sleeves and cutoffs that must have been in his closet since high school. He was sweating and breathing hard, blocking Nick and laughing, waving his arms as if he were no older than the boys. He looked hot and male and, to Rachel, utterly irresistible.

She glanced over and found Marta looking at her.

"Cam hasn't talked about it?"

"He's working on a new book, and not, to Kendy's dismay, about the family ghost. I think that now the question of Jack's death has been resolved and he knows he didn't commit suicide, he's at peace in a place inside that might never have known peace." Her hands on the bag of chips were still. "It's as if he's done this for Jack and now he's content to turn over to Pete the job of bringing those responsible to justice."

"I'm just so glad that another tragedy was averted when Jason didn't kill him." Marta shoved an empty bowl for the chips across to Rachel. "Dying instantly would have been too quick and humane. After what Monk Tyson did, he deserves to suffer more."

"Without a doubt." She thought of the anguish in Jason as he'd talked about Tyson's abuse. And the awful moment when he almost pulled the trigger. There were so many boys damaged. Ward had appeared in her office at school the day after and she'd been able to refer him and Jason to a good therapy program.

It was the weekend now, and five days since Tyson's arrest. The furor was still ongoing. Understandably, the town had been shocked and horrified. Parents were still reeling, questioning how such a predator could have moved about so freely in their midst for so long and nobody knew. But those who knew—the boys themselves—had been diabolically manipulated, aided and abetted by a town intoxicated by a coach's incredible successes. In the end it had not been the victims who brought Tyson down, but his own arrogance.

Loud whoops from Cam's driveway stirred the two women into action. "Oops," Marta said, doling out plastic forks. "Get the food ready. Here they come."

Rachel opened the door to the kitchen where her mother was mixing dressing for coleslaw. "The brisket's in that big pan," Dinah said, pointing with a whisk. "It's ready and so is this as soon as I toss it together."

Rachel gave her mother a kiss on the cheek. "Thanks, Mom. There are going to be four hungry guys out there in just about half a minute.'' Lifting the pan, she went to the door and bumped it open with her hip. "Come on out as soon as you're done, okay?"

"Hey, gals, what's for dinner?" Pete said, wiping himself down with a towel and dropping into a lawn chair to catch his breath. Cam, rummaging in an ice chest, tossed him a beer.

"Brisket and the trimmings," Marta said, giving him a stern once-over. "You're too hot. Cool off first."

Pete popped the top on the beer. "Yes, ma'am, that's just what I was thinking." He tilted the can and swigged nearly half of it down. "Aah, only one thing better than cold beer on a hot day." He winked at her.

Marta gave him a scalding look and tipped her head toward Nick and Ward, who stood drinking soda and grinning.

"I'm having water," Cam said virtuously.

"Water?" Everybody looked at him.

He grinned and poured it over one foot. "Nick spilled Gatorade on my foot and it's sticky. I need to clean it off."

Pete tossed him the towel. "Great game, you guys," he said to Nick and Ward. "And the next time you think you can take us old-timers, we play for money."

Marta stared. "You won?"

Pete shrugged modestly. "I don't like to brag."

Nick sputtered and choked on his root beer. "Next time, old-timer. And we don't spot you guys nothing."

Marta winced. "Please, not in my hearing. I'm an English teacher."

Cam came up behind Rachel and kissed her on the side of her neck. "How's it goin', sugar?"

"Good. Very good." She tilted her head to expose more skin to him and glanced up to see Kendy and her camera pointed at them. "Kendy, must you?"

"I'm making a family album," Kendy said. "For when I get old."

It warmed her heart that Kendall had accepted so naturally her relationship with Cam. And Nick, too. Cam, himself, had

laid the foundation. Their lives would have been much different had he not been next door and simply there for them.
Of course, there would be rocky times ahead, she expected
that. Divorce was never an easy thing, and Ted had much to
do to make amends to their children, but he seemed sincere
about trying and Nick and Kendy would be forgiving as long
as he proved to do just that.

When Cam's arms slipped around her waist, she let herself
lean back against him for a moment, feeling lucky and loved.
She glanced up, met Marta's eyes and smiled in tacit wonder
at how things sometimes work out. Marta and Pete had set
the date for their long-delayed marriage. And as soon as Rachel felt Nick and Kendy were truly accepting and ready, she
and Cam would take their vows. They would be a family
again, and it would be a joy living in the house Cam had
restored with his own hands.

"Speaking of family," Marta said, rising from the table,
"I've got something for you, Cam." She reached for a folder
she'd tucked between two of Dinah's potted begonias. "I
knew I had put this away for safekeeping years ago, but I
couldn't remember where. I don't keep everything my students write, even when I see real talent. As a writer yourself,
you'll see what I mean when you read it." Slipping a clip
from the folder, she handed it to Cam. "Once in a while,
there'll be a student whose work just takes your breath
away." She smiled. "This boy was one of them."

Cam turned the folder up to read the label on the tab. Jack
Ford. Pain bloomed in his chest, blade-sharp. His hand was
unsteady and the letters of his son's name blurred as a great
wave of regret and grief rolled over and in him. He'd never
known of Jack's talent and it was a bittersweet gift to know
it now. But still a gift. He somehow managed a smile of
thanks and gently set the folder aside to be savored later.

Rachel, guessing the mix of emotion in him, slipped her
hand into his, lacing their fingers, tight and warm. Across the
way, Kendy's camera was focused on them. She wondered,
when she looked at the "family album" years from now,

what would show on their faces only five days after such a telling moment in their lives. Then, turning back to the table, she picked up a plate and handed it to Cam, smiling into his eyes. Nick, watching, gave them a thumbs-up. This was not a day for regrets, but for new beginnings. When Kendy next pointed her camera, there were smiles all around.

KAREN YOUNG

66471	FULL CIRCLE	___ $5.99 U.S.	___ $6.99 CAN.
66306	GOOD GIRLS	___ $5.99 U.S.	___ $6.99 CAN.
66679	PRIVATE LIVES	___ $6.50 U.S.	___ $7.99 CAN.

(limited quantities available)

TOTAL AMOUNT	$_____
POSTAGE & HANDLING	$_____
($1.00 for one book; 50¢ for each additional)	
APPLICABLE TAXES*	$_____
TOTAL PAYABLE	$_____

(check or money order—please do not send cash)

To order, complete this form and send it, along with a check or money order for the total above, payable to MIRA Books, to: **In the U.S.:** 3010 Walden Avenue, P.O. Box 9077, Buffalo, NY 14269-9077; **In Canada:** P.O. Box 636, Fort Erie, Ontario, L2A 5X3.

Name:_____

Address:_____ City:_____

State/Prov.:_____ Zip/Postal Code:_____

Account Number (if applicable):_____

075 CSAS

*New York residents remit applicable sales taxes.
 Canadian residents remit applicable
 GST and provincial taxes.

MIRA®